ONCE UPON A BAD BOY

A Sometimes in Love novel

Melonie Johnson

St. Martin's Paperbacks

Published in the United States by St. Martin's Paperbacks, an imprint of St. Martin's Publishing Group.

ONCE UPON A BAD BOY

Copyright © 2019 by Melonie Johnson.

All rights reserved.

For information address St. Martin's Publishing Group, 120 Broadway, New York, NY 10271.

ISBN: 978-1-250-19307-0

Our books may be purchased in bulk for promotional, educational, or business use. Please contact your local bookseller or the Macmillan Corporate and Premium Sales Department at 1-800-221-7945, ext. 5442, or by email at MacmillanSpecialMarkets@macmillan.com.

Printed in the United States of America

St. Martin's Paperbacks edition / June 2019

10 9 8 7 6 5 4 3 2 1

Also by Melonie Johnson

Getting Hot with the Scot
Smitten by the Brit

*To the long-haired guy I worked across the
hall from at the mall.
At sixteen, I didn't know you'd become the wonderful
husband and father you are today . . .
I just thought you were cute.
So glad I found my HEA with you.
And yes, you're still cute.*

CHAPTER 1

SPRINKLES. SADIE GOLDOVITZ braced her feet on the mat, bent her knees slightly and twisted sideways, pulling her elbow back. *No, Glazed.* She rotated, hips twisting as her arm shot forward, fist flying. Her cross punch landed with a solid thwack, knocking the sparring bag sideways.

"Nice one," her trainer, Jim, grunted from his position behind the bag.

Sadie nodded. She knew better than to waste air replying.

Sure enough, a beat later Jim steadied the bag and barked, "Again."

Her body responded instantly to the command, dropping back into fighting stance, legs braced but not locked, core tight. Her left fist slammed into the bag in a quick jab, followed by another cross with her right. Jab, cross. Jab, jab, cross. Her thighs burned. Her hands, curled inside her boxing gloves, were an aching, sweaty mess. But she continued the punching pattern. Jab, cross. Jab, jab, cross.

A rebellious little blond curl escaped her ponytail and

proceeded to flop around face, but Sadie ignored it, focusing on the rhythm of her movements. Jab, cross. Jab, jab, cross. She glared at the bag, returning to her happy place. *Glazed *with* sprinkles.*

The asshole curl was now stuck in her eyelashes, but she didn't have the extra energy or breath to blow it away, so she kept going, inhaling and exhaling with each blast of her fist. The round had to be over soon. Unless Jim had decided to screw with her and extend the drill time. She wouldn't check, though. Last time she'd glanced at the clock, she'd earned an extra burpee for each second she'd had left.

Sadie hated burpees.

Jim knew this, of course.

She kept going. Another jab and cross. Two more jabs followed by a cross. She pictured the glass case of the donut shop, the gleaming rows of unholy bliss awaiting her perusal. She would take her time, absorbing the heavenly smells and carefully considering all her options before making her selection.

Her Friday donut was the proverbial carrot on the end of the stick. A reward for enduring another week of hell training for the lead role in a new action movie. Sadie had spent the summer honing her body into a fighting machine, preparing to step in to the ass-kicking boots of Jamie, the dynamic heroine of *Fair is Fair.*

For inspiration to stick to her brutal exercise regimen, she'd taped a poster of Linda Hamilton in her *Terminator 2* glory days to her bathroom mirror, admiring Sarah Connor's guns every morning as she brushed her teeth. For motivation to stay on her strict diet plan, Sadie had started her Friday donut ritual. Knowing she could pick whatever she wanted from that glass case of bliss, even if it was just once a week, gave her enough willpower to see her through each day.

Plus, there was no limit on how much she thought about that one donut. Fantasies were calorie-free and Sadie indulged often. Maybe she'd try something totally different today. Something *extra* sinful. With frosting. Loads of it. Her stomach rumbled with anticipation as she twisted her middle, winding up for another punch combo.

"Gold!" Jim yelled.

She faltered mid-swing, her fist grazing the bag. "What?" she snapped.

"Time's up."

"Oh." She relaxed. "Thank God."

"Thank me." Jim chuckled and helped her remove her gloves. "I called your name at least three times. You were in the zone."

"Yeah, the donut zone." Hands finally free, Sadie flexed her fingers and shoved the annoying curl out of her face. Too long to leave down, but too short for a decent ponytail, the best she could manage with her hair looked more like a mushroom about to explode from the top of her head.

"What's this about donuts?" Jim asked, frowning.

"It's Friday." Sadie grabbed her water bottle and chugged.

"And?" he grunted, hands on hips.

"And, I made it all the way through this week's training."

"What do you want, a sticker?" He raised an eyebrow.

"No. I want a donut." Sadie pointed her water bottle at her trainer and squeezed.

"Hey!" Jim sputtered, blocking the spray of water. "You're going to mess up my 'do."

"Dude, nothing could mess that up." Sadie rolled her eyes at him. Jim was very protective of his hair. "And one donut a week is not going to mess up my training."

"Only one?" He raised both eyebrows this time.

"Only one." She held up her hand, palm out. "I promise." She dropped her hand and poked at her bare sweaty stomach. "Would these abs lie to you?"

"They better not." Jim smirked. "Or I'll add another hundred lemon squeezers to your sets next week."

Sadie grimaced. "Noted."

"I don't want to see all my hard work go to . . ." he paused, eyeing her torso, ". . . waste."

"*Your* hard work!" She moved to punch him.

He turned, absorbing her swing with the meat of his shoulder. "Not bad. Your right hook is getting pretty boss."

"Thanks." The agony of the last sixty minutes faded at her trainer's words. Jim didn't dole out compliments often.

"When do you finally get to start kicking ass for real?" he asked, tossing her a towel.

"Filming starts Monday." She wiped the sweat from her forehead.

"Nervous?"

"Hell, no." Sadie tucked the towel around her neck. "I've been waiting for a part like this since I started acting." She took another swig of water. Becoming Jamie was her chance to prove to the world she was more than the spoiled little rich girl she'd been playing on a soap opera for the last several years. Prove she was more than the spoiled little rich girl the tabloids continued to describe her as. She was tired of the catty accusations, the assumption that because she came from a powerful, wealthy family, she had more connections than talent.

Sadie swallowed past the resentment burning in her throat. "This movie could make or break me," she admitted. "I'm just glad to finally get started, you know?"

"Oh, yeah." Jim nodded. "I've had matches like that. Big ones where it felt like my career was hinging on the outcome. Spend all that time training, when what I really wanna do is just get in the ring already." Her trainer crossed his arms over his massive chest. "But that's how it works. You gotta put in the time first. You want it, you gotta earn it." Jim narrowed his eyes, giving her a once-over. It was a fighter's look, sizing her up. "You think you've earned it?"

Sadie met his gaze head-on, mimicking his serious tone. "I've definitely earned that donut." She bent her arms and flexed.

"Whoa, put those guns away, girl." Jim held up his hands in mock surrender.

Laughing, Sadie flexed some more. For the first time in her life, she had defined, visible muscles and couldn't resist the urge to show off a little. She'd never worked harder in her life than she had the past few months, preparing for this role.

As if reading her thoughts, Jim added, "Seriously, Gold, you've been working your ass off. I'm proud of you."

"You are?" Sadie's cheeks flushed.

"I said so, didn't I?" He grinned at her, grabbing the towel off her neck and snapping it. "Now get outta my gym. Go get your *one* donut."

Half an hour later, Sadie tucked a damp curl behind her ear as she examined the day's selections in the bakery case. She'd showered and traded her tight sweaty workout clothes for her favorite pair of jeans and a loose, comfy

T-shirt, but hadn't taken the time to blow-dry her hair. Every minute spent getting ready was another between her and her donut.

One of the few benefits of having workouts that started at the unholy hour of five in the morning was that she was done by six. Which meant, if she showered fast, changed faster, and speed-walked, she arrived at Stan's in time for when they opened the doors at six thirty. Often, she was the first one there, giving her first pick of the freshly stocked case. Even better, she could take her time deciding, since the morning rush, which usually kicked off around seven, hadn't gotten underway yet.

Glazed, sprinkled, glazed with sprinkles. Chocolate, double chocolate, chocolate cake. Coconut cake. Sadie bobbed up and down, gaze roaming hungrily over the mounds of carbs, glistening with sin. *Peanut butter, peanut butter banana. Strawberry, blueberry, raspberry. Lemon curd. Pistachio. Maple.* She licked her lips, tasting the name of each flavor.

Her mouth was watering, and she hadn't even gotten to the hand pies or fritters yet. Sadie bent over, hands braced on her thighs as she stared into the case. She was still engrossed in the bounty on display when a hard smack to her backside made her jump in surprise.

"What the hell?" Sadie swung around, fist clenched.

"I thought that might get your attention," a husky, sultry voice teased.

"Ana!" Sadie relaxed at the sight of her best friend, green eyes twinkling, full red lips curving in a mischievous smile.

"In the flesh." Ana tossed her mane of thick waves, black as a raven's wing, over her shoulder.

"I wasn't expecting you." Sadie reached out to give her best friend a hug. "You're lucky I didn't punch you in the face for that ass grab. I'm told my right hook is getting pretty boss."

"I bet." Ana returned the hug. "But since your face is currently buried in my boobs, let's call it even."

Sadie snorted and stepped back. Where she was petite and barely topped five feet, Ana was tall and generously proportioned. Which yes, put Sadie at about breast height. She smiled up at her best friend. "I thought you couldn't make it today."

"I decided I couldn't pass up our new Friday tradition." Ana glanced at the glass case. "Have you ordered yet?"

Sadie turned back to the selection of donuts. "I can't make up my mind." She sighed. "I'm thinking I need frosting today. But I can't decide which I want more, maple or chocolate."

"Get them both."

"Oh no, I can have only one."

"Or what? The calorie gods will curse you?"

"No, but my trainer will. He threatened me with extra lemon squeezers."

Ana curled her lips in revulsion. "I don't know what those are, but I do know the only lemon I want squeezed is the one dribbled over a nicely grilled bit of barramundi or going into a Lemon Drop martini."

"Will you split with me? We can have half of each."

"Ugh, the things I do in the name of friendship." Ana sighed dramatically, impressive cleavage heaving. "If you insist. Get the donuts. I'll buy the coffee."

After ordering, they slid down to the other end of the counter. The clerk handed Sadie a bag, and she pulled out both donuts and set them on a napkin. She sliced each one down the middle, then rearranged the pieces so half of both was on each napkin. She pushed one of the napkins toward Ana.

"I'm going to take mine to go. I can't stay long," Ana admitted. "I have a party for twenty-five mermaids to prepare for."

"What time does the party start?" Sadie asked, putting Ana's portion back in the bag.

"Not 'til eleven." Ana poured a measure of cream into her coffee. "But the mother of the birthday mermaid wants me there early."

"How early?"

"If she had her way, since last night."

Sadie laughed. "One of those types, huh?" Ana ran a catering company that specialized in uniquely themed upscale parties, and with every mom on the North Shore looking to outdo the other, her services were in high demand.

"You have no idea." Ana stirred her coffee. "It's bad enough I let the woman bulldoze me into agreeing to be there by seven."

"It's almost seven now."

"Which is why I can't stay long." She offered Sadie the carafe of cream.

Sadie shook her head. "No dairy."

"You can do donuts but no dairy?" Ana's lips twitched.

"That part isn't so bad. It's the protein bars that are the worst." Sadie shuddered.

"Not your favorite?" Ana asked, smirking.

"They taste like a dead banana." Sadie made a face. "No, if a banana were murdered, and someone made a chalk outline of the crime scene, that's what they taste like."

Ana let out a snort of laughter. "And you eat this atrocity? On purpose?"

"Three times a day."

"I don't think I could ever subject myself to such torture." Ana raised an eyebrow. "Are you sure you're not some kind of masochist?"

"Ha. The workouts make me wonder sometimes." Sadie fiddled with her two donut halves. "By the way, thanks for saving me from extra torture by avoiding temptation this morning."

"Happy to help." Ana beamed at her. "I've missed you. It's been nice having you back in Chicago. Monday night margaritas, Friday morning donuts, Sunday bike rides." She snapped the lid back on her coffee cup. "I know once filming starts, I won't see you as much."

"I'm still going to be around, but yeah, it's going to get rough soon."

Ana sipped her coffee. "Will you be able to ride this weekend?"

Sadie nodded. While her best friend despised most types of exercise, Ana loved cycling, was almost religious about it. For Ana, Sunday rides were like church. "This Sunday should be fine. After that, I don't know." Sadie took a sip of her own coffee. She'd gotten used to drinking it black, but she'd never love it. When this movie shoot was over, she was going to have *all* the lattes. "I'll have a better idea of my schedule after today."

"Ooh, the table read is this afternoon, right?"

"Yep." Sadie grabbed another bag and stuffed her donut halves inside.

"Wait, after all that fuss, and you're not even going to eat it now?"

"I want to walk out with you." Sadie carefully placed the bag inside her purse. She licked a stray smidge of maple frosting from her finger and groaned with pleasure. "Besides, the longer I wait to eat this, the better it will taste."

"Delayed gratification only works up to a point." Ana eyed her up and down pointedly. "Trust me, you don't want to end up with a stale donut."

Sadie followed Ana toward the exit. "Why do I get the feeling we're not talking about food anymore?" she asked, weaving her way through the now-crowded shop. Morning rush was in full swing.

"Why do I get the feeling sucking frosting off your finger was the most action you've had in weeks?" Ana shot back, juggling her coffee and donut bag as she reached for the door. At that moment, it swung open and the guy entering stepped to the side, holding the door for them. "Thank you." Ana flashed him a flirty smile as she sailed past.

Sadie hurried after her friend. "Are you saying what I think you're saying?"

"You've heard the expression use it or lose it, right?" Ana glanced over her shoulder and wiggled her fingers. "He's cute."

Sadie glanced back. Door guy was still standing there. He returned her friend's wave and grinned.

"Great smile." Ana paused, watching as he turned to head into the shop. "Ooh, and a great butt." She began to retrace her steps. "I think I'm going to grab his . . ."

Sadie yanked on Ana's arm, holding her back. "You're going to grab his what?"

"His number." Ana gazed down at Sadie, face full of innocent curiosity. "What else?"

"Aren't you already late for your mermaid mom?"

Ana bit her lip. "Darn. You're right." Her smile turned sly. "Maybe *you* should get his number instead."

"Me?"

"Why not?"

Sadie sputtered.

"When's the last time you got a guy's number?"

More sputtering.

"Now that I think about it, when's the last time you've been on a date?" Ana pressed. "Ever since you moved back to Chicago, you've been . . . different. What happened to my flirty dirty partner in crime?"

"I don't know what you mean," Sadie hedged.

"Please," Ana snorted. "You're talking to me, remember? I *know* you. And I know something is up," she added, her tone losing its playful edge.

"Nothing is up," Sadie denied, uncomfortable with the sudden turn in the conversation.

Silently, Ana stared down at Sadie, one raised eyebrow doing the talking for her.

"I mean it," Sadie insisted. "With all the training and prep work for the film, I haven't had time to think about anything else."

"Is that true?" Ana asked quietly. "Or is it really more about how, now that you are back here to stay awhile, you are thinking of something in particular. *Someone* in particular."

Half-formed dreams swirled through Sadie's mind. She shook her head, scattering them before they could take shape. She wasn't going there. Not now, not ever. "I've just been busy, that's all. Okay?" She stared up at her friend. *I can't talk about this. Please don't make me talk about this. About him.*

Awareness flickered in Ana's green eyes. An acknowledgment of all that Sadie left unsaid. She backed off, voice picking up its light teasing tone again as she clucked her tongue and said, "No one is ever too busy to get busy."

"What is that supposed to be"—Sadie smirked, playing along—"some kind of mantra?" She sucked in a grateful breath and waited at the curb while Ana walked around to the driver's side of her car.

"A motivational slogan." Ana opened her car door. "My mom has been into needlepoint lately. I'll see if she can sew that into a pillow. What do you think?"

"I think you're weird." Sadie shook her head and leaned on the convertible's passenger door. The same shade of emerald as Ana's eyes, the car was fun and sexy, just like the woman who drove it.

"Very," Ana agreed. "But I can't help it, I come from a long line of weirdos." She set her coffee in a cup holder and settled into her seat. "Can this weirdo give you a ride?"

"Thanks, I'm good." Her apartment wasn't far, and Sadie enjoyed walking through her neighborhood. Every city had its own vibe, and after living in New York for six years, it was nice to be back on home turf. September in Chicago could be unbearably hot and steamy, but this morning was promising to be one of those awesome end-of-summer days that held a kiss of fall. And the steady breeze blowing in off the lake didn't hurt either.

"That's debatable," Ana teased, clicking her seat belt. "Look, I totally get how important this movie role is to you, but you know what they say, all work and no play . . ." She turned the ignition and revved the gas suggestively.

"Ana," Sadie warned.

"I'm just saying." Ana shook her pink-and-white striped bag from Stan's. "Treat yourself." She tossed the pastry bag on the passenger seat. Over the roar of the engine, she added, "Don't let your donut get stale, okay?"

Before Sadie could form a reply, Ana was pulling out of the parking space with the practiced ease of a lifelong Chicagoan. With a wink, she blew Sadie a kiss and tore off down North Broadway.

Standing at the curb, Sadie hollered after the convertible's retreating bumper, "My vagina is not a donut!"

CHAPTER 2

AFTER SHOUTING ABOUT her vagina on the edge of Boystown, where one lovely passerby assured Sadie her hoo-ha could be whatever she wanted it to be, she recovered a modicum of dignity and decided to take Ana's advice to treat herself. Not with the cute guy's phone number, but with her favorite pastime: shopping. Rather than head home, she'd hit the Gold Coast, giving her credit card a workout almost as intense as the one she'd done at the gym this morning.

By the time she'd schlepped the bounty of her retail therapy back to her Lakeview East apartment, it was well after noon. The production meeting was scheduled for two and was all the way across town. Sadie barely had time to change, so she traded her T-shirt for an adorable sleeveless silk blouse she'd just bought, slapped on a pair of sunglasses, and hauled ass.

As she navigated her way through the giant warehouse studio to the conference room, she rubbed her palms against her jeans, trying to quell her sudden bout of nerves. This was just a table read, nothing to get worked up about.

She'd done plenty of them before. Though admittedly, most of those had been for college productions. They'd been fun. Usually held over a big family-style dinner at the director's house, first reads were a chance for the cast and crew to meet in a casual setting, hear the director's vision for the play, and get a sense of their expectations for the characters.

During her time spent on the soap opera *Hope General*, table reads didn't really happen. Occasionally the director or executive producer would schedule a meeting to discuss upcoming episodes, which meant a fast and furious debriefing. Sometimes she'd get lucky and catch a glimpse of her character's story arc, but Sadie had learned not to put much stock in those moments. Too often the writers decided to change something, reworking the storyline, shifting events, swapping love interests. By the time the next round of scripts was ready, everything would be different.

Prior to getting cast on the soap, Sadie's handful of movie roles had been too small to earn a place at the table. Literally. Instead, an assistant would be on standby, reading the lines for all the smaller roles. This would be her first official read as a principal with a spot at the table. A spot she'd busted her ass to earn. Sadie took a deep breath, then notched up her chin and strode into the meeting like the leading lady she was.

"Sadie, hey!" A hand waved at her from near the head of the table. Ryan, the leading man and her costar. His warm smile did much to settle her nerves. They'd met during initial screen tests prior to final casting. He had a carefree California vibe that seemed authentic rather than cultivated. Easy on the eyes, of course, but easygoing too—goofy and adorable. She liked that about him and was looking forward to working together.

Like her, Ryan had gotten his start in television, playing a lovable slacker on a sitcom. He'd successfully made the jump from television to movies with a big part in a blockbuster sci-fi last year, and Sadie was hoping this movie would do the same for her career.

"Hey, Ryan." She returned his smile, sliding into the seat next to him. "Ready to do this?"

"I was born ready." He swiveled back and forth on his chair. "And you can call me Ry. Like the bread." Ryan gave her a goofy grin, white teeth flashing in his charmingly boyish face.

"Sure thing, Ry Bread," Sadie agreed.

"Ugh, on second thought, don't." He groaned and swiveled his chair again, casting a longing glance at the coffee bar set up in one corner of the room. "Any mention of carbs makes me . . . what's the word?"

"Homicidal?" she suggested.

"Exactly." His gaze drifted back to the piles of pastries and bagels. "I'd kill for a donut right now . . . if this diet doesn't kill me first. No lie, I think my stomach is eating itself." He sighed and rubbed his flat belly, six-pack rippling beneath the fitted cotton of his V-neck T-shirt.

Now it was Sadie's turn to laugh. Was she a horrible person because she found it comforting to know he'd been undergoing the same brutal diet and exercise training regimen? Taking pity on him, she reached for her purse and unzipped it. "If the situation is that bad . . ." She flashed him the bag from Stan's.

Ryan's eyes grew round. He licked his lips. "Is that . . . ?"

"It is." She opened the pink-and-white striped bag and covertly tilted it toward him.

He leaned forward, but rather than peek inside, he inhaled, breathing deeply. "Oh, sweet baby Jesus on a hamster wheel," he moaned, closing his eyes.

"Right?" Sadie nodded in understanding.

"Where did you get that?" he asked, breathing in another lungful of donut-scented goodness and looking at
her with wonder, like she was some magical donut fairy.
"I haven't had Stan's since LA. I didn't even know they
had them around here."

"Oh yeah, there's a few in the city." Sadie shrugged.
"One is a couple blocks from my gym."

"Where's your gym?" he started to ask, then stopped.
"No, wait. It's better if you don't tell me. There's no way I
could control myself."

"It's my biggest weakness too," she confessed. "I only
allow myself one every Friday."

"T.G.I.F," Ryan spelled out reverently.

"Tell you what." Sadie grinned, taking pity on him. "I
already ate half, but if you promise to keep my secret, I'll
give you half of my other half."

"Deal." The word shot out of his mouth as his hand
shot into her purse.

"Hey!" She slapped his wrist. "Slow down, Ry Bread."
She glanced around, a few other people had joined them
at the conference table, while several still congregated in
the corner by the food. Sadie recognized Dave, one of the
production leads, and some other familiar faces from prior
meetings. People she'd rather didn't know about the half-
eaten breakfast pastry crammed in her purse. She'd already been fitted for wardrobe and didn't need their judgy
stares sizing her up. "I meant we could share this *later*."

"Oh." He withdrew his hand sheepishly. "Okay." Ryan
watched, face full of longing, as she closed the bag and
zipped up her purse. "You promise you'll give me a taste
of your donut later, though, right?"

Sadie choked. Damn Ana and her ridiculous meta-
phors. Wishing she could choke her best friend, Sadie

composed herself and nodded. She patted her new costar's cheek. "Later," she repeated, then leaned closer, whispering in his ear, "I promise."

"This looks cozy." Someone observed from behind them, the low male voice tinged with a hint of mockery.

Sadie froze. *No way.* She hadn't heard that voice in more than ten years. But she recognized it immediately. *No freaking way.*

Maybe she was wrong. She was probably wrong. She had to be wrong.

Beside her, Ryan turned toward the voice. "Bo! Hey, man, what's up?"

Bo. The name slammed into her gut, as if someone had written it on a piece of paper, tied it to a boulder, and hurled it straight at her.

Oblivious to her sudden discomfort, Ryan stood, shaking hands with the person behind them. Sadie remained frozen. She had not been mistaken. How did this happen? What was he doing here?

"Sadie?" Tugging on her elbow, Ryan provided the answer. "Say hi to our stunt coordinator, Bo Ibarra."

Not trusting her ability to stand, Sadie glanced over her shoulder. "Hi." She smiled weakly then forced herself to look up, meeting his gaze. "Stunt coordinator, huh?"

"That's right," Bo said. His light brown eyes were exactly the same. Still that unique tawny shade that reminded her of an Irish halfpenny she'd once found in her nana's coin collection, still framed with the most incredibly long and ridiculously thick eyelashes she'd ever seen. His hair was darker, only streaks of the golden blond she remembered glinting here and there. And shorter, much shorter. Last time she'd seen him, it had brushed his shoulders. But what hair Bo had chopped off on top of his head, he'd made up for on his face.

A full beard covered his lean cheeks, hiding the cleft she knew dimpled the center of his chin. The fact she was aware of that feature despite it being hidden from the world felt . . . intimate. Sadie squirmed in her seat, recalling all the times she'd pressed her lips to that dimple. Dragging her attention away from that spot, she noted the beginnings of laugh lines creasing the corners of his eyes. She wondered if besides the cleft, the beard hid more laugh lines around his mouth.

Had there been much laughter in his life? She hoped so.

"Bo-dacious is one of the best in the biz," Ryan continued, patting Bo on the back. "Soon as my agent told me we'd be filming in Chicago, I got on the horn and insisted they hire you, man." Ryan turned to Sadie. "Ain't nobody better to have your back than Bo-dacious here."

"Dude, come on, I told you to knock it off with that Bo-dacious crap," Bo said, taking the sting out of his words with a light punch at Ryan's arm.

"You have a stunt company?" Sadie asked, unable to mask the surprise in her voice.

"I do," he said. "Windy City Stunts."

"I've heard of it." Sadie nodded. "But I didn't . . ." She hesitated. "I didn't know it was your company."

"It is." His mouth twisted.

The answer was spoken softly, but his words were sharp. Biting. An accusation. An acknowledgment of the fact she'd not bothered to stay up to date on what he'd been doing in the years since . . . well, in the years since she'd last seen him.

She hadn't. She'd been afraid to. And she never thought she'd see him again. Certainly not here. Not now. Not like this.

Digging deep, Sadie got to her feet and turned to face Bo. He seemed bigger than she remembered. Not in size exactly, not taller or thicker, but sturdier. More substantial. The last time she'd seen him, they'd been teenagers. A man stood before her now.

"That's great," she managed.

"Yeah, I started with some freelance gigs. Did that for a couple of years before helping form WCS. Now it's become the number-one source for stunt performers in Chicago."

The pride in his voice was unmistakable, and well-deserved. The company had an excellent reputation—even she knew they were the go-to company to hire in this city.

"Wow. I'm happy for you," Sadie said, and meant it too. Despite everything that lay between them, everything that had happened, she was truly glad to see him doing so well.

"Hold up." Ryan glanced between her and Bo. "Do you two know each other?"

For a moment, neither of them answered.

"Yeah." Always the braver one, Bo spoke first. "We were friends as kids."

"Yep," Sadie agreed brightly. Too brightly. "Friends." Throat tight, eyes stinging, she added, "Although it's been a long time. Ten years, I think?"

"Eleven," Bo said, eyes never leaving her face. "But who's counting."

Sadie's heart began to beat faster, wild and fluttery, thumping against her sternum like a bird trying to escape its cage. She knew exactly how many years it had been. Despite her best efforts, she'd never been able to stop keeping track.

"Small world, huh?" Ryan chuckled, either completely oblivious to the tension zipping around him or a better actor than she'd realized. "I met Bo last year when I guest-starred on an episode of *Chicago Rescue*. He set up this amazing stunt, right? An explosion that sent me flying out a twelfth-story window." Ryan brushed one palm over the other, pumping a hand skyward, as if to demonstrate his airborne body.

Sadie's skin crawled at the thought.

"Got any cool stuff like that planned for us, man?" Ryan asked, eager as a kid about to ride a roller coaster.

Sadie hated roller coasters. Hated heights of all kinds, actually. She didn't even do well with escalators. Bo, of course, knew this.

Fuck. She jerked her head toward him. Would he use that knowledge against her? He could. Easily.

"I have some ideas," Bo answered Ryan, but kept his gaze on her, his tawny eyes giving away nothing.

"Do stunt coordinators usually come to first reads?" Sadie asked, struggling to hide the wave of anxiety crashing through her.

"Occasionally." Bo shrugged, the thick line of his shoulders rising and falling. "Depending on the complexity of the stunts, directors will sometimes ask me to sit in on a read, so I can get a feel for things. Identify potential problems."

As he talked, he'd begun rolling up the sleeves of his shirt. Sadie tried not to stare as the strong masculine lines of his forearms were revealed. What was it about a man rolling up his sleeves that immediately upped his hotness factor? And with a guy like Bo, whose hotness level was already off the charts, it simply wasn't fair. "Is that what you're doing today? Identifying potential problems?" *Because she could think of a few.*

Bo looked at her, a knowing twinkle in his eye, as if he was aware of how discombobulated she was. "For one,

I'll decide which stunts I think are suitable for the actors to perform themselves."

"Oh?" Sadie rubbed her palms on her jeans.

A grin curved one corner of his mouth as he nodded. "Don't worry, I'm not here to make anyone do anything that makes them uncomfortable." The teasing edge of his smile eased the vise around Sadie's heart.

"Morning, team!" The director, Sylvia, coasted into the room, fist-bumping people as she made her way toward the head of the table. "RG!" She fist-bumped Ryan. "MG!" She fist-bumped Sadie.

"MG?" Bo asked under his breath.

"Sylvia likes to use initials," Sadie whispered back. "It's her thing."

"But your initials aren't . . ." He paused. "Oh, right. *Mercedes.*" His voice vibrated with a low chuckle. "I'd almost forgot."

Sadie didn't need to look at him to know his smile had taken on an edge of cockiness she remembered all too well. She'd bet he was remembering the conversation they'd had when they were kids. Sadie had been eight, and Bo nine, when he'd first learned her full name was Mercedes Esther Goldovitz. Much to her chagrin, he'd found it hilarious. A girl named after a car.

But now? Was he laughing with her, or at her? Did it matter? As an actress, the public knew her as Sadie Gold. Aside from Sylvia, who'd seen Sadie's full name on a contract and had been calling her MG ever since, the only person who referred to Sadie as Mercedes was her mother, the one who had made the ostentatious decision to name her daughter after a luxury automobile in the first place.

Once upon a time, Bo had called her something else.

Something special. A secret name, just for her. A name Sadie long ago accepted she'd never hear again. She'd sealed the memory of it in a box and locked it away, along with all their other memories. Other secrets.

One of Sylvia's assistants began passing out scripts, and Sadie dropped back into her chair. Ryan returned to his seat on her right, and Bo claimed the open spot on her left. The nervousness she'd felt earlier transformed, became something different. Sadie focused on the little bundle of energy buzzing around inside her. She fiddled with the corner of her script, trying to pin the feeling down. Was it fear? Trepidation?

Next to her, Bo shifted in his chair, and the entire left side of her body grew antennae, tuning in to the man sitting beside her. The buzzing sensation intensified.

Suddenly, Sadie recognized the feeling.

It was hope.

CHAPTER 3

ALL THROUGH THE reading, Bo did his best to stay focused on the task at hand. Today was his first time representing the company for a production of this magnitude, his first time handling a big-budget action film, and he couldn't afford to fuck it up. The last thing he needed was a distraction—yet that's exactly what was sitting right next to him.

Thoughts swirled through his head, question after question spinning their wheels, kicking up dust while doing three-sixties in his mental parking lot. Ever since Bo had learned *she* was going to be Ryan's costar, he'd been preparing himself to deal with it. To deal with her. It wasn't like he could back out of this commitment. The opportunity had been too good to pass up. What he'd told Sadie was only half true. Yes, he was the owner of Windy City Stunts, but it was a partnership. The primary owner was Vic, a crusty old fall guy who'd started an early version of the company when Bo was still tooling around on bikes with training wheels.

When Vic asked Bo to come on board and help officially

form WCS, Bo had focused most of his time coordinating projects for the local TV shows that filmed perennially in the city while Vic took on the film productions that came through. Bo had organized stunts for a few movies, but to date, nothing big had been under his solo command. The plan had always been for Bo to eventually take complete ownership of WCS, but when it came down to it, Vic was finding it hard to let go.

Bo got it; he did. Vic loved his job and letting go of the company wasn't a decision the tough old bird would make lightly. Nor should he. But Bo never would have agreed to a partnership if he'd thought WCS wouldn't one day be his. Lately, he wondered if he'd made a mistake. If, like his father, he'd end up stuck running someone else's business, putting all his time, sweat, and energy into something that belonged to somebody else.

For the past two years, every time WCS took on a film, even when Bo was head coordinator, Vic couldn't resist jumping in at the last minute and taking control. Bo didn't mind, exactly. He appreciated Vic's expertise and understood why it was hard for the guy to back off. But it was time Bo had a chance—not only to show Vic what he could do, but to prove to himself he had what it took to run the company on his own.

When Ryan put in a good word for Bo with the executive producer of a big-budget action film based on a best-selling novel set in Chicago, it was the perfect opportunity. Due to WCS's reputation, Bo was sure hiring their company had been a given, but thanks to Ryan, Bo's name had been requested specifically, forcing Vic to step aside and let Bo take the reins.

All Bo had to do now was manage to hold on to them. There was a lot of publicity surrounding this movie. If things went as well as Bo hoped, the success of this gig should be enough to finally convince Vic to let go permanently.

Scribbling notes in the corner of the script, Bo did his best to ignore the woman next to him, ignore how she sat there looking casual, sexy, faded jeans hugging her legs. Ignore the honey-smooth caress of her voice whenever it was her turn to read. Ignore the warm, sweet scent of her. For Chrissakes, she smelled like freshly baked sin.

It should be easy to ignore Sadie. Especially since, apparently, the opposite was true. She found it easy to ignore him. The fact she hadn't known he was working on this project—hadn't known anything about what he'd been doing with his life at all—stung. Eleven years. Had she never bothered to check in on him, never typed his name into the search bar or looked him up on social media? Not even once?

Nope. Apparently, she'd just gone on with her life as if he'd never existed.

Why was he surprised? That's exactly what he'd told her to do.

He just hadn't realized it would be so easy for her. It hadn't been for him.

The director finally wrapped up the meeting with a reminder that her assistant would be sending out call sheets for the first week of shooting later that day. Once everyone had been dismissed and began filing out of the room, Bo hurried after Sadie, questions still churning.

Before he could catch up to her, Ryan intercepted him with a dude-bro punch to the shoulder.

"Man, I can't wait to get started. This shoot is going to be *sweet*. I can do the jump off the silo, right? We don't need a double for that."

"I need to think about it," Bo hedged. "Consider the logistics first."

"Why don't I take you out for a drink and we can look at the logistics together?" Ryan suggested.

"Sure," Bo agreed, tracking Sadie as she moved closer to the door of the conference room.

"Wait." Ryan's face fell. "I can't have beer. Too many carbs."

For a second Bo thought the guy was going to burst into tears, but then Ryan beamed with fresh enthusiasm. "What if I buy the beers and watch you drink them?"

"Like some kind of alcoholic voyeurism?" Bo snorted, beginning to shake his head no, but paused and changed his mind. "You know what? Sure, I'm in." He owed Ryan for the referral and besides, he'd say anything to get the guy out of his way. Sadie had stopped to talk to someone, now was his chance.

"Great, man." Ryan slapped him on the back. "Tonight, then. It'll be fun."

Bo nodded, relieved he was finally free. But before he could head toward Sadie, Ryan beat him to it. Bo watched in mute frustration as the charming lead actor bent his head low to whisper in Sadie's ear.

Clutching her purse to her chest, she giggled. Bo's heart clenched at the sound. A moment later, Ryan was leading Sadie out the door of the conference room, the two of them wearing matching looks of clandestine mischief.

He watched them go, shocked at the sudden rush of jealousy heating his blood. This was dangerous. Bo needed to get his shit together and relax. Be rational. Professional. If Ryan and Sadie wanted to sneak off together for a bit of . . . whatever it was they were doing, it wasn't his business. Why should he be surprised? It made sense. The two of them were going to be spending a lot of time together, and it was not unlikely something would develop between the costars. Bo saw it all the time on set.

Holy hell, with the number of fights and stunts this script called for, he'd be spending a lot of time with them too. With her. But while performers dating each other was common and widely accepted—often even expected—a stunt man dating an actress, especially a lead actress, was not.

Bo hoped Ryan planned to make good on his offer, because he suddenly found himself needing a drink.

That evening the actor did, indeed, follow through, which was how Bo found himself propped on a bar stool in the trendy brewery conveniently located around the corner from the studio. Bo was on his second beer and Ryan was on his second chick. He took a swill of his porter and eyed Ryan in the act of getting girl number two's phone number.

Thanks to its location, the brewpub was a hot spot for people in the biz to hook up. Or, even more common, for those looking to hook up with someone in the biz. The flirting had started the moment Ryan had walked in, making Bo wish he'd picked a place under the radar. After girl number two blew them both a kiss and bounced off, Bo decided to give the actor a piece of his mind. "What the fuck, dude?"

"Huh?" Ryan gave him a blank stare.

"If you're messing around with Sadie, what are you doing chasing tail here?"

Ryan chuckled.

Embarrassment washed over him. Bo regretted bringing the subject up, but it was out there now, so he forged ahead. "Look, it's not really any of my business, except for the fact that I have to work with both of you." *There's also the fact that the thought of you hurting her makes me want to rip your head from your shoulders.*

"No, man, you got it all wrong." Ryan shook his head, still laughing. "Sadie and I are just friends. I don't like to taint the well, if you know what I mean."

Bo raised a brow.

"I'm serious. I don't date costars. Something always goes wrong and it ends in disaster." Ryan cracked open a bottle of mineral water and took a swig. "It's like that old saying, don't shit where you eat." He smirked. "Well, kind of. My rule is don't fuck where you work." Another chuckle. "It's like my mantra."

"You should see about getting that put on a T-shirt," Bo muttered.

"That's not a bad idea." Ryan grinned at him across the table, eyes gleaming with impish curiosity. "What gave you the idea I'm messing around with Sadie?"

"The two of you seemed extra *friendly* when I first walked in today. And then, after the read, when you rushed off together . . ." Bo trailed off. "Whatever. Obviously, I must have been mistaken."

"Dude," Ryan said, staring at Bo. "Duuuuuuuuude."

"What?" Bo snapped.

"You like her."

"What is this? Fucking kindergarten?"

"You do, you totally have feelings for her." Ryan leaned across the table wiggling his eyebrows. "What's up between you two, anyway?"

"Nothing." Bo stared into his beer. Once upon a time, she'd been his everything. "I told you, we knew each other as kids."

"Uh-huh, yeah. That *nothing* seemed like a whole lot of *something* to me." Ryan shook his head. "The tension between you two was thick enough to choke an orca."

Shit. He hadn't covered up his feelings as well as he'd thought. "You noticed that, huh?"

"Come on, man. I'm not a complete dumbass." Ryan straightened up on his stool. "I'm actually a better actor than people give me credit for. It's not just this hot bod, you know." He winked, pressing a quick kiss to each of his biceps. "Though, that is why you saw me sneaking off with Sadie earlier."

"Because of your hot bod?" Bo's grip tightened on his glass as he raised it to his mouth. Again, white-hot jealousy rushed through him, singeing his insides. *Fuck.*

"Chill, bro. I told you, it's not like that." Ryan watched, face full of longing as Bo chugged his beer. "We're both stuck on this evil diet as part of the movie prep. It's killing me. For real. I thought I was dying today, and she saved me."

"Okay," Bo drawled, not sure where this hyperbole was headed.

"No, really. She had a donut stashed in her purse. And not just any donut, a *Stan's* donut. It was like a freaking miracle."

Bo stared at him. *Well, that explained the warm delicious smell.*

"I'm telling you, she saved my life." Ryan leaned an elbow on the table. "Just ask my fans. I've been filming myself when I have to eat the crap on my meal plan. Making little videos so they can watch me suffer for my art, that kind of thing."

At that moment, a woman Bo predicted would become girl number three walked up to their table. "Hey," she purred. "Aren't you Ryan Gratt?"

"Hey, yourself," Ryan shot back. "Aren't you my date tomorrow?"

Bo hid a smile in his beer. The actor had dropped his voice to a deep gravelly rumble. To Bo, it sounded ridiculous, like a cartoon caped crusader, but the chicks seemed to lap it up. The woman leaned in closer and ran her hand along Ryan's arm, fondling his muscles.

After exchanging numbers and making plans to meet up later, the woman sauntered off. Ryan watched her go with an appreciative sigh. "Yeah, the diet sucks and the training blows, but it's all worth it."

"Because it scored you a role in a big movie?"

"No, man. Because it's scoring me all the pussy I can eat."

Bo shook his head at the guy's crass goofiness and finished up his drink. "Just don't go overboard. I need you well rested for Monday."

"Don't worry." Ryan wiggled his eyebrows. "I plan to spend most of my time in bed this weekend."

Exhausted, Bo wanted nothing more than to head home and spend the weekend in bed himself. But somehow, with memories of a hot blonde who smelled like fresh-baked temptation taking up all the space in his head, he doubted he'd be getting much sleep.

CHAPTER 4

WAY TOO EARLY on Sunday morning, while normal people were still sleeping, Sadie was on a mostly empty L train, taking the purple line north out of the city to meet Ana for their bike ride. She'd had over twenty-four hours to process the fact she would be spending the next few months working with Bo Ibarra. And still, it seemed unreal. Seeing him had been unreal.

Sadie may have never expected to see him again, but that didn't mean she hadn't imagined the moment over and over in the last decade. In the hundreds of thousands of times her mind had played out various ways their paths might cross one day, she'd never managed to come up with this scenario. It was almost enough to make her believe in fate.

Almost.

Exiting the train, Sadie headed east. From the first time she'd read the script, she knew she wanted the role of Jamie. More than anything she'd ever wanted, ever. Well, except for one other thing. And, strangely enough, thanks to this movie, that was suddenly, unbelievably, happening too. Because deep down, Sadie had always wanted to see Bo again.

A buzz of energy zinged through her, the same way it had on Friday when she'd sat next to him. At first, she hadn't recognized the charged hum of nerves fluttering around inside her, because it had been so long since she'd felt it. *Hope.* She wrapped her arms around herself, holding the feeling close.

Sadie turned the corner and headed down the path toward the bike trail. A blast of wind hit her full in the face, and she ducked her head, pulling her hood up.

"You're late," Ana called from across the trail's parking lot, voice rising over the steady crash of the waves rolling in on the Lake Michigan shoreline.

Sadie squinted through the wind and glare coming off the lake to see her friend leaning against a van with GLASS SLIPPER EVENTS, the name of Ana's party planning company, emblazoned on the side. Two bikes rested on their kickstands nearby, frames glinting in the morning light, helmets hanging by their straps on the handlebars. "What time did you get here? Sunrise?"

"Maybe." Ana grinned, standing up and stretching. She grabbed one of the helmets and handed Sadie the other. "Ready to roll?"

"Let's get this over with," Sadie grumbled, strapping the helmet on. "What kind of ride do you have planned for us today?" she asked, bending over to loosen up her hamstrings. "Long?" She stood, kicking a foot up behind her and grabbing her ankle, stretching her quads. She switched legs. "Or really long?"

"Hey, riding season is almost over," Ana protested, pulling two water bottles out of the van before locking it. She tossed one to Sadie, then shoved hers into a wire holder secured to the bike frame.

"Which means you're adding extra miles each ride to . . . what? Make up for all the rides you're going to miss once winter hits?" Sadie shoved her water bottle into the holder on the other bike.

"Something like that." Ana chuckled. She grabbed her bike by the handlebars and headed across the lot.

"Why don't you just ride indoors during the winter?" Sadie wondered, following behind her friend.

"I do ride a stationary bike in the winter. But it's not the same." Ana slipped her feet into the stirrups on her pedals and eased onto the trail. She rose from the saddle and started pumping hard, picking up speed.

"Ana, wait!" Sadie called, hopping onto her borrowed bike and hurrying to catch up. It never ceased to amaze her how damn fast her friend was on two wheels.

Forty-five freaking minutes later, Ana finally slowed down, and Sadie pulled up next to her, breathing hard. "Well, I got my workout for today," she wheezed.

"Says the one who's supposed to be in shape," Ana snorted.

"You've always kicked my ass on a bike."

"True." Ana grinned. She let go of one of the handlebars and patted her leg. "It's thanks to these babies." Bending to grab her water bottle, she sat back up and took a quick chug before adding, "Thick thighs save lives."

Sadie choked on her water, snorting with laughter. "Put that on a T-shirt."

"Already done, my friend." Ana stashed her bottle and began to pick up the pace again.

"Not yet!" Sadie groaned, falling behind as she wrestled to put her own bottle back. "Can't we take it easy for a little bit?" She flung an arm out toward the lake. "It's a gorgeous day, let's enjoy it."

When Ana still didn't slow down, Sadie called out, "I have something important to tell you!"

That got her friend's attention. Ana squeezed her brakes, chin jerking over her shoulder as she watched Sadie catch up. "Well?"

"Give me a sec," Sadie huffed, sucking in air. She could run mile after mile. Deadlift twice her weight. But get her on a bike and she was toast. After a few minutes pedaling at a more leisurely clip, Sadie had her breath back . . . but not her words. She'd wanted to talk to Ana about Bo, but now that the moment was here, she couldn't work up the nerve.

"Does it have something to do with the movie?" Ana asked, impatient as she forced herself to maintain a slower pace.

"Yes and no." Sadie guided her bike around a curve, checking to make sure the way ahead was clear.

"Something happen at the read? Is your costar a dick?"

"No, nothing like that. Ryan is fine." Sadie shook her head. "Fun, even." She tugged at the zipper of her hoodie with one hand. Now that she'd worked up a sweat, the breeze felt good. "I shared my donut with him."

"That was fast," Ana snickered.

"Will you stop with the euphemisms!" Sadie reached over to shove her friend, but Ana pedaled out of reach. Drawing even with her again, Sadie continued, "My costar is not the problem. It was someone else at the meeting."

"The director? I thought you said you loved Sylvia."

"I do love Sylvia, she's great. I'm thrilled to be working with her."

"Then who?"

"I'm trying to tell you!" Sadie snapped, exasperated.

"Well, you're not doing a good job of it. Spit it out already. What happened that was so important? Who was at the reading?"

"Bo," Sadie said, before her courage left her again.

"Bo?" Ana skidded to a halt. "*Bo* Bo?"

Besties since their first day of posh, overpriced preschool, Ana had known Sadie a long time. She knew everything that had happened with Bo.

Almost everything.

Sadie squeezed the brakes on her handlebars and wheeled around, turning her bike to face Ana's. "Yeah."

"Whoa."

"I know."

Around them, other bikers zipped past. In the distance, a whistle blew, a soccer or lacrosse game starting on one of the many fields adjacent to the path.

Wordlessly, Ana reversed directions and together they began the trek back. After a few minutes of riding in silence, she finally asked, "How is he?"

"Good," Sadie said, throat dry. "Really good." *He looked really good too.*

"I wouldn't have pegged him as an actor."

"He's not; he's the stunt coordinator."

Ana nodded. "Now that, I can totally see."

"He's in charge of all the stunts for the movie. He choreographs the fights and will be overseeing everything. Overseeing me."

"Are you freaking out?"

"Yes, I'm freaking out!" The dam burst, and Sadie began to ramble. "My first call is tomorrow morning, and *of course* it's for one of the fight scenes. How am I supposed to keep it together when he'll be there—on set—babysitting me."

"Babysitting you?" Ana blinked.

"It's when a stunt coordinator watches over a scene, to make sure the actors don't get hurt or whatever." Sadie's stomach twisted. "He'll be watching everything I do."

"First of all, you know better than to think of it like that. He's not watching *you*, he's watching your character, your performance. Babysitting, like you said. And second . . ." A twinkle appeared in Ana's emerald eyes. "Maybe this is your chance."

"My chance for what?" Sadie wondered. "My chance to finally find out why the guy I wanted to spend my life with dumped me without explanation?"

"I was thinking it's your chance to try again," Ana mused. "It's been ten years."

"Eleven," Sadie growled, pedaling faster.

"Eleven," Ana amended, matching Sadie's pace, "and now fate has brought you two back together."

"We are *not* back together."

"Not yet."

"Ana!"

"Are you saying you don't have feelings for him?"

Sadie didn't respond. She didn't have to.

"I know you, Sadie. I know all about your boxes. And let me tell you, you can cram your feelings into a box, slam a lid on top, and lock it up, but the stuff is still inside. Eventually, something is going to make you drop that box, busting it open. And when that happens, look out."

"What do you suggest I do about it?" Sadie demanded, breath coming harsher. "I can't just wave a magic wand and *poof!* All my feelings disappear."

"Please. You know you can't wish your feelings away." Ana glanced over at her. "You have to deal with them."

Easier said than done. "How?"

"Channel all that angsty emotional shit into this fight scene you're so worried about."

"I think I like the magic wand option better," Sadie grumbled.

"Even fairy tales don't work like that." Ana laughed and took off, flying ahead as she yelled, "Race you to the van!"

Tightening her fingers on the handlebars, wishing she could ride fast enough to escape the memories in those boxes, Sadie leaned forward and chased after her friend.

Later that afternoon, after she'd helped Ana load the bikes back into the van and choked down a protein bar, Sadie stood in her shower, letting the hot water soak into her sore muscles. Meanwhile, Ana's words soaked into her brain.

Like her best friend had said, Sadie had a habit of boxing up her emotions into a dark corner. *Compartmentalizing.* She'd developed the trick early on in her acting career, and found it worked just as well off the stage as on. At this point in her life, shutting away problematic emotions to focus on the task at hand wasn't just a performance trick, it was a survival tool.

Why deal with all those messy feelings when you could ignore them?

The urge to do it again, right now, was strong. Sadie wanted to take the joy and fear and worry and wonder and every other nuance of emotion bubbling up inside of her ever since seeing Bo and shove it in a box. Conveniently, she already had one with his name scrawled across it in big angry letters. Being near him had loosened the lid, brought things long buried to the surface.

Sadie closed her eyes, the memory of their last night together rising like steam from her shower, enveloping her. Senior prom. The night he'd told her it was over—they were over.

"It's over, abeja."

His words ringing in her ears from across the years, Sadie's eyes snapped open. She grabbed her loofah and began to scrub, her skin turning bright pink beneath the rough, angry strokes.

She hadn't been angry that night. She'd been too stunned, too confused to feel anything beyond disbelief. It had been the night of her prom, and despite his reservations, Bo had agreed to be her date. The night had been going well. The dance had been fun, and even though Bo wasn't the biggest fan of most of her classmates, he'd seemed to enjoy himself well enough. He'd definitely enjoyed the time they'd shared in the back seat of his car between the dance and the after-party.

Then he'd dropped her off to freshen up with her friends and went to park the car. The after-party was on a cruise ship on Lake Michigan. Sadie had stood on the gangplank, waiting for Bo, worry creeping up inside her as the minutes ticked by.

Setting the loofah aside, she leaned her head back into the shower spray. Beads of water drummed against her shoulders, drowning out the rising thump of her heart, reminding her of the sound of Bo's footsteps on the dock, the relief she felt when she caught the flash of his white dress shirt in the light from the streetlamps dotting the pier.

She'd hurried toward him and reached for his hand. But when she'd grabbed his fingers, he'd winced and tried to pull away.

Slicking her hair back, Sadie stared down at her own hands, recalling how Bo's had looked that night. The streak of dark bruises along his knuckles. After that, she'd noticed other details too. The way his tie hung limp around his neck. One sleeve of his shirt ripped. And a dark stain on his collar.

Blood.

She'd demanded to know what happened, worried he'd been in a fight. But he'd shrugged her off. Sadie turned her face into the spray as the memory of what happened next washed over her. He'd told her it didn't matter. Said *they* didn't matter. And when she'd tried to reach for him again, he'd stepped back, avoiding her touch.

With a voice like sandpaper, Bo had looked Sadie in the eyes and told her he never wanted to see her again.

"It's over, abeja."

Sadie braced her hands against the slick tiles of her shower, water streaming down her cheeks, mixing with her tears. It had been so long since she'd let herself cry over him, over them, over everything they'd lost. The memory stirred the lid on another box, one she kept hidden even deeper still—deep, deep down. Wrapped in chains, anchored to the deepest, darkest, most hidden part of her heart.

With a vicious pull on the faucet, Sadie turned off the water and mentally resealed the lid before any tendrils of the memories trapped inside could escape, reach out, grab hold. Ana may know about Sadie's boxes, but she didn't know what was hidden in this particular box. Sadie had never told anyone. And she never planned to.

No. This box would stay locked and buried. Sadie was determined to make sure it would never be opened, its contents never spilled.

After drying off, Sadie took her time applying lotion, rubbing the cream on with slow, soothing strokes. As it soaked into her skin, a calm settled over her, emotions drifting back below the surface. She tugged on a pair of sweats and decided to spend the rest of her Sunday snuggled on the couch with some wine and cat videos.

Wrapped in a blanket, laptop propped on her knees, Sadie sipped a glass of merlot and poked around the internet, grinning her way through a series of clips involving cats who delight in terrorizing dogs three times their size. She clicked on the next video and gasped at the sight of a huge, shaggy Irish wolfhound.

Flynn. Her heart squeezed. The dog in the video looked just like Flynn, the furry best friend of her childhood. Though technically her grandmother's dog, everyone knew Flynn belonged to Sadie—or rather, they belonged to each other. Sadie had been four when Flynn was born, and from the moment puppy and girl met, a bond was formed.

A bittersweet ache spread through her chest. The same sensation she'd felt at the end of every summer, when it was time to head back home, leaving her nana and Flynn behind. The first few years, Sadie had begged her mother to let Flynn come with them. But the answer was always no. The city was no place for a dog like Flynn. He was too big, too loud, too messy . . .

She hated having to leave him behind. Hated having to say goodbye.

Just like she'd hated saying goodbye to Bo at the end of every summer.

Ugh. Sadie downed the rest of her wine. She'd managed to avoid thinking about him for more than an hour, but here the man was, creeping back into her thoughts.

Bo had been her first everything. Her first crush, her first kiss, her first boyfriend. Her first love, her first lover . . . her first heartbreak. And while she'd gone on to have many more kisses with many more boyfriends and several lovers, she'd never *loved* any of them. And certainly none of them had broken her heart.

Though, one could argue, you can't break what's already broken.

She reached for the bottle and refilled her glass. Growing up, Sadie had spent every summer vacation with her grandmother. From early June to late August, while her parents traveled the globe, visiting hotels around the world for her dad's job, Sadie was sent to the Murphy family estate, the stables and meadows becoming her world.

She'd met Bo the summer she was seven, and he'd become part of her world too. A year older, he was reckless and bold and daring. Like Flynn, Sadie couldn't imagine Bo in the city. He was too wild, too free—unlike anybody she knew back home. When she was with him, she felt wild and free too, the summer days stretching into an endless adventure.

Well, not actually endless. Near the end of each August, one of her parents' spotless fancy cars would roll up the driveway to her nana's estate, come to fetch her home. Sadie could count on one hand the number of times her mother and father came themselves. Usually they sent a nanny, or sometimes just their driver. And once, they forgot to send someone at all.

That was just fine with Sadie, she'd have been perfectly happy to stay with her grandmother year-round. Then she could play with Flynn all the time and see Bo every day. His father was the stable manager for her grandmother's estate, and Bo and his family lived on the property in the carriage house, just a short walk down the hill, across the meadow, and through a patch of trees. Sadie had walked the path so many times, she could do it blindfolded.

As far as Sadie knew, Bo's family still lived there. It was part of the reason she hadn't returned to the Murphy estate in years—eleven years, to be exact.

Who was she kidding? It was the only reason.

She took a long pull on her wine and sank deeper into the couch, assailed by a sudden wave of guilt. Unlike the fearless heroine she'd spent the past summer preparing to become, Sadie was a coward. The last time she'd set foot on the estate had been the summer after Bo had broken up with her. That horrible, horrible summer.

Don't think about that. Back in the box. Close the lid. Lock it tight.

Sadie stared into her empty glass.

In the years since, Sadie had made every excuse imaginable to avoid going out to her grandmother's home. She'd spent time with her nana when the family gathered for events in the city. Visited with Nana when she came to her parents' house for holidays. Sadie convinced herself that was good enough.

The lie had been easier to buy when she'd been living in New York. But Sadie had been back in Chicago for months. And still, she'd avoided making the drive north. If she was honest, it was why she'd put off getting a car. Anything to help validate her own bullshit.

That night on the pier, when Bo had closed the door on them—slammed it in her face, really—Sadie had told herself that in order to move on, she would have to keep that door closed. For years she'd managed to keep it shut, resisting the urge to tug on it.

She pictured Bo, standing in the conference room, eyes she knew so well flashing in a face that had changed so much. She ached to fill in the details, to know how the boy she remembered had become the man she'd met.

Sadie pulled her laptop closer and fiddled with the keys, fingers hovering over the letters of Bo's name.

The door was already open. What harm would there be in taking a peek?

CHAPTER 5

ON SUNDAY EVENING, Bo raced his motorcycle down the long winding road to his parents' home. Leaves the shade of marigolds kicked up in his wake. This early in the season, the fall color was just beginning to show, but the corn was already high. The tall stalks swayed in the fields, their silken crowns gilded with golden light as the September sun sank toward the west.

Bo slowed to a crawl and made the turn onto a gravel drive. A few moments later, he rolled to a stop next to his family's dusty old pickup truck. After ditching his helmet, he grabbed his saddlebag and bypassed the house, heading for the nearby stable.

The familiar smells of horse and leather, dust and hay assailed him as he strolled down the aisle between the stalls. The stable doors were open wide, allowing the evening breeze to flow through, dulling the more acrid scents. Horses knickered as he past, ears flicking with interest, a few curious muzzles peeking over the top of their stall doors. He patted their velvet noses, but kept moving, boots scraping on the stone floor.

Pausing in front of the last stall in the aisle, he tugged the pack off his shoulder and unbuckled it. As he bent over, rummaging inside the bag, something warm and firm nudged the top of his head. Bo glanced up, smiling at the big beautiful dark eyes watching him. "There you are," he murmured, reaching out to stroke the mare's neck. "How are you, old girl?"

She nudged him again, harder this time, and he chuckled. "Impatient, aren't we?" he teased, pulling out the treats he'd brought. Bo turned around, facing away from the horse. She headbutted him right between the shoulder blades. "Hey," he grunted. "No peeking." He grabbed a fistful of chopped carrots in one hand, and sugar cubes in the other.

Turning around again, Bo held up both fists. "Which will it be today, bella dama?"

The mare leaned closer, nostrils quivering as she sniffed his hands. After a moment, she knickered, head bobbing in excitement over his left hand. "You're so predictable." He chuckled, opening the fist with the sugar cubes.

"Uncle Bo?" a small voice called.

"Back here, Toby. By Stella."

"Abuela says not to give her any sweets," the little boy warned, scurrying down the aisle toward him.

"Uh-oh," Bo said as Stella licked the last traces of sugar from his palm. "Too late." He grinned down at his nephew. "Are you going to tell her?"

"Nah." Toby screwed up his face. "She never lets me have sweets neither."

"Never?"

"Well, *not* never," the boy admitted with all the irritated acquiescence his seven years could muster. "Mamá made cherry-cola cake for dessert tonight, and Abuela promised I could have the first piece."

"Cherry-cola cake, huh? That's my favorite." Bo smiled.

"I know. That's why Mamá made it."

"Here." He offered Toby the carrots in his right hand. "Why don't you give these to Stella."

"Abuela says you're s'posed to eat your veggies first."

"That's good advice," Bo agreed. "But once in a while, it's okay to break the rules." He stopped, glancing down at his nephew sheepishly. "Um, don't tell her I said that. Or your mom, for that matter."

"They have too many rules anyway," Toby grumbled. He lifted his hand toward Stella and the mare reached forward eagerly.

"Easy now," Bo warned. "Make sure to keep your hand flat, palm up. You don't want her to mistake one of your fingers for a carrot."

"I *know*," the boy huffed, his voice smarting with indignation.

Bo backed off, reminding himself his nephew knew what he was doing. Like Bo, he'd grown up around horses, riding almost before he was walking. Still, Bo kept an eye on Toby's hand while the boy's precious little fingers were in chomping range of Stella's strong white teeth.

"It tickles." Toby giggled as Stella's soft thick lips roamed over his palm, looking for more.

Bo smiled, loving the sound of his nephew's laughter. There was nothing quite like it in the world. He brushed his hand over Stella's forelock absently, watching Toby. His nephew's blond hair glinted golden in the warm shaft of evening sunlight spilling in the open doors of the stable. Bo glanced outside, the sun had dipped lower, long shadows creeping across the meadow beyond the stable yard. He looped his saddlebag over his shoulder. "Come on," he ordered, swooping Toby up and tossing him over his other shoulder. "We better get inside and wash up."

He tickled Toby in the ribs and was rewarded with shrieks of glee.

"One of your abuela's rules I know better than to break," Bo said as he headed toward the house, arm locked around his nephew's middle, holding him in place, "is never show up late for dinner."

Hands clean and folded, Bo bowed his head as his father said grace. Sunday dinner was sacred in the Ibarra family. You didn't miss it unless you were bleeding, and only then if the injury was life threatening. Though he'd moved out and gotten his own place several years ago, Bo still made the hour drive to his parents' house every week.

"Amen," Dad's gruff voice concluded the prayer.

Like a pistol shot at the start of a race, everyone jumped into motion at once. Bo's mother set about pouring iced tea while his father began slicing the roast. Bo reached for the basket of rolls. Across the table, his sister spooned vegetables onto Toby's plate, much to the child's displeasure.

"Tobias," Bo's father chided, "you are going to eat every one of those green beans. Your mother grew them herself."

"Yes, Granda," Toby grumbled, cramming a green bean in his mouth.

"Better give me some of those too," Bo said, holding his plate out to his sister. As she scooped out a serving, Bo winked at Toby. "I hear there's cake later."

"It was supposed to be a surprise." His sister shot her son an accusing look, her smile taking out the sting.

"Cherry-cola cake? I *am* surprised." Bo grinned at Luna. "What are we celebrating?" A thick, rich chocolate cake sweetened with cherry cola and slathered with just the right amount of fudge frosting and topped with maraschino cherries, his favorite dessert was usually a treat his sister reserved for special occasions.

"Your new job," Luna said. "You start filming tomorrow, right?"

"Yeah, but it's not really a new job," Bo hedged. "Just another project for Windy City Stunts."

"Just another project," Luna echoed in a mocking voice. "You're working on a Sylvia Jensen movie!"

"Who?" Mom asked.

"Sylvia Jensen." His sister glanced at their mother. "She directed all those superhero movies." Luna returned her attention to Bo. "My big brother has hit the big time."

"You get to work with superheroes?" Toby asked, eyes bright with excitement.

"Not exactly." Bo leaned across the table. "This movie is about a girl who fights for justice and stands up for what she believes in. She's a hero, but no cape or superpowers."

"Oh." Toby's face fell.

"She does have to ride a horse, though," Bo added.

"Oh?" With typical exuberance, Toby's curiosity bounced back. "Fast?"

"Very fast." Bo nodded. "To escape the bad guys." He washed down the last of his roll with some iced tea. "That's part of my job, to make sure everyone's safe while on horseback."

From the head of the table came a grunt. Bo glanced up. His dad's attention was on his plate, but Bo knew that grunt had been meant for him. Dad had never been a big fan of his career choice. Bo pushed his food around, stomach churning with guilt. He knew his father still resented the fact Bo hadn't taken over for him here at the estate. Dad had never been able to understand why Bo would refuse such an opportunity.

As the story went, Bo's father had come here from Ireland with barely more than the clothes on his back. The position of stable manager for Murphy Farms was an answer to a desperate man's prayers, providing a steady, if not lavish, income, as well as use of the carriage house and surrounding property. Dad had been able to settle down. Get married. Raise a family.

But everything, from the beds they slept in, to the table they ate on, was owned by the Murphy family.

Sadie's family.

From a young age, Bo had known that the world was divided between the haves and have-nots. His dad liked to say fortune came with the flip of a coin. And Bo knew which side of the coin he fell on.

And which side Sadie did.

After Dad's accident, Esther Murphy, Sadie's grandmother, had insisted Bo's family stay in the carriage house. The house and gardens were theirs to use until his dad's death. She'd also asked Bo if he wanted to take over management of the stables. The offer made sense. Bo knew the property and the horses as well as his father and had already been helping with many of the responsibilities for years. Plus, if Bo accepted, his family could remain in the carriage house for another generation.

It seemed like the perfect solution. Grateful for the opportunity and what it would mean for his family, Bo came very close to accepting. But the thought of pouring everything he had into a place that belonged to someone else, that he could never truly call his own . . . didn't sit well with him.

He didn't want to step into his father's shoes, he wanted to stand on his own two feet, earn his own way, be his own boss. It's why it was so important he eventually took over Windy City Stunts. To make it his.

And then, of course, was the issue of Sadie. Did she even know what had happened to his father? The arrangement her grandmother had made? Probably not. She hadn't had a fucking clue about his life, so why would this be any different? As far as Bo knew, she hadn't set foot on this estate in a decade. He doubted that was a coincidence.

Sadie may not have kept up with what he'd been doing all these years, but Bo had stayed informed about her. He'd already known where she'd planned to go to college in Chicago, and knew she moved to New York City right after graduation. He'd followed her career faithfully, knew every cheesy commercial she'd made, the movies she'd had minor roles in, every television show she'd appeared on. His abuela wasn't the only one who watched every single episode of that angst-fest of a soap opera Sadie had starred in.

Ever since he'd found out she'd been cast in this movie, even though he'd been worried about how she'd react to seeing him, he'd been looking forward to seeing her. Bo had expected Sadie to be angry, to hate him even. But he hadn't been prepared for her initial coldness. Her calm aloofness. The fact she'd not known a single thing about what he'd been doing in the years since she'd seen him last.

It was like she hadn't thought about him at all. Her indifference hurt worse than her anger.

"Can we have cake now?"

Bo cast a grin across the table at his nephew, grateful for the distraction.

"I still count three green beans on that plate, mijo," Luna observed. She looked over at Bo. "And your uncle Bo has a whole pile left."

At Toby's accusing glare, Bo crammed a forkful of green beans in his mouth.

"I can't wait to see that escape scene on the big screen," Luna said, watching her son as he ate the last of his vegetables one bean at a time. "I read the book and thought the story was amazing. Did you know the author is from right here in Chicago? And young? Like my age."

Bo chewed, watching his sister in stunned silence. Luna didn't ramble often. She really must have loved that book.

"Who did they cast in the lead?" Luna asked, attention shifting to Bo. "Anyone I've heard of?"

Green beans lodged in Bo's gullet. *Oh, you've definitely heard of her.* He forced himself to swallow. "Sadie Gold," he mumbled, bracing himself for his sister's reaction. She'd never been a member of the Sadie fan club.

"Sadie?" Luna's voice rose. "Sadie Goldovitz?" She leaned back in her chair, staring across the table at him. "You're working with that spoiled little b—"

Their father cleared his throat, loudly. Swearing was not allowed at the dinner table.

Luna shot a quick glance at her father, then her son, before flicking her eyes back to Bo. "Brat?"

Bo stared down at his plate and poked at his remaining green beans. Ever since they were little, Luna had despised Sadie. But his sister had never told him why, so Bo had decided it was some female thing and given up trying to figure it out.

"Isn't that Esther Murphy's little granddaughter?" his mom asked. "The one who would stay with her during the summer?" She smiled at Bo. "You two used to be inseparable, gallivanting all over the place."

"That was a long time ago," Bo said, cheeks heating.

"Never had time for anyone but each other," Luna grumbled.

Bo glanced at his sister. Had she been jealous? Was that her problem?

"Little Sadie. A movie star." Mom sighed. "I remember when she was on that show Abuela likes, the American telenovela." His mother waved her hand, searching for the title.

"*Hope General*," Luna said. "Yeah. She played a spoiled brat on there too."

"Pfft, that's just her TV character, mija. I thought Sadie was a lovely girl. And I know our Bo certainly thought so." His mother cast a playful look his way. "It's been so long since I saw her in person, though. How does she look?"

"Good," Bo grunted. *He should have stayed in the stable.* "Stella looks good too," he observed, desperate to change the subject.

As he hoped, his mother immediately took the bait, nodding. "She does, doesn't she? Poor old girl."

"Isn't Stella the same age as you, Uncle Bo?" Toby asked.

"That's right, we were born a few months apart." Bo's heart tugged with affection for the sweet aging horse. Lippizans tended to live longer than average, but at thirty, the mare was nearing her end. At best, she had five more years, though likely it was closer to only two or three. He sighed, filled with melancholy at the passing of time.

"Mamá?" Toby asked, tugging on Luna's arm. "Uncle Bo isn't going to die soon, is he?"

"What? No, baby," his sister assured her son, running a hand over his sandy-blond hair, so like his own had been at the same age, and likely how Bo's dad's had been as a boy too.

In terms of rolling the genetic dice, Bo and his sister had managed to split things evenly. While Bo had Dad's brown hair and Mom's coppery eyes, Luna had inherited their mother's black hair and Dad's green eyes.

And while Toby's hair would likely darken to the same shade as his uncle and granda, his eye color was altogether different—blue as a robin's egg—most likely from his father's side. But Bo couldn't know for sure, and he would never, ever ask. Like her feelings for Sadie, Luna refused to discuss Toby's father.

"I'm not going anywhere, little man," Bo assured his nephew. "Horses are different than people. They don't usually live as long."

"That's sad," Toby said, lip quivering.

"It is," Bo agreed. "That's why it's important we do everything we can to make sure Stella is as happy as we can make her while she's still with us."

"Is that why you bring her sweets whenever you come visit?" Toby asked.

"Bonifacio Maguire Ibarra," his mother drew his full name out, the syllables ricocheting around the dining room, her voice laced with accusation, "have you been giving that horse sugar cubes again?"

"Huh?" Bo blinked, face a mask of innocence as he glanced up from his plate. He slid a peek at his nephew. Toby's lips were sealed shut, but the kid was shaking in his chair, vibrating like he was about to burst from holding the secret inside. Bo wasn't sure how much longer the little guy could last. "How about some cake?" he suggested.

His sister rose from the table and went to the kitchen. Toby scuttled off his chair and hurried after. Eager to sneak a lick of icing while his mother sliced the cake, and likely equally eager to escape Abuela's scolding.

"Relax, Mom." Bo offered her an appeasing smile.

"You shouldn't give Stella sweets, it's not good for her."

"I only gave her a few and made sure she had some carrots too."

His mother made a face, but he could tell she was caving.

"Come on now, Mami. The old girl needs a little sugar in her life," Bo said, adding a little sugar to his voice for her too.

As he knew she would, his mother shook her head, a reluctant smile curving her mouth. He leaned across the table to press a kiss to her cheek.

"Fine," she relented, patting his head with affection. "But only a little. I don't need her developing diabetes." A small animal veterinarian by trade, his mother didn't specialize in horses, but she'd been around them long enough to provide basic care. Though the stables were technically not her domain, Bo's mother viewed every animal on the property as her responsibility.

His sister reappeared, Toby at her side, carrying a plate loaded with a giant slice of cake.

"Whoa, little man, that's a lot of cake."

"It's for you, Uncle Bo."

Bo watched, heart as full as his stomach was about to be, while his nephew carefully walked the plate to the table and set it in front of Bo. "Gracias, sobrino."

Toby nodded, face beaming with pride. "Mamá let me cut it myself." He paused, face squishing up. "Well, she let me help."

"You might have to help me too. I don't know if I can eat this all by myself."

"'Kay." Toby nodded, scrambling back into his seat. "After I'm done with mine."

"Deal." Bo laughed, and waited until his sister was

done serving everyone and had returned to her own seat. "Thanks for this, sis," he told her.

"Just make sure I get a ticket to the movie premiere," she shot back.

"You still want to go now that you know who's playing the lead?" he teased.

"No le hace." Luna rolled her eyes. "It was a really good book."

"I guess so." Bo laughed. "I'll see what I can do." He dug into his cake, wanting to groan with pleasure as the sweet rich fudge melted on his tongue. If he ate this entire piece, he'd likely be the one developing diabetes, but it'd be worth it.

"How's the garden?" Bo asked.

"Not bad." Luna licked a bit of icing from the prongs of her fork.

"Not bad," their father harrumphed. He stabbed at his cake. "Your sister is selling vegetables at five farmers' markets now, and has business deals with flower shops all over town."

"Really?" Bo looked at Luna. "That's great."

"Dad's been a lot of help." She sidestepped the compliment, cheeks growing rosy beneath her tanned skin. "The farmers' markets will be winding down soon, but homecoming season is starting, so I'm getting lots of orders for corsages."

When Luna first started the garden, Bo had been hesitant to ask her too much about it. It was a sensitive subject for his sister. Eight years ago, after getting pregnant with Toby when she was still a teenager, she'd given up her dreams of leaving home to study agricultural design in California. Instead, she'd poured her heart and soul into designing a garden here, selling the organic vegetables and homegrown blooms at local farm stands.

Luna had a real talent with plants. A natural green thumb with an eye for arrangements. Bo had always admired his sister's ability to take the curve ball life had thrown her and keep swinging. She impressed with him with the way she managed to juggle everything.

From the beginning, Toby's father was never in the picture. If his sister chose to raise her son as a single mom, that was her business. At least, by Luna living here, Mom and Dad were able to help with Toby.

"Uncle Bo?"

Toby's tug on his sleeve pulled Bo back to the dining room table. He smiled down at his nephew. "Yes, sobrino?"

"Are you going to finish your cake?"

Bo laughed. "Tell you what." He split the large slice down the middle. "How about we share?"

Toby eagerly agreed, and they both dug in. Bo's thoughts drifted to the start of filming tomorrow. Working with Sadie wasn't going to be easy, but he was so close to getting what he wanted, he could almost taste it. If the movie ended up being the blockbuster everyone was predicting, Bo was confident he'd have the leverage he needed to convince Vic to let him take over. Scooping up another forkful of cake, Bo vowed to do everything he could to ensure the film's success.

CHAPTER 6

INHALE. HOLD, TWO, three, four. Exhale. Hold, two, three, four. Sadie breathed, slow and deep, moving through the centering exercises she always did right before a performance. She'd been doing the same routine for years, from standing backstage during college shows to waiting for her cue on *Hope General*, to now, when she was due on set in less than five minutes.

Usually Sadie waited until she was actually on set before running through her exercises, but while sitting in the makeup chair, she'd realized she was on the verge of completely losing her shit. Shit, which lost, would take way more than five minutes to find again. She took another deep breath.

Or attempted to. As soon as she began sucking in air, the makeup artist yelled at her.

"Knock that off!" Zara waved her powder brush with an air of menace and warned, "Unless you want to walk out of here looking like you have three boobs."

Sadie choked back a laugh and glanced down at her

chest, where Zara was busy making her cleavage camera ready. Through the magic of highlight and contour, encased in a tight leather vest (and a damn good bra), Sadie's not-quite-a-B-cup rack had never looked so impressive.

Doing her best to hold still, Sadie inhaled slowly.

"Nervous?" Zara asked, darkening the shadow between Sadie's breasts.

"No," Sadie lied. After all, what did she have to be nervous about? She was only minutes away from shooting the first fight sequence in the film that would either make or break her career. This role was the chance Sadie had been waiting for ever since quitting the soap—ever since she'd decided to become an actress, really. A once-in-a-lifetime opportunity.

But with great opportunity came great risk. There was a reason films that did poorly at the box office were called bombs. If the movie failed, her chance at a career on the big screen would be blown. *Kaboom.*

Worse, it would give power to the whispers that had been circling around her for years. Rumors claiming she'd only gotten her role on the soap opera because of who her family knew, not what she could do. Insinuations that her career was based on connections, not talent.

The thing was, the best rumors began with a kernel of truth. Her father may be in the hotel industry, but he had a lot of friends in the entertainment business. Friends who attended the same charity events, played golf at the same country clubs, vacationed at the same resorts. Friends who did favors for each other. And Sadie *had* landed an audition for the soap thanks to someone her dad knew. But despite what the websites reported, she'd won the role on her own.

Nobody seemed to care about that part of the story,

though. Not even after she'd earned an Emmy for her performance as the emotionally scarred poor little rich girl on *Hope General*. All they saw was what she played on TV. The spoiled socialite. The pampered princess. Sometimes Sadie wondered if she'd made a mistake taking that role. But she'd long ago decided life was too short for regrets. She'd made a choice. She had to live with it.

For better or for worse, those choices had brought her here. To this moment. This movie could put her on the path to joining the ranks of her idols. Playing Jamie could help her become what she'd always dreamed of: the leading lady in a Hollywood hit.

No pressure, right?

If she sifted past all that, Sadie knew it wasn't just the future of her career that had her panicking. Right now, the critics and the reviewers and the box office numbers were a distant rumble. A problem for tomorrow.

No, her current freak-out was centered on one person. The man who would be watching her every move *today*.

Again, Sadie considered Ana's advice. Should she try it? Open her Bo box on purpose and tap into those feelings? It was too personal. Too dangerous. What if she lost control and couldn't get the lid back on? What then?

Better to keep her emotions tucked away. Do things the way she'd always done them. Compartmentalize.

Bo watched as Sadie went through the paces in a fight scene involving a trio of generic villains. She ducked under a punch, the timing smooth and perfect. Villain Number One finished swinging, the weight of his body sending him tumbling. As Villain Number Two charged forward, Sadie pulled out of her crouch, pivoting on her left foot as she swept her right leg up in a roundhouse kick aimed at his solar plexus.

Again, the timing was exact, and played out as choreographed, down to the millisecond. The guy went flying backward, tumbling onto the crashmat. On a technical level, the sequence had been perfect. But something was missing.

Bo rubbed a hand over his face and gave the signal to run the sequence again. This was supposed to be an easy first day. But as he watched Sadie move through the choreography, he knew something wasn't right.

"Cut!" Sylvia ordered, pulling off her headphones.

Maybe the director sensed something was off too. Bo let out a breath. *Good*. Well, not good, exactly, but at least he wasn't imagining problems where there weren't any. He was finding it hard to be objective today—being around Sadie so much was fucking with his head. Making him doubt his instincts.

Sylvia hopped down from her perch and crossed to the actors, her assistant Tanya trailing behind her. "What's the problem, MG?"

"Nothing." Sadie glanced at the director. A flicker of unease passed over her face. "Why? Was something wrong with the take?"

"The timing was flawless, the choreography spot-on." Sylvia rubbed her fingers together, as if trying to conjure an explanation out of thin air. "But we're missing something." She turned to Bo. "Do you get what I'm saying?"

Bo moved closer, mentally reviewing the footage. As the scene played back in his mind, he realized what had been bothering him. "Yeah." He nodded at Sadie. "Her punches don't look real."

Beside him, Sadie sputtered. He swore he could feel her hackles rising. Bo jerked a thumb at his trio of fighters. "They're doing their job and selling the hits." He shifted his gaze in Sadie's direction. "But I'm not buying your delivery."

"He's right, MG." Sylvia frowned, her gaze bouncing back and forth between them. "Why don't you take a minute and go over the choreo a few more times? I'll have the crew take five."

"But," Sadie began.

Decision made, the director walked off, telling her assistant to announce a break.

By the way Sadie bristled, back going ramrod straight, jaw clenching in a smile that was all teeth, Bo could tell she hadn't appreciated his critique of her performance.

There'd always been so much pride in her—an endless need to prove herself.

And the thing was, he knew she could do this. The pieces were all there. She just needed a little push. Something to get her fire going.

The thought gave Bo an idea. A slow smile spread across his face. Just like when they were kids, the fastest way to get Sadie to do something was to tell her she couldn't.

But he had to play it just right.

Bo adjusted his features, hiding his grin and furrowing his brow in concern. "I don't know if I can make this work." He heaved a sigh, adding a little extra *tsk* of frustration for her benefit. "You're not ready."

"What did you say?" Sadie stiffened and turned to stare at him.

"I said, you're not ready." Bo held his ground, even though her stricken face looked as if she'd been the one hit in the solar plexus by a roundhouse kick—delivered by him.

"Of course, I am." She glared, eyes narrowed, mouth pinched, ready to spit nails. "I spent my entire summer preparing for this role, hours of conditioning, followed by more hours of training."

"Exactly. That's your problem."

"What are you talking about?" She crossed her arms over her chest.

Don't look. Bo did his best to ignore how the shift of her body pressed her breasts together, soft creamy curves threatening to spill over the tight line of the leather vest she wore. He had to hand it to the costume designer, the sight alone was worth the price of admission. "I'll show you." He jogged over to grab one of the prop dummies.

He set the life-size weighted foam figure in front of Sadie. "Punch it."

With a glare that said she'd rather punch *him*, she did what he asked. Dropping into a fighter's crouch, Sadie drew her fist back and slammed it into the dummy.

It was a good hit, he'd give her that. And her form was perfect. But it was missing heat.

"Harder," Bo ordered.

Sadie pulled back and drove her fist forward again.

"Harder," he repeated, wanting to goad her, push her. "You're not trying, princess."

"I *am* trying!" Sadie's back stiffened. "Don't tell me I'm not trying." Her arms shot out, jabbing choppily at the dummy's torso. "And don't call me princess."

"Loosen up." He wrapped a hand around one of her tight fists. The scrape of her knuckles against his palm was electrifying. Bo cleared his throat, covering his reaction with a gruff command. "This isn't the gym. You're not wearing gloves. You're going to break a finger."

"I'll give you a finger," Sadie muttered, jerking out of his grip.

Bo chuckled. *There she was.* There was his little bee, the sharp sting of her temper, the fire he used to know.

Nice to see it was still inside her. It was that fire that likely drew Sylvia to cast Sadie in the role of Jamie. He just needed to coax it out of her. "Relax," he told her, making a point to keep his own voice overtly calm and cool. A tactic he was betting would have the opposite effect on her.

He was right.

Infuriated, she drew back her arm and swung, fist smashing into the dummy's torso.

"Is that all you got, *princess*?" he taunted.

Taking a step forward, Sadie threw another punch. A wicked right hook that took him by surprise. "Not bad," he observed. Even though Bo was damn impressed, he purposely kept any note of approval or praise from his voice as he moved to stand behind her. "Again."

She grunted, clearly pissed now, and swung again.

"That's it." Bo spoke low in her ear. "That's my girl." He felt more than saw the shiver ripple through her.

Awareness radiated between their bodies, an undercurrent of tension.

"I'm not your girl," she snapped, whirling around to face him, eyes blazing. "What's the point of all this, anyway? I told you, I spent my entire summer learning how to throw a punch."

"Fake punches," he snorted.

"Yeah, I'm *acting*. It's supposed to be fake."

"You know what happens when you learn to throw a fake punch?" Bo stared down at her. "It looks fake."

"R-i-i-i-g-h-t," she spoke slowly, her voice dripping with sarcasm, "it's supposed to."

"No. It's supposed to look real."

"You're saying you want me to throw *real* punches?" Sadie crossed her arms over her chest again. "I think the other actors might take issue with that."

"No." As if pulled by an invisible string, his gaze dropped to her cleavage. "I'm saying I want you to *learn* how to throw a real punch."

"Weren't you listening? I told, you. I spent the summer—"

"That's practice, not passion," he said. "You need to know what it feels like."

"The script calls for my character to take an arrow to the shoulder," she sniped, "should we shoot me with one of those for real too?" She leaned toward him, breasts straining against the front of her leather vest.

Bo swallowed. She had to know what she was doing. What it was doing to him. "Why would we do that?" he asked, forcing his attention back up to her face.

"So I know what it *feels* like."

"If we need to," he began, deciding to yank her chain. "Sure. Thanks for the suggestion."

Her eyes flew to his, wide with horror.

"I'm joking," he assured her, pleased to have regained the upper hand.

"That's your idea of a joke?" she spat. "Someone needs to work on his sense of humor."

"I've been told that before," he agreed, mouth quirking.

"You take things too seriously." Sadie studied his face, violet eyes probing, as if she were trying see into his head. Read his thoughts. "Always have."

Bo was quiet for a long moment. It was the first time since the table read she'd acknowledged their past. Finally, he said, "I take my job very seriously." He moved even closer, filling her space. He liked that she stood her ground, didn't shy away. "Something you should appreciate as it's what's going to keep you safe." His eyes caught hers. "All I'm asking is that you trust me, okay?"

"Oh, is that all? You, of all people, are asking for my trust?"

Her bitter laugh hit him in the gut harder than any punch she'd thrown today. Bo's jaw clenched. Their conversation had shifted in a direction he wasn't prepared to go. There was a lot they needed to talk about. But not here. Not now. Struggling against the impulse to touch her again, he ran a hand through his hair. "This isn't about us, Sadie. This is about my job. And yours."

She breathed in, slow and deep, the rise and fall of her breasts . . . hypnotic.

A brisk cough snapped Bo out of his trance. He glanced up to see Tanya standing behind Sadie, lips pinched. *Nicely done, dumbass.* Jesus, she must think he was a total perv. Not the reputation he was looking to build.

"Sylvia wants to get started again in five," the assistant said, tapping her pen against her clipboard.

"Got it." Bo nodded.

Sadie glanced over her shoulder. "Thanks, Tanya."

After the assistant and her clipboard had scurried off, Bo cocked an eyebrow at Sadie. "Well, princess? What's it going to be?"

"Fine." Sadie narrowed her eyes, hands on her hips. "I'll trust you." After a beat she added, "As my stunt coordinator."

"Good enough," he said, a bastion of willpower as he kept his gaze locked on hers. He had to pull it together. She was right. He was her stunt coordinator. Time to do his fucking job and keep his eyes—and his mind—off her tits.

"I'll make this quick," Bo said briskly, getting down to business. "The thing you need to remember is that unlike getting stabbed with a knife or, say, shot with an arrow, which is all about reaction, throwing a punch is all about intent, what emotion drives the action."

"I understand that." She cocked her stubborn little chin at him.

"Yeah? Then show it. I wasn't seeing any emotion from you in the scene. There wasn't any passion, any fire. You were too focused on the mechanics." Bo shook his head. "Get out of your own way by getting out of your head. Let loose. Feel it more. Let it flow through you."

Her mouth twisted in a curious half smile. "Use the Force?"

Bo's breath caught as dozens of memories flipped through his brain at hyperspeed. His pulse jumped to light speed. A *Star Wars* reference? She was going to kill him. He pulled it together and cocked a smile at her. "*Yeah*. Exactly." He crossed his arms and ran with her little joke. "Trust your instincts. Obi Wan knew his shit."

Sadie laughed and the sound rippled through him, lighting up places that had long been dark. She looked up at him, violet eyes glinting with something other than irritation . . . something he couldn't quite figure out.

Whatever it was, he liked it. Bo's chest swelled, filling with a warm glow. "Think you're ready now?"

She nodded. Her smile was fierce, her face determined. "I'm ready, flyboy."

"Then let's try it again," he said, unable to keep an answering smile from his face as the warmth spread all through him. "For real this time."

CHAPTER 7

EXHAUSTED, SADIE HURRIED to catch the "L." Her butt had barely hit the seat when it started buzzing. She pulled her phone out of her back pocket, ready to click ignore, but stopped when she saw Ana's face on the screen. She slid her thumb over the answer key. "What?"

"Hello to you too, sunshine," Ana replied. "Where are you?"

"Heading home."

"You're done filming for the day?"

"Yeah," Sadie grumbled. "Finally."

"Great, I'll tell the girls we'll see you soon."

"What?" The question was more of a yawn.

"It's Monday," Ana reminded her. "Aren't you coming?"

"Shit." Sadie slumped into her seat. *Margarita Monday*. "I forgot."

"What? It's Bonnie's last night in the States!" Ana said.

"Yeah, I know, I know." Sadie stifled another yawn. "I'll be there." She peered out the grimy window of her train car. "Give me about twenty minutes."

Eighteen minutes later, Sadie slid into the booth next

to her friends at their favorite Mexican restaurant, a place they'd been frequenting since college, when the Monday tradition first began. Over the years, everyone had to miss the weekly meet-up sometimes, but Sadie had missed out the most. Moving to New York after graduation, she'd only made it occasionally when she was in town for a visit.

It had been nice falling back into the old routine. To have the whole gang together again. After their jaunt overseas for Cassie's wedding last month, for the first time since college, the five of them had managed to meet consistently for the rest of the summer. But the reunion would be ending soon. Delaney's fall semester at a preschool in the burbs had started, and she wouldn't be able to make it into the city as often. Sadie's film schedule would be keeping her busy, and Ana's catering business would be picking up for the holidays. Cassie had Logan, her newlywed hot Scot husband to entertain and a thriving career in broadcast journalism. And tomorrow, Bonnie was headed for England, to move in with her new fiancé.

"When's the wedding going to be?" Sadie asked, pushing the basket of tortilla chips out of reach.

"Are you planning to have it here in the States or in the UK?" Delaney wondered. "Because if you have it over there, and we end up all together back in England for a third year in a row, that will just be bananapants." She knocked back the rest of her drink and waved at their waitress for a refill. "Not that I'm complaining."

"Ooh, you and Theo could get married on a boat on the Thames, since that's where you two first met." Ana's emerald eyes twinkled. "Then it really would be just like Ariel and Prince Eric."

"Slow down. We haven't set a date yet." Bonnie stared

at the antique gold band on her finger, her cheeks turning the same shade of ruby as the garnet stone in the center of the setting.

"Uh-oh," Cassie began, brow furrowing with concern. "Not this again."

"What is it with dudes proposing and then stalling on setting a date?" Delaney huffed, taking the fresh pitcher of margaritas from the waitress and refilling everyone's glasses.

"Actually, he wanted to pick a date," Bonnie began, eyes still on the ring, cheeks growing even redder. "I was the one who insisted we wait." She glanced up. "I'm just not ready yet."

"Of course not," Cassie agreed.

"Completely understandable," Sadie added.

Barely five months ago, Bonnie had still been engaged to Gabe, her long-term boyfriend. Sadie had always hoped the pair would make it. Partly because she wanted her friend to have her happily ever after, but also, selfishly, it would be nice to know that childhood sweethearts could last. That it could happen.

She should have known better.

But despite the fact Bonnie's ex ended up being a cheating dickhead, her story turned out better than anything in one of Ana's Disney movies or Cassie's romance novels. After a summer teaching at Cambridge, Bonnie was now engaged to an actual duke. Theo, her new fiancé, wasn't a royal duke, but he *was* a real prince of a guy. Sadie said as much. "Theo's a good man. I'm sure he's fine with waiting until you are ready."

Bonnie nodded. "He said he understood if I didn't want to get married anytime soon, but hoped I'd wear his family's ring." She smiled, radiant in her happiness. "He told me I looked good wearing his future."

"Aaaw!" Their entire booth collapsed in a collective swoon.

"That is the sweetest thing ever." Cassie beamed at her friend.

"It's just like the line from *Some Kind of Wonderful*." Delaney sighed dreamily.

Bonnie gave her a blank stare. If you needed a line from Shakespeare or Jane Austen, she was your girl, but quote anything from the last two centuries and she was lost.

"The eighties' movie?" Delaney glanced around at the rest of them. "Anyone?"

Sadie shrugged. Obsessed with films from the 1930s and '40s, her expertise was the Golden Age of Hollywood. She looked to Ana for help, but her best friend shook her head, just as clueless. A Disney addict, Ana's movie knowledge was limited to cartoon princesses and animated rodents.

"Unbelievable." Delaney tossed her strawberry-blond ponytail over her shoulder. "The line is at the end of the movie. It's what Keith says to Watts when he gives her the earrings he bought with his college fund."

"He blew his college fund on a pair of earrings?" Bonnie gasped, horrified at the prospect.

"Trust me, it's very romantic," Delaney assured her.

"Well, it sounds like Theo's proposal was very romantic." Sadie smiled at Bonnie. Raising her glass, she added, "A toast, to the future Mrs. Theodore Wharton."

"That reminds me," Cassie said after they'd all clinked glasses. "Whenever you do get hitched, will we have to start calling you 'Duchess'?"

"Or 'my lady'?" Delaney wondered.

"The proper address is 'Your Grace.' But please don't call me that." Bonnie paused, grinning wickedly. "Unless we're having tea with Theo's mother."

"The dragon lady?" Cassie asked.

"Ooh, that would totally frost her scones." Delaney nodded approvingly.

"Totally," Bonnie agreed, giggling. "But enough about me. You started filming today, right, Sadie? How did that go?"

"Yes, Sadie? How did that go?" Ana teased, mouth quirking with mischief.

"Fine." Sadie gave her bestie a warning glance. But it was too late, the others had picked up on Ana's tone.

"Just fine?" Cassie probed. A journalist, her senses were always attuned to potential dirt. She swiped a finger through the salt rimming her glass. "Have you run into any problems on set?"

Sadie stared at her own naked glass. No salt for her, she couldn't risk getting bloaty. *Have there been any problems on set? Hmm. How about having to work with the love of my life? The guy who dumped me eleven years ago without any explanation? But now he's back and doing things like asking me to trust him and looking all hot and . . .* "Not really, no," she finally said.

Ana cleared her throat meaningfully.

Sadie ignored her.

"All right, you two," Cassie said, glancing between them. "What aren't you telling me? Something is up." She pinned her reporter's stare on Sadie. "Is it your costar?"

"Who, Ryan?" Sadie shook her head. "No, why?"

"He's like almost forty. And yet had zero trouble getting cast as an action hero. Doesn't that piss you off?"

"It's the way it is." Sadie shrugged. "Because he's a man."

"Because he's a man," Cassie repeated in an angry growl. "Meanwhile, you got all kinds of grief because you're turning thirty soon."

"Thanks for the reminder." Sadie wanted to growl too. Her birthday was on Halloween, which was fast approaching. *Thirty.* The thought of leaving her twenties scared her enough to be worthy of the holiday. She'd wanted to accomplish so much before that milestone, but had wasted too many years stuck in neutral.

Not anymore, though. Finally, her career was moving in the direction she wanted it to go. She shouldn't be dreading her birthday, she should be celebrating it. "Maybe I'll throw a party," Sadie mused.

"Oh no, *I'll* throw the party." Ana rubbed her hands together. "And since it's on Halloween, I'm thinking costumes are a must."

"You just want an excuse to wear your Cinderella dress," Sadie teased.

"Actually, I just bought a new one," Ana confessed. "Belle."

"A costume party would be so much fun!" Bonnie fizzed, and then her face fell. "But I'm going to miss it."

"No way." Sadie reached across the table for Bonnie's hand. "You need to come back for my party. You *have* to be there."

"But." Bonnie hesitated.

"No buts," Sadie insisted. "I'll pay for the damn plane tickets; I don't care. I'm not going to face turning thirty alone. I want all my girls to celebrate with me. And their guys too. Bring Theo."

"Ooh," Ana piped up. "You can dress up as Ariel and he can be Prince Eric." She chuckled. "Count me in on the airfare if I can see that."

"Where will this grand event take place?" Delaney wondered. "The Waldorf?"

"I dunno," mused Ana. "That's where she had her twenty-first, remember?"

"Who can forget?" Delaney snorted. "It was epic."

"My parents planned that party." Her father's position for the elite hotel chain came with lots of perks, including access to luxury suites for slumber parties. Sadie frowned. "But I'm trying to escape the image of spoiled little rich girl, you know?"

"I have an idea." Ana stuck a chip in the guacamole bowl, swirling it around. "We could have the party on my family's yacht."

"Like that doesn't scream rich and spoiled." Sadie rolled her eyes.

"Well, I *am* rich. That's nothing to be ashamed of; it's just a fact. And what's wrong with wanting to spoil my best friend on her birthday?" Ana argued.

"You're worried about letting your best friend throw you a party on her private yacht." Delaney shook her head, ponytail swinging. "A champagne problem if I ever heard one."

"I'll even do the catering myself," Ana added. "Consider this my present to you. And you know it's rude to refuse a present."

A smile tugged at the corners of Sadie's mouth. "Fine. If you insist."

"I do," Ana said. "I also insist you invite your hot co-star."

"Are you serious?" Sadie laughed. "Ryan's sweet, but he's not the sharpest tool in the shed."

"Who cares how sharp his tool is as long as he knows how to use it," Ana purred, raven eyebrows quivering with mischief.

"Ana!" Sadie chided as her friends erupted into tequila-fueled giggles.

"What?" Ana frowned. "When did you become such a nun?"

"Shut up, I'm not a nun," Sadie sputtered. "It's just, that's my costar you're talking about."

"It's not like you're married to him. But fine, let's talk about someone else," Ana said agreeably.

Too agreeably. Sadie's neck prickled.

"Let's talk about Bo."

Crap. Well, she walked right into that one.

"Wait. As in your first boyfriend Bo?" Delaney demanded. "*The* Bo?"

"The I-lost-my-virginity-to-him-at-fifteen Bo?" Cassie asked.

"The I-puked-giving-him-a-blow-job Bo?" Bonnie added.

"I wasn't fifteen, I was sixteen," Sadie muttered, sinking lower in the booth. Usually, nothing embarrassed her, but right now she wished she could disappear into the cracked vinyl.

"But you did puke, right?" Bonnie asked. "I am remembering that part of the story correctly?"

"Yes, I puked. Ugh. Why are we talking about this?" She felt like puking right now.

"Yeah, why *are* we talking about this?" Delaney echoed.

"Because *the* Bo is currently Sadie's stunt coordinator," Ana announced.

"What?"

All heads swiveled to Sadie.

"It's true." She slunk lower. Any farther and her chin would be resting on the table. "I haven't seen him since I was eighteen. When he broke up with me at prom," she blurted.

"He broke up with you on prom night?" Delaney sputtered.

A bitter laugh escaped Sadie. "Yep. He dumped me in

the middle of prom. Didn't even attempt to ease the blow with some line about being friends, just told me we should never see each other again."

"Why didn't you ever tell us about this?" Cassie demanded.

"It's not really something I like to talk about." Sadie forced her voice to remain neutral and struggled to keep her mind from drifting to other things she refused to talk about. "The point is, I took him at his word. I never looked him up, never checked in on how he was doing."

"Never?" Cassie asked, doubtful.

"Never." Sadie was firm. She sat up straighter, frustration giving her strength. "For the past eleven years, I've done everything I could to avoid him, even staying away from my own grandma's home. I've never done a search for him on social media or anything. I was shocked to find out he was working on the film. I had no idea he'd gotten involved in stunt work. But . . ." she glanced at Ana, ". . . after our bike ride yesterday, I did a deep dive on the internet."

"Oh!" Bonnie leaned forward. "That's how I learned Theo was a duke."

"Bo is definitely not a duke," Sadie assured her.

"Well?" Ana prodded, one brow quirked. "Find anything interesting?"

"Does he have a criminal record?" Delaney wondered.

"Embarrassing viral videos?" Cassie suggested.

"Is he married?" Bonnie asked.

"None of the above." Sadie shook her head, laughing.

The redhead grinned at her, freckles bunching playfully. "Then it can't be that bad. Besides"—Bonnie reached across the table again, and this time she was the one to take Sadie's hand—"if there's one thing I've learned over the last few months, it's that the past is prologue."

"Huh?" Sadie gave her friend a bit of side-eye. "Are you quoting Shakespeare?"

"When isn't she?" Cassie snorted.

"When she's busy quoting some other dead guy," Delaney quipped.

Cassie laughed with appreciation and high-fived Delaney.

"Make fun of me all you want, but it's true." Bonnie glowered at the two of them in annoyance before turning back to Sadie. "What happened with Gabe taught me it's important to remember your past is part of you. It sets the stage for what's to come. You can start a new chapter, or even a new book—but the things you've done, the people you've loved, are all part of your story, you can't change that." Bonnie gave Sadie an empathetic squeeze. "Bo was part of your past. Like it or not, now he's part of your present."

Sadie squeezed back. Her friend's words hit closer to home than she knew.

The question now, the one that niggled way in the back of her brain and tugged on the far corner of her heart, was, could he be part of her future?

CHAPTER 8

"LET ME GET this straight. You want me to jump through a glass window?" Sadie stared at Bo, wondering if he'd lost his mind.

"No, I want your stunt double to jump through a glass window." Bo pointed to the platform soaring above their heads, where a woman, dressed in the same outfit as Sadie, stood waiting. "You just have to watch." Bo crossed his arms over his chest.

Sadie was watching, all right. Her eyes followed the movement of his arms, latching onto the swell of muscle bunching beneath his skin. The polo shirt he wore stretched tight across his chest, the short sleeves hugging his biceps in that way she'd always found irresistible. God, why did she have to be such a sucker for arm porn?

It was like he had giant magnets hidden in his biceps, making it impossible for her to stop staring. Sadie swallowed hard and shifted her gaze, studying the logo of the stunt company embroidered over one sculpted pec. "And then what?"

"And then you'll jump."

"What?"

"Through paper, not glass." He leaned closer, speaking low so only she could hear. "Trust me, remember?"

His breath tickled the side of her neck, and Sadie fought off a shiver. Same as the first day of filming, when he'd stood behind her and whispered in her ear, tension hummed between them. Did Bo feel it too?

If he did, he didn't show it. But they were on set, surrounded by cast and crew. She needed to remain professional, which meant one: not lusting after her stunt coordinator, and two: not doubting the abilities of said stunt coordinator.

Or at least not let any of that show—the lust or the doubt.

She watched Bo climb the ladder to the platform. Shit, that was really high. While he reviewed the scene with Emily, her stunt double, Sadie fought to repress the rush of fear building like a tidal wave inside. Her chest felt tight, throat closing as she struggled to get more air in her rapidly shrinking lungs. She closed her eyes and forced herself to take slow, deep breaths.

"You okay?"

Sadie blinked. Bo had come down from the platform and was standing next to her again. She gave him a curt nod as places were called.

Once the cue to start filming was given, Bo bent his head. "Watch what she does," he said, his voice a quiet command in her ear as Emily took off running. The stuntwoman hit her mark and leapt into the air, twisting her body so her shoulder made contact first. The breakaway glass shattered, and she burst through to the other side, curling into a ball, head tucked, chin against her chest as she hurtled toward the ground, hitting the crash mat in a smooth roll.

It was over in seconds.

On Bo's signal, the crew went into motion, cleaning up the glass and resetting the window. "Now it's your turn."

Sure enough, in place of the breakaway glass, a large piece of thin blue paper was being fitted into the window frame.

Bo pulled Sadie over to Sylvia's observation deck and pointed at one of the monitors.

Emily joined them as they reviewed the footage. "What do you think?"

"Perfect." Bo flashed Sadie's stunt double a grin. "You were great, Em."

Jealousy ripped through Sadie, a hook with wickedly sharp barbs scoring her heart.

"Sadie," Bo called, turning to her.

"What?" she snapped.

"Are you paying attention?"

"Yes." She was definitely paying attention to how he was paying attention to *Em*.

Sadie needed to get a grip, fast. Jealousy was not her style. And her stunt double hadn't done anything wrong. Yet Sadie was ready to tear Emily's hair out, even if it was a wig designed to match her own.

"You better be," Bo warned. "You may not be jumping through glass, but there's still a level of risk." He pointed at the screen replaying Emily's jump. "See how she uses her shoulder? You want that to be your first point of contact." He paused the replay and looked at Sadie. "If you don't want to do the fall, we can just film you coming through the window.

"I think we'll get a better take with the full jump and roll, though," Sylvia interjected, cocking her head at Sadie. "What do you say, MG?"

Sadie swallowed, glancing at Bo.

"I agree with Sylvia," he said, before she had to ask. "The full run would play better on camera."

"Then that's what we'll do," Sadie said, voice brittle, despite her attempt to sound confident.

Bo narrowed his eyes, studying her. "How about you go through a few practice runs with Emily first?"

"How about you mind your own business?" she snapped, marching toward the ladder.

"You are my business," he snapped right back.

She whipped around to stare at him

"This. This is my business," he amended. Clearing his throat, Bo stepped past her. "If you insist that you're ready, then come on. The gag is all set," Bo said, gesturing for her to follow him.

Gag. The slang term for a stunt was quite appropriate. Because that's exactly what she wanted to do right now. Sadie swallowed bile and forced herself to climb up the ladder behind Bo, too nervous to appreciate the up-close-and-personal view of his tight, jean-clad ass. Nausea churned with each step, her feet heavy, her head empty. All the blood in her brain seemed to be pooling in her boots.

Did she look as pale as she felt? Probably not, since she was in full makeup. Reaching the top of the ladder, Sadie inched onto the platform. Her legs felt like strands of dry spaghetti, ready to snap.

"You sure you don't want to run through it with me?" Bo asked, watching her closely.

If she'd thought he was mocking her, Sadie probably would have told him to shove it. But his voice was soft, tinged with genuine concern. She nodded. "Maybe once."

"Okay." He grinned, mouth curving with the tiniest hint of roguish smugness. "Once."

As he walked her through the gag, Sadie pictured

the face she'd last seen in the mirror before being called to the set. The face of Jamie. A rebel. Fierce. Resolute. Brave. She didn't feel any of those things right now, but if she focused on channeling Jamie, maybe she could.

"We won't start until you give the signal, understand?"

She nodded again, feeling oddly detached from her body.

"I'll be right over there," he promised, indicating a spot off to the side.

Numbly, Sadie looked to where Bo pointed and nodded. It was well within her line of vision; she'd be able to see him the whole time.

"Abeja," he whispered, "nothing happens until you're ready."

Abeja. Her heart flared to life. How long had it been since Bo had called her that? His nickname for her, strange and yet achingly familiar, broke through the haze that had settled around Sadie. She nodded again, this time with more conviction. Then she sucked in a breath, holding it down deep inside.

She would not show fear. She would not panic. She was not Sadie. She was Jamie. She didn't feel faint while riding an escalator or cringe at the thought of climbing a ladder. Sadie exhaled and clenched her fists, digging her nails into her palms. The needling pain grounded her, gave her enough of a toehold to keep from falling into the abyss of terror that was waiting for her, if only she let go.

But she would not let go. Slowly, she relaxed her fist, uncurling her fingers one by one. As each finger released, she chanted under her breath. One finger. *You are in control.* Two. *You are in charge.* Three. *You call the shots.* Four. *You can do this.* Five. *You will do this.*

Shaking out her left hand, she took a deep breath and repeated the process on the right. Again, with each command, a finger relaxed, and she stepped a little further into the skin of her character. By the time the last words faded from her lips, shaking out her right hand, she was Jamie. And Jamie was ready.

Double-checking her position on the platform, Sadie took her mark. The hum of activity around her dimmed, and she turned to Bo, eyes locking on his. His gaze never left her face as he waited for her signal.

She notched her chin up, drew her belly into her spine, took a breath, and lifted her hand. He nodded, his movement like the flick of that first domino, sending everything tumbling in quick, precise succession.

Here we go.

Sadie leapt into motion, boots striking the platform rhythmically with solid confidence as she picked up speed. By the time her brain caught up with her body, it was over, and she was laid out on the crash mat, breathless as she stared up at the camera crew. *I did it.* Sadie's heart soared inside her chest. *I fucking did it.* She whooped with joy.

Golden-brown eyes appeared over the edge of the mat. "All good?"

"I did it!" Sadie crowed.

"You sure did," Bo agreed, pressing down on the edge of the inflatable mat and rolling her toward him.

Straight into his arms. She got to her feet, holding on to Bo, legs wobbly as adrenaline pumped through her veins, hard and fast, making her giddy. "I fucking did it!"

"Mm-hmm." He cocked an eyebrow and helped steady her. "Now get back up on that platform and do it again."

After several more runs, Sadie was finally allowed to take a break. She settled gingerly into a chair. Everything hurt.

"Sore?" Bo asked, plopping down in the chair next to hers and handing her a water bottle.

"A little." Sadie turned the cap, trying to ignore the sudden crackle of awareness zinging along her nerves. "No offense, but what made you decide to do this for a living?"

Bo chuckled softly. "Do you remember that time I jumped off the roof of the tractor barn?"

Sadie's eyes widened, surprised he'd brought up the past so lightly. "I do." She recalled the details and smiled ruefully. "I also remember it did not go well."

"No, it did not," Bo agreed. "But I didn't give up. I kept practicing. Teaching myself how to fall from a great height without getting hurt."

"I'm not sure that can—or should—be taught."

"Why not? With enough practice, I learned how to develop body rolls that allowed me to land safely." He paused, a sheepish grin crossing his face. "Relatively safely. I still get a few thumpers now and then."

"Thumpers?"

"Bruises."

"Oh." Sadie carefully rotated her shoulder. "After today, I think I have more than a few of those." And she'd thought the gym kicked her ass. "You were always jumping off stuff."

"I was a stupid kid."

"I would never call you stupid." Sadie took another sip of her water, watching him from the corner of her eye. This was easier than she'd expected, talking about their past. It felt okay. Good, even. "Reckless? Yes. Impulsive? Maybe. I never knew what wild adventure you would dream up next."

"Neither did I." The sheepish grin was back. "It's funny you use the word 'dream.' That's exactly what I would do. I saw myself doing these amazing things in my dreams, and figured, if I can do them there, I can do them in real life too."

Sadie looked at Bo, not sure if he was pulling her leg. She realized she hoped he wasn't. She liked thinking he believed in his dreams. "Maybe I should give that a try sometime." She glanced up at the window frame she'd somersaulted through. "Though I hope, after getting through today's nightmare of a stunt, the rest of this week will be a piece of cake."

CHAPTER 9

A FEW NIGHTS later, Sadie stood in her apartment's bathroom, her best friend crowding in next to her. "Thank you for coming over." She smiled, meeting Ana's reflection in the mirror.

Ana returned the smile, reaching for Sadie's hand and squeezing. "Of course."

"I feel like I'm getting ready to go into surgery tomorrow or something," Sadie admitted. "Not preparing to cut my hair."

"Well, you *are* preparing to cut off a piece of you," Ana said, running a hand through Sadie's locks. "Several pieces, if you want to get technical."

Sadie watched in the mirror as her blond waves swished around her ears. Her hair was already short, but in less than twenty-four hours, it would be much, much shorter. Tomorrow she'd be filming what Sylvia called the "transformation scene" and Sadie was nervous as hell. She hadn't expected to be this anxious. Only a few days ago, she'd jumped out of a window. Multiple times. This was nothing compared to that. No big deal.

Or so she'd thought. After she'd left *Hope General*, eager to break away from the identity of Simone, the character she'd played, Sadie had chopped her hair to just above her shoulders. On the soap, she'd been contractually obligated to keep her hair long and straight, a Barbie-perfect curtain of golden silk.

When she'd first read the script for *Fair is Fair* and come across the hair-cutting scene, Sadie had been excited. It was a powerful moment, a chance to really stretch her acting chops. She and Sylvia had talked about it, and they'd both agreed it would be a much more moving scene if Sadie cut her hair for real. By herself. On camera. But now that the time had come to go through with it, Sadie was scared. The scene called for her character to take a scissors to her head and violently hack away at her hair until "nothing but stubborn scraps remained."

Reading over the scene in preparation for the next day, Sadie had decided to try practicing in her apartment. Not cutting her hair for real, but going through the motions, visualizing the process. Unfortunately, the more she'd stared at herself in the mirror in her bathroom, the more terrified she'd become.

Her motivational poster of Linda had been no help either. Sadie tried to remind herself she was supposed to be a badass. But even Sarah Connor got to keep her hair. She'd ended up calling Ana in a panic, begging her to come to over.

"I didn't take you away from anything important tonight, did I?"

"Nah, I was just hanging at my folks' place." Ana rummaged through a tote bag emblazoned with the image of a glittery glass slipper on top of a cupcake, her company's logo. "Aha!" She pulled a snarled tangle out of her bag.

"What the hell is that thing?" Sadie eyed the mass in

her friend's hand. "A dead animal? Where did it come from?"

"Calm down, it's a wig." Ana shook the monstrosity, sending long spidery black curls swinging. "I got it from my mom's closet."

"Why am I not surprised." Sadie grinned with affection. Her best friend was fond of saying she came from a long line of weirdos, and Ana's mother was undoubtedly the weirdest of them all. Zany and eccentric, with the energy (and attention span) of a toddler, Mrs. Kaufman was constantly starting a new project or indulging in another hobby. God only knew what escapade had led to the wig. "Why did you bring it here?"

"So you can practice, obviously." Ana slapped the wig on Sadie's head.

"Oh!" Sadie perked up, peering at herself through the messy strands. "That's actually a good idea."

"You're welcome." Ana smirked and began to adjust the wig. "I figured it didn't matter what color it was."

"No, this is fine. It's perfect." Her panic eased a little. "You sure your mom won't mind if we cut it?"

"Are you kidding?" Ana waved a hand. "Hack away. I think I saw a least a dozen more wigs in her closet, easily. One of these days I'm going to figure out what to do with all the bizarre junk she's collected."

"How is your mom, anyway?"

"The same. Running circles around the rest of us. I went over there to help plan the menu for Rosh Hashanah."

"Damn. I completely forgot." A ripple of guilt fluttered over her. Her family wasn't big into most of the traditional celebrations, but they usually gathered for the High Holidays. Sadie couldn't care less if she saw her parents, but she didn't want to miss a chance see her nana. "This weekend, right?"

"Mm-hmm."

"What are you planning to bake?" Sadie asked.

"I think the easier question would be, what am I *not* planning to bake?" Ana laughed.

"Details," Sadie ordered while Ana continued to fuss with the wig.

"Everything is apple-based. Apple cake, apple Bundt cake, apple cupcakes, apple challah, apple rugelach, apple kugel . . ."

"I get the idea, Bubba Gump," Sadie said drily.

"I'm planning to go apple picking Saturday morning. You want to come with?"

"Where? Apple picking?" Sadie made a face.

"At Wunderlich Farms. They have do-o-o-nuts," Ana crooned in a blatant attempt to lure her.

"They do, huh?" A smile tugged at Sadie's lips.

"Yep, amazing apple-cider donuts. Totally worth a few hours of manual labor." Ana's green eyes blazed with mischief. "Maybe we could . . ."

Sadie shoved the wig's matted curls out of her face and narrowed her gaze at her friend. "Maybe we could what?"

"Maybe we could convince a few strong men to come along," Ana suggested. "Your strapping costar, perhaps? And a certain hunky stuntman?"

"No." Sadie shook her head so fast, the wig slipped sideways. "No way."

"Come on," Ana cajoled, readjusting the wig. "With their help, we'd be done in less than half the time. It'll be fun."

"Fun?" Sadie raised an eyebrow doubtfully.

"Yes. Fun. You remember what fun is, don't you? You used to have fun. You used to *be* fun." Ana pouted.

"I've just been so busy with this movie and—" Sadie stopped. Her excuses sounded lame to her own ears. "You know what? You're right. I haven't been much fun lately. I'm sorry, Ana."

Ana's pout turned sympathetic. "It's okay. I get it. You're under a lot of pressure." She smoothed the wig back from Sadie's brow. "It would do you good to let off a little steam."

Sadie nodded. Her best friend had a point. She needed to relax. Loosen up. Her knuckles tingled as she recalled Bo wrapping his hand around her fist, telling her to do just that. But being around Bo had the opposite effect. Made her tense. Turned her into a bundle of nerves. On top of being ridiculous levels of attracted to the man, she was also still angry with him. Still hurt. Those feelings hadn't gone away. Because she hadn't dealt with them.

There just never seemed to be a good time to bring that stuff up. She'd hinted at it the other day, but he'd side-stepped her. In his defense, it had been the right thing to do. Midway through filming a stunt was not the best time to start unloading your emotional baggage.

Perhaps, if she spent some time with Bo away from the set . . .

"Okay," she blurted, before she could change her mind. "I'll do it."

"You'll come apple picking?" Ana asked, perking up.

Sadie nodded. "And I'll ask the guys if they want to come."

Ana started to clap, but Sadie held up a hand. "I'm not making any promises. For all we know, they'll both have plans."

"Oh, please." Ana rolled her eyes. "I guarantee you they'll say yes."

"Do you have a crystal ball you're not telling me about?"

"Call it intuition."

"Well, did your intuition tell you that you'll have to pick me up? I can take the train up to you. Save you a trip into the city."

"No problem." Ana laughed. "But when are you going to get a car? Your mother is probably having a conniption over the thought of you riding around the city on *public transportation*."

Sadie snorted. Whenever Ana mimicked Sadie's mom, she added a haughty nasal accent. It was well-deserved. While Ana's mother may be guilty of impulsive and often eccentric purchases, she wasn't fixated on money or the place it bought her in society . . . unlike Sadie's mom. Maureen Goldovitz was an elitist snob.

Like Ana had said, there was nothing wrong with being rich, but there *was* something wrong with people who thought having more money equated to being a better person. In Sadie's experience, the opposite was usually true.

And while Sadie knew riding the train and taking buses didn't make her a better person, it did help teach her to appreciate the advantages she'd grown up with, including luxuries like a car with a personal driver at her beck and call. When she'd lived in New York, she'd managed fine without a car, but now that she was back in Chicago, Ana had a point. "You're right."

"About your mother or the car?"

"Both," Sadie groaned. It was time to stop making excuses. "I really do need a car, especially before the cold weather hits. I'll go sometime this week."

"Good. Does that mean you've decided to stay here for the winter?"

"Yeah." Sadie nodded. "Filming wraps up mid-November, but I don't have plans to leave. At least not until after the movie premiere happens in the spring."

"And then what?"

Sadie shrugged. And then she would be a star? The glamorous leading lady with her pick of movie roles, as she'd always dreamed of being? Her stomach tightened as she considered the future. "You sure you don't have a crystal ball?"

"Trust me," Ana deadpanned, "if I did, I'd have used it long ago to figure out where my prince charming is hiding." Ana picked up the scissors, snapping them open and closed. "Now come on, Rapunzel, let's chop off that hair."

Sadie smiled feebly, taking the scissors. "Tell me I can do this."

"You can totally do this," Ana promised, adding, "and if it's a disaster, I'll help you pick out a new wig."

"Gee, thanks," Sadie grumbled. "Just not from your mother's closet this time, okay?"

On set the next day, Sadie went over her lines while the crew ran a final sound and light check. Over in one corner, under Bo's supervision, Ryan was warming up with some practice moves. Sadie took a deep breath and let it go slowly, running through her calming exercises more out of habit than necessity. The chat with Ana last night had helped her feel much better. She was glad she'd asked her best friend to come over.

Sylvia came bustling up, Tanya at her shoulder. "Ready, MG?"

"Ready!" Sadie smiled.

"Now, don't freak out," Sylvia warned, "but I made a few changes to this scene."

"Oh?" Sadie immediately started freaking out. But she kept that to herself.

Ryan sauntered toward them, Bo trailing behind. "What's up, boss?"

Sylvia held out her hand to Tanya, who passed her a tablet computer. The director scrolled her finger down a line of text. "This scene is a huge turning point, right? But I've always thought the lead-up was missing something. I want to punch it up a bit."

"You want me to add a few more moves to the fight sequence?" Bo asked.

The director shook her head. "We've got plenty of action, what we need is a little more romance."

"Romance?" Sadie and Ryan asked in unison.

"Yep." Sylvia nodded. "Don't worry. Most of the scene doesn't change." She waved a hand toward Sadie. "Jamie will take the scissors and face herself in the mirror, but before she goes through with it, Christian busts in and tries to stop her. The fight scene will happen as choreographed, but I want to end it with a kiss."

"Who kisses who?" Sadie asked.

"Christian kisses Jamie."

"Am I angry or scared?" Ryan wondered.

"Both," Sylvia said. "And desperate. You don't want her to cut her hair and join the rebellion. You're worried that if she chooses to leave her old self behind, she'll leave you behind."

"Do you want this to be a wide or close shot?" Bo asked.

Sadie turned to look at him. His voice seemed strained, mouth a hard line in the shadow of his beard. Was something bothering him? Was it the thought of her kissing Ryan?

"Wide," Sylvia instructed. "But I do want a few flash cuts, to focus on their faces."

"Got it," Bo said while Tanya furiously scribbled on a notepad.

Sylvia pointed at Ryan. "Remember, you think once

Jamie takes this step and becomes part of the rebellion, she'll never be the same—that you'll lose the woman you love. You're desperate to keep her from changing."

"That's good stuff." Ryan grinned, rubbing his hands together.

"And you"—Sylvia focused on Sadie—"you're ready to break away from your old life. Like Christian, you're also scared things will change forever. But unlike him, you accept change must happen, and you're angry he's trying to keep you from fulfilling your destiny. His attempt to use your feelings for him to stop you will strengthen your resolve, force you to reach deep down inside yourself for the strength to move forward."

The director held up the scissors. "That's when you will return to the mirror, and with each snip, you will cut away your regrets, your mistakes, the trauma and heartache of your past. This is about so much more than cutting hair. As your appearance changes on the outside, you will transform on the inside. In the end, you will be reborn."

Sadie took the scissors from Sylvia, head and heart pounding as she threaded her fingers through the cold metal loops of the handle. This was too close, too raw. Too real.

Back in the box. Close the lid. Lock it tight.

"Hey," Bo murmured. "You okay?"

Sadie glanced up. The concern in his eyes almost undid her right there on the spot. She got a grip on her emotions, fist tightening on the handle of the scissors and nodded. "I'm fine." She was pleased to hear her voice come out smooth and steady. Strong, even.

Because like Jamie, she *was* strong. Sadie turned and marched toward her place on set. "I'm ready."

* * *

Bo watched Sadie as she took her mark, steps confident and sure. She didn't fool him, though. Something was up. Something was bothering her. A lot.

Was it this scene? Because that sure as hell was bothering him.

The director's words echoed in his mind. Bo knew the desperation Sylvia described. The fear of being left behind. Forgotten. He knew the anger too. He'd tasted all of it, standing on a pier, knuckles bruised, face bloodied.

The signal for the scene to start sliced through his memories, and Bo shifted his attention to the set, forcing himself to focus on the action—to do his damn job. Anytime you added another element to a fight scene, like a pair of fucking scissors, there was additional risk for something to go wrong.

He trained his gaze on the actors as they struggled for possession of the prop. Ryan made a grab for the scissors, latching on to Sadie's wrist. As choreographed, she twisted, yanking her arm and sending him hurtling into a coffee table.

One, two, three. Ryan flowed through the move, pivoting to land on his back, the table exploding beneath him as planned. Made of balsa wood, the prop crumpled easily. The crash didn't sound very impressive, but they would fix that in post-production.

Body tense, Bo assessed the actors for damage. All the proper precautions had been taken, but things could still go wrong. If he sensed either of them were hurt, he'd signal for a break. Everything seemed fine, though, and he relaxed as Ryan shifted smoothly into the next part of the sequence, rolling to his feet and charging toward Sadie.

It was a tricky combination that required the actor to come in low and fast. Bo narrowed his eyes, watching as Sadie subtly bent her knees. Not so much that it would show she'd anticipated the move, but enough to allow her to brace for impact.

A millisecond later, Ryan thrust his shoulder into Sadie's torso and hefted her off the ground, effectively sandbagging her. From here, it looked as if she's had the wind knocked out of her, but as long as she kept her core tight while Ryan hefted her over his shoulder, she'd be fine. In seconds they'd hit their mark for the final moment.

And then, as Sylvia had instructed, Ryan bent his head and pressed his lips to Sadie's.

Even though the kiss wasn't part of Bo's choreography, wasn't his job or his business, fuck if he would tear his eyes away from the action. He shouldn't care that they were kissing. They were actors, and this was supposed to be fake, as Sadie had reminded him the other day.

And he'd told her she needed to learn how it felt for real.

Something rattled deep in Bo's chest. Growing up with little to call his own, Bo had developed a hell of a possessive streak. Some might call it jealousy, and maybe it was. All he knew was that once he claimed something as his, nobody better fucking mess with it.

Sadie wasn't an object to be owned, wasn't his property. Bo got that. But once upon a time, she had been *his*.

And he'd let her go.

Like Ryan's character, Christian, Bo knew what it was to fear the woman you loved was about to head down a path you couldn't follow. But unlike Christian, Bo hadn't tried to force Sadie to stay with him.

Instead, he'd forced her to leave him.

Bo still believed he'd done the right thing. Done what was best at the time. Back then, they'd lived in different worlds. Their lives so far apart, they might as well have been on different planets, in different orbits. He never could have imagined their paths would cross again, and definitely not like this.

Shaking away the memories, Bo packed up his personal feelings and buckled in for a long day. Even though this run went perfectly, multiple takes were required to ensure Sylvia and her team had all the angles and shots they wanted.

Several hours and more *fake* kisses than Bo cared to count later, the director announced she was ready to move on. Bo could chill now, his job in the scene was over. But he wanted to watch Sadie perform this next part. Besides, he'd decided he wasn't leaving the set today without talking to her. He'd put it off long enough.

How much to tell her, though? Was there anything he could possibly say that would make Sadie understand what he'd done? Or why? She was still pissed at him—that much he knew from the bits of the past that had leaked into their interactions on set.

What would happen once he'd explained himself? What did he hope for? Forgiveness? Friendship?

A second chance?

Lost in thought, Bo was caught off guard when he looked up and realized they'd starting filming again. The entire soundstage was still, silent save for the sharp metallic *snip* of the scissors echoing in a haunting rhythm. He glanced around at the frozen crew, following their rapt gazes to where Sadie stood on one side of a prop mirror, its open frame allowing the camera to zoom in on her face. A lump formed in the back of Bo's throat as he turned to watch her, mesmerized like everyone else.

Jaw tight, cheeks shining with tears, striking violet eyes staring straight into the lens as she grabbed clumps of her hair, Sadie's pain was a tangible thing. Dark and bitter, it floated on the air, settled all around him. Seeped into his skin.

When it was over, when her hair was nothing but a mass of short, spiky thatches, Sadie dropped the scissors. They clattered to the floor, and the jarring sound broke the spell. The room exhaled—as if everyone had collectively been holding their breath and had let go at once.

From somewhere in the back, a crew member began to clap. Soon others joined in and moments later, the entire production staff was on their feet, applauding Sadie's performance.

She dipped her chin and ran a hand over her newly shorn locks, then bowed, acknowledging their approval. As the clapping subsided, Sadie hurried toward the director's platform and fell into conversation with Sylvia.

Bo collapsed into one of the camp chairs. He'd known she was a good actress, but *whoa*.

Ryan sauntered over, eating something from a plastic container. Bo glanced at the contents, mouth curling in distaste at the substance that defied description. He wasn't even sure it was food. "What the fuck is that shit?"

"That's a good guess," Ryan joked, scooping up a forkful. "But I don't think it's actually shit. Not this time. When I posted a picture, one of my fans suggested it might be tofu Swedish meatballs." He shoved the gooey, congealed mass in his mouth and chewed.

Bo recoiled, but morbid curiosity prompted him to ask, "What's it taste like?"

With some effort, Ryan swallowed his mouthful. "Shit."

Bo laughed. "Guess I was right the first time."

"What's so funny?" Sadie asked, sidling up next to Ryan.

"My dinner," Ryan snarked, setting the container aside.

"Holy monkey balls, that was amazing, Gold. You're good. Really good." Ryan raised a hand to give her a high-five.

The jealous asshole in Bo decided to assume the actor was talking about Sadie's jaw-dropping performance just now, and not referring to her kissing skills from earlier.

"Ah, thanks," Sadie murmured, sinking into the chair next to Bo's.

"It was very . . . *real*," Bo agreed.

She froze, turning to look at him, cheeks pale and streaked with the remnants of her tears.

"Hey," he began, "once we wrap for the day, do you want to go somewhere and talk? Maybe grab a drink?"

Violet eyes guarded, she considered him. After a moment, her face relaxed and a small apologetic smile ghosted her lips. "I appreciate the invite, but I've got a date with Zara. She's going to try and tame this mess for me." She ran a hand over the top of her head.

"Dude." Ryan chortled. "I think she just shot you down with the sorry-I-can't-I'm-washing-my-hair excuse."

"What? No." Sadie turned to Bo. "I mean, I really can't tonight. But," she hastened to add, "if you're not busy on Saturday, I do have an idea."

"I'm not busy," Bo said, pulse tripping. "What did you have in mind?"

"Apple picking."

"Pardon?" Bo asked.

"Apple picking," she repeated. "At an orchard."

"Well, that sounds delightfully domestic," Ryan cooed, dropping into the chair on Sadie's other side.

If part of his paycheck didn't currently depend on the bastard's good looks, Bo would have considered decking the annoying fucker. Instead, he kept his attention on Sadie. "Since when do you go apple picking?"

"I don't," Sadie admitted. "It was Ana's idea. You remember my best friend, Ana?"

Bo nodded, the name conjuring memories of a girl with long black hair and bright green eyes who'd always reminded him of his sister. He'd liked Ana. She was one of the few people from Sadie's world who'd treated him kindly. With respect.

"Who's Ana?" Ryan asked.

"A friend." Sadie smiled.

"A hot friend?"

"Come apple picking with us on Saturday and see for yourself." Sadie winked. "I've been told there'll be donuts."

"What time?" Ryan asked eagerly.

Before Bo knew it, he'd been roped in to what felt an awful lot like a double date at an apple orchard this Saturday morning.

CHAPTER 10

SATURDAY, OF COURSE, was gorgeous. Sadie woke to a brilliant blue sky, not a hint of a cloud anywhere to be seen. She'd secretly hoped it might rain. But nope. Today just had to be a storybook, Hallmark-movie-perfect fall day. She moped to the bathroom and almost screamed when she turned the light on. Her hair. Holy shit, her hair.

Zara had cleaned up the worst of the damage, shaping the ragged strands into a funky asymmetrical bob. No, a bob was too generous a word for the amount of hair left on her head. A pixie cut, maybe? Though that still sounded cuter than what Sadie had going on. More whimsical.

There was nothing whimsical about the way she looked right now.

Groaning, Sadie set about brushing her teeth. She didn't feel very whimsical either. She could admit to herself, she was a vain person. She usually liked the way she looked and almost always felt pretty. But this morning, she *did not* feel pretty. Acknowledging that stung. It was just her hair. Her face hadn't changed. Her eyes were the same, still the unique violet most people assumed were contacts. Her nose, her cheeks, her lips—none of it had changed. And yet, she felt different. Stripped. Unpretty.

Maybe she'd take Ana up on her offer to go wig shopping. And not just to appease her vanity. So far, Sadie had flown under the media radar. The movie had been getting some early buzz, but most of it was focused on the author of the book the film was based on. As publicity for the film ramped up, however, Sadie was sure to be recognized around the city more often, especially with such a . . . unique look.

Because she needed to feel more like herself, and *not* because she was seeing Bo today, Sadie took extra care with her makeup. Then she slipped into some of her frilliest underwear. An adorable matching set the color of ripe cherries with lace scallops trimming the bust and hips.

The only thing she loved shopping for more than shoes was lingerie. Her friends gave her shit for having a panty addiction, and Sadie didn't bother to deny the accusations. They were right. She couldn't help herself. She adored underthings. Fun and flirty or sexy and sassy, Sadie loved it all. And bought it all.

And she always had to match her underwear to her outfit. Which was why she decided to wear a dress in the same cherry-red color as her panties. A comfy cotton number in a gingham pattern. Not too fancy and not too short, the hem fell just above her knee.

It might not be the most practical outfit to go apple picking in, but she didn't care. She did draw the line at visiting an orchard in heels, though. Forgoing her closetful of designer shoes, Sadie chose a pair of sensible, sturdy Converse sneakers. With one last look in the mirror, she decided she looked quite stylish. Cute, even.

Less than an hour later, she was waiting on a bench at the train station, staring at the toes of her sensible, sturdy sneakers.

"Don't we look adorable," Ana said, sliding on to the bench next to Sadie and checking out her haircut. "I love it."

"Really?"

"Really," Ana assured her, gaze dropping to take in the rest of her. "The Chucks are cute too."

"Thanks." Sadie smiled, grateful Ana didn't make a big deal about her hair and relieved she didn't give her any shit about the dress. Sadie wasn't in the mood to explain herself. Not even to her best friend. "Bo's meeting us at the orchard. Ryan's train should be here any minute now."

As if on cue, a roll of thunder rumbled down the tracks and a train hurtled into the station. Sadie scanned the crowd of people spilling out on to the platform and caught a familiar figure walking toward them. Wearing faded jeans and a hoodie, a pair of aviator sunglasses hiding most of his face, Ryan was dressed to blend in. With one hit movie already under his belt, her costar was much more likely to be recognized than she was.

"Morning." He leaned over and ruffled Sadie's newly shorn locks. "Wow, Gold."

"Hey now, don't do that," Ana said, standing up, her husky voice sharp with an edge of warning.

"Huh?" Ryan's arm fell to his side, and he glanced up in surprise.

Sadie waved a hand between them. "Ryan, this is Ana."

"Nice to meet you." His gaze snagged on Ana's chest, but quickly kept moving up to her face, where it stayed.

Hmm. He was smarter than she gave him credit for.

"Hi, Ryan," Ana purred, voice low and almost dangerous as she shook his hand. "You wanna keep this hand? Don't touch her hair like that again."

Well, this was off to a great start. Sadie glanced at her costar, gauging his reaction.

Rather than be upset by Ana's threat, Ryan seemed amused. He relaxed, easing into a lazy grin. "She doesn't mind." He cocked an eye back at Sadie. "Do you, Gold?"

Okay, maybe not that smart. "Actually." Sadie also stood, pulling herself up to her full height, all five feet and one-half inches, maybe even more, if she counted the spikes of hair sprouting from the top of her head. "I do mind."

Ryan's grin faded. "You do?" He looked dumbfounded, as if such a possibility had never occurred to him. "Look, if I crossed a line," he mumbled, groping for an apology, "I'm sorry."

"Here's a piece of free advice," Ana said, emerald eyes flashing. "A good rule of thumb is to never touch a woman, never touch *anybody,* unless you know for sure they are cool with it."

"You're right. That's good advice." Ryan nodded. "Thanks." He cleared his throat, his words sincere as he turned to Sadie. "Sorry about that. It won't happen again."

"Apology accepted." In what was quickly becoming a habit, Sadie brushed her hand over the top of her spiky new do. "And I can understand the temptation. It *is* pretty wild, right?"

"I'm telling you, I love it," Ana insisted, leading them across the platform toward the parking lot. She clicked a button on her key fob, unlocking her car. "It looks freaking amazing. Totally badass. Like a rock star." She got in the driver's seat and tilted her head, considering her reflection in the rearview mirror. "Maybe I should give the style a try."

"Are you kidding?" Ryan piped up from the backseat. "How could you even think about getting rid of all that gorgeousness?"

Ana shifted her focus, narrowing her eyes at him in the rearview mirror.

"Right." Ryan shrunk back, looking sheepish and contrite and ready to hide in the trunk. "Not my business."

"You're learning." Icy glare melting, Ana's lips softened into a smile. "I do appreciate the compliment, though."

At the playful shift in her tone, Ryan perked up, mood bouncing back with the ease. "I could go on, you know."

Ana laughed. A husky, flirty sound. "Maybe later, cowboy."

Climbing in next to Ana, Sadie hid a smile. The games had begun.

Bo parked his motorcycle in the shade of a wooden shack and glanced up at the sign hanging from the side of the building advertising HOMEMADE CIDER DONUTS Another sign swung below it, the words HOT AND FRESH painted in bright red letters.

He scanned the busy parking lot. All around him, people bustled past. Families pulling wagons and pushing strollers, couples holding hands, everyone laughing and smiling in the September sunshine. For the hundredth time, he wondered what the hell he'd been thinking. Why had he agreed to come here today?

Before he could climb back on his bike and get the hell out of there, a sleek emerald convertible rolled to a stop in front of him. The car door swung open and a pair of Converse sneakers stepped out, crunching on the gravel. Bo's gaze traveled over the sneakers, up the lean curve of muscled calves, past the pretty dress, to the even prettier face. Eyes the color of the flowers that grew in the meadow back home met his.

Those eyes held the answer he'd been looking for—the reason he'd agreed to be here. No one ever made him feel the way Sadie did when she looked at him. All these years later, her eyes still held the same magic—still put the same spell on him.

Bo glanced away, catching his reflection in the side mirror of his bike. *Take a good look, man.* He'd been feeding himself a line of bull. Sure, he wanted to find a moment to talk to Sadie about their past. But not only so he could clear the air. He wanted to know if she still had any feelings for him.

Because he sure as hell still had feelings for her.

The car door shut, knocking Bo out of his musings. "You came," Sadie said, her tone clearly indicating she'd had her doubts.

"I did." Bo nodded. She didn't need to know he'd been seconds away from backing out.

"When did you get a motorcycle?" she asked, glancing over at his ride.

"A long time ago." He kept his voice neutral. She also didn't need to know he'd traded in his car for the bike the morning after they'd broken up. Didn't need to know about the little issue of a smashed windshield he'd had to deal with.

"Sweet ride," Ryan said, breaking the rising tension as he hopped out of the back seat, slapping Bo on the shoulder in greeting.

"A chopper," Sadie's friend Ana added, full lips quirking. "Very bad boy of you."

"She's not a chopper."

"But are you still a bad boy?" Ana rejoined.

Bo chuckled, grinning at the dark-haired woman he

hadn't seen since they were teenagers. "Nice to see you again, Ana."

"Nice to see you too." Ana patted Bo's cheek. "I like the beard."

"Thanks." Bo glanced at Sadie, wondering what she thought. She'd not commented on it, and he sure as hell wasn't about to ask.

"Yeah," Ryan added with a teasing smirk. "It's very bad boy."

"Come on." Bo pulled Ryan toward a booth where an attendant was handing out baskets. "Make yourself useful."

An hour or so later, perched on a tree branch, Bo squinted against the afternoon sun, watching as Ryan stretched his arm to reach the apples Ana was pointing to from her spot on the ground below.

"Hey, careful, man," Bo warned. It would suck if one of the leads in his film got injured, and not even on the damn set. He hadn't been thrilled at Ryan's suggestion to sneak off to a quiet part of the orchard and break the "no climbing" rule, but he'd been outnumbered. Ana had been excited at the prospect and Sadie had seemed game too, so Bo had shrugged and grudgingly followed them to a far corner of the orchard. If nothing else, he'd keep an eye out and make sure they stayed safe and weren't caught. And to be fair, when it came to climbing trees, Bo had years of practice.

"Chill, dude, I got it." Ryan snagged the fruit. "Ready?" he called down to Ana.

"Let me have it!" Ana shouted, holding the basket out.

"I'd love to, sugar," Ryan muttered under his breath as he let the fruit drop.

"What was that?" Bo hissed, snapping off an apple from a nearby branch.

"You heard me." Ryan raised his sunglasses, peering through the leaves to wink at Bo. "Have you ever seen such lush, round, perfect . . . apples?" He grinned wolfishly and glanced back down, his vantage point offering a clear view of Ana's cleavage. "Incoming!" he called, sending more apples falling.

Bo shook his head, doing his best not to ogle the cleavage hovering below him as he tossed a few apples down to Sadie, who also stood waiting holding a basket.

When both baskets were overflowing, Bo and Ryan carried them to Ana's car while the girls headed inside the donut shack.

"You and Ana, huh?" Bo asked.

"If I'm lucky." Ryan set his basket on the back seat of the open convertible.

"But what about your rule?" Bo pressed, settling his basket in next to the other and making sure both were secure.

"What about it? Coworkers are off limits. But friends of coworkers are fair game." Ryan glanced over at the shack. "Hot and ready," he said, chuckling as he read the sign. "Perfect."

Bo snorted and followed Ryan back to the shack. The guy was incorrigible. But as long as Ana seemed to welcome his advances, it was none of his business. They found the girls waiting on the other side of the little wooden building, where picnic tables had been set up in an open patch of grass.

Ryan took the seat next to Ana, which left Bo the spot next to Sadie. As he settled onto the bench, his skin tingled, an electric current arcing in the space between his body and hers. Bo gripped the rough wood of the picnic table, fighting the urge to move closer, to fill that space, to touch her.

Across from them, Ryan showed no such reserve, scooting closer to Ana until he was right next to her. "Hey," he said.

"Hey, yourself," Ana shot back with a flirtatious wink. She reached for the paper sack sitting on the table. "You're not fooling me; I know you're just trying to get your paws on my donut."

Beside Bo, Sadie make a choking sound.

"Are you okay?" He turned to her, ready to clap a hand between her shoulder blades, move behind her and do the Heimlich, get her on the ground and perform mouth-to-mouth. *Whoa, slow down there.*

Sadie nodded. "Fine." She glared across the table at her friend.

"Bo?" Ana asked, her voice sweet as honey. "You like to eat donuts, don't you?"

"Um, sure," he said absently, his brain still caught on the image of Sadie, spread out on the grass, his body bent over her, mouth on hers. "Who doesn't?"

Again, Sadie choked.

"Are you sure you're okay? Can I get you some water or something?" He glanced around, catching sight of a brightly painted tent set up on the other side of the picnic area. "What's that?"

Ana glanced over her shoulder. "That?" She turned back to face him, grin almost as wolfish as Ryan's had been earlier. "That's the Garden of Eden."

"The what now?" Bo asked, sure she was pulling his leg.

"The Garden of Eden, it's like a beer garden, but instead they sell hard cider."

"Sounds pretty good. I could use a drink right about now. Anyone else?" Three hands shot in the air. Bo excused himself and headed for the tent. Aside from a drink, he could also use a few minutes to pull himself together.

When he got back to the table, the mood was jovial, the girls laughing at a story Ryan was telling them. "What's so funny?" he asked, setting the tray of ciders down.

"I was just telling them about my life before I became an actor," Ryan said.

"I can't believe you actually lived in a van down by the river." Ana shook her head.

"Not a river, the ocean," Ryan corrected. "This was Hawaii, remember? I lived in a van down by the ocean." He grinned as the girls burst into giggles again.

Hilarious. A pang of jealousy darted through Bo as he scooted back onto the bench, next to Sadie. He wanted to be the one to make her laugh, the one to bring out her smile.

Across the table, Ana was leaning on her elbow, studying Ryan with affection, like he was a cute little puppy she wanted to take home and play with. "Let me get this straight," she began, "one day you are homeless, on a beach in Hawaii, and the next you're cast in a movie?"

"That pretty much sums it up, yeah." Ryan nodded. "Look, I know I'm lucky. But I don't take any of this for granted. Success came to me in the blink of an eye; I know I can lose it all in the blink of an eye too."

"I'm impressed," Ana said. Admiration now mixing with the affection.

"So am I," Sadie added.

Bo remained silent, lost in his thoughts. In some ways he envied the actor's easy success. Unlike Ryan, Bo had to bust his ass for every step he'd moved forward. He'd worked damn hard for everything he had. Hell, he was still working hard, doing everything he could to achieve his dreams. Owning the stunt company was just the start.

Setting the serious thoughts aside, Bo reached for one of the plastic cups and tossed back a healthy swallow. Cold and sweet, the cider kissed the back of his throat before hitting his belly with a bang.

"Careful," Ana warned. "This stuff might taste like apple juice, but it packs quite a punch."

"You're not kidding," he said, already sensing the start of a nice little buzz as the alcohol swept through his veins.

"Oh yeah?" Ryan asked, face skeptical as he grabbed a cup.

"You might wanna go easy, man," Bo suggested.

"Dude, do you know how long it's been since I had a drink?"

"Exactly." Bo didn't want to get up in the other guy's business, but he knew Ryan hadn't been drinking while training for the film and was worried the actor's tolerance wasn't very high right now.

"Relax, Bo-dacious." Ryan brushed Bo's concern away and raised his cup, throat working as he downed more than half in one gulp. The actor gasped and wheezed. "Wha . . . whazz in . . ." he began, words not fully coherent as he stared into his cup. Finally, he got control of his mouth again and turned to stare at Ana. "What the hell is in this?"

"Forbidden fruit." Ana grinned wickedly. "Fermented apples soaked in brandy barrels." She pulled a donut out of the bag and held it up to Ryan's mouth. "Here, take a bite of this. It'll absorb some of the booze." She pushed the bag toward Bo. "You better eat one too."

Bo picked up the bag, but before he reached in and grabbed one, he turned to Sadie. "Want one?" he offered.

"Of course." She took a donut from the bag and set it on a napkin in front of her. "Thanks."

Bo nodded, mesmerized as she licked cinnamon and sugar from her finger.

She glanced his way. "Aren't you going to have one?"

"Huh?" he asked, focused on watching Sadie's lips move. There was a speck of cinnamon in one corner of her mouth. He wanted to lean forward and lick it from her lips.

"Bo?"

"What?" He shook himself. "Oh. Yeah. Thanks." He took the last donut from the bag.

She smiled at him, and he felt his skin flush from head to toe. It could be the effect of the cider, but he doubted it. He took a big bite, barely tasting it as he chewed and swallowed, watching her do the same.

"You really like that donut," he said, letting the first thought that popped into his mind fall out of his mouth. *Smooth, man.*

Luckily, she didn't seem offended. "It's delicious." She laughed, sucking more sugar from her fingers.

Bo squirmed on the bench.

"Donuts are my favorite food group," she went on, oblivious to his sudden discomfort.

"Donuts aren't a food group!" Ana interrupted, giggling.

Bo looked over, taking in Ana's pink cheeks. She'd obviously been imbibing in the cider as well. It seemed nobody would be going anywhere for a little while.

"Fine," Sadie acquiesced, "they're my favorite treat."

"I don't know if I could pick a dessert as my favorite," Ana mused. She turned to Ryan. "How about you? If you could only eat one dessert for the rest of your life, what would it be?"

"Hmm." Ryan leaned in closer to Ana and whispered in her ear.

Her eyes widened, and she burst into giggles again.

Bo took another pull on his cider, he could guess what Ryan's answer had been.

"Your favorite dessert is cherry-cola cake, right?" Sadie asked, her voice almost shy.

"That's right." Bo looked at her over the rim of his cup. There was that ache again, throbbing in his chest.

"I remember your sister would make it for you on your birthday," she continued, reaching for the remaining cup of cider on the tray and taking a sip. "She never liked me very much."

"Who, Luna? She liked you fine."

"No, she didn't," Sadie insisted before taking a long pull on her drink. "Luna hated me," she said, and then grew quiet, staring down into her cup.

An awkward silence settled between them. Meanwhile, Ana and Ryan continued their mating dance on the other side of the table. Bo gazed into his own cup, almost empty. He'd wanted to talk with Sadie about their past, but now that the opportunity had arrived, he didn't know how to proceed. The time still didn't feel right. If he could get her alone for a few minutes . . .

The loud clanging of a bell shattered his thoughts. Bo glanced around, bewildered. "Is there a fire?"

"It's a hay ride!" Ana squealed with inebriated delight. She jumped up, pointing at the approaching horse-drawn wagon. "Let's go!" She grabbed Ryan's arm, then stopped and looked at Sadie. "Are you coming?"

Sadie turned to Bo. "Want to?"

Did he want to lie in a pile of hay, Sadie's soft warm body curled against him? Yes, yes he did. "Sure." He gathered up the cups and napkins, cramming everything into the empty donut bag and tossing it in a trash can on his way to join the others lining up to climb aboard the wagon.

Bo got in, then turned and offered Sadie a hand up. When her fingers touched his, sparks skittered up his arm. He tightened his hold reflexively, pulling her close for the space of a heartbeat before letting her go. Then he found an open area in the wagon and sat, yanking off his leather jacket and laying it on the straw next to him. "Here," he said to Sadie, patting the spot he'd made for her, grateful when she didn't protest, but simply dropped down beside him.

"Thanks." She bent her knees and tucked her bare legs up under the hem of her dress, until only the toes of her sneakers peeked out.

"No problem." He pressed his back against the wooden slats of the wagon, resisting the urge to wrap his arm around her shoulders.

Before long, they were all settled in, bumping slowly down a worn muddy track, the creak of the wagon wheels and steady thump of the horses' hooves threading with the conversations of the other passengers. Bo cast an eye over the group, smiling as he watched a pair of toddlers tussle over who got to sit on their mother's lap. Eventually, they both won, their mom scooping them up and plopping them each down on one of her legs.

Seeing them reminded him of Toby. His nephew was older than those two, but the little guy would like this place. Bo recalled what Sadie had said about Luna. He bent his head, pressing his mouth close to Sadie's ear. "She didn't hate you, exactly. She was just jealous, you know."

"Who?"

Bo hesitated. He shouldn't have brought up the subject

again. He should drop it. Or make something up. But before he could say anything else, Sadie caught on.

"Your sister?" she asked.

"Yeah. Luna didn't hate you so much as she hated how much time we used to spend together."

"But I only saw you during the summer," Sadie protested.

"Didn't matter. You were encroaching on her territory." There was more to it, but Bo wasn't about to take that turn down memory lane. It was a detour sure to lead to disaster.

"How is your sister, anyway?" Sadie asked.

"Fine. Good." He stretched his legs out in front of him. "She runs her own business. Grows and sells organic vegetables. Flowers too." For some reason, he refrained from mentioning Toby. Another detour he wasn't ready to make.

"She always had a green thumb," Sadie mumbled, her voice sounding sleepy.

Bo was feeling kind of drowsy too. The afternoon sun was warm, and the rhythmic creak and sway of the wagon was like being rocked in a cradle.

Beside him, Sadie began to relax, her body leaning into his. The weight of her head on his shoulder felt so shockingly familiar, Bo could almost believe the last eleven years hadn't passed, that they hadn't been apart all that time. How often had they been together just like this? Snuggled in a pile of hay, her head tucked under his chin.

He shifted, grief twisting his heart as he settled her more firmly against him. A longing for all the days and weeks and months and years he hadn't gotten to share with her. But he had to let that go, had to stop mourning what he'd missed.

Besides, he had no one to blame but himself. He'd been

the one to make the choice, to walk away. He'd fully believed their lives had been headed in different directions, that a future together was impossible and would lead to nothing but pain. He'd even had the bruises to prove it.

Had he been wrong to let her go? All this time, Bo had consoled himself with the belief he'd done right by Sadie. Told himself he'd sacrificed what he wanted, so she could have what she needed.

Maybe, he swallowed, regret burning in the back of his throat, maybe he'd been wrong.

Because here they both were.

He'd come here today wondering if she still had feelings for him. She did. He knew it. Good an actress as Sadie was, she couldn't hide it from him completely. He'd known her far too intimately for far too long not to recognize it. The tilt of her head. The way her body instinctively leaned toward his. The warm weight of her gaze when she thought he wasn't looking.

Was he as transparent to Sadie? Could she read him as easily? Did she know he still had feelings for her? Bo hadn't been prepared for the depth of emotion that washed over him when he saw her that first day. Walking in to the view of Ryan whispering in Sadie's ear, he'd immediately wanted to beat the shit out of the actor.

This was dangerous territory—on both a personal and professional level. If he was smart, he'd follow Ryan's policy and avoid getting involved with Sadie. Though at this point, Bo wasn't sure if that was even an option.

Hell yeah, it's an option. You can make the choice. Right now. When they got off this wagon, he could distance himself from her, redraw the lines of their relationship, make it clear he wanted to keep things strictly professional. But even as he thought it, Bo knew he would do no such thing.

Seeing her again made his pulse race, his heart hammer. Being near her made everything come alive inside him. The only thing Bo could compare it to was how he felt while doing a stunt. The kind of rush he only got when jumping off the side of a building. But better.

Feeling like he was lined up on the edge for a jump now, Bo finally gave in to temptation and wrapped his arm around Sadie's shoulders, tugging her even closer, until her cheek rested on his chest, pressed firmly over his pounding heart.

CHAPTER 11

SADIE OPENED HER eyes. They'd stopped moving. The hayride was over and all around her, people were rustling through the piles of straw, exiting the wagon. But she didn't want to leave. Not yet. Maybe not ever. She wanted to stay exactly where she was.

How many times had she dreamt about this? Fallen asleep to the memory of how it felt to lie against Bo, her head on his shoulder, cheek against his chest. This wasn't a memory. Or a dream. Right now—his chest rising and falling with each breath, his heart thumping gently beneath her cheek, slow and strong and steady—these things were real.

"Time to wake up, abeja," he whispered, fingers stroking over her earlobe.

Sadie shivered. "I am awake."

"We need to get off the wagon."

"Do we have to?"

"I'm pretty sure we do, yeah." He chuckled, a low rumble in his chest.

She closed her eyes and buried her face against him, absorbing his laughter, his scent.

"Come on," he said, tugging her up with him. "Should I carry you?"

Yes, please.

"No, thanks." Sadie steadied herself and made her way off the wagon.

Bo retrieved his jacket and hopped down after her.

That had been kind of him, to set the jacket out for her, so she didn't have to rest her bare legs on the straw. Sadie knew from firsthand experience how itchy hay could be against naked skin. For that matter, so did Bo.

Heat bloomed in her belly as memories assailed her, the two of them in the hayloft of her nana's stable, evening light spilling in from the west, making the dust motes sparkle in the air. Everything seemed to have a touch of magic when Bo was around, always had. Ever since the first time she'd met him, when she'd been seven years old and covered in glitter.

She'd been up before the sun, so early it was still dark more than light, the trees a patch of swollen shadows curving toward the sky like the bellies of sleeping giants. Sadie smiled, remembering how determined she'd been that morning, marching across the dew-kissed clover, a glass jar of magic sand in the pocket of her robe.

Glitter. Which she'd planned to use to help her catch a fairy. Sadie had grown up on her poppa's stories about the Wee Folk and was convinced a colony of the magic people lived in the woods at the edge of the meadow. As the sun began to rise in the east, streaks of purple giving way to pink, she'd known it was almost time.

Her poppa always said the fairies returned home from their nightly adventures with the dawn. It was the only opportunity to catch one. She'd pulled the jar of glitter from her pocket and popped the cap, spilling some into her palm.

Then a voice came from the shadows, unexpected, startling her. She'd stumbled, the jar of glitter flying, coating her in a shower of sparkles. And when she'd glanced up, smearing more glitter across her face as she tried to brush the hair out of her eyes, she'd caught sight of him.

Bo.

Sadie stole a glance at the man walking beside her now, recalling the boy he'd once been. Eight years old. Astride a white horse that looked as if it'd galloped straight off the pages of a fairy tale. His fingers had been tangled in the horse's mane, his brown eyes shining like two lucky pennies in the morning light as he stared down at her. She could still recall every detail of that first encounter. How he'd smelled. Of leather and horses. Of wet grass and sunwarmed hay. How he'd come from the west, silent as a wraith. She'd believed Bo was one of them. A fae prince.

Brushing stray bits of straw from her dress, Sadie brushed aside the memories. At least she didn't have pieces of hay hiding in her hair. There were some benefits to her new haircut. Self-consciously, she reached up and attempted to smooth the spiky locks that were probably sticking out all over the place thanks to her impromptu carb-and-cider-induced nap.

Sadie glanced at Bo, watching as he tugged straw from his own hair, taking the opportunity to drink him in while he was distracted. Her thirsty gaze roamed his richly tanned skin, his long sooty lashes, and his eyes that defied description, a shade of brown so light as to be almost golden. Tiger eyes. It was those magic eyes that had convinced Sadie that Bo was fae—a fairy-tale creature—too beautiful to be a real boy.

Emotions bubbled up, and Sadie shoved them back

down. She crammed and crammed, mentally smacking the lid of the box closed, hammering it in place to nail it shut. She'd almost gotten everything locked back down when Bo glanced at her, the afternoon light catching the gold of his eyes.

Air hitched in her throat, in that awkward little spot between swallowing and breathing. He winked at her, and the lid blew off the top of her box. In her mind's eye, she pictured it flying skyward, rotating end over end as it disappeared into the clouds above the orchard.

Well, hell. Sadie forced air through her windpipe and returned Bo's grin with a weak smile. *She was going to need a bigger box.*

"Where did Ana and Ryan go?" she asked abruptly.

Bo tipped his chin toward a fenced animal pen. "Ana wanted to feed the goats."

Sure enough, her best friend was bent over a wooden railing, holding out handfuls of pellets. Standing beside Ana, Ryan's gaze was glued to her ass.

Lips twitching, Sadie sidled up to her costar. "Enjoying the view?"

"He's staring at my butt, isn't he?" Ana asked, not bothering to look up from the white-and-tan spotted goat whose head she was scratching.

"Guilty as charged," Ryan admitted without a hint of remorse.

"Honesty." Ana stepped back from the fence, wiping her hands on her recently admired behind. "I like that."

"I also might have sneaked a peek down your shirt earlier too," Ryan admitted, his face the picture of earnestness.

"Yeah, I know," Ana acknowledged with a husky chuckle.

Sadie knew that chuckle. If Ryan played his cards

right, he'd be getting more than a peek later tonight. Ana never let anyone get away with ogling her unless she wanted them to. Sadie caught her friend's eye and a signal passed between them. They'd been communicating without words since their finger-painting days.

Having worked with all kinds of characters, Sadie knew Ryan's type. A happy, carefree kind of guy. Dumb but not stupid. Not even dumb, exactly. Clueless might be more accurate. Attractive . . . hot even. But an accessible kind of hot, with warm, friendly eyes and an easy smile. Adorable and lovable. Like a puppy. It was easy to see why the box office loved him. Women longed to take care of him, rub his belly, and give him treats or something. Men too.

"What?" Ryan asked, catching her studying him.

"Nothing," Sadie said quickly, not about to admit she'd been comparing her costar to a canine. On silent feet, Bo joined them at the fence, and Sadie's skin prickled with awareness. If Ryan was a puppy, Bo was a fox. A falcon. Something predatory. Not in a sly, cunning way, but in a watchful, serious way. You didn't want to bring him home to snuggle, you wanted to give him a wide berth and pray you didn't piss him off.

But at the same time, you couldn't help wondering what it would be like to get close to such a creature, earn its trust. She'd had Bo's trust once, long ago. And he'd had hers. But that was in the past. Lost, along with everything else they'd shared. An old, familiar ache burned in the back of her throat. "Did you have fun on the hayride?" Sadie asked, seeking distraction.

"I did." Ana chuckled again. "How about you? Did you have a nice nap?"

"It was very nice, yes." Sadie glanced over at Bo, heart catching as she watched him cooing to a charcoal-gray

billy goat, who stared up at him with adoring eyes while
he stroked a hand up and down the goat's back. She didn't
blame the creature; she'd be besotted too if Bo were petting her. Sadie turned back to Ana. Her friend raised an
eyebrow and another signal passed between them.

"Wow, it's getting late," Ana announced. "We'd better
get going, I have a ton of baking to do."

"Baking?" Ryan perked up, as if he were playing
bingo and his winning number had just been called. "You
bake?"

"Oh, yeah. You know all those apples you helped pick?
They need to be turned into a whole lotta kugel."

"Kugel." Ryan moaned lustily. "I love kugel."

"*Everybody* loves kugel." Ana chuckled. "We are talking about a pasta cheesecake—two comfort foods rolled
into one—that's Jew magic right there."

"An old girlfriend of mine used to make it sometimes."
Ryan closed his eyes, clasping a hand to his chest. "Mitzi.
God, I miss her."

"Do you miss her or her kugel?" Ana teased, moving
to stand closer.

What Sadie didn't miss was how her friend used the
opportunity to press her boobs against Ryan's chest. She
could watch those two flirt some more, or she could help
move things along. "Hey, Ryan, I bet Ana could use some
help in the kitchen."

"That's a fabulous idea," Ana purred, patting Ryan.
"Tell you what, you can come over to my place and help me
bake." She let her fingers trail up his arm, lingering over
the swell of his muscles. "And I'll let you have all the kugel
you can handle. Do you know how to heat up an oven?"

"I've been told I'm good at turning things on." Ryan
wrapped his hand around Ana's, helping her give his biceps a good squeeze.

Sadie couldn't stop a snort of laughter from escaping. These two were perfect for each other.

Ryan glanced over at her. "You don't mind, do you?"

"Why would I mind?" Sadie wondered. Did Ryan think she'd be jealous?

"Wasn't Ana planning to give you a ride home?"

"I'll give Sadie a ride," Bo broke in.

"You will?" When she'd jumped in to help Ana score some time with Ryan, she hadn't considered the logistics.

"I will." Bo met her gaze, and Sadie thought she caught a challenge in the glint of copper shining in his eyes "If that works for you."

"Didn't you come here on a motorcycle?" she asked, already knowing the answer. It wasn't like she could forget how he'd looked as they'd pulled up next to him in the parking lot. The image of Bo, standing next to his bike, leaning against the sleek curves of chrome and leather, looking cool as fuck and hot as hell, was burned into her brain.

"Yeah, I rode my bike. Is that a problem?"

There was definitely a challenge in his eyes. She'd seen that look before, many times. Usually right before he dared her to do something risky.

"The problem"—she balled her fists at her hips—"is that I don't have a helmet."

"You can use mine."

"What will you wear?"

"Are you serious?" He raised his eyebrows. "You do remember what I do for a living?" Bo shook his head, dismissing her argument. "Trust me, sweetheart, I can take one ride on my own bike without a helmet."

He had an answer for everything, didn't he? So smug, so infuriatingly confident. She'd been looking for excuses, a reason to stall, and he'd knocked them down with ease. Sadie bet Bo knew exactly what he was doing too.

"Fine," she snapped, wishing she still had some hair to whip around. "Let's go." Sadie stomped off toward the parking lot, not waiting for the others to follow. She was acting like a petulant child, but she didn't care. He always could get a rise out of her.

In the best and worst ways, Bo knew exactly how to push her buttons.

Bo hurried to catch up to Sadie as she marched across the grass.

"Here." He handed her his jacket. "Wear this."

"Why?"

"I know it's warm today, but it's going to get chilly once we get on the road. And if anything happened, this would help protect your skin." He eyed her bare legs. "It'd be better if you were wearing jeans, but—"

"What? You're going to give me yours?" She slipped into his jacket and shot him a sassy little smirk. "Should we trade? You wear my dress and I wear your pants?"

He should say yes, just to yank her chain. He almost did. Bo didn't have a problem putting on a dress. No, the problem was he liked how she looked in that dress far too much. Not to mention he was looking forward to having her bare thighs pressed against him. "I'm good," he said, crossing his arms over his chest.

"If you say so." She mimicked his stance, folding her arms, chin notched at a cocky angle.

Bo smothered the smile threatening to break across his face. She'd kill him if she thought he was laughing at her right now. And he wasn't. Not exactly. It's just, she looked so ridiculously adorable, standing there in his jacket, hands lost somewhere in the sleeves, the bottom of it reaching past her knees, longer than her dress.

On second thought, it was probably for the best he hadn't taken her up on the offer to trade outfits. That dress of hers wouldn't leave much to the imagination if he wore it.

"Everything okay here?" Ana called, interrupting their standoff.

"Yep, everything is peachy," Sadie replied, voice acid and sugar at the same time, like the candy his abuela always gave him. Sweet on your tongue, but with a kick that made your cheeks feel like they were being pinched from the inside.

"I'd make a joke about picking apples, not peaches, but I can't think of one, so pretend I did." Ryan grinned.

"Then I'd make a joke about low-hanging fruit," Ana countered. She turned to Bo. "No fancy stunts on that thing, okay? That's my best friend you've got there."

"And my costar," Ryan added.

"I'll take good care of her," Bo assured them.

"This best friend and costar can take care of herself," Sadie huffed, reaching for the helmet hanging from his handlebars.

"Of course you can." Ana leaned in for a hug.

"Thanks, man. I owe you one." Ryan clapped Bo on the shoulder. "See you next week. We start filming at the stable, right?"

Bo nodded. "You've ridden a horse before?" He assumed the studio wouldn't have cast the guy unless he had some equestrian experience, but actors were known for inflating their resumes. "Equestrian experience" could translate to rode a pony once at the town fair.

"Oh, yeah, plenty of times." Ryan waved his hand with exaggerated casualness.

"Western or English?" Bo pressed.

"Western. I've never been able to handle myself in one of those prissy English saddles. It's like surfing on half a board." The actor slanted him a smile that said he was aware of Bo's little test, before hopping into the passenger seat of Ana's car.

After the convertible had taken off, leaving nothing but a puff of gravel dust in the parking lot, Bo turned back to Sadie. She was still struggling with the helmet, trying to adjust the visor.

"Here, let me help you."

"Mmmpfh."

"Huh?"

"Mmmpfh mmmfff mmm!"

He flipped the face shield up. "What was that?"

Violet eyes glared up at him. Sadie tugged at the lower half of the helmet, pulling it away from her mouth. "I said this thing is too heavy! What's it made of—Sheetrock?"

"Fiberglass, mostly." He checked the helmet's fit, making sure it was secure. "It's a little big, but you'll be fine. And yeah, I know it feels heavy at first. You'll get used to it."

"But—"

He flipped the face shield back down, effectively cutting her off. *Nice. That was convenient.* Bo popped out the passenger foot pegs on the rear of the bike. "Now listen, when you get on, you need to put your legs exactly where I tell you. I don't want you accidentally getting burned by the exhaust pipes. And stay away from the muffler." He indicated the areas to avoid. "And when I stop, don't try and put your feet on the ground. Keep them on the pegs. Got it?"

The helmet bobbed back and forth. Bo hoped in understanding.

This was a bad idea. Why had he been so quick to jump in and offer to give her a ride home? There were too many variables here, too many things that could go wrong. Shoving his doubts aside, he took a breath and climbed on his bike. Since it was already done, the best thing he could do now was focus on what could go right.

"When you're ready," he told her, grabbing the handle-bars and flicking his chin over his shoulder, indicating she should get on behind him.

Faster than he'd expected, Sadie climbed on. Bo dug his boots into the gravel, bracing his legs and maintaining the bike's balance while she adjusted her weight, strad-dling the seat behind him. She tucked the ends of her dress beneath her, securing it around her thighs before pressing her legs against his.

He reached back and grabbed one of her hands, tug-ging it over his hip. "Hold on tight, but not so tight you can't maintain your own balance."

The helmet bumped against his shoulder blades as she nodded again.

"That reminds me, if you need to get my attention, like if you need a break and want me to pull over, squeeze my leg. Twice, like this." He gripped her thigh and slowly squeezed and released, and then did it again.

Jesus. The feel of her beneath his fingers, the contrast of smooth soft skin and firm lithe muscle. Bo's mouth went dry.

"If it's an emergency," he added, voice rasping a little, "and you need me to pull off the road immediately, then squeeze three times very fast." He wrapped his hand around her leg again and squeezed in three quick successions.

She raised her arm and gave him a thumbs-up.

"Okay, then." He put the bike in neutral and opened the choke. "Here we go." Bo jumped down on the starter.

The engine roared to life, and he revved it a few times, warming it up. Sadie scrambled closer. Her thighs pressed hard against his, arms clamped around his waist. "Not too tight, remember?"

Immediately, she loosened her hold. "That's it," he praised her, not sure if she could hear him over the rumble of the motor. He wasn't too worried. Sadie had been riding horses since she was a child; he knew she could handle riding a mechanical one.

Bo walked the bike backward out of his parking space. As he'd instructed, she kept her feet firmly planted on the pegs. Beneath the cool leather of his jacket, her breasts pressed against his back. At the base of his spine, he could already feel the heat of her seeping through his jeans. Sweet Lord, this was going to be a long ride.

Slipping on his sunglasses, Bo gathered himself and prepared to endure the hour drive back to the city. He swung the bike through the parking lot and headed east, the late afternoon sun riding low behind them.

They'd been on the road about thirty minutes when Sadie squeezed his thigh, twice, slowly. A break, but not an emergency. He nodded. After another mile or so, a gas station appeared over a rise. Bo checked his mirrors before switching lanes and pulled into the tiny parking lot.

He cut the engine. Behind him, Sadie wiggled off the bike. He was pleased to note how she diligently kept her legs far from the areas he'd warned her about. After easing the bike onto its kickstand, Bo dismounted.

She was struggling to escape the helmet.

"There's a trick to it," he said, helping her slide it off.

"Thanks."

They were standing so close, Bo could feel the soft rush of air on his skin as she sucked in a breath. Her cheeks were flushed, and her hair stuck up in every direction, a rebellious army of golden spikes. His fingers itched to smooth a hand over the messy locks, to trace the delicate line of her nose and chin. Bo cleared his throat. "Why did you want me to stop?"

Sadie tilted her chin and studied him. "Do you know where you're going?"

"Uh, yeah."

"Are you sure?"

What was that look she was giving him right now? Bo couldn't decide if she was confused or curious or something else.

"Yes, I'm sure. I said I'm taking you home, remember?" He stared at her, wondering if the helmet had cut off oxygen to her brain.

"Oh, I remember that part," she assured him. "What I can't remember is the part where you asked me where I live."

Bo opened his mouth, about to remind her he knew exactly where she lived but then stopped, mouth still hanging open as he realized his mistake. He snapped his jaw shut. He knew where Sadie *used to live*. Eleven years ago.

"My parents still live there, so you wouldn't have been completely wrong," she continued, as if reading his mind. "Wouldn't that be a treat for my mom?" Sadie smirked. "To see me roll up on the back of a motorcycle?"

Bo's mood dipped. If Sadie believed Luna didn't like her, Bo *knew* Sadie's mother hated him. Maureen Goldovitz had made it clear Bo was not fit company for her daughter. Hell, the woman didn't think he was fit company for her house. On the few occasions they'd interacted, she'd treated him like that dog Sadie used to have. "On the back of *my* motorcycle? She'd shit a brick."

"I'm not convinced my mother does that." Sadie grinned. "Shit, I mean. It's not ladylike."

Despite himself, Bo laughed, some of the tension easing out of him.

"I'm thinking she'd be more likely to demand to see what tattoos I'd gotten," Sadie mused. "What about you?" A curious glint flickered in her eyes as her gaze roamed over his body. "Do you have any tattoos?"

Tendrils of lust snaked through Bo, curling at the base of his spine. *He wanted her.* His balls ached, heavy with need, cock stiffening in the tight confines of his jeans. If she kept staring, she was going to get an eye full for sure. But Bo stood his ground, determined to let her look as long as she liked. "See anything interesting?" He quirked an eyebrow.

Sadie quirked an eyebrow right back. "Maybe you have one hiding where I can't see it."

"Maybe I do."

Her gaze drifted over him again, scrutinizing his body, head to toe.

Everywhere those violet eyes landed, Bo felt it like a brand on his skin. *Fuck.* She could tattoo him with just a look. "Tell you what." He took a step toward her. "Why don't you come back to my place."

"Your place?" Sadie drew back, eyes flaring wide. "Why?"

"I was thinking," Bo drawled, "maybe, if you ask *very nicely*, I'd show you my tattoos."

"Ha! You do have one! I knew it," Sadie crowed. "Wait." Her gaze darted to his. "*Tattoos*, as in, more than one?"

Bo leaned in close, whispering low in her ear. "Only one way to find out." With a wink, he moved past her and climbed onto his bike. The weight of her gaze was doing things to his body. Things he needed to get under control before she got back on behind him. He glanced over his shoulder, tilting his sunglasses, giving her the full force of his stare. "Well?"

She licked her lips, chest rising and falling rapidly.

Was she nervous? Probably. He sure as hell was. Bo couldn't believe he'd invited her over to his place. But he had, and no way in hell he was backing down now. "Are you coming?"

"How do I know you're not bluffing?"

"You don't." Bo cocked his head. "Get on the bike, princess," he ordered.

"Excuse me?" Sadie jerked her chin up

"You heard me. Now, get on." He revved the engine. "I dare you."

As Bo knew she would, Sadie crammed the helmet back on her head and got on.

And just like that, his night got a whole lot more interesting.

CHAPTER 12

ON THE DRIVE into Chicago, Sadie had plenty of time to lose her nerve. More than once, she considered changing her mind. Several times she almost reached out to grab Bo's thigh, give him the signal to pull over again, tell him to drop her off at home instead.

But she didn't. Instead, she kept her arms locked around his waist, holding on for dear life as he raced down the highway. It was a strange dichotomy of sensations, to feel simultaneously both terrified and safe. Familiar too.

How many times had she sat behind him on a horse just so, legs straddling his, her breastbone pressed to his backbone, gripping his hips tightly as he galloped across the meadow. Only then, she'd watched trees pass in a blur while her cheek rested against the broad planes of his back. Now, Sadie watched buildings speed by from behind the muffled darkness of his motorcycle helmet.

She should have insisted Bo wear the helmet. He was the one driving—the one sitting in front and taking the full brunt of air blasting him in the face while whizzing down the road at sixty-plus miles an hour. But it wasn't just Bo's comfort she was concerned about. Without the helmet in the way, she could close her eyes against the wind and tuck her face into the dip between his shoulder blades like she used to. Let his body protect hers. She longed to do it now. Ached to watch the world fly by while she hid, sheltered against him.

Finally, he exited the highway. Dusk was creeping over the city, the streetlamps clicking on as he weaved through evening traffic. After a few more blocks, Bo slowed down and maneuvered the motorcycle into a narrow spot in front of an older brick building. He parked and cut the engine.

Sadie eased off the bike gingerly. Her thighs felt like jelly donuts. Once she had control of her legs again, she stepped onto the sidewalk and removed the helmet, staring up at the building. "This is it?"

"Yep." Bo pointed to a large picture window on the second floor of the building. "Right up there." He took the helmet from her and headed toward the walkway, leaving Sadie no choice but to follow.

She glanced around, taking in her surroundings. "Hey, I know that place," she said, recognizing the sign for the Rebellion brewery a little farther down the street. "We're in Logan Square, right?"

Bo nodded.

"We're actually not too far from my apartment."

"Really?" He punched a code into the security panel. "Where's that?"

"Lakeview."

"That *is* close." Bo shook his head. "Who'd have thought." A strange expression crossed his face.

Did he feel it too? The sense that no matter what happened, no matter what they did, they'd been on a collision course, destined to crash into each other once more. Sadie was tempted to ask, but before she did, a buzzer sounded, releasing the security latch.

"Let me guess." Bo smirked, holding the door open for her. "You're in one of those fancy new condos."

Sadie notched her chin up haughtily but didn't answer him. There was no reason to. He was right, and she knew he knew it.

"They're nice enough, I suppose." Bo shrugged. "If you're into that sort of thing."

"You mean a great view, new appliances, and a foyer that doesn't smell like sausage?" Sadie asked, trying not to be offended, since she was, indeed, into that sort of thing.

"My foyer doesn't smell like sausage," Bo argued.

Sadie took a dramatic sniff.

Bo inhaled and wrinkled his nose. "Fine. You're right." He led the way up the stairs, calling over his shoulder. "Some people might view that as a perk, you know."

"Who?"

"People who really like sausage."

Sadie snort-giggled. "Look, I'm just saying there's nothing wrong with liking something fresh and shiny and new." She followed him down a narrow but well-lit hallway.

"And I'm just saying I like this old, smelly place." At the end of the hall, he paused, digging in his front pocket for his keys. Unlocking the deadbolt, Bo twisted the knob and swung the door open. "Welcome to my humble abode." He let her through, closing the door behind him.

Not until she'd stepped inside his apartment did Sadie realize how curious she'd been to see where Bo lived. He flicked on a light, and she tried to look everywhere at once, wanting to absorb every detail. It was a loft space, not too big, but open and airy. She spotted the tall picture window she'd seen from outside and moved toward it, gazing out over the street below. While the view wasn't awesome, it could certainly be worse.

Sausage-scented foyer aside, it fit him, this place. Hardwood floors, rough-beamed ceiling, exposed brick. A galley kitchen lined one wall, and a punching bag hung from a rafter. A grin curved one corner of her mouth as she pictured Bo, shirtless, working the bag over, sweat beading on his chest, trickling down his body, trailing along those alleged tattoos he had.

"Don't worry," he said, interrupting her thoughts and nodding toward the punching bag. "I'm not going to make you go a few rounds." He gave her a smile dripping with sin. "Unless you want to."

"I'm good, thanks." She swallowed, suddenly too warm, and unzipped his jacket. "And thanks for the letting me borrow this." Sadie slipped the thick leather off her shoulders and held it out for him.

"No problem." He took the jacket from her, their fingers brushing. Electricity jolted up her arm.

Sadie jerked her hand away, turning to examine the rest of the space. His decorating style could best be described as spartan. Aside from the punching bag, there were the requisite bachelor-pad leather couch and flatscreen TV. On the same wall as the picture window was a counter-height desk, a laptop, and piles of paper scattered across its surface.

"This is a nice place," she told him. "It looks good."

"You look good," he said.

The blunt observation caught her off guard. "Thanks," Sadie mumbled, running a self-conscious hand over the top of her hacked-off hair. She felt the weight of his gaze as it moved over her, taking in the details of her appearance the same way she'd taken in his apartment.

"Well," she declared, covering her sudden bout of nerves with a show of bravado. "I came, I saw"—she wrinkled her nose and flashed him a teasing smile—"I smelled."

"Hilarious," Bo growled.

"I took your dare." Sadie waggled her fingers at him. "Now stop stalling and pay up."

"Fine." Bo lifted his T-shirt, twisting so she could see the inkwork trailing up the left side of his ribcage.

It took Sadie a moment to even notice the tattoo, she was too busy noticing other details. Like all the toned skin suddenly on display. She cleared her throat. "Are those flowers?" Sadie leaned forward, eyes narrowing as she looked closer.

"Oh," she breathed. "It's a thistle." Her voice was so soft, it could barely be called a whisper. She lifted her chin, gaze questioning, knowing she was looking at him with eyes the exact shade of the ink coloring the spiky petals in his tattoo.

It couldn't be a coincidence. Could it?

Bo remained silent. Golden tiger eyes giving nothing away.

She returned her attention to his side. A second later she gasped. Nestled atop one of the thistle buds was a honeybee—tiny translucent wings fluttering right below Bo's heart. She raised her face to his again, and this time there was no question in her gaze, because this time she knew.

It wasn't a coincidence.

Sadie reached out, wanting to trace the delicate lines of the tattoo with her fingers.

"My turn." Bo shifted away from her, pulling down his shirt. "Truth or dare?"

"But that's only one," Sadie protested. "I dared you to show me *all* your tattoos."

"Odd. That's not how I remember it," Bo tsked. He crossed his arms over his chest, cocky and smug. "I think you're scared of what I might dare you to do."

"Hardly," Sadie scoffed, lying her ass off.

"Well, then?" Bo quirked an eyebrow at her. "Truth or dare?"

She decided to retreat gracefully. Lose the battle but win the war. "Truth."

A triumphant smile spread across his face and Sadie wilted. He'd *wanted* her to pick truth.

"Fine. Yes. You played me," she groaned, admitting defeat. "What do you want to know?"

His tiger eyes prowled down her body and back up again, slow and lazy, a cat in the sun.

"What?" she asked again, her voice rising, demanding a response.

"Do you remember, abeja? How it felt when I touched you?"

"No." *Was it getting hot in this place?*

"Liar." His voice was a throaty chuckle, low and dirty. "This is supposed to be a game of truth. Are you sure you don't remember?"

Sadie clamped her lips shut. She should tell him to go to hell. But she couldn't even draw enough breath to answer his question. Which was fine, since denying it would only give him another excuse to call her a liar—and he'd be right. Of course she remembered what it felt like when he touched her.

"I remember exactly how you felt the first time I touched you, abeja." He reached up, one finger tracing the scooped neckline of her dress. "How perfectly you fit in my hand."

There was a flash of white teeth as he bit his full lower lip. The tip of his tongue peeked out, and Sadie's nipples tightened in response. *It was definitely getting hotter in here.*

Then Bo was touching her. His palms slid along her sides, grazing her ribs. His thumbs stroked slowly up, barely brushing against the sensitive undersides of her breasts. Sadie closed her eyes, aching for him to reach up and cup her. *Slow, breathe in and out. Slow . . . easy . . . slow.* Sadie took shallow, quiet breaths, not wanting to let him see how he affected her, not wanting to let him know how much she wanted him to keep touching her.

But when she trained her gaze on Bo, the look in his eyes told her he already knew.

"Okay." She panted, trying to ignore the gentle pressure of his hands. "You win. I remember."

"Do you?"

"You know damn well I do." She scowled, the sexual frustration flooding her veins feeding her temper as well. "There. I gave you the truth. Now you owe me the other half of *your* dare. You were supposed to show me the rest of your tattoos. Remember?"

"Oh, that's right." He brushed his thumbs up again, higher this time, almost reaching her nipples—almost. "I guess we're both forgetful," he murmured, continuing to stroke his thumbs back and forth along the tender under-curve of her breasts.

Smart-ass. Sadie closed her eyes. Her lungs ached, her breasts ached. Worse, her heart ached, beating hard and fast, and her nipples were so rigid, she was surprised they hadn't poked holes right through her fancy silk bra.

Bo shifted the pattern of his touch, stroking up the slopes of her breasts, the pads of his thumbs coming closer and closer to her sensitive nipples, but never quite getting there. Reaching just high enough to tease without offering anything more.

The tingling was drifting lower now, heat spreading through her, from her breasts down to between her legs. A moan escaped her throat. She wanted more.

With Bo, she always wanted more.

"What was that?" Bo asked, leaning toward her, head tilted with inquiry.

"I didn't say anything," Sadie gritted through her teeth, holding back another moan as his thumbs came closer than they had yet. If he thought he could make her beg . . . well, he was probably right.

She remembered how it felt to have him touch her, how her body fit with his, but she also remembered how it felt to touch him. The thought sparked an idea. Regaining a sliver of control, Sadie fought to gain the upper hand.

"Actually"—she trailed her fingers along the waistband of his jeans—"I remember something else."

"Oh?" Interest flared, lighting his eyes with copper fire.

"Mm-hmm." *Two can play at this game.* Placing her palms on his hips, she began to brush her thumbs back and forth across the tight denim. Sadie mimicked Bo's movements, her slow gentle strokes coming just into teasing range of the swell of his cock. "If I recall, you didn't fit quite as perfectly in my hand."

His breathing grew ragged.

"But it was such a long time ago." She furrowed her brow in mock confusion. "Maybe I'm remembering it wrong." She let her thumbs drift, the soft slow strokes barely brushing the hard ridge of his erection, trapped inside his jeans.

He groaned, the guttural sound making her belly tighten, her panties instantly wet.

Sadie had been enjoying turning the tables, but her plan was in danger of backfiring. She ached for Bo to touch her, but even more than that, she ached to touch him. Each time she stroked him, teased him, she teased herself too.

Before she knew it, her fingers were working his belt buckle, tearing at the button on his fly, eagerly tugging the zipper down. Through the soft cotton of his briefs, she traced the hard outline of his cock with her palm, and it was exactly as she remembered, thick and hot, the length of him more than she could handle, even with both hands. One thumb slipped inside the tight waistband, stroking the satiny head.

Another groan tore from Bo's throat, raw and male.

Sadie's insides clenched at the sound, and she wrapped her fingers snug around his tip.

He jerked, thrusting himself deeper into her hand, and a bead of moisture kissed the pad of her thumb. His body's instant reaction to her was intoxicating. She circled the head of his cock, rubbing the slick stickiness into his skin, and he shuddered. Wanting to touch more of him, she moved to push his clothing out of the way.

But before she could continue her explorations, he pulled back, out of her grasp. She reached for him again, but he stopped her, locking a hand around her wrist.

They were both panting now, breath coming quick and sharp, chests rising and falling rapidly. Bo stared down at her, searching her face.

She understood what he was asking. This wasn't a game anymore. Where they were heading was dangerous. Sadie didn't care. She wanted Bo, any piece of him she could get. Even if it was just here, just this moment, it was more than she'd thought to have of him ever again.

"I'm guessing you don't have any tattoos down there then," she teased, keeping her tone light, determined to restore the playful mood.

He relaxed his grip, the tight lines around his mouth easing. "No," he confirmed, following her lead and playing along. "Not there."

She pulled her arm back and tapped her chin in speculation. "Hmm . . ." She let her gaze rove over his body. Thanks to her handiwork, his jeans were undone, belt hanging loose, fly spread wide, the thick swell of his cock pressing against his briefs, tip visible above the band.

Bo noticed her staring but didn't move to adjust his clothing. Didn't cover himself. Like he'd done earlier in the gas station parking lot, he stood still and let her stare. It was another dare.

Sadie's mouth went dry, everything wet in her body heading south. With effort, she lifted her gaze to his, forcing her attention to stay focused on his face. "Okay, so where *are* your other tattoos, then?"

His grin returned, slow and sexy.

Holy shit was she in trouble.

In one smooth motion, Bo grabbed the ends of his shirt and tugged it up and over his head.

Yep, serious trouble.

He turned away from her, giving her his back. Which at least made it easier to look at him without her gaze constantly straying to the teasing glimpse of cock on display. And she'd thought his biceps were a magnet for her attention.

The view from this side wasn't bad either, though. Soft denim molded over a firm, tight ass. Above the waistband of his jeans, the tapered muscles of his torso expanded gloriously, spreading up to the broad line of his shoulders.

Sadie stared at the valley running down the middle of his back, the shadow cast between the slopes of his lats and traps. Unlike a lot of guys she saw at the gym, Bo wasn't bulging with muscle, but rather he was packed with it, defined and delicious. She wanted to taste him, to run her tongue along the groove of his spine.

Instead, she reached out and traced the shadow with her finger. His body tensed at her touch, sending everything rippling. Sadie enjoyed the show, stroked her palms up over his bare shoulder blades, watching in fascination as the sculpted muscles danced beneath her hands.

"Aha!" She narrowed her gaze, catching the small circle of ink at the top of his right trapezius. "Found one." She leaned in, studying the tattoo in the dim light from the one lamp he'd lit. "The moon?"

He dipped his head, nodding once.

"For your sister, Luna, right?" she guessed.

Another nod.

Warmth spread through her. He had always been fiercely protective of his little sister. The best of big brothers.

She didn't have any siblings. Giving birth once had been more than enough for her mother. Sadie had always been jealous of Ana, who had both an older brother and a younger sister. Ana would joke about being the forgotten, unloved middle child, but it was always only that—a joke. Her friend loved her siblings fiercely, a love that was returned just as fiercely. Sadie envied that bond. She and Ana were as close as sisters. Ana would be the first to insist they *were* sisters. But Sadie knew it would never be quite the same thing.

Warmth flickered in her heart, flames of love and affection for her best friend. If it hadn't been for Ana, Sadie wouldn't be here right now, in Bo's apartment, perusing his half-naked body. Smiling, she continued her inspection. Another tattoo perched atop Bo's other shoulder, the same size and similar in design to the moon. "The sun?" she asked.

"Yeah."

Was that a note of wariness in his voice? Maybe he was self-conscious about the tattoo. Did it represent him? The symbolism made sense. If Luna, with her dark as midnight hair, was the moon, that would leave Bo to be the sun. Easy enough to imagine, with his golden-brown hair and eyes.

Sadie wanted to ask him more about the tattoo, to see if she was right about what it stood for, but before she could, he bent his head and pointed at the nape of his neck.

"This is the last one."

Going up on tiptoe, Sadie peered closer. It was a pair of hearts. One inked with the colors and pattern of the Irish flag, the other with that of the Mexican flag.

"For your parents." It was a statement, not a question. She knew his mother was a second-generation Mexican American, who met Bo's father when he came to America in the eighties, seeking asylum from the troubles in Northern Ireland.

"It's beautiful," she whispered, tracing the vine that wove between the hearts, binding them together. Sadie didn't want to stop touching him, so she ran her hand along his back, counting the tattoos as she passed them.

"One." She pressed her palm to the pair of hearts.

"Two." She circled the moon on his right shoulder before sliding her hand across to the sun on the left. "Three."

Sadie moved, walking around him, fingers trailing over his ribs, never breaking contact as she came to stand in front of him. She stroked up and over the flower stem, slowly outlining the points on the thistle. "Four." She brushed her thumb over the bumblebee. "Is that it?"

"That's it." Bo's voice was a low rumble vibrating beneath her hands.

His skin felt different here, not as smooth. Sadie stepped closer, her height putting her at the perfect position to study the flower carefully.

He stiffened.

"There's a scar here." Her brow furrowed as she caught sight of the ribbon of healed flesh completely hidden within the design of the tattoo. She'd missed it the first time he'd shown her, and never would have noticed it if she hadn't been touching him, hadn't felt the raised seam on his skin. The wound was old, but it must have been deep to leave such a lasting mark.

"What happened?" she asked.

He was silent for so long, she wasn't sure he would answer her.

"Accident," he finally bit out.

She didn't press, but waited, fingers stroking gently over the scar, hoping he would continue.

"Dad and I were driving the carriage back to the barn." His voice was clipped, as if he had to force each word through his teeth. "Dad was on the box, but it should have been me. I knew he was tired. He'd been up long before sunrise to deal with a new foal. But he insisted he was fine. You remember how he was." He glanced down at her, a rough laugh easing some of the tension around his eyes.

Sadie smiled. She did remember.

"So, I let him drive while I took the backstep and held on to the tailboard. It was dusk. I should have been paying attention. Then I might've caught sight of the bucks racing across the meadow and warned my dad."

"The deer spooked the horses?" Sadie asked quietly.

Bo nodded. "Took Dad completely by surprise. He lost control of the reins and the horses tore off. We hit a bump and the carriage flipped. I went flying off the back, but Dad, he got trapped underneath."

"Oh God," Sadie breathed, her heart filling with dread. When she'd asked about his parents, he'd said they were fine. "Bo, your dad, he isn't . . ."

"Dead?" He swallowed. "No." The barest hint of a smile touched his lips. "As Mom says, he's too stubborn to let the devil have him yet."

Sadie waited, knowing there was more, and it wasn't good.

"Dad's alive and well. Still kicking." He stopped, grimacing. "Well, not literally. The accident messed up his back, did something to his spine. The doctors couldn't fix it. He's paralyzed from the waist down."

"Oh, Bo, I'm so sorry." Sadie had no idea. She'd closed herself off completely from everything to do with Bo, and that included everything that happened at the estate.

"Don't be. I told you, Dad's fine. He's made peace with it. The last thing he wants is anyone's pity."

"Of course. I didn't mean to imply . . ." Sadie searched for the right words. She remembered Bo's father. How, like Bo, he'd been full of boundless energy, always in motion. To imagine that restless, robust man constrained to a wheelchair . . . She stopped that thought in its tracks, realizing she was making assumptions she had no business making.

"You're absolutely right," she said. "Your dad deserves better than my pity."

"Yep, so let's move on." He swept his hand through

the air, dispelling the somber moment. "You've seen all my tattoos. I've fulfilled my dare, and as a bonus, I just shared a truth. Which means it's definitely my turn." He bent his head closer, lips to her ear. "What's it going to be? Truth? Or Dare?"

CHAPTER 13

NERVES STRUNG TIGHT, Bo waited for Sadie's answer. How the hell had this day gotten so far off track?

It was wild enough she was here, in his apartment. But he'd just exposed himself. Given her a piece of his past, revealed a bit of his soul.

Fuck. Speaking of exposing himself. Bo suddenly remembered his fly was open, revealing something a little more . . . tangible. He glanced down. Rock-hard, his cock was still imprisoned inside his briefs, the tip escaping, pressing flat against his stomach. The whole time he'd been standing there, talking about serious shit, his dick was popping out of his pants.

This could only happen with Sadie. Things with his little abeja were never normal. Damn, he'd missed her. He'd missed everything about her. The way she laughed, the way she jerked her chin up to stare him down when he annoyed her. He missed touching her, watching her skin flush with desire.

And clearly, the rest of him missed her too. He really should adjust his pants and cover himself. But at this point, it was almost more awkward to do something about the situation than it was to continue ignoring it. So, he stood there, waiting for her to decide.

Truth or dare? Bo wasn't sure which he wanted her to choose. He knew exactly what he'd say in either case. Had both already picked out.

She was nibbling her bottom lip, working it back and forth while she debated her options. He watched as her gaze drifted over him, catching how her eyes bulged when she caught sight of his bulge. Sadie let out a squeak.

"Something wrong?"

"Um, your, ah . . ."

"Dick is still out?" Bo's mouth twitched, a juvenile snicker on the verge of escaping. He couldn't help it. How had she forgotten his pants were undone? She'd been the one to undo them.

"Is that . . . comfortable?" she asked. Still staring at his groin, she licked her lips, and now it wasn't his mouth that was twitching.

"Well, you gaping at it isn't helping," he said mildly.

"Oh." Her eyes darted away, but almost immediately returned. "I meant . . ." With obvious effort, she returned her attention to his face. "I meant, is it comfortable . . . to have it, um, stuck like that?"

"Not really, no." Again, he was struck by the absurdity of this moment. Of their conversation. Only with Sadie. "Have you decided yet? Or should I pick for you?"

That got her attention.

"You'd pick for me?" She narrowed her eyes at him, considering. "Why?"

"Why not?" He knew she was searching for the trap hidden in his words, but there wasn't one. Not really. In his mind, either choice was going to lead them down the same path. If he was honest with himself, from the moment they'd begun playing, he'd known where this game was going. "Because you take too long to decide."

Her face flushed. He'd hit a nerve with that one. He knew he would. But it worked. His comment goaded her into action.

"Fine." She sniffed. "Pick."

"Truth," he responded immediately.

Her eyebrows lifted with surprise. Which told him she'd been expecting him to say dare this time.

He had plenty of things he'd like to dare her to do. But what he wanted now was more of the truth. "Did you miss me?"

It was unfair of him to ask that question, seeing as he was the one who'd broken things off between them. But their conversation from that first day at the reading still stung. The knowledge she'd not looked him up, not once in all those years, burned a hole in his gut. As seconds ticked by and Sadie remained silent, the burning sensation intensified, a sharp pain ripping through him.

After a freaking eternity, she finally nodded. "Yes, Bo. I did. I missed you."

He let out a breath, the ache easing a little. Bo loved hearing her say his name. Loved the way her upper lip dipped to kiss her lower one as her mouth formed the single syllable. He'd missed that too.

He was an asshole for wanting this from her, for needing it. She owed him nothing. And yet, he couldn't stop himself from asking for more. "Did you . . ." His voice faltered. "Did you think about me?"

A kaleidoscope of emotions flickered across her face, so many and so fast, he had no hope of deciphering them all. There was pain there. Pain he'd caused. He couldn't expect her to give more of herself without giving something back. "I missed you." Bo reached for her hands.

"So damn much." He squeezed her hands inside his. "I thought about you every day, abeja. Every. Fucking. Day."

"I thought about you too," Sadie whispered. She swallowed, licked her lips, voice a little stronger as she added, "All the time."

He lifted her fingers to his mouth, pressing a kiss to her knuckles.

She giggled.

Bo froze, staring down at her. What the hell did she find funny about this?

"I'm sorry," she blurted. "But it tickles."

"What tickles?"

"Your beard." Sadie pulled her hands from his grasp and reached up, exploring his face with her fingertips. She stroked his beard. "It's soft."

"You sound surprised." He held still as she continued to touch him, her thumbs rubbing along the sides of his jaw and under his chin, where his beard gave way to smooth skin.

"I've never kissed someone with a beard before," she murmured.

"Well then," he said, bending toward her, "it would be my pleasure to be your first." He kissed her then, pressing his lips to hers.

She kissed him back, her mouth moving beneath his, opening without reservation or hesitation as he slipped his tongue inside.

The shock of it, so familiar and yet so new, rocked through him. Hot, slick, sweet. "You taste so good, abeja." Bo nibbled at her lips. "Sweet. So fucking sweet." He reached up, grasping the short spikes of her hair between his fingers and tugging her head back, forcing her mouth to open wider as he kissed her again, tongue going deeper, swallowing the delicious little sounds she was making in the back of her throat.

She leaned into him. Bo moaned into her mouth, relishing the press of her perfect little tits against his bare chest. Sadie reached between them, her hand wrapping around the exposed head of his cock, picking up where he'd stopped her earlier.

Bo had no intention of stopping her now.

Like before, she wrapped her fingers around the tip, her grip firm and sure. But it wasn't enough.

Luckily, Sadie seemed to be thinking the same thing. She tugged on his pants, working his jeans and briefs down over his hips. He reached for the hem of her dress, and their arms got tangled. Bo broke the kiss.

"Hold on," he rasped, stepping back and shucking off his boots. When he looked up from tugging off his socks and discarding the rest of his clothes, he saw she'd managed to kick off her sneakers and was in the process of slipping out of her dress.

The soft fabric fluttered to the ground. But Bo barely noticed.

"Ho . . . ly . . . fuck," he breathed. A scrap of cherry-red silk lay between her legs. More red silk hugged her breasts, lifting the gently rounded mounds high, frilly lace trim barely hiding the pale pink of her nipples.

"You are *beautiful*, mi tesoro." He gently touched one of the delicate straps of her bra. "I want to taste you," he told her, fingers stroking over the lace, teasing her. "I want to lick and nip and bite you." Bo dropped to his knees, arms wrapping around her waist, teeth grazing the strip of lace at her hips. "I want to suck your clit," he said, mouth hovering over the little red triangle of silk, "right through these sweet fucking panties."

"Oh." A trill of surprised laughter escaped her. "You always did cut to the chase."

Bo stared up at her. "Is that a yes?"

Sadie answered him with her body. Arching her back, hips thrusting toward him, she threaded her fingers in his hair, her nails an erotic scrape against his scalp as she urged him closer, pressing his mouth to her pussy.

"I'll take that as a yes," he said, lips curving in a smile as he brushed them over the silk covering her curls.

She whimpered, legs trembling.

"Come here." Bo helped her to the floor. She lay back, and he nudged her legs apart, cupping his hands behind her knees as he bent over her. "Quiero comerte la panocha."

"I know what that means, bad boy," Sadie panted, voice raw and husky with lust. "You've got a very naughty mouth."

"Sí," Bo growled. "And I'm about to put it to work on you." She was already wet, so incredibly hot and lusciously wet. He stroked her, circling his tongue around the tiny bud before making good on his promise and sucking her through the delicate silk.

Sadie moaned, her hands fisting in his hair. "More."

Bo chuckled, remembering this side of her, the greedy, demanding side. He fucking loved it. Hands on her thighs, he spread her wider, pushing her legs higher, over his shoulders, until her heels were resting against his back. He breathed her in, savoring the earthy tang of her arousal on his tongue, teeth nipping her tender skin with tiny teasing bites.

Sadie dropped her arms to the side, palms slapping the hardwood floor as she bucked her hips and begged, "More."

"Whatever you want, abeja." Bo wrapped his fist around the lace at her waist. "You want more; I'll give you more." He yanked once, hard. The fabric ripped and fell away, leaving her bare to his touch. He slipped a finger inside, relishing the soft slick feel of her.

She gasped at the invasion, but then her body tightened around him, and she moaned his name. The sound shivered down his spine, made his balls ache.

"That's it." Bo pumped his finger back and forth, hungry for each gasp, each thrust of her hips. "Come on, abeja," he urged her on, finger moving deep inside her, tongue flicking over her sticky sweet heat. "Come for me, honeybee." He felt the tremors begin in her legs and braced himself, covering her with his mouth, sucking hard and fast, taking her over the edge.

She cried out, and he was lost in her, riding out the wave of her orgasm, so close to fucking coming himself he thought he was going to burst into flames. But he didn't stop, he continued to suck and stroke her until the last shudder crashed through her body, until her legs fell slack, ankles slipping from his shoulders. He pressed a final kiss to her swollen clit and collapsed against her, cheek resting on her belly.

The rapid rise and fall of her abdomen began to slow as her breathing returned to normal. Bo shifted, rolling to his side and propping his chin up with an elbow. Sadie's eyes were closed. He watched her in silence for a moment, wondering if she'd fallen asleep.

"I'm not asleep," she muttered, reading his mind, voice a little croaky, as if she'd been screaming. Which, he smiled, pleased with himself, she had.

Sadie cracked open the eye closest to him. "What are you smirking at?"

"Who me?" Bo asked, feigning innocence.

"Yes, you." Sadie rolled onto her side and faced him, mirroring his position, leaning her chin on her elbow, both eyes open now. "Don't forget, I know you. I know that smug little grin of yours. You're quite pleased with yourself, aren't you?"

"Did I please you?" he asked.

"You know you did."

"Then yes, I'm pleased with myself." He tried to contain it, but the grin stretched across his face again. "I like that about you."

"You like what about me?" She quirked a brow. "My orgasms?"

He chuckled. "I like how you don't hide your pleasure from me. I've always liked that. Always liked your honesty."

A shadow flickered in her violet gaze, but before Bo could question it, she was smiling at him, eyes bright and clear. "And I like your beard."

"I was wondering about that," he admitted. "First time, huh?"

Sadie nodded, eyes flashing with delight, like a child with a new toy. "First time a guy with a beard has kissed me . . . anywhere." She wiggled her eyebrows.

Bo grinned at her innuendo, but a dark thought crossed his mind like a storm cloud. What other baby-faced cabrón had kissed her . . . everywhere? Eleven years was a long time. Who had she slept with? How many others had there been? It wasn't really any of his business, and yet, the need to know burned inside him, an angry jealous impulse.

"What's wrong?"

"Nothing's wrong," he mumbled, struggling to push the possessive thoughts out of his head. He had no right to feel this way, no claim on her. But something about Sadie always turned him into a caveman. Made him want to pound his chest and drag her to his lair.

"Are you sure nothing's wrong?" She glanced down between their bodies. "Ah," she said, a sly smile slinking across her face as she tilted her chin to gaze back up at him. "I think I figured out what's bothering you."

"It's not that—" he began, but she cut him off, pressing a hand to his shoulder and shoving him onto his back, straddling him in one smooth rolling motion.

"You were saying?" she asked, her lithe thighs pressing against his.

Fuck, she was strong. "It's not that bad," he amended, finally managing to shove the questions and concerns away. He needed to get over himself. Especially with her body draped over his like it was now.

"Not that bad, huh?" She glanced pointedly down, where his cock was pointing straight up.

"You have a point," he couldn't resist saying.

She laughed, settling herself more snugly atop him.

Bo sucked in a breath, savoring the sensation of her slick heat against him, an acute reminder that he was naked, and, except for her bra, so was she. "Sorry about your panties."

"That was one of my favorite pairs." Sadie glanced at the discarded scrap of silk "But . . ." She turned her gaze back to him, one eyebrow lifted. "I'd say it was worth it."

Again, Bo was struck with the urge to pound his chest, caveman style.

"Though maybe I should take this off," she added, reaching behind her and undoing the clasp on her bra, "just to be safe."

Safe. Shit. "Hey, before things go any further, I should get something."

"I think we're okay for now," she assured him.

"We are?" His tongue felt thick in his mouth, his head fuzzy. He was having a hard time concentrating, too distracted by the sight of her pretty little tits bouncing in his face. "Wait. Are we talking about the same thing? What are you talking about?"

"I'm talking about the fact that you don't have to do anything but lay back and relax," she purred, one hand wrapping around the base of his cock.

"Oh," he mumbled, brain completely useless now. "Okay."

She stroked his length, slowly moving up and down, her fingers covering every inch of him with painstaking care. Bo had done it too, when he touched her. Relearned her body. Adjusted to what felt completely familiar and yet so new.

He closed his eyes and gave himself over to her, wanting to let Sadie take her time. He just wasn't sure how much longer he could keep it together.

When her hand was replaced with the hot wet stroke of her tongue, Bo jerked. His eyes snapped open and he stared down at her, mesmerized. She was bent over him, on her hands and knees, and in the dim light he could just make out the pink of her tongue as it slid along the rigid length of his shaft.

Sweet motherfucking hell. Sweat broke out on Bo's forehead. He fisted his hands at his sides, clenching and unclenching against the hardwood floor. He wanted to reach up, rake his fingers through the rough spikes of her hair, and guide her mouth down over him.

But he held back, suddenly recalling all too well what had happened the first time she'd done this with him.

Again, Sadie had the uncanny ability to read his mind. She froze mid-lick and glanced up at him. "You're thinking about *that*, aren't you?"

"No!" Bo protested, too quickly.

She sat up, lips pursed.

"I mean, yes, it crossed my mind," he amended, "but only for a second."

"That was a long time ago, you know," she said peevishly.

"Right. You're right," Bo agreed, desperate for her to continue what she'd been doing.

"I'm pretty good at it now, actually," she added, tone growing defensive.

"Ah, okay." There was that rush of jealousy again.

"I've even given lessons."

"Lessons," he repeated. Had he heard her right?

"Well, I helped Ana give a lesson. With popsicles."

Bo didn't say anything. He couldn't. He was struck speechless. Instead, he laid there, flat out on the floor of his apartment, while she straddled him and defended her talent for giving blowjobs. This had to be the singularly most bizarre experience in this department he'd ever had.

What the hell did he do now?

Studying her from beneath his lashes, Bo was struck by a realization. *Sadie was embarrassed.* Which was silly. It had happened, as she said, a very long time ago. And with practice, they'd eventually managed to figure things out just fine. He couldn't say why that particular memory had surfaced. Maybe because, in some ways, this was like their first time all over again.

She needed to get out of her headspace, forget he'd been thinking about her mortifying first attempt at this. Bo propped himself up on his elbows, looking Sadie straight in the eye. "Go for it, then."

"What?"

"I dare you," Bo said, voice laced with challenge.

"You're daring me." Her eyes narrowed. "To do *that*?"

"Sí." Bo relaxed, lying back with feigned casualness, crossing his arms behind his head. It was a bold move. A gamble he was betting she couldn't ignore. He gazed up at her. "I dare you to give me the best fucking blowjob of my life."

Her eyes blazed, and for a second, Bo feared he'd calculated wrong.

But then Sadie smiled, licked her lips . . . and damn, if she didn't deliver.

CHAPTER 14

SADIE FINISHED WASHING up and turned off the water. As she dried her hands and face with a towel, she studied her reflection in the mirror over Bo's sink. She was still getting used to seeing herself with the new haircut. Still had to take a moment to remember that the person staring back was her.

She glanced around Bo's bathroom. The space was surprisingly neat and clean. Maybe not that surprising. He'd always been tidy. A minimalist who liked everything organized. Meanwhile, she was a clutter bug and a bit of a slob.

She tried to picture her stuff spread out on the bathroom counter. Her toothbrush next to his. Her piles of makeup and skin-care products and hair stuff beside his aftershave and razor. *Wait, does he even have a razor?*

His beard was growing on her, especially after what had just gone down on his apartment floor. That had been a new experience for her. It was strange to be with Bo again. Not unlike the sensation she had when looking in the mirror. The same, but different. New . . . yet not.

Strange and scary. But thrilling too.

With a sigh, Sadie folded the towel and hung it back on the rack. She had to be careful. Locked in a subterranean chamber of her heart, she could sense her feelings for Bo stirring. Still contained, but yearning to break free. What they'd shared today had been fun, but it was physical. Something they could still step back from. The trick was not letting her emotions get involved.

Being with Bo was a risk, like standing on a cliff, a raging river churning far below. As long as she didn't get too close to the edge, she was safe. The problem was, Sadie wasn't sure how far she could flirt with the edge before the ground gave way beneath her feet, before she fell into the river and was swept away. The only thing to do was watch her step.

With one last look in the mirror, Sadie smoothed her dress over her hips and opened the bathroom door.

"C'mon, dude, don't give me that face." Bo's voice carried across the open space of his loft, apologetic and cajoling.

Who is he talking to? Sadie looked around the room but didn't see Bo anywhere.

"Hey, I get it, you're annoyed with me."

There was a light on in the kitchen area. She followed the sound of Bo's voice and discovered him crouched down behind the island, head inside a cabinet.

"Bo?"

"Yeah?"

"Who are you talking to?" Sadie came around the side of the island.

"Clark."

"Who's Clark?" she wondered, trying to see past his broad bare shoulders into the cabinet.

Bo eased back, resting on his heels and glancing over

at her. "Clark is my grumpy-ass cat." He directed his gaze back inside the open cabinet. "Aren't you, buddy? Aren't you my crabby tabby?"

Sadie bit her lip, holding in the idiotic grin threatening to split her face. *Crabby tabby?* A decidedly grumpy yowl sounded from inside the cabinet. "What's his problem?"

"What isn't his problem?" Bo grumbled. "For starters, His Highness is pissed I've been gone all day, annoyed I didn't feed him the second I walked in the door, and likely irritated I allowed you, another human, to invade his domain."

"Is that all?" Sadie laughed. She scooted closer, poking her head into the cabinet.

"Careful," Bo warned. "He's got a wicked right hook."

"So do I."

Bo's chuckle rumbled behind Sadie as she peered into the dark interior of the cabinet. The space beneath the island was deeper than she'd realized, and it took her a moment to spot the ball of black-and-white fur curled up in the far corner, feline face peering at her from between a stack of stove pots. "Oh, you *do* look pissed," she told the cat.

Clark just glowered at her.

"Where's his food?" she asked.

"I didn't get it ready yet," Bo said, then raised his voice for the benefit of the cat. "I was waiting for the little jerk to get his stubborn ass out of the cabinet first."

"Why don't you bring him his dinner and see if that lures him out?"

"Because I'm not giving in to his manipulative tactics."

She popped her head up and offered Bo a sympathetic smile. "I don't think you're going to win this one."

"Then I guess someone is going hungry tonight," he huffed.

Sadie ducked her head inside the cabinet again, repressing another grin. She knew Bo would cave, likely sooner rather than later. His mother was a vet, and he'd always had a soft spot for animals. But for his sake, she played along. "Did you hear that, Clark? No dinner for you."

The cat mewed, an apathetic noise that clearly stated he didn't give a fuck.

Bo snorted. "I hope you like it in there, buddy, because that's where you'll be spending the night."

Another mew.

"Why the name Clark?" Sadie asked as she leaned farther into the cabinet, trying to get a better view of the cat's face. "Is it supposed to be like Clark Kent?"

"That little despot is no superhero," Bo muttered. He stood, and as Sadie predicted, caved and pulled a can of cat food from another cabinet.

She glanced at Clark, giving the cat a wink. "Is it just Clark, then? Or part of something else?"

The whir of an electric can opener filled the air, and the cat scuttled forward.

Carefully, Sadie reached a hand out. Clark hesitated, remaining just inside the cabinet, and eyed her with disdain. "Aren't you a handsome fellow," she cooed, studying the cat's face while he continued to stare at her, unimpressed. "He has a mustache," she said, noting the thin stripe of black fur under his nose. "It makes him look like—"

"Clark Gable," Bo supplied, setting a bowl of food on the floor.

"Exactly!" Sadie laughed, a beam of surprised pleasure shooting through her. Clark skittered past, ignoring the human in the way of his evening meal. She watched the cat dig into his bowl for a moment and then got to her feet. "Do you remember watching that movie with me?"

"Which one?" Bo's eyes were downcast, thick lashes a sinful sweep across his cheeks as he kept his attention on the cat. "You made me watch so many of them."

"True." Sadie leaned against the island's countertop. "I did." A rush of fond memories filled her. Long summer nights spent cuddled together on the fluffy sofa in her nana's den, slowly working their way through her grandmother's extensive collection of old movies. Sadie loved the classics, full of romance and adventure, with glamourous heroines and dashing heroes. Growing up, her crushes had been Cary Grant, Gregory Peck, Errol Flynn . . . and Clark Gable.

Like the thistle tattoo, she couldn't help but wonder at Bo's choice of name for his pet. Another coincidence that seemed anything but accidental. She filed the thought away for later and smiled up at him.

"I was thinking of *It Happened One Night*," she named one of her all-time favorites. Clark Gable as the rogue reporter, and Claudette Colbert as the spoiled rich heiress. She adored their snappy banter, the way they got under each other's skin. Most importantly, she loved how different the two characters were, how wrong they seemed for each other and despite all that, how they fell in love anyway.

"Ah yes. The walls of Jericho," Bo murmured, a Gable-worthy smirk on his lips.

"I knew you'd remember." She met his eyes, and the moment stretched out, the air between them growing charged.

An angry yowl from Clark broke the spell.

"Wow. You really are a crabby tabby." Sadie glanced

at the cat scowling next to his now-empty bowl. "Is he still hungry?"

"Nah," Bo snorted and bent to pick Clark up. "He just wants his after-dinner belly rub." Nestling the ball of fur in the crook of one arm, he scratched the cat's soft, fluffy tummy.

"And people accuse me of being spoiled." Sadie shook her head, taking in the picture of a sexy bare-chested guy and cranky yet adorable kitty. If her panties weren't already in a shredded pile on the floor, they'd be in danger of flying off right this very minute.

Her bra was still on the floor somewhere as well. She couldn't believe they'd done that. Well, she could. It had been all too easy to let her body take over, to give in to wanting him. After accepting Bo's very explicit challenge, Sadie hadn't done more than slip her dress back over her head before escaping to the bathroom. She'd needed a minute to pull herself together.

Now, watching Bo cuddle with Clark, a cat he'd named after one of her favorite childhood heroes, she was on the verge of falling apart again. Sadie stared at the furry body tucked against Bo's chest. Just above the cat's twitching ears, she could see the edges of Bo's tattoo. The tip of a violet-colored thistle bud. The curve of a bee's wing. *Abeja.* Honeybee. His special, secret name for her.

Why did you do it? She ached to ask him. *Why did you leave me?* She could taste the questions on the tip of her tongue, filling her mouth with the bitter ashes of regret.

"What is it?" Bo's voice caught her by surprise.

"What?" She blinked at him.

"Your face." He set Clark on the ground and moved toward her. "Something's upsetting you." He was right in front of her now, his warm strong body trapping her against the island. He reached up and traced a finger over the furrow between her brows. "Please, abeja. Tell me what it is."

Sadie shook her head, tears burning like acid in the back of her throat. She couldn't speak, couldn't answer him. If she opened her mouth now, she wouldn't be able to stop the questions from tumbling out.

Instead, she reached up, her palms against his cheeks as she pulled him down to her, pressing her lips to his. She nipped his bottom lip with her teeth, and when his mouth fell open on a gasp, she slipped her tongue inside, wanting to taste him, needing the passion between them to burn away the bitterness.

Bo groaned, but he didn't resist. Instead, he moved closer, arms wrapping around her waist. As if sensing her frantic need, he tightened his hold and lifted her onto the island. Stepping between her legs, he shifted his grip to her hips and slid her across the counter, pulling her flush against him.

His belt buckle scraped against the bare skin of her inner thighs. A sweet sting that made her wrap her legs around him and rake her nails down his naked back.

"*Fuck*," Bo breathed the word into her mouth, chasing after it with his tongue, thrusting between her lips, again and again. She welcomed the invasion, opening for him, sucking him deeper into her.

As if making up for the many years they hadn't spent kissing each other, Bo and Sadie kissed and kissed and kissed. Time spiraled out and all she knew was the heat of his mouth, the slide of his tongue against hers. Suddenly, his hands were on her ass and he was lifting her.

"Hold on to me," he told her, the command a harsh rasp against her lips.

Head fuzzy, a little drunk from all the kissing, Sadie

nodded, locking her ankles around Bo's waist and gripping his shoulders as he carried her across the loft in
sure, quick strides. Still kissing her, he passed through
a screened partition but didn't stop moving until he'd
reached the bed and collapsed with her onto the mattress.

All around Sadie, from every side, his scent filled her.
The subtle tang of sweat mixed with the spice of his soap,
sun-warmed leather and the breeze off the lake. Sadie lay
beneath Bo on his bed and breathed him in, shivering at
the contrast of being pressed between cool crisp sheets
and hot muscled man.

The whole time he'd been carrying her, Bo hadn't broken their kiss, but now, he tore his mouth from hers, only
to press more kisses along the curve of her jaw. His beard
tickled her skin as he bent his head and slowly licked
down the column of her throat.

Then his mouth was moving again, face buried in
her breasts. Sadie closed her eyes and sifted her hands
through the cool, silky strands of his hair, cradling his
head as he suckled her through the thin layer of cotton.
She moaned and arched her back, offering more of herself. He responded instantly, tugging at the neckline of
her dress with his fingers, nipping at her with his teeth.

It wasn't enough.

With a growl, Bo sat back and yanked her dress off
her shoulders. She wriggled, helping him pull the sleeves
down her arms until, at last, she was free, the top of her
dress bunched around her waist. He bent over her, palms
pressed into the mattress on either side of her as he feasted
on her breasts, his mouth hot and hungry.

Sadie was hungry too. Starving. A ravenous ache was
building at her core, a yawning emptiness needing to be
filled. Jolts of electricity pulsed through her with each tug
of his lips on her nipple. She skimmed her palms down

the planes of his back, relishing the stretch and pull of his muscles. Needing more of him, Sadie reached between them, feeling for his belt. The clasp slipped open easily, and for the second time that night, she found herself unzipping Bo's pants.

He released her breast and sat up, eyes hooded as he stared down at her, knees locked against her hips. With slow, deliberate movements, Bo took over, gripping the belt and sliding it through the loops of his jeans. The *shush* of the leather as it glided across the denim was an erotic whisper, a hint of what was to come.

Eager to touch him again, Sadie reached for the opening of his fly, but he stopped her.

"No, abeja, not this time." He took hold of both her hands, wrapping the belt around her wrists.

Sadie sucked in a breath at the kiss of leather on her skin.

Bo paused. "Are you okay with this?"

She stared up at him. Was she okay with this? Was she okay with *any* of this? Not just being tied up by Bo, but being here, in his bed, with him. There was the edge of that cliff again. Need and excitement roiled through her, and the answer tore from her lips, reckless and desperate. "Yes."

"Good." Bo cinched the belt tighter until it was snug. He raised her arms over her head, wrapping the other end of the belt to the metal rail lining his headboard. "Still with me?"

She nodded, heart pounding in her chest.

"I need to hear you say it, abeja." His eyes pinned her to the mattress, dark and intense.

"I'm with you." Her voice tremored with anticipation, words barely more than a whisper. She loved hearing him call her that. Every time Bo used his nickname for her, a shiver of pleasure rippled inside her. It was like smelling chocolate chip cookies baking in the oven. The promise of something warm and sweet and delicious.

"Good," he said again. "Because if those clever hands of yours were free, I don't think I'd make it long enough to do all the things I want to do with you." His voice dropped to a low growl. "Do *to* you."

"Oh?" she breathed.

"Mm-hmm." Bo looked her over, as if debating where to start, what to do first. He stood and reached for her dress, still bunched at her waist, slipping it over her hips and down her legs, letting it drop to the floor.

Having lost the rest of her clothes earlier, Sadie was completely bare to his gaze. Bo hovered at the edge of the bed, staring down at her. Even if she had the urge to cover herself, she couldn't, not with her hands tied the way they were.

But to her surprise, Sadie wasn't embarrassed at all. The way he was looking at her, eyes flickering with appreciation, made Sadie feel beautiful. Made her want him to look at her, admire her. His gaze continued to roam over her body, the weight of it like a caress. Her skin tingled, nerve endings firing as surely as if he'd touched her.

The recessed space that formed his bedroom was filled with shadows, but the light coming in from the other side of the panel, coupled with the glow from the city beyond the window, allowed her to see him well enough as Bo slid his fingers into the waistband of his jeans and cupped himself. Eyes trained on his movements, Sadie watched as he took his thick shaft in both hands, one fist on top of the other.

"You like this, don't you?" he asked, circling the base of his cock with his fingers. "You like watching me."

She nodded. Her heart was racing, breath coming short

and fast as she continued to stare at him. Keeping a hand on his cock, Bo eased his jeans over his hips. Once his pants were on the floor and he was naked, Sadie licked her lips.

Soft wicked laughter drifted over her. "Oh, my sweet abeja. I do like how much you enjoy watching me do this." His voice was a low rumble as he continued to stroke himself. "But I think you're going to enjoy watching me do something else even better."

And with that, he released his cock and dropped to his knees at the edge of the bed. Sadie stared down the length of her own body, meeting his eyes above the juncture of her thighs. Gaze never leaving hers, he spread her legs and began to lick her.

Oh my God. Oh, dear God. Sadie wanted to close her eyes but couldn't seem to make herself. She couldn't look away, couldn't even blink. Somehow, the way he was staring at her heightened everything he was doing. She felt a thousand times more sensitive, each lazy stroke of his tongue making her body spasm in a mini orgasm.

Hot and aching, she was desperate for more of him. She wanted to hold his cock in both her hands and touch him the way he had, but she couldn't, her arms were still trapped over her head, belted to the bedframe.

Bo had no such restrictions, and when he thrust a finger deep inside her, his movements swift and sure while his tongue continued to flick over her clit, Sadie shut her eyes and let herself take the pleasure he was giving her.

"So. Fucking. Sweet," Bo ground out, the words coming in harsh pants.

Legs still shaking with aftershocks, Sadie lifted her head and met his gaze.

Smiling up at her, mouth wet, Bo's tongue darted out and he licked his upper lip.

Sadie shivered as if she'd felt the stroke of that tongue up the center of her body. She moaned, welcoming him as he climbed back onto the bed in a slow, primal crawl. His thick, hard heat brushed against her thigh, her belly, her chest. Straddling her torso, Bo hovered above her, palming a breast in each hand.

As she watched, Bo fitted himself against her chest. His fingers kneaded her flesh, plumping her small globes, pushing them together as he slid his shaft in the tight space between. Her body trembled. The friction of his silken skin gliding back and forth, the way the calluses on his hands scraped her sensitive nipples as he cupped her, grinding himself against her . . . after all that had already happened, all he'd done to her, Sadie didn't think it possible, but she got even wetter.

Chin pressed to her sternum, she kept her gaze locked on the motion of his body, watching how, with each upward thrust of his hips, the tip of his cock came closer to her mouth. Unable to resist, she reached out with her tongue, tasting him on his next pass.

Bo froze. "Is that what you want?" he asked, voice rough with excitement, laced with lust. His eyes were no more than shadows in the dim light, but she could see his mouth clearly, saw the flash of white teeth as he smiled down at her. He shifted on the bed, moving even closer to her mouth. "You want to taste me?"

She nodded. He was so close now, the movement caused her mouth to brush along his length. Sadie jerked her hands, needing to touch him. But they were tied tight. So she touched him with her lips and tongue instead, feeling him the only way she could.

"That's good," Bo told her, pressing into her. She opened her mouth, sucking him in. "So good," he groaned, a deep guttural sound she could feel like a throbbing pulse all the way through his body and into hers.

"I want to fuck your mouth," Bo rasped. He pulled back, then thrust again, just a little bit, not too much, careful not to go too far. "Would you like that?"

In wordless assent, Sadie nodded and opened her lips wide, scoring him with her teeth as he pushed deeper into her mouth. She felt him shiver, and did it again, trailing her teeth along the delicate ridge of his flesh.

"*F-f-f-uck*." He pulled back, grappling with the belt still wrapped around her wrists.

With a violent tug, he freed her, and Sadie reached for Bo, touching him the way she'd been dying to since the moment she'd watched him touch himself.

She stroked him hard and fast, then long and slow. Just for the hell of it. Because she could. Because she loved knowing she had the power to drive him wild.

But Bo had the power to drive her wild too. As he neared his climax, hips pumping faster, cock jerking in her hands, he reached between them and found her slick heat once more, taking Sadie over the edge with him.

CHAPTER 15

BO LAY ON his side, watching the first streaks of early morning sunlight play in the wild thatch of blond hair on the pillow next to his. Sadie. In his bed. Sound asleep, sprawled out on her side, sheet skimming the hills and valleys of her lithe form. The slope of her shoulder, the dip at her waist, the rise of her hips.

He wasn't sure how long he'd been watching her sleep. He wasn't sure what time it was now. And he didn't care. Bo could stay like this all day, lying next to her until the room filled with shadows and it was dark again. His chest tightened as visions of last night stole his breath.

The things he'd done to her. The things she'd done to him. The things they'd done together in this bed. But they hadn't done everything. Whether intentional or not, there'd been a line they hadn't crossed.

Glancing up, Bo saw his belt was still wrapped around the brass bar of his headboard, buckle glinting above Sadie's head. He'd finally freed her hands as he'd been on the edge of exploding, finishing in the delicious grip of her clever, wicked fingers.

When they both lay spent, quiet and still, he'd placed a kiss on the inside of each wrist before pulling her close, his body spooning hers. The feel of her curves tucked into him—the delicate arch of her spine brushing his chest, the soft firm swell of her bottom nestled snugly against his hips—it was all so familiar, Bo wanted to weep. It was absurd, made him think of corny, sappy things. Like how she was the missing piece of him, what he needed to be whole.

Sometime in the night, long after her loose limbs, quiet breaths, and slow steady heartbeat told him she'd fallen asleep, Bo had uncoiled himself from around her, rolled onto his back and stared at the rough beams bracketing his ceiling, trying to make sense of things.

Last night, he and Sadie had come crashing together like summer lightning, rolling in fast and furious. But now that the storm had passed, he wasn't sure where they stood, or where they should go from here.

Did she want more from him? Did he want to give her more? Bo was an all-or-nothing kind of guy. He liked to deal in absolutes, and he didn't do things halfway. If he started falling for Sadie again, he'd have to make a choice. Either go all in or get the fuck out.

Slowly, listening to the soft hush of Sadie's breathing, Bo's mind finally started to clear—or at least go blank. He closed his eyes and began to drift off. He was on the verge of sinking into sleep when something batted him on the shoulder. Something sharp and furry. Bo turned his head to the side and cracked one eye open. Clark's mustached face hovered directly in front of him, so close that when Bo exhaled, the cat's whiskers fluttered.

Clark, you asshole. Bo gave the cat a one-eyed glare before closing his eye again, rolling onto his stomach, and burying his head in the pillow.

But the cat would not be ignored. A moment later, Bo felt the prickle of four paws on his back, warm fur tickling his neck. "Clark, if you bite my ear, I swear to Christ, I'll turn you into a saddlebag," Bo threatened, his morning voice a low, scratchy rumble.

Expecting a cranky meow, Bo was unprepared for the feminine giggle that sounded from behind him.

Neither was Clark, apparently. The cat jumped, letting out a yowl as he pawed at Bo's bare back.

"Ouch! Hey, knock it off." Bo rolled sideways again, and the cat squawked with displeasure, scrambling off Bo's back and taking up residence on his head instead. "This is not an improvement," he muttered, swiping at Clark's tail as it threatened to suffocate him.

Another giggle rippled across the sheets.

Bo shoved at the cat, trying to see around the mound of fur.

"You don't know how badly I want to make a comment about having a face full of pussy right now," Sadie said, her voice deliciously husky with sleep and laced with humor.

He chuckled, amused and turned on at the same time. "If you do, then I might have to make a comment about how I had the same problem last night."

She gasped in mock outrage.

At least, he thought her outrage was fake, he still couldn't see her to read her expression. "That's enough, Clark. Get your furry ass off my face." With effort, Bo pried the clinging cat off his head, careful to avoid the flailing claws.

The cat let out a howl of fury and leapt out of Bo's grasp, landing on the bed between the two humans.

"Aw, he's just staking his claim," Sadie said, sounding like she was on the verge of bursting into giggles again as she watched Clark paw at the covers and settle himself squarely in front of Bo.

Face finally free of feline interference, Bo studied Sadie. With her attention focused on Clark, he felt safe to look his fill. She lay on her side, facing him, elbow tucked beneath her ear as she rested her head on the pillow opposite his. One leg stuck out of the blankets, sheets wrapped around her middle and tucked tight above her breasts, the bare skin of her shoulders glowing softly in the pale morning light. God, she was beautiful. He loved everything about her, from the peek of naked toes to the wild spikes of blond hair that stuck out every which way.

Bo wanted to reach out and run his hands through the sexy, sleepy mass, but he held back. "What did it feel like?" he asked, before he could think better of it. "To . . . you know . . ." He pointed at his own head. "Cut it all off."

Sadie shifted on the pillow, glancing up at him in surprise.

Maybe it had been a bad idea to bring this up, but it was too late now, he'd have to press forward. "It bothered you. Didn't it?"

"Um," she hesitated, mouth working. "Yeah. It was harder than I expected," she admitted with an embarrassed little laugh. "This is going to sound shallow, but I was afraid I wouldn't be pretty with short hair."

"You're still pretty," he assured her.

"Thanks, but I wasn't fishing for compliments." She gave him a half-hearted smile. "Don't get me wrong, I like hearing I'm pretty."

"It's the truth." He lifted one shoulder. No. The truth was, she was gorgeous. Knock a man to his knees breathtakingly beautiful. But Bo sensed something more lurking beneath that lovely surface. "Is that really all that was bothering you?"

"Well," she began, then hesitated, fiddling nervously, fingers twisting in the sheets.

An undercurrent of emotion drifted around her; he could feel the ebb and flow of it, an urge to be pulled into deep water. Bo waded in slowly. Tentatively. "It must have been hard, undergoing such a dramatic change."

She nodded mutely.

Bo waited, knowing better than to push her. Instead, he lay still, giving her time to collect her thoughts.

Finally, she took a breath, like she was preparing to dive in. "It's something Sylvia said. About cutting away regrets."

"Do you have regrets?" he ventured to ask.

"Do you?" she shot back.

Definitely entering deep water here. Now he was sucking in a breath. "I think everyone has regrets." Bo pressed an elbow into his pillow, hand propping up his head. "Wanna tell me about it?"

"Not really."

"You used to tell me everything," he said quietly.

Her eyes snapped up to his and Bo worried he'd overstepped.

"That was a long time ago," she finally said, turning her attention back to his cat.

Bo got the hint. He watched as she made funny faces, attempting to mimic Clark's cranky scowl.

"You really do look like Clark Gable." Cautiously, Sadie reached out with one finger, stroking the stripe of fur beneath the cat's nose. "Like a little Rhett Butler."

"Accurate," Bo agreed. "Since frankly, he doesn't give a damn."

Sadie bust out laughing, peals of feminine giggles that made Clark recoil. The cat meowed peevishly and scrambled off the mattress, bounding out of sight.

"Aw, I scared him away," Sadie pouted.

"Don't worry, he'll be back soon," Bo assured her, focusing on that pout. He wanted to sink his teeth into her lush lower lip. Biting his own lip instead, Bo raised his gaze to hers. "He hasn't had his breakfast yet."

"Breakfast. Now there's a good idea."

"Are you hungry?" Bo thought of her pussy comment, a smile tugging at the corners of his mouth. His humor quickly turned to lust as he remembered how it felt to have his face buried between her legs, tasting her with his tongue. His bedroom suddenly felt too warm, his skin too tight on his bones.

"Starving," she assured him.

"Me too," he growled, scooting across the bed and rolling her onto her back. He was starving for her, hungry for her body. He craved her taste, her touch. It had been more than ten years since he'd had her, and Bo realized he wasn't close to getting enough. He bent his head, gliding his nose up her neck, inhaling the warm sleepy smell of her soft skin. He nipped her ear.

She laughed.

"What's so funny?" He pulled back, staring down at her.

"You yell at your cat not to bite your ear, and then you bite mine?"

He grinned. "That wasn't a bite, it was a nibble," he protested. "Trust me, there's a difference. That little demon has been known to draw blood."

On cue, a god-awful wail filled his apartment. "Speak of the devil," Bo groaned.

"That's him?" Sadie asked, eyes wide as another ear-splitting yowl shattered the quiet morning.

"Fuck, yes, that's him." Bo groaned. "I need to feed the tyrant before he wakes the neighbors. Or decides to piss in my shoes." He pressed a kiss to her throat, unable to resist licking her there, just once, hoarding the salty sweetness of her on his tongue. Then he crawled out of bed, yanked on his jeans, and headed for the kitchen.

He'd just set the bowl of food in front of Clark when Sadie appeared from behind the screen separating his bedroom from the rest of the loft. She was wearing his shirt, the hem skimming her thighs. She crossed the room toward him, and as she passed the big picture window, the morning sunlight streaming in turned the faded cotton translucent, outlining every curve beneath in exquisite detail.

Bo about swallowed his tongue.

"I see you've fed Mr. Grumpy Face." She glanced down at Clark, whose grumpy face was buried in his bowl.

He nodded mutely.

"What about me?"

"Huh?" He struggled to catch up, mind stuck several paces back, still on the moment she had passed in front of the window. There was something intensely erotic about how she'd looked standing there in his shirt, the seemingly innocent white cotton becoming the fucking hottest thing he'd seen in a very long time. "What about you?"

"What are you going to give me?"

How about I press you up against that window and give it to you from behind? As soon as he thought it, the image bloomed vividly in his brain. Sadie facing the window, breasts crushed to the glass, nipples tight and puckered, poking through his shirt. He'd press her palms to the window and bend her over, only a little, just enough to give him room to slide between her thighs, then he'd grab her hips, thrust up into her, and—

"Um, Bo?"

"Yeah?" he croaked, mouth dry.

"Are you okay? You seem a little flushed." She eyed him with concern, coming closer as if she was going to check his forehead for a temperature.

"I'm fine," he snapped, harsher than he meant to. If she touched him now, she'd be up against that window in a heartbeat. "What was it you wanted?"

"Some breakfast? I didn't eat lunch yesterday, unless you count that donut and cider. And we were too, um, busy, to have dinner last night."

"Oh, right." Heat crept up his neck, and not from lust this time. He was an ass. He hadn't even thought to offer her anything to eat or drink. "Sorry about that. God, I'm a terrible host."

"I wouldn't say that." One corner of her mouth lifted in a lascivious smirk. "Overall, I think you've been quite attentive to your guest's needs." She winked, but then her face turned serious. "However, if you don't feed me soon, there is going to be trouble. You won't like me when I'm hangry."

He laughed. "What are you, the Hulk?"

"Worse." She glanced back down at Clark, who'd taken a break from his meal to lick his paws, underwhelmed by their conversation. "You better watch it, mister. I might decide to steal your food."

Clark blinked at her, whiskers twitching above his namesake mustache.

"Don't worry, Clark, she's not going to eat your food," Bo assured the cat. Clark made a mew of annoyance and stalked off, tail swishing. Bo snorted with laughter. "Let me take a quick shower, then I'll whip you up some eggs."

She made a face.

"That's right, you don't like eggs." Bo grinned, a dozen memories floating through his mind from when they were kids.

"No, it's good. Eggs will be fine."

"Are you sure?"

She nodded, her mouth stretching in the long-suffering smile of a martyr. "They're part of my nutrition plan for the movie."

"Well, help yourself to whatever you want out of the fridge. I'll try and be fast. I don't want you collapsing from starvation before I get back." Sadie shot him a scathing look, and he hurried out of the kitchen before she could tan the skin off his hide with her tongue.

Though, Bo thought as he turned on the taps, that might not be such a bad thing. He stepped under the hot spray, wishing he'd thought to invite her to join him. He really was a terrible host. He didn't entertain at home often. When he wasn't on a set working, most evenings it was just him and Clark and whatever Chicago sports team was playing that night on TV.

Soaping up, Bo returned to the fantasy of Sadie at the window. He'd always loved it when she wore his shirts, had ever since the first time they'd been together. *Shit.* No wonder it was such a turn-on for him. The memory of Sadie, straddling him in the hayloft, wearing his shirt, the faded cotton clinging to her sweat-slicked curves, was a permanent fixture of his fantasies.

Bo lathered shampoo into his hair. If he didn't start thinking of something else fast, he'd be in the awkward position of jacking off to the memory of making love to the younger version of the same woman he'd been with last night. A woman who was only a few feet away in his kitchen.

He stepped under the spray to rinse, his mind drifting

again to their first night together. How afterward, they'd curled beneath the blanket, her back nestled to his front, just as they had last night. Making love to her for the first time had made Bo feel closer to Sadie than ever. Like they were part of each other. Maybe that was why they'd avoided taking that step last night.

Back then, the new physical intimacy had made him want to share everything with her. Give her everything. They'd talked of the future. Whispered about their dreams. He'd told her about how he wanted to run his own stable. Something he built himself. And she'd told him how she wanted to be a famous actress and travel the world, going to all the places her parents went each summer without her.

Looking back, that should have been Bo's red flag right there. It was painfully obvious that they'd wanted different things out of life. But he'd always been a fool when it came to Sadie. And in that regard, it was beginning to look like nothing had changed.

Mixing business and pleasure was a risk he always avoided. Sadie, however, was the exception to every rule. Bo would have thought that now, more than a decade older, he'd have finally managed to grow the fuck up. Hell no. She spared him half a glance and he was on his knees.

If word got out that he was getting a little too friendly with the lead actress on the company's biggest project, Vic would have his balls in a sling.

He rinsed off, letting the hot water beat against his skull, hoping it would pound some sense into him. Maybe it would work better if he switched the faucet to ice cold. Though if he walked out of here and found Sadie still wearing his shirt, Bo doubted a swim in the Arctic could cool him off.

CHAPTER 16

SADIE LISTENED TO the sound of water running and tried not to think about Bo, naked and wet, droplets trickling down the muscled hills and valleys of his pecs and abs. She should have followed him into the shower. If he'd offered, she probably would have.

But since he hadn't, she took him up on what had been offered, and went to rummage in his fridge. Like everything else, his refrigerator was neat and organized, so clean it was almost indecent. Spic and span and sparse.

There was a pint of orange juice, a carton of eggs, some veggies, several bottles of beer, a square of cheese, and a plastic container. That looked promising. Sadie was about to pull the container out for further inspection when her phone chimed. Recognizing her best friend's ring tone, Sadie's brain delivered a series of urgent, brief messages.

Ana.

Sunday.

Their bike ride.

Shit.

Sadie dove across the apartment for her purse. "Hello, Ana?"

"Oh good, you're alive."

"Sorry about missing our bike ride this morning, you didn't wait for me too long, did you?"

"Actually, I missed the ride too," Ana admitted.

In the background, Sadie heard a familiar male voice exclaim, "Oops!"

"Ryan's still at your place?"

"Mm-hmm," Ana hummed an affirmative. "I don't think he really expected me to make him help bake, but he is." There was a sound of crashing metal. "Sort of."

Sadie laughed. Leave it to Ana. "Please tell me you made him wear an apron." Her best friend had a collection of vintage aprons.

"Of course. One of my frilliest."

"Nice." Sadie could just imagine what her costar looked like dolled up like a 1950s' housewife. "Pics or it didn't happen."

"What about you?" Ana asked. "Did a certain former boyfriend make you breakfast this morning?"

"Bo's in the shower right now, but he promised to cook for me after."

"Oh, well done, sir," Ana said approvingly.

"Well, I haven't actually eaten yet," Sadie reminded her, "so I'm reserving judgment on his skills in the kitchen."

"What about his skills in the bedroom?" Ana purred.

"Ana!"

"Okay, okay, fine." Ana paused. "But you two did it. Right?"

"Just because the last time I was with the guy was in high school doesn't mean you can act like a teenager now," Sadie grumbled. "And yes, we did it. Sort of."

"Sort of? What the hell does that mean?" Ana wondered. "You know what? I don't need to know. Just tell me one thing," Ana demanded. "Was it good?"

Good? Not the word she'd have chosen. Amazing. Mind-blowing. That was a little more accurate. "Um, yeah." Sadie bit her lip. "Very good."

"Okay, now I want details," Ana begged.

Images of Bo wrapping his belt around her wrists, shackling her to his bed, his beard scraping her thighs as he took her with his mouth filled Sadie's mind with plenty of *details*.

A crash reverberated over the phone, interrupting Sadie's mental replay.

"I'm sorry," Ana apologized in a rush. "I've gotta go before your costar burns down my kitchen."

"I need to get going too," Sadie assured her.

"Are you spending Rosh Hashanah with your folks?" Ana asked.

"Unfortunately." Sadie sighed, she'd once again conveniently put that out her mind. "I wish I could hang out with your family. They're much more fun."

"I won't argue with the truth." Ana chuckled. "We Kaufmans are an entertaining bunch. But your nana will be there, right? She's fun."

"Yeah. It will be good to see her. I haven't really talked to her since Passover. I'm a terrible granddaughter."

"I'm sure she would disagree." Another crash. "Okay, that's my cue. When will you be free to chat? I still need details, you know."

"I'm not sure. We're shooting at a stable next week. Call times are all over the place."

"No problem, we'll figure something out."

They said their goodbyes and just before they hung up, Ana said, "Hey, Sadie?"

"Yeah?"

"My nonexistent crystal ball sees a handsome bearded bad boy in your future."

"You're incorrigible." Sadie grinned, heart filled with gratitude for her silly, sweet best friend.

As she ended the call, the water in the shower turned off. The sudden silence in the apartment brought Sadie back to herself. She still needed to get dressed. In a flurry of movement that had Clark squawking up a storm as he scrambled out of her way, Sadie scurried around the apartment, grabbing her clothes.

By the time the bathroom door opened, she'd managed to get her bra strapped on and slip her dress over her head. Her panties were a lost cause. Sadie wasn't sure how she felt about walking around sans underwear while in a dress. She thought of Logan, her friend Cassie's husband. Was this how the Scot felt when he went around wearing his kilt? Going commando or . . . what had Logan called it? *Regimental.*

Sadie giggled, recalling the Scot's rolling *R* as he'd said the word in a teasing brogue.

"What's so funny?" Bo asked, stepping into the bedroom.

"I was just thinking of my friend's husband not wearing underwear," Sadie said, not sure if she should elaborate. Then realizing how it sounded, decided to explain about the kilt.

"Better him than me." Bo shook his head. "I like my boys safe and sound."

Her gaze dropped to the fly on his khakis. Sadie's cheeks heated as she recalled the way his snug boxer briefs had kept everything pinned down, so to speak.

"And now you're thinking about my dick, aren't you?" Bo teased, a wry smile playing about his lips.

"Maybe," she admitted, an answering smile tickling her mouth. No point denying it. Her stare had been rather obvious. She watched as Bo pulled on a pale green dress shirt. The color looked fantastic on him, brought out the gold highlights in his brown hair and made his tawny eyes glow. Sadie heartily approved. But she also felt a little underdressed, and not just because of her missing panties.

"You look nice."

"You think I look nice?" His grin widened, reaching almost ear to ear now, warming her in its glow.

Sadie shifted her gaze, watching as Bo did up his shirt, his deft fingers flying over the buttons. She caught a glimpse of the thistle bud as it disappeared behind the pale green linen. "Why don't you have any tattoos on your arms?"

"Work."

"Huh?" He'd finished with the shirt and was now rolling up the sleeves. *Oh, sweet baby Jesus.* Sadie looked away from the tantalizing sight of Bo's strong, sexy forearms. It would not do to get this turned on when one was not wearing any panties. "How is getting a tattoo on your arm more work than getting one on your back?"

"No. *For* work. When I'm a stunt double, it's best if I don't have a lot of visible ink that would require a lot of makeup or need to be edited out in post-production."

"That makes sense." Her stomach chose that moment to let out a ferocious growl. Sadie glanced around, looking for Clark, wondering if she could get away with blaming the cat. No such luck. Besides, by the look on Bo's face, he'd heard her loud and clear.

"Wow. I better get started in the kitchen before you really do try eating Clark's food."

"Ha." Sadie followed him out of the bedroom, pausing

by the bathroom. "Um, you don't happen to have a spare toothbrush, do you?"

"Just use mine."

"Yuk." She recoiled.

"Are you serious?" Bo looked up from pulling ingredients out of the fridge. "Do I need to remind you what else of mine was in your mouth recently?"

"That was different."

He heaved a sigh that clearly said, *You test my patience, woman.*

"Never mind, I'll just use my finger." She escaped to the bathroom and closed the door. Sadie knew she was being a little ridiculous, but this wasn't about her being difficult—this was about doing something as domestic and personal as sharing a toothbrush. And what that meant. To her.

But she sure as hell wasn't going to explain that to Bo. It was bad enough he was making her breakfast. She squirted toothpaste on her finger and scrubbed her gums. Better to let him think she was acting like a spoiled princess. It wouldn't be the first time someone accused her of it.

After washing her hands, Sadie finger-combed her hair as well, which basically amounted to rearranging the spiky locks into a different yet equally messy formation. She took stock of herself in the mirror and shrugged. It would have to do.

By the time she returned to the kitchen, Bo had already started coffee and arranged two place settings on the island. Butter was sizzling in a pan on the stove and he was busy cracking eggs into a bowl.

"Wow," Sadie murmured. "Impressive."

"Welcome to Bo's Bed and Breakfast." He grinned, swinging a towel over his shoulder.

"Anything I can do to help?"

"Make some toast?" he suggested, pointing to a shelf.

"I can handle that." Sadie reached for the loaf and pulled out a few slices. "There's a question I've been wanting to ask you."

"Just one?" Bo cocked his brow.

"For now," she said, popping two pieces of bread in the toaster.

He poured the egg batter into the pan, and then turned his attention back to her. "All right," Bo agreed, tone wary. "One question."

Sadie wondered if he was worried she'd ask *that* question. The one she'd wanted to ask last night. She still burned to know the answer, to understand why, in a blink, he'd decided they were over. But she would play it safe today. Keep things close to the surface.

Thanks to Bo's pillow talk about regrets, she'd already spent enough time swimming deeper in her emotional whirlpool than she was comfortable with this morning.

"How did you end up doing stunt work? When we were kids, all you ever talked about was owning your own stable." Whenever they'd daydreamed about the future, Bo's plan had always been the same. He wanted his own horses on his own land.

"It was the accident, actually," Bo said, one hand absently rubbing his side, over the area where the tattooed scar lay hidden beneath his shirt. "That's what started it." He flipped the omelets and set the spatula down. "I'd told you I was thrown from the carriage. Compared to what happened to my dad, I was lucky. So freaking lucky." He stared at his calloused palms before squeezing his hands into fists. "But the fall still messed me up pretty bad."

"What happened?"

"I busted some ribs. Punctured a lung."

"That's awful." Sadie sucked in a breath, aware of the air filling her own lungs and imagining the horrible pain he must have endured.

"Yeah, well, like I said, I was lucky. The doctors said it could have been a whole lot worse. I could have ended up on a ventilator for life. Or landed just a little bit differently, lacerated my aorta or busted my liver and then that would have been it." Flicking off the stove, he picked up the pan and slid the omelets onto their plates.

"My God, Bo." Sadie winced, cold dread icing her insides. For years, Bo could have been dead, and she wouldn't have known because she'd been so damned angry and stubborn and scared.

But he'd survived. He was alive and well. That was all that mattered.

Sadie stared at her plate. The summer she'd been thirteen and Bo fourteen, the same summer he'd kissed her for the first time, Bo had ended up in the hospital with a concussion after getting kicked in the head by a horse. It was horrible. She'd felt so hopeless, so worried for him. But at least she'd been there. By his side as much as she could be.

When Bo was released, the doctors said he needed to rest his brain, which meant he couldn't read or watch TV or even talk much. So Sadie would ride to the carriage house every day. She'd sit by Bo's bedside and hold his hand, reading books to him and sometimes just sitting in the quiet with him. Letting him know she was there—would always be there.

But she hadn't always been there. He'd been hurt in that carriage accident—badly—and she hadn't been there for him. She hadn't even known it had happened. Sadie was struck with the illogical urge to comfort Bo now, to soothe the pain even though it had happened long ago.

"Maybe I missed something," she said, forcing herself to remain nonchalant as she poked at the omelet with her fork. "How did getting thrown from a carriage lead you to decide you wanted to throw yourself off buildings for a living?"

Bo bit into a piece of toast and chewed thoughtfully for a moment. "It was almost like it was meant to be."

Sadie glanced up, startled. "What do you mean?"

Bo shrugged, stirring his coffee. "Looking back, I can see how it came together. Like the pieces were all there, and the accident was the thing that set everything in motion."

"How?" Sadie swiveled on her stool, staring up at him.

"Well, I'd always been good with horses, right? And after an, um, incident, I decided to take up martial arts."

"You did?"

He nodded, finishing off the piece of toast.

"Wait, what incident?" Sadie frowned.

"Doesn't matter," he said, brushing it aside. "Between the riding and the fighting, I had developed a . . ." he paused, mouth curling in a self-deprecating smirk, ". . . a unique skill set."

Bo pushed his fork through the eggs on his plate. "It was a couple of months after the accident. I was doing better, but Dad was still in really bad shape. I'd take him to his physical therapy sessions. There was this one guy there, about my father's age, Vic LaSalle. A cranky old guy, even more stubborn than dad."

"Is that even possible?" Sadie teased, rewarded with a chuckle from Bo.

"Yeah, well, the two of them, Dad and Vic, would go at it together. Talk smack and drive the rehab staff up the wall as they tried to one-up each other during their PT sessions."

Sadie smiled. From what she remembered of Bo's dad, it was easy to picture the scene he painted.

"Anyway, turns out this guy Vic was a stuntman and coordinator who'd gotten injured on a job." Bo scraped a pat of butter on another slice of toast. "Vic also had a side gig going where he'd help casting directors out, match up stunt guys he knew with projects filming in the city."

"Like a talent scout?" Sadie asked.

"Sorta, but nothing that organized. Vic ended up re-cruiting me because he had a call for someone who could ride a horse. Right place, right time kind of thing. That job led to another and another and so on. At first, it wasn't formal or anything, I'd pick up gigs based on what I looked like: height, weight, the usual. But then I started getting more assignments because of what I could do—or more to the point, what I was willing to do. There was al-ways a show needing someone ready to throw themselves off a building or run through a wall of fire." Bo smirked. "I got a lot of work that way."

"Sounds like you," Sadie said drily, thinking of all the wild, reckless stunts Bo had pulled when they were kids.

"Yep." The smile he gave her now was pure impish boy. The fae prince she'd once believed him to be.

Sadie melted like the butter on Bo's toast.

"A lot of action films were coming to Chicago, televi-sion series too. Vic was getting hit up to place performers so often, I suggested he turn it into an actual business. It was my idea but his contacts, you know? We became partners and formed Windy City Stunts." Bo took the last bite of his eggs. "I turned that haphazard list of his into an official collective. Created a central database of pro-fessional stunt people in the Chicago area. Fall guys, fight guys, wheel guys."

"Wheel guys?"

"Stunt drivers, guys who can do all the fancy car-racing shit."

"Girls can do that shit too," Sadie pertly informed him.

"If you say so." Bo wiped his mouth with a napkin, but Sadie caught the teasing grin beneath.

She narrowed her eyes. *He was baiting her.* "You better watch it, or I'll have my friend Cassie do an exposé on underrepresentation of females in the stunt industry."

"To be honest, she'd probably have a story," he admitted. "But not with WCS. I'll have you know, our best wheelie is a woman. Alexis." Bo shook his head. "The shit Lexie pulls on a motorcycle scares even me."

"Wow. Now that I'd like to see."

His grin widened. "Also, I recently cast a female stunt double for this action movie that's filming in Chicago. I think you may have heard of it?"

"Now you're patronizing me." Sadie rolled her eyes.

Bo changed the subject, glancing at her almost empty plate. "You liked your eggs, then? The omelet was good?"

"I can't believe I'm saying this, but really good." Sadie speared the last bite and popped it in her mouth. "Even Jim would approve of that breakfast. Now he won't have an excuse to torture me more than usual."

"I'm assuming Jim is your trainer?" Bo asked.

"Trainer, dungeon master, whichever."

"Sounds like he's doing a good job." Bo laughed. "Are you finished?"

She nodded and waited at the table while Bo took the dishes to the sink. And yes, she did check out his ass as he walked away. Even in khakis, the man looked good.

Suddenly Sadie recalled she was not wearing any underwear. Holding on to the edge of her dress, she primly slid off the stool and gathered up the butter and juice to put away in the fridge. Spying the container that had caught her interest earlier, Sadie pulled it out and held it up. "What's in here?

Rinsing the plates, Bo tossed a glance over his shoulder. When he saw what Sadie was holding, he gave her a slow, sexy smile, lips parted, nipping his tongue between his teeth. On any other guy, she would have thought the move was ridiculous. But he managed to make it radiate sex.

Which made Sadie extra curious about the contents of the container. Shutting the fridge, she set it on the counter and popped off the lid, a sugary-peppery aroma tingling in her nose. She didn't even have to look in the bowl to know what was in there, the scent triggered a host of special memories, making her hop in excitement. "Mexican fruit salad!"

Her mouth began to water, lips tingling in anticipation of the sweet and spicy treat. Sadie set the lid aside and admired the gorgeous bouquet of colors formed by a mix of tropical fruits and chili flakes. She reached into the bowl and plucked out a chunk of pineapple, popping it into her mouth.

"Oh, God," she moaned, as flavor exploded on her tongue. "I haven't had this in ages."

"Slow down there, chica impaciente," Bo chided, grabbing a spoon and a dish.

"I know that one," Sadie said around another bite of fruit. "Girl impatient. No, wait. Impatient girl."

"Bueno." Bo scooped a heaping spoonful of fruit into the dish and handed it to Sadie. "Do you remember why?"

Sadie licked lime juice and chili flakes from her fingers and thought for a minute. She closed her eyes, pulling the memory out of hiding. "Because Spanish flips the noun and adjective." Her eyes popped open, and she grinned, recalling a snarky teenage Bo's explanation. "That way you know what it is before you know what it's like."

"Muy bueno." He clapped his hands.

"Gracias." Sadie bowed. When they were kids, Bo had taught her some Spanish. And her first lesson took place the same day she'd tried ensalada de frutas for the very first time. Sadie's cheeks heated, and not from the spices. There'd been another first that day as well.

"Here." Sadie pressed a piece of watermelon to Bo's lips.

He opened his mouth, thick dark lashes fanning out against his tan cheeks as he watched her slide the fruit in.

The sight did funny things to her insides. Sadie shifted her attention back to her bowl, selecting what looked like a cube of mango. Spicy heat prickled on her tongue, the contrast making the tart sweetness of the fruit even sweeter.

She licked her lips, almost certain she felt the weight of Bo's gaze on her mouth. "Do you remember—"

"Yes."

"How did you know what I was going to ask?" Sadie demanded.

"Give me a little credit, abeja." Bo took the bowl from her hands and stepped closer, then closer still. He tilted his head.

She tilted hers.

He leaned forward, brushing the tip of his nose against hers.

Sadie remembered this. The soft tickle of his nose. The way her thirteen-year-old heart had thundered like a stampede of horses. She couldn't say how long they'd stayed like that, only their noses touching.

Until finally one of them, or maybe both of them,

shifted the tiniest bit. But it was enough. Their lips touched. And Sadie's heart had jumped fences.

Closing her eyes, Sadie let the memory take her. She could still recall the delight she'd felt when she discovered closing her eyes made kissing even better. With her eyes closed, she could focus completely on Bo's mouth, savor the taste of him, warm and spicy sweet—a little ticklish—but in a good way. A way that didn't make her want to laugh, but made her tingle from the inside out.

When she opened her eyes, coming back to the present moment, Bo was right there. Staring down at her, his gaze golden brown and intense.

And Sadie could. Not. Breathe.

"How old were you, again?"

"Thirteen," she whispered.

"Which means I was fourteen," Bo mused. "A decent age for a first kiss." He shook his head, a secret smile stealing over his features.

"What?" Sadie asked.

"It's just," he hesitated.

"Bo?" Sadie could swear he was blushing beneath his beard. What on earth could make that man blush? "Tell me!"

"It's just, in the shower today . . . I remembered another first we shared."

"We shared a lot of them," she reminded him.

"I think it was the fact you were wearing my shirt that triggered this memory."

"Oh," Sadie said. "*Oooh*." Now she was blushing too. She cleared her throat, moving to the sink to wash her sticky fingers. "Thanks for the fruit salad."

"Thank my abuela." Bo joined her at the sink, rinsing his hands as well.

Again, the domesticity of the moment jarred her.

"She watched every episode of your show, you know. *Hope General*."

"That's sweet."

Bo nodded and handed her a towel. "I did too."

Sadie almost dropped the towel. "You did?" She didn't know what to think about that. Wasn't sure how she felt about it.

"The show was kind of a train wreck, but you were good."

She laughed. "Thanks?" Sadie folded the towel, trying to collect her thoughts. "And thanks for the hospitality." She handed the towel back to him. "While I've had a lovely time at Bo's Bed and Breakfast, I probably should be getting back to my place soon."

"If you don't mind another ride on the bike, I can drive you home," he offered.

"Um, yeah," Sadie began, "about that." She smoothed her dress over her hips. "I'm going to need to borrow some sweatpants or something. It was one thing to ride on a motorcycle while wearing a dress. But to ride in a dress and no panties . . . um, no. Hard pass."

"Wait." Bo stared at her. "All through breakfast you weren't wearing any . . ." His eyebrows rose as his gaze drifted lower, focus sharpening, his tawny eyes making Sadie think of tigers, or jaguars, or other sleek cats stalking their prey through the tall grass.

Oh. Her breath quickened, coming in shallow gulps as he moved closer. *She was the prey.* Sadie backed up. A moment later her butt bumped against the kitchen island.

And a moment after that, he was on her. A fierce growl erupted from his throat, and Sadie experienced a flash of déjà vu as he leaned into her, hefting her onto the counter, his hands reaching under the hem of her skirt.

Bo dragged his fingers up the bare skin of her thighs, reaching around to cup her ass and pull her closer.

Whoa. Beneath the thin fabric of his khakis, Sadie could feel every inch of him—every very thick and very hard inch. "Maybe Cassie's Scot is on to something," she teased. "Walking around sans panties. Commando. This is what does it for you?"

Bo drew back, face taut with desire. His eyes flashed as he bent closer, brushing his nose against hers. "*You* are what does it for me, abeja," he said, voice achingly tender. "Only you."

CHAPTER 17

A FEW DAYS later, Bo sped south down Lake Shore Drive, the wind off Lake Michigan seeping through his jeans and whipping down the neck of his leather jacket. The chill bite in the air a clear indication fall was in full swing. Somehow, the fact that the year had passed into October had slipped his notice. They were almost half-way through filming *Fair is Fair*. By mid-November, shooting would be over, and the project would move to post-production.

While at a stoplight, Bo mentally reviewed his work calendar. Next up was a holiday episode for *Chicago Rescue*. He'd signed the contract for that assignment ages ago and was concerned about how close it bumped up against the end of his current schedule. If anything were to go wrong and delay the filming on this movie, Bo would be in a bind.

That was the last thing he wanted. He needed to show Vic he had everything under control, and part of that was being able to juggle multiple shooting schedules. Currently they were on target. But the call he'd received this morning from one of Sylvia's assistants asking Bo to come to the studio made him wary.

They were supposed to begin a week and a half of filming at a stable the production company had rented. It was a tight schedule with little wiggle room. Luckily, aside from the nip in the wind, the weather was perfect. Sunny and clear, the leaves just beginning to change. And the forecast called for more of the same all week, so they were good there.

The weather had been perfect this weekend too. In fact, everything about this weekend had been perfect. The time he'd spent with Sadie had been better than perfect . . . he didn't have the words. Bo hadn't wanted the weekend to end. He'd even been considering risking the wrath of his family and skipping Sunday night supper until she'd told him she had to get going.

At first, he'd felt like an idiot for getting carried away, and the disappointment had struck deep. But she'd explained she needed to be at her parents' house by sundown for the start of Rosh Hashanah. Bo should have remembered it was the Jewish New Year. Just as he'd taught her bits of Spanish and shared pieces of his family's culture with her as they'd grown up, she'd done the same for him.

A horn honked behind him, and he startled, realizing the light had turned green. Waving a hand in apology, Bo tightened his hold on the bike's handlebars and hit the gas. He needed to get his head straight. Especially since he would be working closely with Sadie pretty much every day these next two weeks. The fact they'd be shooting at a stable and riding horses together guaranteed there'd be minefields of memories to navigate.

Bo parked his bike in the lot behind the warehouse housing the studio and made his way to the conference room, wondering why Sylvia had called a meeting here.

The production had taken a break on Monday for the Jewish holiday, but the plan had been to resume filming on location.

Maybe there was an issue with a permit at the stable, or maybe the set team hadn't finished their prep work. *Or . . . maybe the lead actress decided she couldn't work with the stunt coordinator after spending a weekend fooling around in bed with him.*

He tucked his helmet under his arm. That last thought was ridiculous, but it kept creeping back. Probably his guilty conscience. He shouldn't be messing around with Sadie. As he told himself over and over, getting involved with her was opening a can of worms for a host of reasons, both personal and professional. But he hadn't been able to help himself.

Bo knew the risks and had been willing to take them for a chance to spend time with her. And what was he worried about anyway? They'd said goodbye on perfectly good terms. Better than good. At least, he'd thought so. True, he hadn't talked to Sadie in the three days since, but she'd been with her family. He hadn't wanted to bother her, and he hadn't expected she'd contact him.

Entering the mostly empty conference room, Bo was surprised to see Sadie pacing back and forth, from one end of the room to the other.

Okay, maybe he did need to worry.

Bo nodded to Ryan and the handful of other team members who were gathered around the coffee station. He tried to catch Sadie's eye, but she had planted herself at the farthest side of the table and was currently staring at her phone like she wanted to set it on fire.

What the hell was wrong?

Before he could find out, Ryan waved him over. "Bodacious. What's with this surprise meeting, anyway?"

"No clue." Bo tore his gaze away from Sadie. "It's right there in the name. *Surprise*."

"Ri-i-ight." The actor nodded. "Good point." Ryan flopped back in his chair and picked up a pen, clicking it on and off, over and over again. *Click-click. Click-click.*

Bo shook his head and hurried over to Sadie.

"Un-fucking-believable," she seethed.

"What?" Bo sank in to the seat next to hers.

"This." Sadie slapped her phone down on the table.

Bo leaned forward, scanning the text on the screen. It was an article from *411 on 312*, a local Chicago entertainment industry buzz site. The kind of internet rag that mostly covered celebrity bar fights, breakups, and—he narrowed his gaze, skimming the article that had apparently pissed off Sadie—boob jobs.

"According to this, you recently got breast implants."

"Thanks, Captain Obvious," Sadie snarled. "I read it. Of all the bullshit stories tabloids have written about me, getting my boobs done is one of the most patently false yet."

Bo recalled how her breasts looked that first day of shooting, round and full as they swelled above the line of her vest.

"Did you?" Ryan asked, barging into the conversation.

"What do you think?" Sadie made a noise of disgust.

"That first day on set," Ryan said, scooting his chair closer. "That leather vest?" The actor held up his hands. "I'm saying this with the utmost respect, but I, uh, couldn't help but notice you looked extra . . . perky."

"That was makeup and a really good bra." She glared at him.

"Wow. Really?" Ryan whistled.

Shit, man, stop talking. Bo was too concerned for the guy's safety to be mad at him for copping to checking out Sadie's rack. Also, he'd been guilty of doing the same thing.

"Yes, really." Sadie bristled with outrage. "You don't believe me?"

"I didn't say that," Ryan backpedaled, finally sensing danger.

"I'm telling the truth."

"I'm sure you are," Bo agreed soothingly, glancing around the conference room. While he loved the fire in Sadie, sometimes it burned out of control. Once riled, his little abeja had quite the temper. "Is this what the meeting is about?"

"No," Sadie snapped. "This is fucking bonus material."

Click-click. Click-click.

Sadie jerked her gaze toward Ryan, shooting him a look that said her costar was one click away from having that pen ripped out of his hand and shoved up his—

"Mind if I borrow this?" Bo grabbed the pen from Ryan.

"Huh?" Ryan blinked, oblivious to the fact Bo had probably just saved him from a grievous injury. "Oh, yeah. Sure."

Sadie sent Bo a grateful look, and then resumed stewing.

He knew she was upset about the article, but why was she acting like nothing had happened between them? Not that she could, or should, do anything obvious. They had to keep things under the radar. But still, she could give him some clue . . .

Sylvia breezed into the conference room, Tanya and several other assistants wafting behind her like little bows tied to the streamer of a kite.

The minion assistants began distributing packets to

everyone in the room, while Tanya pulled out a chair for Sylvia and handed her a cup of coffee.

Sylvia took the coffee but ignored the chair. Remaining standing, she addressed the group. "We have a situation, people."

"I can confirm Gold *did not* have a boob job," Ryan announced.

"What?" The director gaped at the actor, bewildered.

Bo shook his head, wondering if Ryan had hit his California stash a little too hard over the long weekend.

"Tanya, what's RG talking about?"

The assistant promptly handed Sylvia her phone, opened, Bo presumed, to the *411* story.

The director scanned it briefly, then shoved the phone away. "I don't have time for this nonsense." She cast a glance down the table at Sadie. "MG, did you get breast implants?"

"No, I did not."

"Excellent, I'm sure wardrobe will be pleased to hear they don't need to refit you." Sylvia took a sip of her coffee and got down to business. "The reason I called you all in here today was because this morning, I received word Birchwood Stables had a fire last night."

The room erupted into concerned murmuring. Sylvia took another sip of coffee and held up her hand. "Luckily, none of the staff or horses were injured. But the property sustained significant damage. My location scout has informed me we will not be able to begin filming at Birchwood as scheduled."

More grumbling.

"How far will this set us back?" Bo asked. This kind of unexpected delay was the exact sort of shit he'd been worried about.

"Hard to say." The director nodded to her assistant.

Tanya took the coffee and handed Sylvia a copy of the packet that had been distributed. "According to our current production calendar, we were supposed to arrive on location at Birchwood today, with calls running through . . ."

"Next Wednesday," Tanya supplied. "We also were holding the rest of next week on reserve."

"This means we're looking at a setback of one, maybe two weeks." Sylvia flipped a page. "Any chance we can bump the final fight sequence at the mall?"

One of the head production editors, an uptight guy Bo had privately nicknamed Annoyed Dave, sighed heavily. "I already have the permits for that signed-off and ready. I'll have to contact the mall's property manager, reapply to have the area secured for the new dates."

"Is that a problem?" Sylvia pressed.

"Not for me," Dave said, though his tone implied it was a huge problem. "However, I can't speak for the person I'll need to convince to speed this new request through."

"That's not our only problem," Mark, another production lead, spoke up. "We chose those dates for Birchwood to take advantage of the fall color."

"We can edit most of that in post-production." Sylvia waved her hand.

"Some of it, yeah. But there's something to be said for the real thing, you know? Once the leaves start falling in earnest, it's going to be hard to re-create that lush autumn feel. Push those dates back another few weeks and who knows what we're looking at."

"Snow," someone muttered.

"In October?" Sylvia scoffed.

"It's unlikely, but not impossible," Mark said. "This *is* Chicago."

Bo nodded, along with a few other locals who knew this area's unpredictable seasons all too well.

"Speaking of impossible . . ." Annoyed Dave swiveled on his chair, ". . . I'm guessing this means we need to find a new stable, with the right specifications for our shoot, somewhere within an hour's radius of Chicago, that can be available for us to film on location, starting tomorrow?" By the end of this litany, both the man's voice and his eyebrows had climbed several notches.

"That about sums it up," Sylvia agreed. "Is *that* a problem?"

The production manager's face turned a fascinating shade of puce, but he didn't respond.

In the silence that followed, Ryan retrieved his pen from a distracted Bo and resumed clicking.

Bo glanced furtively at Sadie, worried that a certain pen tip might end up in Ryan's neck soon. He shifted in his chair, reaching out to nab the clicking time bomb before Sadie committed homicide.

"Yes, Bo?" Sylvia asked.

"What?" He glanced up, startled.

"Did you have something to add?" Sylvia cocked her head, waiting.

Every head in the room followed suit, swiveling in his direction. Bo swallowed, realizing by raising his hand he looked like, well, like he was raising his hand. He couldn't admit he was just trying to steal a pen before the lead actor was impaled by his pissed off costar. Bo scrambled for an answer. "We need a new stable."

"Yeah, we got that," Annoyed Dave ground out. Still purple with frustration.

The man needed to relax before he had a coronary. Bo was worried too. If this schedule fell behind, he was fucked. And it would not be the fun kind.

Bo glanced at Sadie again. And just like that, he had the answer. The perfect solution. It was so simple and so obvious, he wondered why Sadie hadn't suggested it herself. She was probably too ticked off and distracted. Bo straightened, turning his attention back to Sylvia. "I know a replacement location for Birchwood."

"Oh really?" Sylvia finally took a seat at the table. She waved at Tanya, who held up her clipboard, prepared to take notes.

"Yeah," Bo continued. "A stable about an hour north of here. Nice place. I know the specs. It's got everything our set needs." He thought he heard Sadie gasp. She was probably realizing what "nice place" he was talking about. She could thank him later. Bo smiled, feeling rather awesome for saving the day. He glanced at Mark. "Couple of meadows for the wide shots edged with plenty of forest for that fall color you're so hot for."

"What about horses?" Chuck, the head wrangler, piped up. "I'm guessing Birchwood already had to relocate their stock while the stables are being repaired. Not sure we want to risk moving the animals again so soon."

"This place has access to some of the best horses in the world," Bo assured them. "Used to taking direction and being around crowds."

"And you're sure the place is available for us to rent on such short notice?" Annoyed Dave asked, voice doubtful, though his expression bordered on what could almost be called hopeful. "The owners won't have a problem with a film crew descending on them in less than forty-eight hours?"

"No problem at all," Bo promised. "I know the owner." He hitched a thumb toward Sadie. "So does she." Why didn't Sadie speak up? He didn't want to take all the credit. After all, she'd be the one who would likely be making the arrangements.

"You know the owner of this stable too, MG?" Sylvia glanced between Bo and Sadie.

"I do, actually." Sadie smiled weakly. "It belongs to my grandmother." Then she turned to Bo and shot him a look that made him think she was plotting to steal back that pen and use it like a blow dart gun on his windpipe.

It was not the response he'd been expecting. What was her problem? She should be happy he'd thought of a solution. Now they'd be able to stick to the current shooting schedule. Annoyed Dave wouldn't risk going into cardiac arrest by having to reapply for permits, and Bo would have a chance to spend time with Sadie. Despite the intense schedule, there would be some downtime. Bo knew exactly how he wanted to fill those free moments. With her.

But first, he needed to figure out why she still seemed so upset. He tried to catch her attention all through the rest of the meeting, but she ignored him. The second after Sylvia wrapped things up, Sadie hopped out of her chair like a spooked filly and bolted for the door.

"Hey," Bo called, hurrying after her. "Hey, wait up." He started jogging to catch up with her as she speed-walked down the hall, supple little legs jerking angrily. "Sadie! Slow your roll."

"Slow my roll?" She stopped, pivoting to face him as he quickly covered the remaining distance between them. "Did you get lost somewhere in the last decade?"

"You wouldn't have known if I had." *Damn, where did that come from?*

Her eyes widened, and she turned away from him, picking up her pace some more.

"Hold on!" He reached for her hand. "Please."

Sadie yanked her arm free, but she didn't run away. "What do you want from me?"

"I want to know what's wrong."

"You want to know what's wrong?" she fumed. "Let's see, I need to go call my grandmother and let her know a film crew will be descending on her property. *Tomorrow.*"

"Wait, you're upset about that? Your grandma won't care. I know her. If anything, she'll be thrilled."

"You don't know everything, *Bonifacio.*"

Sometimes Bo wished Sadie had never learned his full name. Only his mother called him that—and only when she was irritated with him. Bo hated it. It made him feel like a grubby, little boy. He fought the infantile urge to go hide in a corner and sulk. They wouldn't get anywhere if they were both throwing a temper tantrum. "You're right. I don't know everything," he admitted, forcing his voice to be calm, neutral. "Why don't you tell me? Why are you so mad?"

She remained silent, but he could feel the anxiety rolling off her in waves as she stared down at the scuffed concrete floor of the warehouse hallway.

"Sadie, look, if I messed up, I'm sorry. I really thought this was the perfect solution. But if it's going to make your grandma upset, I'll see if I can find someplace else—"

"No. It's fine. I mean, I'm not upset about that. Exactly." She looked up at him, face drawn tight. Something was bothering her. A lot.

Bo's stomach clenched. "Then what are you upset about?"

"You're going to say it's stupid."

"Sadie, I promise. I won't."

She wrung her hands. "It's just, I worked so hard to get this part. I wanted it so bad, but more importantly, I wanted to earn it on my own." She took a breath and continued. "I know you won't understand, that you'll think

I'm complaining about something I should be grateful for, which makes it even harder to explain . . . but it sucks when people assume you've never had to work for anything in your life. That it's all just been handed to you."

Prudently, Bo kept his mouth shut. He'd thought exactly those things about many people many times. Probably even about her once or twice.

"I had to deal with that shit following me the entire time I played Simone. The rumors my daddy bought me the part. The hints that I wasn't good enough to be a success on my own." She was talking faster now, words coming out in quick, angry bursts. "This movie was my chance to show everyone I could do it. That I had what it takes. That I was good enough." She stopped, voice breaking.

And for the first time, Bo realized Sadie struggled with the same fears he did. She wanted the same things. Respect. A chance to prove herself. To be judged by her own merit. Seeing the picture from this angle, a light bulb went off. "You're worried if word gets out the movie is filming on your family's estate, people will assume that's how you got the part."

"Bingo." She sniffed. "I can see *411*'s next headline now. 'Washed-Up Aging Soap Star Makes Big Splash with Granny's Cash' or something."

"Sadie. You are *not* washed up, and for fuck's sake, you are certainly not 'aging.'"

"Oh yeah? I'm turning thirty at the end of this month."

Bo chuckled, he couldn't help it.

"Stop laughing, this is serious. Once this story gets out, who's going to believe I got this part on my own?"

"First of all, I don't think where we end up for a week of filming is much of a story, but if it does hit the news, so what? The studio's PR team can easily point out there was an issue with the original location and emergency measures were taken. The dates will show that you were cast long before the choice to film at your grandmother's estate was made. You have an entire conference room full of people to corroborate the facts."

"Ugh, you don't get it! The tabloid people, they're not concerned with facts. Exhibit A, my invisible boob job! And the people who like to read these stories aren't interested in facts either. All they need to do is skim a click-bait headline and *bam*, their mind is made up."

"Who cares?"

"I do! What people think of me matters. It matters to me, and it matters to my career."

"Then prove the rumors wrong."

"What?"

"Sadie, I know how hard you've been busting your ass. Anyone who's seen you in action on set knows, beyond a shadow of a doubt, that you earned this role by yourself. Once people see the film, they'll know too."

"You think so?"

Her voice sounded so small, so fragile, it crushed him. "I do." He brushed a finger under her chin, lifting her face to his. "But what I think doesn't matter, abeja. What do *you* think?"

"I think . . ." She stared into his eyes, twin flames of hope slowly coming to life as she embraced what he was saying. "I think I need to call my grandma." A tentative smile quirked her lips. "And then I need to buy a car."

A few hours after the emergency meeting, Sadie pulled out of a car dealership in her new sporty but sensible coupe. "That was fun." She smiled at Bo, strapped in to the passenger seat next to her. "Thanks for coming with me."

"Eyes on the road, please," he said, gripping the oh-shit handle above his window.

Sadie rolled her eyes. "I may have never bought a car by myself before, but I do know how to drive one."

Bo snorted. "When was the last time you were behind the wheel of a car?"

"You don't have to come with me," she huffed. "You're welcome to get out and go ride your crotch rocket home, and I'll drive my shiny new car to my shiny new apartment by myself."

"I told you, I'm coming with you," Bo gritted out. "I want to make sure you *and* the car get to your place in one piece."

Sadie changed lanes, snaking between two other cars with ease. "See? I got this. It's like riding a bicycle."

A ripple of laughter floated through the car.

"Are you making fun of me?" she demanded.

"No." Bo laughed again. "I'm remembering that time you tried to surf on your bike."

"Oh." Sadie felt her cheeks flush. "That's not a good example of what I meant. I don't plan to try riding down a hill while standing on the roof of my car anytime soon."

"I still can't believe you did that." Bo shook his head, awe in his voice. "What were you? Ten?"

"Yep." Sadie snorted. "And of course, I did it. You dared me to." She could still picture her bike, sea-foam green with a turquoise banana seat. It was the banana seat that had started the whole escapade in the first place. They'd been riding their bikes up and down the gently sloping back roads for most of a lazy summer afternoon and were getting bored. Bo got the bright idea to speed down a hill with no hands, then did it again while holding on to his handlebars, knees balanced on his bike seat.

Sadie had decided, with the wisdom of her single decade on earth, that thanks to her longer seat, she could probably one-up Bo and coast down the hill while standing. Bo had dared her to give it a try, and the next thing she knew, she was flying, feet balanced on her seat, legs straight, fingertips barely hanging on to the ends of her handlebars. She managed to make it all the way to the end of the hill before the bike veered sharply, hit some gravel, and skidded, sending Sadie flipping over the handlebars to land in a field on her back, staring up at the blue summer sky.

"I've seen a lot of stunts in my day and done more than my fair share of dangerous ones, but that is still one of the ballsiest, most cold-stone awesome performances I've ever witnessed," Bo said, voice holding more than a touch of admiration. "I'll never forget how you calmly got up, dusted yourself off, and got back on your bike, continuing on your merry way like it was no big deal."

Sadie grinned. The part she remembered most about that day was the look on Bo's face, a little shocked and a whole lot impressed. "At the risk of ruining all the major cool points I earned," she began, glancing over at him, "I have a confession."

"You hired a stunt double," Bo deadpanned. "I knew it."

"No!" Sadie laughed. "It was definitely me, but I was completely stunned by the fall. The wind had been knocked out of me. Honestly, I think I was in shock at the time. Getting up and climbing back on my bike wasn't really a conscious decision. I just did it."

"Seriously?" Bo chuckled, the warm rumble of his mirth rolling over her. "Well, whatever the case, it was still pretty badass. Your cool points are safe."

"Thanks." They drove in companionable silence for a while, lost in memories.

After some time, Bo asked, "Was that the same summer we tried to re-create the bridge scene?"

Sadie frowned, thinking hard. "Bridge scene?"

"You know, in *Star Wars*, when the controls for the bridge don't work, and Luke and Leia swing across."

"Oh, that's right!" Sadie shook her head, smiling. She'd completely forgotten about that. They'd tied a bed sheet to a rafter in her grandma's barn and swung from one side of the loft to the other. "I think that was the summer before, when I was nine."

"Really?"

"Uh-huh. I remember because I had never seen the movie before we watched it together." While Bo usually put up with watching all her "hokey old-fashioned" movies, sometimes Sadie compromised and watched what he wanted. And while she didn't like the films he picked as much as her beloved classics, she could admit she did enjoy them. Especially the ones with kick-ass Princess Leia, a fierce leader who wasn't afraid to take charge and call the shots.

"You know, I think I've unconsciously been modeling parts of Jamie's personality on Princess Leia."

"I can see that," Bo agreed. "You remind me of her a little bit."

"Who? Princess Leia?"

"Sure."

"Well, you remind me of the scoundrel, what was his name?"

"Han Solo."

"Right, him." Sadie made the turn into the parking garage below her building. An assigned space came with her apartment, but she'd never had to park here before, so it took her a moment to figure out the numbering system. She cruised down the aisle slowly, watching for her spot. "Maybe I am a little like Leia," she admitted, rounding another corner and glancing in his direction.

"What's that smile for?" Bo asked suspiciously. "Why are you looking at me like that?"

"Like what?" Finally, Sadie found the number correlating to her apartment and pulled in. She turned off the engine. "I was just thinking, I can relate to Leia."

"Yeah?" His voice was a quiet rasp. In the shadows of the garage, the dark interior of her car suddenly felt very intimate.

"Yeah." Her own voice was low and throaty. "I can appreciate her fondness for a scoundrel."

"Is that so?" Bo's eyes were fixated on her mouth.

"Mm-hmm." She pressed her lips together. Then she leaned across the seat and whispered in his ear, "It's hard to resist a good bad boy."

Bo chuckled. Low and rumbly and delicious. "Well, princess," he began, in a voice full of Han Solo swagger, "maybe you should check out my light saber."

"You didn't." Sadie groaned, leaning her forehead on the steering wheel. "I can't believe you went there."

"What? Too corny?"

"That. And even I know Han Solo didn't use a light saber."

"True," Bo admitted. "There's nothing like a good blaster at your side."

Sadie gave him a bit of side-eye. "Can you recite *all* of Han Solo's lines?"

"Try me." He reached for Sadie's hand.

"Hmm." She sat up, enjoying the sensation of his fingers wrapped around hers. "There's that scene where Princess Leia tells Han she likes nice men," Sadie suggested.

"And he says he is a nice man." Bo cocked a smile at her and lifted her fingers to his lips.

"But she says no." Sadie tilted her face up. "You're not, you're—"

Bo interrupted her with a kiss, exactly like Han did to Leia in the movie. He bent his head and pressed his mouth to hers, tongue thrusting deep, the whole kiss coming at her in one overwhelming wave of sensation.

She heard the click of Bo's seat belt as he undid it, and then he was reaching across, unbuckling hers as well. He pulled her closer, dragging her out of her seat, into his lap. Sadie followed his lead, swinging her legs over the center console and straddling Bo. It was a tight fit and not very comfortable.

"Maybe we should have test-driven this aspect of the car before I bought it," Sadie teased against Bo's mouth.

"We can take things for a spin now, if you like," he offered, gripping her hips, thigh muscles tensing beneath her as he shifted on the seat.

Sadie felt him growing hard between her legs. She settled herself more fully on his lap, rubbing her heat against the tight ridge of his erection. She groaned in frustration. There were too many layers between them. But with her knees trapped between the passenger door and the console, there wasn't a lot of room to remedy the situation.

"If my memory serves, this used to work better for us in the back." She wiggled off his lap, slipping between the front seats and climbing into the back. Free to move around a little more, she kicked off her shoes. A reckless, wanton urge seized her, and she shimmied out of her jeans.

"What are you doing back there?" Bo asked.

"I'll give you one guess." Sadie tossed her panties into the front seat, barely missing smacking him in the back of the head.

Bo retrieved the scrap of fabric. Twirling the silk and lace around on one finger, he shifted, angling his torso so he could turn around and look at her.

Whoa. The heat and hunger in his eyes. Amber shards of fire stoking to life.

Sadie shivered. But she didn't look away. In the dim glow from the parking garage's fluorescent lighting, they watched each other.

Fully clothed from the waist up, from outside the car, nothing would seem out of place. Keeping her gaze locked on his, Sadie spread her knees apart, opening her legs wide. Then she raised an eyebrow, a silent dare for him to break their stare first.

He raised a brow in return, eyes not moving from hers.

Their staring contest continued.

She brought one hand between her legs and stroked herself, slowly.

Beneath the edge of his beard, his throat worked, Adam's apple bobbing.

Sadie fought a grin of triumph. She had him now. She shoved her knees farther apart, as far as they could go, and brought her other hand into the mix, fingers gently spreading her folds, opening herself to him.

With a groan, Bo caved. His gaze dropped, thick lashes a dark swath against his cheeks as he shifted his focus to between her legs.

"I win," Sadie gloated.

"If you say so," Bo muttered huskily from the front seat, attention fixed on the movement of her hands.

"You're going to get a crick in your neck if you keep that up," she taunted, still touching herself with lazy strokes. That, too, was a taunt.

"I thought this was a staring contest."

"I already won the staring contest."

"No, this is a new contest."

"But you're not even looking at me!" Sadie protested.

"Sweetheart, I'm definitely looking at you."

"You know what I mean." Her hands stilled.

"Don't stop," he growled.

"What?"

"That's part of the contest." His eyes flicked to hers. "I won't stop watching you touch yourself. If you come before I look away, I win. If I look away before you come, you win."

"Ha." She stroked herself again. "I could do this all day."

"Fine with me." Bo licked his lips.

Sadie gasped. She was throbbing. Wracked with the need to feel his mouth on her, his tongue inside her. The scrape of his beard against her thighs.

Maybe she shouldn't have been such a big talker. His gaze never strayed from her as she continued to work her fingers over the sensitive nub of her clit, slipping inside, feeling the hot slick slide of her own skin.

She wanted to close her eyes. Wanted to throw her head back and give herself over to the orgasm building inside her. But she also wanted to win. Sadie hated to lose. Besides, if she closed her eyes, she wouldn't know if he'd stopped looking. So she kept it up, fingers stroking and teasing her aching, swollen flesh. All the while watching him watching her.

"Close, aren't you, abeja?" Bo teased, his voice a husky hum. "So very *very* close."

"Shut up," she ordered, gritting her teeth.

He chuckled, and that was even worse. Dark and rich and sweet as sin, the low vibrations of his laughter rumbled through the car and along her skin. Making her throb deep inside.

The tremors began, ripples of sensation radiating out. Sadie bit down on a moan as her hips bucked against her own hand.

"You are so beautiful," he praised her. "Let me watch you, let me see you come."

Not sure she could have stopped now anyway, Sadie circled the pad of her thumb over her clit. She cried out, hips lifting off the seat as she got herself off in a series of sure swift strokes.

"Fuck, yes," he groaned, voice thick with approval. "That's it, sweetheart." Bo jerked the handle on his seat and leaned all the way back. Hands on her thighs, he pulled her to him, sliding her wet heat toward his eager mouth.

Never had losing felt so much better than winning. The second his lips found her, tongue slipping inside, Sadie exploded again, shattering with a second orgasm. She collapsed, lying flat out on the backseat, legs like jelly.

Bo moved over her, covering her body with his. He kissed her then, and she tasted herself on his tongue, tart and earthy.

Their kisses continued as she reached between them, seeking the front of his jeans. Her fingers loosened his belt and made quick work of his zipper. Again, excitement built inside her. She'd just come twice, but the weight of him on top of her, the feel of his body on hers, brought back a hundred familiar sensations from nights long ago.

Of stolen moments and pleasure freely given. She hadn't known how special what they had was, hadn't understood how rare. Nobody made her feel like Bo did. The time they'd spent this past weekend had been incredible, but they'd stopped short of that step. Hadn't taken it all the way.

Sadie tugged at the waistband of his briefs, wanting to free his cock so she could trap it inside her body. He groaned, and she sucked the sound into her, kissing him deep, needing to take all of him inside her. Everything he had to give. Sadie lifted her hips, grinding against him, inviting him in. Finally, the smooth head of his erection rubbed against her, skin to skin.

More memories flooded her. Flashes of the last time they'd been together like this, in the back seat of a car, the heat and scent of passion drenching the air . . . and what had happened after.

She froze, muscles going rigid.

It was Bo who broke the kiss. Propping himself up, he looked down at her, his face a blend of shadows in the dark interior of her back seat, his breathing ragged. "Abeja?"

"Yeah?" Dazed, head still foggy with desire, Sadie tried to make sense of the warring sensations tearing through her. Part of her wanted to keep going, to take that last step, to welcome Bo inside her body again. But another part of her recoiled.

"Maybe we should stop." His voice was rough—raw but restrained. Bo drew back from her, pulling his clothes into place.

"Yeah," she said again. Not a question this time. She couldn't do this. Not here. Sadie struggled to sit up, cold without the warmth of Bo's body against hers. Lust curdled as another sensation, familiar as it was unwelcome, settled around her.

She knew this feeling. Knew its shape and weight and texture and taste.

Regret.

CHAPTER 18

BO RODE THE elevator up with Sadie to her condo. Physically, she was standing next to him, but somehow, he knew she was far away. *Years* away. That moment in her car. The velvet darkness of the back seat, the velvet slide of her skin against his . . . had it brought all of it back for her too?

The last night they'd been together.

The night it all went to hell.

The elevator bell dinged. With effort, Bo pulled himself back, away from that moment, and followed Sadie out of the elevator, wishing he could shut out the rest of that terrible night as easily as the elevator doors slid shut behind him.

Bo glanced around as he waited for Sadie to unlock the door to her place. Everything was shiny and new, just as he'd expected. The plush, stain-free carpet lining the hall, the smudge-free walls, the gleaming floor-to-ceiling windows, filling the space, making it sparkle with afternoon sunshine.

The door opened, and she led him inside. Her place

was equally shiny and new. Gleaming gray hardwood floors. Bright white walls. The same floor-to-ceiling windows letting in more of that afternoon sunlight, and a spectacular view of the lake.

"I think we both could use a drink," Sadie said, heading toward her kitchen.

Bo trailed behind her. She indicated a seat for him at the island. Everything here was shiny and new too. Sparkling granite countertops. Pristine stainless-steel appliances.

Popping open the freezer door, Sadie pulled out a bottle of chilled vodka. She set it on the counter and sifted through the cabinets for two glasses. "Here," she said, placing the bottle and glasses in front of him. "You pour."

While Bo measured out the liquor, she went back to the fridge, returning a moment later with a jug of cranberry juice. She set the juice next to her glass and hopped up on the stool beside his. Despite himself, he felt the beginnings of a grin crease his lips.

"I see that smirk," Sadie said, wiggling onto her seat. "Are you laughing at me because I still can't handle my booze straight or because I still can't get on a stool without jumping?"

"Both," he admitted. The steel band that had been constricting his chest eased a little.

Sadie topped off her glass with juice, pausing to offer him some. He shook his head.

"Suit yourself." She shrugged. Setting the jug down, she lifted her glass. "Should we toast to something?"

"To buying a new car?" he suggested. They were playing a new game now—the evasion game.

"Sure." They tapped glasses.

"Salud." Bo tossed back his drink, icy fire smoothing down his throat and heating his belly. "We should name her," he said.

"What? My car?" She sipped her drink slowly. "How do you know it's not a him?"

He snorted and poured another shot. "Fine. It's a him. What's his name?"

Sadie contemplated this, mouth working. "How about Brad?"

"You want to name your car Brad?"

"It was your idea to name the car, not mine."

"Okay, okay." He raised his glass. "To Brad."

They toasted again. Bo took a breath, the alcohol and meaningless chatter making it easier to pretend everything was fine. He polished off what was left in his glass.

"Bo?"

Sadie's voice was soft, but even his slightly inebriated ears didn't miss the thread of tension.

"Hmm?" He held himself still, bracing for what he knew deep in his gut was coming next.

"Why did you do it? Why did you break up with me?"

And there it was. He *knew* she'd been thinking of that night too. How could she not? He'd wondered when she would ask. Was surprised it had taken her this long to demand the answers he owed her. And he did owe her. Bo stared down into his empty glass, debating another shot.

"Why did you leave me all alone?"

Her words punched a hole in his heart. "You weren't alone." Bo reached for the bottle. "You had Ana. And all your other friends."

"I wasn't talking about just that night."

"Neither was I." He glanced around at her shiny, fancy apartment. *You had your powerful family. Your money. Your luxury cars and expensive homes. Your big college plans.* "I realized it was never going to work out between us."

"You just came to this conclusion out of the blue that

night? On *prom night*?" Sadie slammed her empty glass on the counter, a slight flush rising in her cheeks. "Something happened that night. After we . . . after you went to park the car again. Something you're not telling me."

"Let's just say it became painfully obvious to me that we weren't right for each other," Bo ground out. He could still feel the cold bite of the glass pressing into his face as he was smashed against his own windshield. The throbbing pain in his ribs and back as fists pummeled him, over and over and over. "We were too different."

"I saw the bruises on your hands, Bo. I saw the blood. What happened?"

"I was angry." He shrugged, reaching for the vodka and deciding to go for that next shot. "I punched a wall."

"Bullshit. Next you're going to tell me the wall punched back." Sadie took the bottle out of his hand and poured herself another healthy splash, following it up with more juice.

Bo snorted, tossing the drink back. He held his empty glass out to her.

"I know you were in a fight." She poured him another shot, then set the bottle down and pinned him with a stare. "What I don't know is, why?"

He shifted his gaze, refusing to look at her. The black walnut cabinets lining the back wall of Sadie's kitchen were polished to such a fucking shine he could see his reflection. Yeah, he'd been in a fight. With a few privileged pricks from Sadie's school who had taken one look at Bo and found everything they saw lacking. From his hand-me-down shoes to the cheap rented tux to his work-roughened hands.

The liquor was finally starting to worm its way through his system. Numbing the pain. Dulling the memories. But not erasing them. Bo stared down at his calloused hands, rough as ever. He would never be a guy with smooth hands. Never be like those guys from her world. Bo's fingers clenched, curling into fists.

"Yeah, I was in a fight." Bo spun on his stool to face her. "And you wanna know why?" He leaned closer. "Because those assholes were begging for it."

"What assholes?" Sadie frowned.

"Some pendejos you went to school with. Didn't like the fact you were slumming it with someone like me."

"What's that supposed to mean?"

"Don't play dumb; it doesn't suit you," Bo mocked, tone frosty as the chilled vodka in his glass. "You're not naïve either." He shifted his gaze to his hands. "They wanted to teach me a lesson. Punish me for daring to lay my dirty hands on you."

"Bo, I . . ." Sadie began, but then stopped. "I'm sorry that happened to you."

He despised the pity in her voice. He shouldn't have told her. Bo hated talking about this. Hated the feelings it dredged up. The anger. The resentment. The despair.

Because deep down, he'd known they were right.

She reached for his hand, but he jerked it away.

"Please don't do this again," she begged.

"Do what again?"

"Pull away from me." She looked up at him. "What those guys did to you, it was horrible." Her voice took on a hard edge, accusation sparking in her violet eyes. "But you should have told me, not walked away from me."

His temper flared. "They wanted to fuck me up for the simple fact I was fucking you!" The words exploded out of him. Sadie flinched, but Bo wasn't going to let her back away from this. Not after she'd reopened the wound. "Do you have any idea how that feels?"

"Do you have any idea how it feels to know that all it

took was a couple of dickhead rich boys for you to kill what we had together?" Her cheeks were flushed, face hot with anger.

"That fight was the final nail in the coffin." Bo shook his head. "But it had been building for a while. I had plenty of other reasons."

"Like what?"

Bo rubbed a hand over his face. "Do you remember that summer I had a concussion?"

"Of course I do." She looked up at him from her drink in surprise, eyes wary. "I came to visit you every day. You weren't allowed to do anything. No books, no TV, no video games."

"I know," Bo muttered. "Rogue is still one of my favorite stallions, even if the asshole did kick me in the head."

"I can't believe it happened in the first place." Some of the tension went out of her and she poured another vodka cranberry, topping off his glass with a generous dollop of vodka as well. "I mean, I know horses can be unpredictable, but you always had a sixth sense about that stuff."

"I wasn't thinking." Bo raised his glass, watching Sadie. "I'd kissed this beautiful girl for the first time a few days before, you see, and had been walking around like someone who'd had his brains scrambled." He tossed the shot back. "Maybe that kick to the head helped knock everything back in place."

"Maybe," Sadie agreed drily.

Bo blinked, brain pleasantly fuzzy now. "You read me these stories. About gods and goddesses."

"Mm-hmm. The Greek myths. It was my summer reading assignment that year . . ." She paused, nose scrunching. "I thought you couldn't hear me; you were so out of it most of the time."

"I didn't always comprehend what you were saying, but

yeah." He nodded. "I heard you." Through the foggy haze of his brain and the almost-constant nausea and headaches, Sadie had been his one salvation. Her voice wrapped around him, blocking out everything else. Helped him forget the restlessness, the boredom, the pain.

The stories she read took him away from the frustration of being stuck in bed and forced to do nothing more strenuous than stare at the ceiling. Bo traced a finger around the rim of his glass. "There was this one story about Hades."

Sadie set her drink down. "The lord of the underworld?" Her brow furrowed, and Bo could tell she was trying to piece together where he was going.

"Sure. And the woman he fell in love with." He waved his hand. "I can't remember her name."

"Persephone."

"Right. And they were from different worlds. After she married him, she was miserable. She hated living in his world."

"Bo, I—"

"Let me finish." Maybe it was the alcohol, but suddenly it become imperative that he told this story. Made his point. "She was so unhappy that eventually Hades agreed to give her up for half the year and let her return to her own world."

He brushed his hand over her cheek, fingers a little clumsy as he traced the rosy glow. "I never forgot those stories you read to me, and I'll never forget how it felt when I realized that story—it was you and me. We had our summers together. And during that time when I had you to myself, it was completely different than when you went off to live in your other world the rest of the year."

"Bo . . ." she tried again.

He shushed her, trailing his finger down to her mouth, across her smooth, soft lips. "When we were older, and I finally scraped enough cash together to buy a car and visit you in the city, I never felt like I belonged. Never thought I could measure up. All your friends judged me. Except for Ana. And your mother hated me."

"My mother hates everyone."

"Fine." Bo wasn't going to argue with her on that. "But it was then I started to realize that if we stayed together, if our time stretched beyond the magic of those summers, you would miss that other world. I didn't belong in yours, and you would be miserable in mine."

"You were fourteen when I read you those stories. Eighteen when you broke up with me. Which means what you're telling me is you saw yourself in a story—*in a myth*—and then snap! Four years later, you get in a scuffle with some dude bros and decide to do something about it? That's an excuse, Bo. Not an explanation."

"It's a reason." He tucked a finger under her chin, lifting her face to his. "I didn't want it to eat away at us, to slowly destroy us."

Sadie jerked back, away from his touch. "What you did, it destroyed us anyway." She hopped off the stool and began to pace the length of the island, her steps slightly unsteady. "Only it wasn't slowly. It was one big epic explosion." She waved a trembling hand through the air. "Boom. We're over. Done."

Temper back in full force, she turned to look at him, eyes bright and wild with fury. "And then you walked away. You didn't even bother sticking around to view the carnage. To help pick up the pieces. Do you have any idea how *I* felt? How much you hurt me?" She stepped closer, voice cracking under the weight of holding all this in. "I deserved to know why. You should have told me."

"If I had tried to explain, you would have argued. You never would have listened—"

"You're right, I wouldn't have listened to this garbage." Her chin jutted higher. "I would have *fought* for us." Her eyes narrowed, and Bo felt like she was seeing straight through him. "I always thought you were the brave one. Stronger than me. Now, I'm not so sure."

Bo sat, stiff and still, staring at her. But inside, he was crumbling. "I'm sorry I hurt you, abeja." He stood, gathering the remnants of his courage. "But I'm not sorry for what I did. It was for the best."

"For you." Her eyes flashed in a face of stone. Tension crackled like lightning in the air between them.

"No. For us." He took a step toward her. "What I wanted, you already had and didn't care about. And what you wanted? I couldn't give you. I'd never measure up."

"That's not true!"

"No? You didn't want to spend your life at the stables. You wanted to travel the world. Go on shopping sprees and stay in fancy hotels." He scowled at her. "How was I supposed to make any of that happen? My family literally doesn't even own a pot to piss in! Everything we have belongs to the Murphys. To you." Bo sighed and shook his head. "Our lives were headed in different directions."

"You couldn't know that for sure." She glared at him.

"Maybe not," he agreed. "But I believed I was right."

"Really?" She laughed, hollow and bitter. "You thought you—what—that you were Bogie and I was Bergman?"

"What are you talking about?"

"A movie, *Casablanca*. One of my nana's favorites." Sadie notched her chin. "He tells her to go, to leave, that it's for her own good. Says she'll regret it if she doesn't." Her voice shook with emotion, but beneath the anger and bitterness, there was pain. "Sound familiar?"

"You can't compare us to a movie, abeja."

"Why not? You compared us to a book."

Bo held himself in check. He wanted to reach out, to hold her so badly, the ache was physical, ripping him apart inside. But first he needed her to understand. "Here's what I think. Back then, it just wasn't the right time for us. We both had to walk our own path. If we'd tried to do it together, tried to force it, somewhere along the way, things would have splintered, pushing us apart."

"But we ended up here! Together. Right now. In the same place, at the same time."

"I know, it's . . . incredible." Unable to resist any longer, Bo crossed the room to her. "I'm not saying the universe has a plan for us or anything, but maybe—if it did—then this was the idea all along. That we had to go our own ways in order get here. To this moment."

"Why?" She jerked her head back, staring up at him. "To make us suffer?"

Bo sucked in a breath. There was so much pain in her expression. More than he realized. A moment of doubt caused his foundation to wobble. Had he caused all of that?

He swallowed. "I'm not sure," he admitted. "I don't know why."

As if something inside Sadie gathered all that pain up and tucked it away, it suddenly disappeared, her face going blank. Bo sensed it was still there, hidden from view. He wanted to dive into Sadie's soul, seek that pain out and carry it for her. But whatever she was feeling, whatever she was thinking, she wasn't ready to share that with him now. He hoped, one day, she would.

"Please, abeja," Bo begged, reaching one hand out, palm up, an open appeal "No matter what happened in the past, no matter the reason, what's important is that the universe or fate or whatever you want to call it has given us a second chance."

Tentatively, Sadie placed her palm over his. "A second chance, huh?"

He nodded. "The chance to get it right this time."

"Does this mean we're dating now?"

"I'd like that." Bo squeezed her hand. "But with my job as your stunt coordinator, it could look bad. You know how fast a story like this can lead to trouble." He paused, not sure it was wise to point this out, she'd been so pissed earlier. "If we slip and the media picks up on it . . ."

"We won't slip," Sadie promised. "On set, we'll be professional. No hint of anything *inappropriate*," she said, lowering her voice to an exaggerated whisper.

"Nothing inappropriate, huh?" Bo teased, bringing her fingers to his mouth and brushing his lips across her knuckles.

Sadie let out a tipsy giggle.

"It's the beard, isn't it?"

She nodded. "It really is ticklish." She shifted her hand out of his and slid her knuckles along his jaw. "Nothing inappropriate on set. But when we're alone . . ." Her hand drifted down his neck, slid along his collar, fingers resting on the pulse at his throat.

A pulse that was rapidly picking up the pace. Especially when Sadie began undoing the buttons on his shirt.

"We could take it slow," she suggested, fingers fumbling, moving down his chest, releasing more buttons.

"I can do slow," he breathed.

"Yeah?" One doubtful brow rose in challenge.

"Yeah." Bo rubbed his thumb along her bottom lip. "Can you?"

"I bet I can hold out longer than you can." The last button on his shirt slipped free, and she tugged the tails of his shirt out of his jeans.

"Sounds like a challenge to me." He brushed his hand along the line of her jaw, stroked the back of her exposed neck, grinning in triumph when she shivered, nipples puckering, tight buds visible beneath her T-shirt. "Or maybe a dare."

"Oh, it's definitely a dare," she purred. "I dare you not to have sex with me until we wrap."

"Wait." Bo's hand dropped. "What?"

"Well, no going all the way until we're done filming," she amended. "This way we can honestly say we aren't sleeping together." Sadie's laugh was full of mischief. "Technically, that won't be a lie." Her eyebrow quirked again. "Think you can handle that?"

"We can do anything else but that?" Bo mused.

"Anything you can imagine."

"I don't know. I can imagine quite a lot." He cocked a grin at her.

Sadie rolled her eyes. "You'll get it, Solo."

His grin widened. Christ, every time Sadie picked up on one of his *Star Wars* references, Bo got that much more turned on. "I better."

"You will."

"Well then, princess"—Bo bent his head, leaning in close, mouth inches from hers—"I accept your dare."

CHAPTER 19

THE NEXT MORNING, Bo hustled into the Windy City Stunts office, nursing a vodka hangover, a heart full of hope, and a head bursting with a hundred things to do. Things he wanted to do with Sadie. But also things that needed to get done in the next few hours. It hadn't even been twenty-four hours and already Bo knew keeping his personal and professional shit together while separate was going to be the hardest dare he'd ever taken. He might not have agreed to the terms of Sadie's challenge if he hadn't been half a dozen shots under the table, but what's done was done, and he'd never backed down from a dare. He wasn't about to start now.

"Good morning, Bo," the middle-aged woman at the front desk trilled sweetly, greeting him with a warm, motherly smile, her thick Polish accent curling around his name.

"Hi, Claudia." He returned the smile. "Is your husband around?"

"VICTOR!" Claudia shouted, loud enough to knock Bo back on his heels.

"What?" an annoyed bark sounded from Vic's office.

"BO IS HERE TO SEE YOU." Claudia bellowed the words in loud blocks of sound.

"Well, send him in!"

Claudia returned her attention to Bo. "Victor will see you now," she announced, voice once again soft and pleasant. Singsong, even.

Bo hid a grin. "Thanks."

He headed down the hall into Vic's office and plopped into one of the cracked leather chairs they'd salvaged from a set years ago. "When is your wife going to learn how to use the intercom system?"

"Never," Vic grunted. "She enjoys yelling at me too much."

This time Bo didn't contain the grin that split his face. Vic and Claudia's relationship was a constant source of unintentional entertainment.

"What's up?" Vic leaned back in his chair, wheels creaking. "I thought you were headed out to Maplewood for a week."

"Birchwood. And there's been a change in plans."

"Oh?" One salt-and-pepper brow arched.

Bo nodded. "Fire at the stables."

"Shit." Vic frowned. "Anybody hurt?"

"Everyone's fine. No casualties, no injuries. The horses had to be relocated, though, and the facility is shut down for repairs. We can't shoot there."

"Obviously." Vic leaned forward again, shuffling papers on his desk. "Is this going to push you back? I know you're on a tight timetable. You still got that *Chicago Rescue* contract before the end of the year."

"It's fine. I figured it out."

"You did, eh?"

"We're moving the shoot to Murphy Farms."

"Hey, that's where you—"

"Yeah." Bo nodded. "Where I grew up."

Vic chuckled. "Those cowboy days of yours are still coming in handy."

"Seems like," Bo said. "I've already told my crew about the switch. Just wanted to keep you up-to-date, have Claudia change it on the paperwork."

"Sounds like you've got it covered." Vic cocked his head, eyeing Bo. "You didn't have to come in for that, though. My wife *does* know how to use the phone."

"I wanted to talk to you." Bo sat up straighter, hands braced on his knees. "This movie I'm working on . . ."

"It's a big one." Vic smiled. "People are already talking."

"It has the *potential* to be big," Bo agreed. "I'm thinking, now might be the time to start moving forward with the plan."

Vic's smile faltered.

"Just discuss it," Bo hurried to add. "Start getting specs for how we'd make it happen. Maybe draw up some paperwork."

"I don't know, Bo," Vic hedged. "The holidays are coming up and then it's a new year."

"My point exactly. Let's start fresh with the new year. If we get WCS transferred fully over to me before *Fair is Fair* hits the market, that could be a great springboard to relaunch the company."

"Relaunch?"

"You know what I mean," Bo backed off. "Announce the changes, that's all."

Vic scratched his chin. "I'll think about it."

Right. Bo had been listening to that song for two fucking years. Frustration frayed the edges of his temper, but Bo reined it in. "Good." He stood, before he said something he'd regret. "We'll talk more about this later." He held out his hand to Vic.

"Sure." The old guy shook it, grip firm as ever. "Later."

By the time Bo got to Murphy Farms, it was almost noon, and production trucks and vans were lined up along the gravel drive, crews hard at work. He decided to leave his motorcycle parked at his parents' house and head over to where the filming was taking place on horseback. He still went riding on occasion, but he'd been more city boy than country boy for too long. It would do him good to warm up a bit on his own before starting in with the actors.

The stallions were kept in a separate stable on another part of the Murphy property, away from the mares, so Bo didn't see Rogue unless he made a special trip. Murmuring softly, he slipped the bridle into place and cinched it before leading the horse out of his stall. Fall sunlight filled the stable yard. A brisk breeze swayed through the trees beyond the fence, sending leaves dancing across the thick grass.

Rogue tossed his mane, turning into the wind, nostrils twitching. "Feels good, huh, boy?" Bo chuckled, stroking the soft velvet of his muzzle. "Wanna go for a ride?"

The horse bobbed his head. Without preamble, Bo swung up, deciding he'd ride bareback. He didn't want to waste time dealing with a saddle right now, and the urge to feel the wind in his hair, the glide and shift of smooth power beneath him, was a temptation he couldn't resist.

Afternoon sun warm on his back, wind stinging his face and tearing through the horse's mane, they crossed the open field. Rogue's hooves thumped against the ground in time to Bo's heartbeat. In no time, they'd reached the line of trees. With a tug on the reins, Bo slowed to a trot and guided the horse to run parallel along the edge of the meadow until they reached a break in the trees where an old dirt path wound its way through the woods.

Following a path in his mind as well-worn as the one beneath the horse's hooves, Bo's thoughts shifted to Sadie and their conversation last night. Did the universe really have a plan? He couldn't shake the sense it was possible, that seeing Sadie again, being with her again, was inevitable.

In minutes, Rogue had reached the other end of the woods. For a moment, Bo stood at the edge of the meadow, watching the steady stream of activity flow around the estate as various crews carried out the business of prepping the location for filming. They were in for a couple of long days ahead. "Okay, boy," he said, as much to himself as to the horse, "let's go."

A few hours later, Bo stood next to Sylvia in the south glen, comparing notes while Ryan and Sadie rode a practice route together. As he watched them move across the meadow, Ryan on the black gelding and Sadie on the caramel mare, Bo was struck by the fact he wasn't jealous. Rather than a sharp pang of envy that she was in another man's company, Bo only felt joy. She was beautiful to watch on horseback. How could he have forgotten? The flow and symmetry. The rhythm. It was like art or poetry. A piece of music.

Ryan wasn't half bad either. "I'm impressed," Bo admitted to Sylvia. "He really does know how to handle himself on a horse. I knew Sadie could ride, but I had my doubts about Gratt."

Sylvia chuckled. "I had my casting people do their due diligence. I'm well aware of an actor's inclination to pad resumes."

"If what we're seeing now is any indication, as long as

the weather holds, the next few days of shooting are going to be a breeze."

"Don't jinx us." Sylvia watched as they finished the circuit. "But yeah, they do look good out there together."

He nodded. "Not trying to jinx anything, but I think we'll get this wrapped up by Sunday morning."

"Perfect." Sylvia turned to her assistant. "Did you get that, Tanya?"

Tanya mumbled under her breath, scribbling notes on her clipboard. Bo wondered if the girl slept with that thing under her pillow.

On Sunday morning, as Bo had predicted, the crew was prepping for the final sequences with the horses. The plan was to film during "magic hour"—the time just before dawn when natural light spreads evenly across the sky, and Mother Nature provides breathtaking lighting, no special effects or fancy filters required. From his standpoint, it was an easy sequence to shoot, the focus of the scene more on atmosphere than action.

By the time the sun was full up, golden October sunlight streaking through the copse at the edge of the meadow, the shoot had wrapped. Bo did his part, checking in WCS's safety equipment as it was loaded on the truck, all the while tracking a thatch of spiky blond hair. He and Sadie hadn't had a moment alone since that night in her apartment.

All through the shoot, they'd kept their distance and stuck to the provisions of Sadie's dare. Professional. Courteous. But it had been almost a week since they'd talked about anything not related to the movie. A week since he'd touched her. Kissed her. Bo was dying to steal just a few minutes with Sadie.

While the crew packed up the last of the equipment, Bo waved at Sadie. She moved toward him, the rose and auburn shades of the fall morning bathing her in a warm glow. He sucked in a breath. Christ, he could look at her all day. Watch the color of her eyes change with the light. She was so radiant, it was like the dial had reset on the clock, and the sun was rising again.

"What is it?" she asked, catching him staring.

"Nothing. Just . . . you're beautiful," he replied honestly.

A shy, pleased smile curled in the corner of her mouth. The sweet mouth he'd been wanting to kiss for days. Bo glanced around, most of the strike team had finished up. The coast seemed clear for the moment, so he took a risk, leaning in and kissing her. Briefly. Softly.

It wasn't enough. "Come on," he whispered, taking her hand and tugging her toward the stable.

"Where are we going?" she whispered back.

Bo didn't answer, but pulled her inside the tack room, shutting the door and pressing her up against it. "I've been thinking about doing this for days," he said, dipping his head and pressing his mouth to hers.

"Why, Mr. Ibarra, this is highly inappropriate." Sadie giggled. "Are you calling off the dare?"

"No. But can I call a time-out?"

"Hmm," she mused, face scrunching in exaggerated contemplation. "I'll have to consult the rule book. Any other requests?"

"Actually," he began, mouth moving along her neck, "I was wondering . . ."

"Yes?" Her breath tickled his ear.

"My folks still insist on family dinner every Sunday night." He molded his hands over the curve of her jean-clad hips.

"Uh-huh." She strung her fingers through his belt loops.

He slid his hands up under her sweater, caressing the smooth, satin skin. "And since today is Sunday . . ."

Sadie leaned into his touch. "It is . . ."

"Well, if you don't need to get back to the city right away . . ." He flicked his thumbs over her nipples.

"I don't," she breathed. Her fingers had moved from his belt loops to his buckle.

He chuckled, filling his hands with her breasts, squeezing gently. "Would you like to come over for dinner?"

"I'd love to." She slid her hand inside his jeans, wrapping her fingers around his cock.

"So," Bo groaned, "it's a date?"

"It's a date." She grinned up at him.

Bo stared down at her, brain a little numb as he basked in the warmth of her smile. Also, there was the fact his dick was in her hand—that tended to make his brain go on hiatus. Which was probably why he was taken completely off guard when the handle to the tack room jiggled.

"Hello?" a female voice called from the other side of the door. Not Sylvia. Maybe one of her assistants.

Shit. Bo jerked, pressing his palms flat against the door, holding it shut.

Sadie yanked her sweater back down. With lightning reflexes, she sprang into action. While Bo continued to keep the door shut, she made quick work of his buttons, tucking his shirt back in his jeans.

"Easy there," he growled softly. "Watch the equipment."

A snort of laughter escaped Sadie, and she clapped a hand over her mouth.

"Is someone in there?" The door jiggled again.

"One minute," Sadie called, eyes on Bo, warning him to stay silent. "I'm, uh, just changing." She pressed her back against the door and pointed to an alcove on the other side of the room. Bo got the hint. He nodded and hurried over to it, careful to keep his feet silent. Once he was hidden from view, Sadie opened the door and slipped outside.

Fuck, that was close. From the other side of the door, he could hear Sadie weaving some form of explanation. Bo crouched in the alcove, feeling like a naughty little boy. Like Toby when Luna put him in a corner for a time-out. Which, let's face it, he needed a time-out. What had he been thinking?

That was the problem, He *hadn't* been thinking. From now on, if he and Sadie were going to play this game, they'd have to stick to the rules.

CHAPTER 20

HOURS AFTER ALMOST getting caught with her hands inside his pants, Sadie rode behind Bo on Rogue, holding on as he cut through the meadow to his parents' house. She relished the contact. Thanks to the close call in the tack room, they'd agreed to keep their hands off each other on set. No more time-outs. No more risks. They were adults, not horny teenagers. They could act like it.

Unfortunately, being around Bo made Sadie feel *exactly* like a horny teenager.

Bo kept the pace steady, and in minutes, Rogue was trotting up the drive to the carriage house. Originally established as the coachman's residence, it now served as the home for the estate's stable manager. A position Bo's father had held since before Sadie was born.

In the distance, Sadie could just make out the lights of her grandma's house on the hill beyond the trees. The Murphy mansion was gorgeous to look at, stately and impressive. But Sadie had always thought the carriage house was the loveliest building on the property. It was certainly cozier.

Sadie thought again about what Bo had said that night in her apartment. How his family owned nothing. How everything they "had" belonged to her family. She'd never considered what it would have felt like if someone else owned everything she believed was hers. Had never really thought about it. Guilt cramped in her belly. That's what privilege was, right? To have so much you don't even know it.

The baying of hounds startled Sadie out of her musings. As Bo guided the stallion past the main horse barn and toward a smaller stable sitting at the edge of a pasture, the barking grew louder. Sadie glanced toward the kennel, where the pack of hunting dogs were kept. Luckily, Rogue was accustomed to the cacophony and paid it no mind.

A moment later, Bo pulled the stallion to a stop and dismounted before helping her slide down. Sadie assumed they'd have to see to the feeding and rubdown of the horse themselves, but as Bo walked Rogue to his stall, she was surprised to see a groom emerge from the tack room. The two men exchanged a few words, and Bo handed off the reins, patting Rogue's rump affectionately. "Good job today, boy."

"He is a good boy," Sadie agreed, cooing to the stallion as she reached out and stroked his soft muzzle, hot puffs of breath tickling her fingers. The groom nodded politely at her before guiding Rogue away. Now that she thought about it, she shouldn't be surprised her grandmother had hired more staff. Bo was gone, and his father . . .

"Come on." Bo tugged on her arm. They jogged across the yard toward the house. With each step, Sadie grew increasingly nervous. Why had she agreed to do this?

Because you want to see if things can work with Bo. And spending time with his family is a logical step in the right direction.

It may be logical, but that didn't make it any less terrifying. Sadie didn't know why she was so scared. She'd met Bo's family countless times. His dad was gruff and rough around the edges and his sister hated her guts, but his mom was wonderful. Thinking of Bo's mother, Sadie relaxed a little. It would be nice to see Mrs. Ibarra again.

As they neared the house, the screen door swung open and a child stepped onto the porch. Sadie staggered to a halt. It was a little boy. Blond hair the exact shade Bo's had been as a child. The same golden curls she remembered from that first morning they'd met. *No. It's not possible.*

The earth tilted sideways. Sadie hunched over, hands on her knees, and breathed in through her nose. *Don't pass out. Do not pass out.* She exhaled slowly. Eyes squeezed shut, she could still see the image of the boy, his face lighting up with Bo's trademark mischievous grin.

"Abeja?" Bo asked, voice filled with concern. "What's wrong?" She felt his hand on her back, warm and gentle.

She shook her head, unable to speak, the lining of her throat singed with bile.

"Uncle Bo?"

Sadie swallowed. The burning sensation retreated to her stomach. *Uncle?* That made sense. She forced another series of slow, deep inhales and exhales to cycle through her lungs. Finally, she unfolded her body and stood. God, she was an idiot. She glanced back at the porch, at the little boy who still stood there, watching them, head cocked to the side, eyes bright with curiosity.

"Who's she?" the boy asked, directing his question to Bo.

"An old friend," Bo replied. He wrapped an arm around Sadie's waist and asked her quietly, "Are you feeling okay?"

"I'm fine." She gave him a cheery smile, hoping it didn't look as forced and ghastly as it felt. "Just a dizzy spell."

"Let's get you inside and get you something to eat."

Sadie nodded, grateful she didn't have to explain further. After all, how did one go about explaining you'd almost fainted because you saw the ghost of what could have been?

The bile began to creep up again, and Sadie pushed everything back down. The thoughts. The fears. The worry. *Back in the box. Lock it up. Nail it shut.*

Letting Bo lead her up the porch steps, Sadie shuffled along next to him.

With polite formality that she would have found adorable if she wasn't about to have a nervous breakdown, Bo introduced them. "Toby, this is my friend Sadie. Sadie, I'd like you to meet my nephew, Toby."

Again, hearing the word *nephew* helped quell the panic. "Nice to meet you, Toby," Sadie said, even managing to offer her hand to the boy. Up close, she could see he had blue eyes. Robin's egg blue. A lovely shade, but nothing like the jewel tones of Bo's amber-brown eyes or his sister's emerald-green. *And not the violet of her own eyes either.*

Toby shook her hand, mouth quirking as he stared up at her. He didn't have to look too far.

At barely five feet, she wasn't much taller than a . . . "How old are you?" she asked the boy abruptly.

"I'm seven," Toby announced proudly.

That's good. Seven. See? He's not ten. He's not the same. It's not the same. But even as Sadie told herself that, her mind was doing other calculations. If Bo was Toby's uncle, then that must mean this was Luna's child. Sadie was three years older than Luna. Which meant . . .

Sadie's head began to swim again. It was all too horribly, ironically similar.

"How old are you?" the little boy demanded, pulling Sadie back to the moment.

"Toby, you're not supposed to ask a lady's age," Bo admonished.

"She asked me first!" Toby protested.

"He's right, I did." Sadie smiled at the boy, the first genuine smile she was able to muster since laying eyes on him. "I'm twenty-nine now, but I'll be turning thirty soon."

"Wow! You're almost as old as Uncle Bo!"

"Thanks, kid," Bo grumbled, taking the words right out of Sadie's mouth.

"When's your birthday?" Toby asked, ignoring his uncle.

"On Halloween." *Oh, God, that was less than a month away.*

"What? Cool!" Toby's button nose scrunched up in thought. "Does that make you a witch?"

"Tobias!" a voice called sharply from the house. "Supper's ready. Get back inside this instant!" The door swung open and Bo's sister appeared. She turned, green eyes growing cool as she noted Sadie. "Oh. It's you."

"This is Uncle Bo's old lady friend," Tobias explained helpfully. "She's a witch."

The trademark Ibarra smirk tugged at Luna's lips, but she didn't comment. Instead, she held the door open for Toby. "Did you wash your hands?"

"Doing it now, Mamá!" Toby turned and ran back inside.

With one more icy, assessing look at Sadie, Luna followed her son.

Bo caught the screen door before it could slam shut.
"Sorry. Luna is, well, you know Luna, but I probably
should have warned you about Toby." He held the door
open for her.

"What? No. He's fine. You're an uncle. That's great!"
Sadie walked past him, clamping her mouth shut before
she continued babbling.

"Abuela!" Toby's voice reverberated through the walls.
"Uncle Bo brought a friend over for dinner. A *girl* friend!"
the little boy added in a high-pitched singsong voice.

Bo raised his eyes heavenward, and Sadie giggled.

A second later, a blond head appeared around the corner followed by a pudgy little hand waving them forward.
"Hurry up, Uncle Bo," Toby whisper-yelled in that way
only children seem to have mastered.

"It appears we've been summoned," Sadie observed.

"It does appear that way," Bo agreed. "Shall we?" He
offered her his arm and led her into the dining room.

"My goodness. Is that little Sadie?" Bo's mother hopped
up from her chair and hurried around the table to hug Sadie. "Just look at you." Mrs. Ibarra held her at arm's length,
eyeing her warmly up and down. "It's lovely to see you
again, absolutely lovely."

"Thank you," Sadie said. "It's nice to see you too."

"Here, sit next to me." Bo's mother patted a chair
before turning to glower at her son. "Bonifacio. Shame
on you for not telling me you were inviting a guest for
dinner!"

"I'm sorry, Mom. It was kind of a last-minute thing."

"I hope it's not too much trouble . . ." Sadie began.

Bo's mother waved her hand. "It's fine, it's fine. We
have plenty." She sat and pulled Sadie down next to her,

patting her hand. "And really, it's so nice to see you, dear. How is your grandmother? Is she well?" Another glower at Bo. "You should have invited her too, mijo."

Bo froze in the act of sitting down, eyes blinking in mute panic like a deer in headlights.

His mother waved her hand again. "Another time."

Bo's father cleared his throat.

Everyone quieted at once, turning their attention to the head of the table.

Bo had told Sadie about his father's accident, but still, knowing what had happened to someone and facing it in real life were two different things. As a child, whenever she'd seen Bo's dad, he'd been doing something active. Breaking in a colt, training a horse for hunting, harnessing a team . . . To see him in the wheelchair took Sadie back for a moment. But her skills as an actress served her well, and she managed to control the initial sense of shock. She composed her face, recalling what Bo had said. His father deserved better than her pity. And that was that.

Mr. Ibarra ordered grace, and everyone bowed their heads. Sadie followed suit. As Bo's father blessed the meal, Sadie couldn't help sneaking a glance across the table. Head bowed, eyes closed, Bo was behaving himself. Next to him, however, his nephew was not.

Toby caught Sadie's eye, his lips pressed together, cheeks puffing out with suppressed mirth at their shared mischief. Sadie shook her head slightly but couldn't stop a grin from forming as a gurgle of giddy nervous laughter bubbled up inside her too. Luckily, a moment later, Mr. Ibarra called amen, and Sadie could pass off the chortle as a sudden coughing fit.

Winking at Toby, Sadie joined in passing dishes around the table. Meat, mashed potatoes, a few kinds of vegetables. Sadie made sure to be polite and took a bit of everything offered to her. It was all so simple and homey and normal. Whether he knew it or not, *this* was the kind of thing that truly marked her world different from Bo's.

Family dinners like this didn't happen in Sadie's world. Not often. As a kid, her parents would take her to social events sometimes, usually fancy parties with more courses than she could count on her fingers. Food she didn't like, while sitting at a table where children were meant to be seen and not heard. Otherwise, dinner was whatever a maid or cook or nanny or tutor or whoever happened to be on duty that night heated up and left out for her. During the summer, she and her nana would share meals together, and Sadie enjoyed that time, but it wasn't the same as a whole family gathered like this. Not really.

Bo had believed he couldn't give her what she wanted. But what he didn't know was how much she wanted this. Messy table manners and laughter and time spent together. As a family. He didn't know because she'd never told him. She'd held that close. A secret too painful to share.

Sadie's gaze strayed to Toby's blond head again and a pang sliced through her. *Don't do this to yourself.* She locked the what-ifs down, closed the lid, nailed it shut.

Poking at the food on her plate, Sadie concentrated on the sounds around her, the rumble of conversation, the scrape of silverware against dishes, the clock ticking on the mantle, and in the distance, the dogs baying in their kennel. In control once more, she turned to Bo's mother. "I caught part of the fox hunt when I drove in earlier this week."

"You did?" Mrs. Ibarra smiled warmly. "How did the pack look?"

"Excellent. They'd definitely caught the scent already." She smiled, recalling Ryan's reaction. "My costar couldn't believe that kind of thing happened out here."

"You know how rich people like their pointless fancy hobbies," Luna observed, ever-frosty green eyes flicking over Sadie.

Sadie's smile faded. What did Bo's sister have against her? One of these days Sadie was going to say fuck it and just ask.

"I'll admit, it's a bit eccentric," Bo's mother cut in, tone abjectly civil, "but the hounds love it. And what harm is there? It's not like they chase an actual fox."

"They don't?" Toby asked, lips pursing in his chubby cheeks, making him look like a confounded cherub. "What are they chasing, then?"

"Why don't you ask your uncle?" Sadie suggested, glancing mischievously at Bo. "I bet he knows."

"Tell me! Tell me!" Toby yanked on Bo's shirt sleeve.

"Okay, okay. Easy there." He patted Toby on the head and then whispered in his ear.

"Pee-pee!" Toby giggled. "Really?"

"Yep." Bo nodded, mouth quirking in a grin so similar to his nephew's, Sadie's heart squelched. "You know," Bo continued, "you're almost old enough to start marking the trail yourself."

"What?" Toby's robin-egg eyes widened. "Can I, Mom?"

"Absolutely not." Luna's mouth was a grim line.

"Aw, come on, sis. I was about his age when I started."

"You were also jumping off silos at his age," Luna reminded him.

"This is different. He knows how to ride. It's perfectly safe."

"My son will not waste his time pandering to a bunch of bored snobs!"

Bo froze, glaring at his sister over Toby's head.

The mantel clock ticked, punctuating the sudden silence.

Sadie stared at her plate. She could almost hear the unspoken battle waging between the siblings, imagine what was being said. This was her fault. She shouldn't have come. It was clear Luna didn't think she belonged here.

But did Bo?

Caught between his mother and uncle, head down, Toby let out a strangled sound.

"Mijo?" Luna dropped her gaze to her son. "Are you crying, baby?"

Toby shook his head and lifted his chin, revealing a face wreathed in smiles. Shoulders shaking with glee, he sputtered, "They're chasing pee-pee!"

Biting her lip, Sadie tried to suppress the bubble of laughter rising to the surface, but the little boy's chortles got the best of her.

Soon, everyone around the table was cackling, even Mr. Ibarra, who failed to maintain his stern face while declaring the dinner table was no place for toilet humor.

"Sadie, you must tell us about this movie you and my son are working on together," Bo's mother suggested, deftly taking advantage of the moment.

Eager to help steer the conversation in a different direction, Sadie launched into a description of the filming they'd done here at the estate.

"That's nice you were able to use your abuela's stables," Bo's mother observed. "I'm sure the studio appreciated it."

Sadie shrugged. But she could feel Bo's eyes on her from across the table.

"You know," Luna drawled, dipping her fork into her

potatoes, "now that you mention it, I think I read something about that."

"About what?" Sadie's head snapped up.

"About the movie filming on your family's estate." Luna blithely swallowed a bite of food, the cat eating the canary.

"What are you talking about?" Bo demanded.

"It was online. One of those Chicago entertainment websites."

"*411 on 312*?" Sadie couldn't help asking.

"Maybe." Luna paused, and Sadie had the distinct impression Bo's sister was enjoying every second of this. "The usual story. Spoiled rich girl buys her way to the top. Never has to work for what she wants." Luna pointedly dropped her gaze to the perfect half-moons of Sadie's buffed and shining fingernails. "Never has to get her hands dirty."

Stomach churning, Sadie was glad she hadn't eaten too much of her dinner. The last thing she needed was Mrs. Ibarra's meatloaf to make a reappearance.

No. The last thing she needed was to hear the exact thing she'd feared—the thing she'd warned Bo about— was happening. Sadie had told him this would happen, but he'd brushed her concerns aside, made her feel silly and vain for being worried. *Damn it.*

"Luna, would you mind clearing the dishes?"

Luna frowned at her mother but didn't argue.

"I'll help," Sadie announced, springing from her chair.

"That's not necessary," Mrs. Ibarra said.

"Yeah, we wouldn't want you to mess up your manicure," Luna added sweetly.

"Please. I insist." Ignoring Luna, she gathered up her plate and silverware. *Bless your heart too, bitch.*

"Well, that's very kind of you." Bo's mother handed

Sadie her plate, casting a wary eye on her daughter. "And I'm sure Luna appreciates it."

"I'll help too!" Toby piped up.

"No!" Both Luna and Mrs. Ibarra responded instantly.

"Why don't you come say hi to Stella with me, sobrino," Bo suggested. He lifted his gaze to Sadie, eyebrow raised in question.

She nodded, adding his plate to the others in her pile. She was fine. She needed to do this. While Bo hustled his nephew out to the stable, Sadie picked up her stack of plates and headed for the kitchen, preparing for battle.

Luna was standing at the sink, her long cascade of black hair reminding Sadie of Ana. With a start, Sadie realized she'd known Luna for almost as long as she'd known Ana. But unlike her best friend, this woman had *never* liked her. And Sadie decided it was about damn time she found out why.

Crossing the kitchen, Sadie set her stack of dirty dishes on the counter next to the sink.

"We don't have a dishwasher," Luna said, glancing up from the plate she was scrubbing.

"No problem." Sadie ignored the eye daggers coming her way and reached for a towel. Taking one of the clean dishes drying on a rack, she began wiping it down.

Luna set the plate she'd finished washing in the rack and grabbed another. "I bet *you* have one, though," she muttered, voice barely audible over the sound of rushing water. "I bet you have tons of fancy appliances—and a maid, and a cook, and a housekeeper."

"I do," Sadie admitted. "I mean, I don't have *all* those things in my apartment, but I do have a dishwasher." Sadie rubbed the towel in circles around the dish. "And yes, my family has people who prepare their meals and handle the clean-up." She set the dish down. "Is that why you hate me so much?"

"I don't hate you."

"Right," Sadie scoffed. She was tired of the bullshit.

"Fine." Luna shut off the faucet and turned to look at her, green eyes flashing. "I hate you."

Sadie drew back as if slapped. Even though she'd been expecting it, the words still stung. "Why? Because I have money? Because I'm a 'bored, spoiled snob' who wastes your brother's time?"

"You didn't just waste my brother's time, you stole it!" Luna exploded, a simmering volcano that had been waiting to erupt for years. Hot angry words spewed forth. "Every summer. *Every* summer you'd come here and the two of you would run off on your adventures, playing games and having fun and not once . . . not *once* did you invite me!"

"Why would I?" Sadie stared at her, too incredulous to feel guilty about the accusation. "You've hated me from the moment you first laid eyes on me!"

"That's not true."

"No?" Sadie still remembered her first encounter with Luna. "Then Bo has another sister who threw mud at me and told me to go away and never come back?"

"I was five years old! You can't blame me for what I did when I was five."

"Fine." Sadie gripped the towel in her fingers, struggling to remain calm. "What about the time when you were nine and you locked me in the tack room? Or the time you stole my shoes and threw them in the creek? Now that I think about it, you pulled that particular nasty little stunt on me several summers in a row. Then there was the time you dumped paint on my new saddle. I think you were at least fourteen for that one."

"I did it because I was jealous, okay? Is that what you wanted to hear? I was jealous of you, the beautiful fairy princess who lived in the castle on the hill with your pretty clothes and expensive toys. You had everything. And I had nothing." Luna's lip trembled, and for a moment, she looked like the sad, angry little girl Sadie remembered taunting her all those years ago.

"That's not true, Luna. You had a mother and father who spent time with you. You had a brother who loves you."

Luna shook her head, tears glistening in the corners of her eyes. "He loved you more. Every fall, when you'd get in one of your fancy cars to head back to your fancy house in the city, Bo would be miserable. He'd mope around for weeks, and nothing I ever did could cheer him up." She swiped at her eyes.

"I didn't know . . ."

"How could you?" Luna cried, tears running down her face now. "All I wanted was for someone to love me the way he loved you. To look at me the way he looked at you. That's why I . . . I was so desperate to have what you two had, I . . ." Luna stopped, covering her mouth with her hands.

A chill ran down Sadie's spine. "That's why you what?"

But Luna only shook her head. "It doesn't matter." She wiped her face again, in control once more. "Like my dad says, some people are haves, and some are have-nots, and that's just the way it is." She straightened, staring down her nose at Sadie. "To answer your original question, yes, I think you're spoiled. I think you've always gotten everything you've ever wanted, and you take it for granted."

More than a slap to the face, Luna's confession was a punch to the gut. "You talk about my fancy clothes and big houses with servants to do everything, and you're right, that stuff is nice. But I'd give it all up if it meant I could have grown up having the kind of dinner like the one you had tonight." Sadie's voice shook. "You think I take my life for granted? Look around, Luna. You take your family for granted." Sadie tossed the towel on the counter. "And you can't buy that."

Sadie banged out of the kitchen, pausing in the dining room to thank Bo's parents for their hospitality, mortified but certain they'd heard every word of her argument with Luna. Then she let herself out, stomping across the moonlit gravel driveway to the stable, the cold October air cooling her heated skin.

The main stable door was already closed for the night. Sadie made her way around to the tack room entrance on the side of the building and slipped inside. Made to house teams of horses, the carriage stable was the biggest on the property, much bigger than the one closest to her grandma's house. A row of antique lanterns outfitted with LED bulbs stretched overhead, pale circles of light reflecting on the stable floor, creating a gleaming path between the stalls, like stepping stones.

At the far end of the barn, near the very last stall, Sadie spotted Bo and his nephew, petting a lovely, old gray mare, their voices muffled by a symphony of small quiet sounds created by the rustling of more than a dozen horses settling in for the night. Rather than spook any of the animals by calling out to them, Sadie made her way toward the trio, her booted footfalls nearly silent.

Bo was scratching the mare between the ears, while Toby ran his hand up and down her silvery muzzle. Sadie watched as Bo leaned toward Toby, giving the boy his full attention as he listened to whatever his nephew was saying. Bo was a good uncle. He would probably make a good dad.

Sadie didn't even flinch when the ache came this time.

She was getting used to it. Like permanent emotional heartburn.

Bo glanced up, catching her eye as she approached. "You're alive."

"Were you worried I wouldn't be?" Sadie stood next to him, reaching up to run her fingers over the mare's snowy forelock. "Hey there, Stella. How are you, old girl?"

"Do you know she and Uncle Bo have the same birthday?" Toby asked.

"Almost the same," Bo amended.

"I think I did know that." Sadie smiled, but it was bittersweet. The last time she'd seen Stella, the mare had been nearing the end of her prime, which meant now she was likely nearing the end of her life.

Another stab of pain. Sadie placed a hand over the aching spot in her chest, rubbing absently. All those years. All that time. Gone.

"Abeja?" Bo murmured, brow creased with concern. "You good?"

"Fine," she lied, dropping her hand and forcing another, brighter smile. She nodded toward Stella. "This silver beauty was the horse you were riding when we first met, right?"

A soft smile touched Bo's lips. "That's right." The burnished amber of his eyes glowed, his gaze gentle and warm, and Sadie knew he remembered that first encounter at the edge of the meadow as clearly as she did.

"Uncle Bo?" Toby's voice, laced with curiosity, pulled them back from the past.

"Yes, sobrino?"

The little boy moved closer, wiggling around until he stood between Bo and Sadie. "Why did you call your friend a honeybee?"

CHAPTER 21

THE GRANDFATHER CLOCK in the upstairs hall was chiming nine as Sadie waved to Bo from the window of her nana's front parlor. He waved back, then hopped into the pickup truck he'd borrowed from his family to bring Sadie home and headed down the driveway. She stayed at the window, gaze trained on the glowing taillights until they disappeared around the bend.

Bo was headed back to the city in the morning, but Sadie thought she might stay out here a little longer. Between the excellent weather, Sadie and Ryan's ease on horseback, and Bo's expert handling of the stunt choreography, they'd wrapped up filming at the stable ahead of schedule. Sadie wasn't due on set again until the end of the week.

Yom Kippur was in another day. She could stay here until after that. Her family had never been strongly invested in the traditions of their faith, and rarely, if ever, attended services. Ana liked to say Sadie's family was "Jew-*ish*." But there were a few holidays and rituals Sadie managed to grow up with, each holding a sense of comfort in their own way. It would be good to spend some time in reflection. She and Nana could fast together. Light a candle for Poppa. And Sadie could begin to atone for all the years she'd neglected to make her grandmother a priority in her life.

The lilting croon of a fiddle playing an Irish melody drifted from the back of the house. Sadie poked her head in Nana's den. The room was dark, lit only by the flickering glow of the television screen. *Casablanca* had given way to *The Quiet Man*, which could mean only one thing . . . Nana was thinking of Poppa.

"Nana?" Sadie whispered, making her way across the den's thick rug. Her grandmother was curled in one corner of the sofa, nestled under a pile of crocheted blankets. "Are you awake?"

"Mmm," Nana hummed. "I told you I'd wait up for you."

"You did." Sadie grinned at the kick of spunk in her grandmother's voice. "Do you need anything? Can I make you some tea?"

"Not now, doll." Nana lifted one corner of the blanket. "Come snuggle under here with your nana."

Happy to oblige, Sadie crawled onto the sofa, careful not to steal too much of the blanket. Nana reached up and pulled Sadie's head down to rest on her shoulder. Her wrinkled fingers were warm as they stroked Sadie's short locks. Sadie realized her grandmother hadn't said a word about her haircut. That was Nana, though. Appearances didn't matter much.

It was strange to think this woman had raised Sadie's mother. Mom and Nana were polar opposites. Appearances were everything to her mother. Aside from money, Sadie's mom was obsessed with three things. The three W's as Sadie started calling it in her teens: weight, wardrobe, and wrinkles.

Sadie still heard her mother's voice in her head sometimes. Snide little comments about the size of her waist or the choice of her dress. For Sadie's twenty-fifth birthday, her mom had given her a certificate for Botox treatments. Sadie had regifted it to her pain-in-the ass former soap opera costar.

"Nana," Sadie murmured, watching the screen. "Did you name my mom after this movie?"

A chuckle rumbled beneath the blanket. "You're only realizing this now?"

Sadie chuckled too. "I never really thought about it before," she admitted.

"Yes," Nana sighed. "I named your mother after Maureen O'Hara. Shame she didn't turn out more like her."

"Nana!"

"Oh, pish, I'm not saying anything new." Nana kept stroking Sadie's hair. "I love my daughter, of course. But I don't have to like her."

Sadie couldn't help snickering.

"Though she did give me you for a granddaughter. And for that, I can forgive pretty much anything." Nana patted Sadie's cheek. "Now, *you* would have been worthy of the name Maureen. *Mercedes*. Bah. Don't know what she was thinking. Your poppa was the first one to call you Sadie, did you know that?"

Sadie did know, but she liked hearing Nana talk about her grandfather, so she stayed silent and still.

"You were his wee Sadie-kins. Oh, the joy on that man's face when he put you on a horse for the first time."

"You miss him, don't you?" Sadie asked quietly.

"Of course, doll." Nana's voice dropped to a bittersweet whisper. "All the time."

Heart aching for her grandmother, Sadie reached for Nana's hand. Nana and Poppa had been through so much to be together. Childhood sweethearts. Like she and Bo had been. And talk about "different worlds." Sadie didn't know all the details, but she'd heard enough stories over the years to know it hadn't been easy for an Irish immigrant and a Jewish girl living on opposite ends of Maxwell street to be together in 1940s Chicago. Somehow, though, they made it work.

On the television screen, Mary Kate and Sean were sharing a tender kiss in a stormy graveyard. It wasn't as memorable as the movie's iconic, passionate windswept embrace, but still, it was a great kiss. Sadie thought of her nana and poppa, watching this movie together year after year. She squeezed Nana's hand. Their story had been as romantic as any movie. "Let's light a candle for him tomorrow. I think I'll stay here a few more days. Spend Yom Kippur with you."

"That would make me very happy, doll." Her grandmother squeezed her hand in return. "Now tell me, how was dinner?"

"Ugh," Sadie groaned. A dull throbbing warned her a headache was coming on. For a few minutes, she'd been able to forget tonight's fiasco.

"Oh, dear. It didn't go well?"

"I fought with Bo's sister." Sadie let go of her nana's hand and sat up, rubbing her temples.

"Luna?" Nana tsked. "She's such a nice young woman, so pleasant. You should see the flowers she grows. The mums in the dining room are some of hers, you know. Angie picked them up for me at the farmers' market. Oh, and she has the best produce in the entire county, the bread we had the other day was made with some of Luna's zucchini."

"Anyway," Sadie broke in testily, fearing if she let her, Nana would spend the rest of the night listing all the

9262   MELONIE JOHNSON

wonderful plants and vegetables in nice, pleasant Luna's
garden. "She's always had it in for me, and we finally had
it out. In her parent's kitchen."

Sadie leaned back against the couch, watching as the
Duke brawled his way through an Irish village. It was one
of the most ridiculous fight scenes in cinematic history,
but also one of the most memorable. Fortunately, her fight
with Luna hadn't escalated into a boxing match, despite
Sadie feeling like she'd been punched in the gut.

"Well?" Nana prodded. "Did the two of you work it
out?"

"Not really." Sadie shrugged. "I mean, I'm glad I finally confronted her, after all these years but . . ." She
rubbed her middle. "Luna admitted that she hates me."

"Who could ever hate you?" Nana wondered.

Lots of people. God, she still needed to track down
that stupid internet article.

"Nana, do you think I'm spoiled?" Sadie held up her
palm. "Wait. Never mind. You're my grandmother, you
can't answer that objectively."

Nana chuckled. "It's my job to spoil you, but no, doll
face, I wouldn't say you're spoiled. Pampered, yes." Nana
lifted her hand from the blanket and waggled a wrinkled
finger. "Your mother, on the other hand. Oy. Now, there's
a woman who is spoiled." Heaving a sigh, she continued,
"I blame myself. Your grandfather and I, we started out
with nothing. I wanted better for your mother. We gave
her everything." Nana shook her head. "And that's why
she's never happy with anything."

Upstairs, the clock chimed ten.

"It's getting late. How about we get you up to bed?"

"Don't worry about me." Nana waved her hand. "I'll
call for Angie."

"I'm already here." Sadie reached for her grandmother's

arm. "Let me help you." She clicked off the TV, and to-gether, they made their way toward the door where light spilled in from the hallway.

As they shuffled up the stairs together, Sadie was struck by another wave of guilt. Poppa had been gone for years. Aside from the staff, of which Angie was the only in-residence member, Nana was alone in this big old house.

"This is all very sweet of you," Nana said as Sadie helped her into her nightgown.

"It's nothing." Sadie smoothed down her grand-mother's puffs of snowy-white hair. "I should be doing this more often."

"You should be living your life, not taking care of an old woman," Nana barked, showing that spunk again.

"I can do both." Sadie pulled on the covers, tucking her grandmother in. How many nights had Nana done the same for her? Helped her get ready for bed. Tucked her in. Sadie glanced up at the familiar pale blue canopy draped above her grandmother's bed, eyes stinging with unshed tears. She'd accused Luna of taking her family for granted, but Sadie had done the same. "I'm sorry I haven't been a good granddaughter. Can you forgive me?"

"I don't think there's anything to forgive, but if that's what your heart craves, then yes, of course I forgive you." Nana reached out and patted Sadie's hand. "You're a good girl, Sadie-kins. Your poppa would have been proud."

"He would have wanted me to take care of you. Like you did for me." Sadie placed her hand over Nana's, cra-dling the paper-thin skin between her palms. "I promise I'll do better. From now on, I'm going to spend more time with you. Not just this week, but every week."

"I'd like that," Nana murmured, the words slow and drowsy. Her hand slipped from Sadie's, eyes drifting closed.

Sadie sat on the edge of the bed, a tender smile flitting about her lips as she listened to her grandmother's gentle snores. She'd always found the sound soothing. Her wolfhound Flynn had snored too. Louder, of course, long, snuffling snores. Sadie used to rest her head on him while he slept, cheek nestled against his shaggy fur, rising and falling to the steady rhythm of his breaths. There was something so peaceful about listening to another creature enjoy sleep with such abandon. It made Sadie relax too, as if rest could come through osmosis.

She missed Flynn. She missed Poppa. But they were long gone, memories of them a bittersweet comfort. Nana, however, was right here. Had always been here. But she wouldn't always be. Sadie couldn't make up for all the time they'd lost. But she could make the most of the time they still had.

The following weeks passed quickly, a blur of days spent shooting on location around the city, and nights spent with Bo. Challenging as it was, they'd stuck to their pact and had not *technically* slept together. Bo had warned her, he could imagine quite a bit, and holy hell could he ever. He'd found ways to get creative in his bed, on his couch, bent over the kitchen counter—and once, pressed up against the big picture window of his loft—cold glass pressed against her breasts while his fingers pressed inside her heat.

Then there were the quiet times. Mornings when they'd snuggle under the covers, his soft beard tickling her cheek and Clark biting their ears. Jogs along the lakefront together and donut runs after. Nights they'd come home from a long day of filming to veg out on the couch and watch movies.

Faster than Sadie could have predicted, she and Bo

had settled into a comfortable routine. While filming, they were strictly professional. Cordial and polite. But the time they spent together away from the set felt like how their summers used to be. Their own little island of happy away from the rest of the world. A small part of Sadie, the dark graveyard where she kept her boxes buried, held back, wary of the joy, knowing that eventually, the reality boat would barge in. But for the most part, she was able to embrace the moment and enjoy the calm seas and smooth sailing while it lasted.

True to her word, she also visited with her grandmother on the weekends, driving out any time she had a Saturday off and spending the night. It had been lovely, and Sadie tried her best to relish the present, rather than regret the past. Both with Bo, and her grandmother.

It was the last week of October, with about two weeks left on the film schedule, when Sylvia called Sadie and Ryan in for a meeting.

Ryan caught up to Sadie on the way to the conference room, and they headed in together. "I'm looking forward to your party."

"What party?" She blinked, mind still occupied with her lines for today.

Ryan's face fell. "Shit. Did I just ruin a surprise?"

"Oh, *my* party!" Now Sadie's face fell. "Shit. I completely forgot."

"Dude, don't let Ana know that; she's been getting stuff ready for weeks."

"I am the worst friend in the world," Sadie groaned.

"Knock it off, Gold. She knows you're busy." Ryan grinned. "Besides, she's got me to keep her company." He glanced over at her. "Did you pick your costume out yet?"

"No." Sadie shook her head, mentally scrambling for ideas. "I haven't even invited Bo yet."

"Oh, Bo knows."

"Bo knows about the party?"

"Yeah, Ana invited him." Ryan's face fell again. "Uh-oh. Did I screw up that time?"

"You're fine." Sadie followed her costar through the conference room door, wondering what, if anything, went on inside that adorable but empty head of his. "But if I do ever decide to throw a surprise party, remind me not to ask you for help."

"MG and RG! Perfect," Sylvia called from the head of the table. She waved them over. "Come, sit."

Sadie glanced around at the handful of people assembled. Aside from Sylvia, there was Tanya, of course, pouring coffee for two people Sadie assumed were executive producers. Next to Sylvia was a pretty young woman who looked vaguely familiar, but Sadie couldn't place her. An actress, maybe? She wasn't sure. Rounding out the group was a spry woman in a bow tie and glasses. The woman sprung up and headed toward her.

"Sadie Gold?"

"Yes."

"Meg Fay." She handed Sadie a business card.

Sadie took the card and shook the woman's hand. Confident, firm grip. Energetic presence. Great style. Sadie liked her already. "Nice to meet you, Meg."

Meg repeated her introduction to Ryan.

"Cool tie," Ryan observed.

"Thanks." Meg led Ryan and Sadie over to the table. "You both have my card. Don't lose it. Think of that number as the bat signal. Your protection against the bad guys."

Bad guys? Sadie glanced toward the head of the table. *Did Sylvia hire a security detail?*

When everyone was seated, Sylvia said, "I've decided

to hire someone local to handle PR here, and Meg is one the best publicists in Chicago."

Ah, *those* bad guys. Great. Sadie perked up. Maybe Meg could help her figure out a way to bury all the bullshit getting shoveled on the internet.

"You two came in together." She glanced between Ryan and Sadie. "Anything *personal* I need to be aware of?"

"Like, are we dating?" Sadie asked.

"Hell, no," Ryan said. "No offense, Gold."

"None taken," Sadie promised him.

"I don't date costars," Ryan explained.

"Smart man." Meg nodded in approval.

Sadie bit back a secret smile.

Meg gestured to the packet of papers Tanya was passing around the conference table. "Although the film doesn't premiere until May, there's been a lot of on-location shoots around the city this month, so public interest is already hot. I'd like to take advantage of that," Meg explained. "And since the tabloids have started taking an interest too, we'll need to stay ahead of them." Meg cut Sadie a look. "You'll make the rounds on all the networks later, but I want to get you in for a few interviews soon to build some momentum and maintain a positive outlook on the film and its stars. Sound good?"

"Sounds great," Sadie agreed, a little annoyed Meg had signaled her out, but mostly relieved. It would be nice to have someone in her corner fighting the bad guys and their bullshit. "Where do we start?"

"I was thinking some local talk shows, that sort of thing."

"Like *ChiChat*?"

"Definitely." Meg nodded.

"My friend Cassie works for them."

"Cassie Crow?" the pretty brunette next to Sylvia asked.

"Yep." Sadie smiled, again trying to place where she'd seen the young woman. She knew her face, that was for sure. "You know her?"

"The girl shook her head. "No. I'm just a fan. I adore her 'Coming out of the Book Closet' interview series."

"Valerie, I'm so sorry I didn't introduce you," Meg apologized to the brunette. She turned to Sadie and Ryan. "Please meet Valerie Rose the—"

"The author of *Fair is Fair*!" Sadie exclaimed. "Oh, my goodness, I can't believe I didn't put it together sooner." Sadie hopped out of her chair. "It is so nice to meet you." She hurried around the table and gave the girl a hug. "I've been trying to figure out why you looked so familiar. Your face has been staring at me from the back of your book for like a year now!"

Valerie laughed. "When you put it like that, it sounds kind of creepy."

"Thank you for writing the character of Jamie," Sadie gushed.

"Thank you for playing her," Valerie gushed right back.

"Love the energy between you two—and since I'm also Val's publicist, I'm happy to capitalize on this— but let's press pause on the mutual love fest," Meg said, straightening her bow tie. "It's time to get down to business."

Later that afternoon, Sadie was in her dressing room, forcing down a protein bar while reviewing the interview schedule Meg had put together when her phone chimed with Ana's ringtone. "Hey, you."

"Hey yourself." Ana didn't waste any time getting to the point. "You're coming to your own party, right?"

"I'm guessing you talked to Ryan." Sadie swallowed a bite of goo. "Yes, I'm coming." She peeled the rest of the wrapper off and eyed the remainder of her lunch with distaste. "Thanks for inviting Bo, by the way."

"Of course. Have you two decided on costumes?"

"I haven't even talked to him about going yet."

"I figured as much," Ana chided. "Lucky for you, I've got that covered too."

"You picked out our costumes?" Sadie asked, not putting it past Ana, party planner extraordinaire.

"Tempting, but no." Ana let out a low chuckle. "I'm not going to go full fairy godmother on you."

"Then what?" Sadie wondered.

"You'll see," her best friend promised. Sadie could hear the mischievous grin in Ana's voice. "Just promise me you'll pick something that shows off Bo's assets."

Sadie's mouth quirked. "You mean his ass?"

"Exactly."

There was a tap on her dressing room door. "I gotta go, someone's knocking."

"Perfect. See you soon, birthday girl."

Sadie ended the call and hurried to the door.

"Bo!" She glanced up and down the hall, but nobody was around.

"It's okay," he assured her. "I'm here on business."

"So, this is a professional visit then," she teased.

"Not exactly." He leaned one broad shoulder against the doorframe. "I hear there's a costume party we need to get ready for?"

Sadie's cheeks heated. "Sorry I didn't invite you myself. I kind of forgot about it."

"Accidentally on purpose?" Bo joked, reaching for her hand and pulling her into the hall.

"Could be. I've had . . . other things on my mind." She looked up at him, the ever-present sizzle of electricity zinging between them. "I'm glad you're coming to my party."

"Wouldn't miss it." Bo cleared his throat. "But," he said briskly, tugging her down the hall, "we don't have a lot of time."

"Time for what?"

"You'll see."

The note of mischief in his voice reminded Sadie of her best friend. "What are you and Ana up to?"

They rounded a corner, and Bo dropped her hand, maintaining a professional distance as he led her through a maze of several more hallways, all bustling with activity from the various productions filming in the warehouse. "Thirty years old." He whistled. "How's it feel to be on the brink of a new decade?"

"You tell me, old man," Sadie shot back. She was joking, but beneath the banter, this birthday had her on edge more than she cared to admit. She thought of all the usual adages, you're as young as you feel, blah blah blah. But the reality was that in a few days, she wouldn't be a twenty-something anymore. She'd be a thirty-something.

"Harsh." Bo placed a hand over his chest, as if she'd wounded him. "Ah, here we are." He nodded at the set of wide double doors up ahead.

"Wardrobe?" She glanced back at him. "We can't just waltz in there and help ourselves, you know."

"Why not?"

"You're going to get us into trouble," she whispered, but her warning lacked heat. It was hard to resist him when he was like this. Playful. Relaxed. Bo in any mood was tempting, but Bo in a good mood was irresistible.

His golden-brown eyes were sweet as warm honey as he raised a cocky eyebrow, giving her his scoundrel's grin. Bo pulled a keycard from his pocket. "Trust me."

Sadie's heart flip-flopped in her chest. He had to know what that smile did to her. "Lead the way, flyboy."

"I love it when you talk dirty." He chuckled and unlocked the door. "That does give me an idea for our costumes, though."

"What?" Sadie asked, gazing at the endless rows of costumes lining the studio's wardrobe department.

"*Star Wars*," he suggested, weaving between the aisles.

"As much as I admire the rebel princess, I am not enabling your Princess Leia fetish," Sadie warned Bo as she trailed behind him. "No cinnamon-bun Leia."

He glanced over his shoulder, golden eyes flashing as they moved down the length of her body. "I was thinking metal-bikini Leia."

"Perv." Sadie rolled her eyes. "Does every man in the galaxy have that fantasy?"

"Probably," he admitted.

She smirked, tugging an elegantly embroidered velvet coat off a hanger. "*Interview with a Vampire*?"

"No fangs." Bo made a face.

Sadie laughed. "Okay." They both fell silent, sifting through the racks. She paused, reaching for a billowy white shirt. "Oooh, pirates."

"I'm not enabling your Jack Sparrow fetish," Bo countered. "Does every woman have that fantasy?"

"Not me." Sadie turned to face him. "I was thinking about *Captain Blood*. You know, Errol Flynn?"

"Hmm. Maybe." He eyed the shirt speculatively. "Who would you be?"

"Olivia de Havilland's character. Arabella Bishop."

"I'm not sure people would get it." Bo scratched his

chin. "We need something a little more recognizable, abeja."

An idea blossomed in her brain. Bo must have made a similar connection, because just as she opened her mouth, he also suggested, "Robin Hood!"

"It's perfect," Sadie beamed, shoving the pirate shirt back on the rack. "I can be Maid Marian. I have a Ren Faire dress that will work great. And speaking of Renaissance Faires, you . . ." She turned to Bo, gaze dragging slowly up his body. "You get to wear tights."

"What?"

"It's Robin Hood; you *have* to wear tights," Sadie insisted.

"I changed my mind, I'm good with the fangs," Bo declared.

"Oh, no you don't. It's my birthday and you're doing this my way."

Bo leaned forward in a snarky imitation of a courtly bow. "As you wish, m'lady."

CHAPTER 22

ON HALLOWEEN MORNING, at precisely 6:52 a.m., the exact time Sadie had been born, the door to her apartment burst open and Ana, the one-woman birthday brigade, barged in. Making Sadie wish that one, she hadn't given Ana a key to her place; and two, she had been born later in the day. Much later.

Twelve hours later, while Ana gave some last-minute instructions to a trio of servers, Sadie glanced around the yacht's decked-out dining area. Her best friend had out-done herself. In one corner of the room, a bartender was mixing something in a pitcher. In another, a DJ was testing sound and light equipment. Sadie thought she spied a karaoke machine. Ana sauntered over to Sadie and handed her a glass. "Try this."

"What is it?" Sadie eyed the glowing pink liquid warily.

"Your signature birthday drink. I came up with the recipe myself. Bottoms up."

"I don't know." Sadie hesitated. Usually she never re-fused one of Ana's cocktails, but she still had a couple weeks left of filming and didn't need to show up on set with a hangover. That damn *411* site would have a field day.

"What do you mean, you don't know?" Ana scoffed. "It's your birthday. Your fucking thirtieth birthday. You are entitled to relax and enjoy a drink, damn it. Now, bottoms up, bitch!"

"Okay, okay. I'm drinking, I'm drinking." Sadie took a healthy sip from her cocktail.

"Well?" Ana raised her eyebrows expectantly over the rim of her own glass.

"It's good," Sadie admitted. Sweet yet tart, she could barely taste the alcohol, which experience told her meant there was way more in there than she thought. She took another sip, tension easing out of her. Oh yeah, there was definitely more booze in this then there seemed. "You know," Sadie drawled, nose tickling with the promise of a good buzz to come. "You're right."

"Of course, I'm right," Ana replied automatically. After a beat, her mouth curved saucily. "What am I right about?"

"It's my birthday."

"It is."

"My fucking *thirtieth* birthday."

"Yep."

"And it's about time I relaxed and enjoyed it, damn it," Sadie declared.

"Finally!" Ana whooped and raised her glass. "There's my girl. Lord, I've missed you. Let's get this party started!"

Several hours and almost as many signature birthday cocktails later, the birthday girl was beaming, watching her best friend light the candles on her birthday cake. And not just any cake. A *donut* cake. Ana had outdone herself, creating a towering masterpiece built from tiered stacks of homemade donut holes. Ana told her she'd made each layer a different flavor, and Sadie was looking forward to tasting every single kind.

Ana had also said she'd considered designing the tower of donuts to be shaped like a certain part of the female anatomy. And while Sadie was curious to know how that would have turned out, she was glad she didn't have to blow candles off a giant donut hole vagina.

Instead, Sadie prepared to blow out the line of purple candles marching in a row, spiraling around the layers of donuts. Sadie took in the smiling faces shining all around her—thirty candles provided quite the glow to view them by—thirty-one, if you counted the one for good luck, which she did. As her friends sang a rousing rendition of the birthday song, Sadie closed her eyes and prepared to make her wish.

It came to her easily. She blinked, momentarily startled by the realization that what she wanted most in the world hadn't changed for a very long time. Deep down, year after year, her wish was always the same. Sadie blew out the candles, careful to save the good luck one for the end.

Applause burst around the room as the last flame winked out of existence. Sadie studied the wisps of smoke rising in curling tendrils, watching them fade away to nothing. She'd expected to feel a wave of melancholy, a sense of despair about growing older, but instead, she was filled with a buzzing sensation, and not just from her birthday cocktails. No, this was the same feeling she'd had the day of the reading, the day she'd seen Bo again for the first time.

Hope.

She turned, searching for Bo among the crowd. As if knowing she was looking for him, he appeared before her, grinning as he tugged on the long gauzy veil she wore as part of her costume. "You're lucky you didn't light yourself on fire while blowing out all those candles, Maid Marian."

Sadie matched his grin. "I appreciate the concern, Sir Robin."

"Can I get you a piece of cake, m'lady?" he asked, gesturing to where Ana was directing the cutting and serving of her creation.

"Later." Sadie glanced around the crowded room. Everywhere she looked, people were eating and drinking, laughing and chatting. It was nice to see everyone having such a good time, and it had been fun to catch up with friends she hadn't seen since college, but what she really wanted was a few minutes alone with Bo, preferably somewhere quiet. "How about we take a walk first?" she suggested. "Work up an appetite."

With a jaunty bow, Bo swept off his feathered cap and offered her his arm. "Your wish is my command."

Sadie laughed, delighted by his chivalric antics. "Well, I am the birthday girl," she agreed.

He tucked her hand against his side and led her up the steps to a heated glass-enclosed deck. The area was deserted, a stunning view of the night sky spreading out before them, city lights sparkling along the shoreline. "Oh, this is perfect." Sadie sighed with pleasure, leaning her head on Bo's chest and absorbing the quiet. "Thanks for coming tonight."

"Of course."

"And for wearing the tights."

"Excuse me," he huffed, "I was informed these are called leggings."

"Whatever you want to call them, that's one wish granted." She stroked her fingers over his bearded chin.

"The only thing that would have made it better was if you'd shaved this into a goatee."

"Sorry, sweetheart, a man has to draw the line somewhere." Bo tugged at the hem of his costume's leather jerkin. "It's bad enough I feel like everyone can see my balls in this thing."

"Oh?" Sadie's mouth twitched. "I hadn't noticed," she lied, glancing down to admire the powerful swell of his thighs encased in the skintight green fabric.

He chuckled. "So that was your wish, huh? To see me in tights?"

"I thought you said they were leggings," she teased, stepping closer. "And yes, it was my wish, but not *the* wish." She tipped her chin, staring up into his golden tiger eyes. "Not my big birthday wish."

Bo bent his head, mouth almost brushing hers as he asked, "What did you wish for, then?"

"She can't tell you that!" Ana announced, appearing at the top of the stairs and cutting through their quiet moment as neatly as she'd cut the cake. She joined Bo and Sadie on the deck, Cassie, Delaney, and Bonnie trailing behind. Ana clapped Bo on the shoulder. "Why don't you go help yourself to some cake," she suggested.

Bo took in the faces of the women standing in front of him and got the hint. "I think I'll go get a piece of cake," he said.

"Wise man, Peter Pan," Ana quipped, watching Bo head for the stairs. "By the way, your assets look great in those tights."

"I'm Robin Hood," Bo sniffed. "And they're called leggings," he added haughtily, blowing Sadie a kiss before disappearing down the stairs as the girls burst into giggles.

Ana pulled Sadie in for a hug. "Having a good time, birthday girl?"

"I was," Sadie teased.

"Oh, please." Delaney shook her head, her tall dome-shaped black-and-white wig teetering. "The Prince of Thieves has been stealing all your time tonight."

"Goth Marge Simpson is right," Cassie agreed. "The birthday girl needs to spend some time with her friends."

"Goth Marge Simpson?" Delaney frowned at Cassie in confusion.

"Isn't that your costume?" Cassie asked.

"I'm the Bride of Frankenstein for fudge sake!" Delaney adjusted her giant wig again. "And what's up with *your* hair?" she asked Cassie. "You look like you stuck your finger in an electric socket."

More giggles erupted, and Sadie joined in. She'd missed this. Missed hanging out with her friends. Life had been much too serious lately.

"I can't believe you don't recognize Hermione Granger." Cassie pouted as the five of them settled onto plush couches nestled in a sunken section of the deck.

"I can't believe you didn't recognize the Bride of Frankenstein," Delaney shot back. "I wore this to the class party and even my ankle biters knew who I was supposed to be."

"I'm sure your preschoolers would have recognized I was Hermione too."

"Now I get it!" Sadie interrupted before the two of them started brawling over costumes. "That's why Logan is wearing the horrible sweater with the giant letter *R* on it, right? Your ginger-haired Scot is supposed to be Ron Weasley."

"Oh!" Bonnie's eyes widened in belated understanding. "I thought the *R* stood for Reid."

"Why would he wear that as a costume?" Ana wondered, nose wrinkling.

"Because that's his last name," Bonnie explained in her professor voice.

"Right. But it's a *costume*." Ana sighed wistfully. "I was hoping he'd wear the kilt."

Everyone echoed her sigh. At least that was something they all could agree on. They all liked the kilt.

"We talked about that," Cassie admitted. "I suggested Claire and Jamie, but Logan told me he wasn't wearing a kilt outside in the 'fecking Chicago cold' ever again." Cassie grinned wickedly. "Something about Baltic balls."

Snorts of laughter bounced off the glass windows.

"Confession. I've been trying to figure out your costume all night, Ana," Delaney admitted, giving Ana a once-over. "With all that leather and green skin, who are you supposed to be? The dominatrix version of the Wicked Witch of the West?"

"Good guess, but no." Ana raised an arm, showing off her painted green skin. "I'm an alien assassin." She shrugged. "It wasn't my idea. I wanted to be Belle and the Beast, but Ryan wanted to come as Galaxy God or something."

"Star King." Sadie laughed, correcting Ana. "It's from his movie last year. I can't believe you're still seeing him," she teased, glancing at her friend. "Is something more going on between you two?"

"Why does there have to be more? We're both in it for a good time, that's all," Ana insisted. She circled a green finger in the air. "There'll be no riding off into the sunset for us."

"Why not?" Cassie asked.

"Because he's not the one." Ana shrugged.

"Don't worry. Your Mr. Right is out there somewhere," Bonnie promised.

"Thanks, Ariel." Ana snorted. "But I'm beginning to think that's not in the cards for me. I've kissed a lot of frogs, and still no prince."

"Same," Delaney snarked. "This costume is about as close as you're going to see me get to ever being a bride." She patted her oversized wig. "Maybe I'll save this for when I go on sad single-lady cruises. I can hide Bingo in here and smuggle him onboard."

"How is Bingo doing?" Sadie asked. She loved hearing stories about Delaney's pet chinchilla.

"The usual. Spoiled rotten and lavished with affection by his perpetually single owner."

"His owner doesn't *have* to be single," Cassie observed drily.

"Maybe his owner *wants* to be single," Delaney shot back, just as drily.

"You may change your mind," Cassie said, a knowing little smile tugging at her lips.

"Oh, because she's married now, this one thinks she knows everything," Ana teased.

"Yep," Delaney agreed. "And because her sexy Scot of a husband was once a confirmed bachelor, she thinks she has us bachelorettes figured out."

"Knock it off." Cassie shook her head, cheeks flushing. "I'm just saying, never say never. Anything is possible." She looked to Sadie for support. "Right, Sadie?"

"Um, sure."

"I mean, you never thought you'd see Bo again, and now you two are working together, going to parties in matching costumes . . ." Cassie continued.

"Right?" Ana added. "I told her it was fate."

"Do you ever get the feeling you're the butt of a big cosmic joke?" Sadie wondered.

"What about big butts?" Bonnie asked, confused.

"Oh my God, Becky." Delaney rolled her eyes. "That's not what she said."

Sadie snickered. "I mean fate. Destiny. I wasn't sure if I believed in any of that stuff, but I'm starting to wonder."

"Logan's family has a saying." Cassie nodded. "People plan and God laughs."

Delaney raised an eyebrow. "Meaning?"

"I kind of took it to mean that no matter what you do, the universe has its own plan."

"I can believe that." Bonnie shrugged. "Look at what happened with Theo and me. That certainly wasn't in any of my plans."

On the deck below, someone started singing "Sweet Child O' Mine" in a clipped but slightly tipsy British accent.

"Speak of the devil," Delaney snorted. "Or should I say, the duke?"

"Oh dear, I think Theo's discovered the karaoke machine." Bonnie gathered the fins of her mermaid tail and stood. "I better get back down there before he starts in on 'Paradise City.'"

Laughing, the girls headed for the stairs. Bringing up the rear, Ana tugged on Sadie's arm. "Starting to believe I could be right, huh?"

"About what?"

"Fate. You and Bo."

"Maybe." Sadie sighed. She wanted to believe Ana could be right, that she and Bo could have their fairy-tale happy ending, but there was so much more to the story. So much that Ana didn't know. Sadie pushed the dark thoughts away before they had a chance to form. It was her birthday, a night for wishes, for dreams to come true. "What was it that Cassie said? Never say never."

"Exactly." Ana's smile was warm and full of hope and love. "I just want you to be happy. You know that, right?"

Affection pulled at Sadie's heartstrings. She had amazing friends. Another thing she was realizing she took for granted.

"Sadie, are you crying?"

"No." Sadie sniffed, swiping at her eyes. "Okay, yes, I'm crying. But it's the good kind of crying. Besides, it's my party, and I'll cry if I want to."

"Sounds like someone just picked out their karaoke song."

A blubbery laugh burst out of Sadie. God, she loved her friends. "Fine. But only if you sing with me."

"What? And upstage the birthday girl on her special day?" Ana's voice lost its snarky tone. "Seriously. What's wrong? I hate to see my best friend in tears on her birthday."

Sadie shook her head. "I'm not crying because I'm sad. It's because I have the most amazing friends in the world."

"Aw." Ana beamed. "I'd hug you, but I don't want to get body paint all over you."

"Then I'll hug you." Sadie reached up and wrapped her arms around her friend. Like usual, their height difference put her at breast level, giving her an up-close-and-personal view of Ana's very busty and very green cleavage. After a moment, Sadie pulled back, mouth quirking. "That is a *lot* of green boob."

"It was a lot of green paint." Ana cocked an eyebrow. "I promised Ryan he could help me wash all this off tonight."

"Why do you tell me these things?" Sadie asked in mock horror.

With a wicked laugh, Ana pulled Sadie toward the stairs. "Come on, you still haven't had a piece of cake. We better hurry and get you some before Ryan eats it all. Your costar likes carbs almost as much as he likes my tits."

"Didn't need to know that either!" Sadie groaned, hurrying after her friend.

CHAPTER 23

THIS WAS IT. The last big shoot of the movie. Bo's stomach churned as he walked through the scene step-by-step one more time. After all the wild stunts he'd planned. The fights he'd choreographed. The buildings he'd jumped off . . . To have the future of his career hinge on a scene in a shopping mall, well, that was the movies for you.

He'd spent the first half of the week working hand in hand with the actors, their doubles, and the specialized stunt film crew. Running the sequences, reviewing them over and over. Making sure everyone was as prepared as possible before they arrived on set.

Actual time inside the mall was limited. The permits only allowed them to shoot on location after hours. So long as the crew managed to capture the footage they needed and cleared out before the doors opened for business in the morning, they were good.

It was why Annoyed Dave had arranged the permit for a Saturday night. The mall opened later on Sundays, buying them a few more hours. Still, they'd roped off the area where they planned to film and had their own security detail working with the mall cops to ensure nobody ended up somewhere they shouldn't. Not an easy feat considering the size of this shoot.

Dozens of nondescript extras milled around in the holding pen. Bo caught sight of Sylvia's assistant Tanya checking the extras in, ever-present clipboard in hand. The principals were at hair and makeup and would report to the set soon. He glanced at his watch. So far, so good.

"Nervous?"

Bo glanced up to see a gruff beefy man striding toward him.

"Vic!" He hurried over and slapped the old guy on the back. "Couldn't stay away, huh?" Bo kept his voice light while his stomach bucked, nerves kicking in. He'd been hoping Vic would resist the urge to check on him. Tonight's shoot was going to be hard enough without having his mentor there watching.

It was his own damn fault, though. He'd told Vic how important this last sequence was during their conference call last week. Bo had all but dangled a carrot in the man's face. Ah well, since he was here, Bo would make the most of it. "Wanna take a look around?"

"Don't have to ask me twice." Vic chuckled and followed Bo out to the area that had been marked for the set, dodging crews still adjusting lights, running power cords, and arranging mics. Bo walked Vic through the choreography. It was a classic on-foot chase scene, followed by a fight scene that would begin on the ground level and travel up the escalator for two floors before shifting to the third floor of the mall where another foot chase scene would finish off the sequence.

"Isn't there a car chase too?"

"In the parking garage, yeah." Bo nodded. "But we filmed that last week."

"Smart." Vic rubbed his chin thoughtfully. "Who'd you use for wheel guys?"

"Alexis and Mike."

"Nice." Vic grinned. "Did Lexie run Mike's ass into the ground?"

"Like always." Bo returned Vic's grin. "He's determined to catch her, but nobody can handle hairpin turns like she can, and this scene had plenty of 'em."

"You did good, Ibarra." Vic looked around the set one more time. "I hardly feel needed here."

"No offense, man, but that's kind of the point, right?" Bo chuckled, again trying to keep his tone light. "Windy City Stunts is in good hands."

"I know it is," Vic agreed.

"Does that mean you're ready to start having our 'talk' soon?" Bo asked, tired of tiptoeing around the subject. "Be straight with me, Vic. This is the biggest sequence in the one of the biggest projects our company has taken on. If tonight's shoot goes well, then you gotta believe I'm ready to take on WCS solo."

"I already believe that, Ibarra," his boss said softly. "Wouldn't have gotten into business with you in the first place otherwise. When we formed this company, I told you it would be yours one day, and I meant it."

"Then what's the hold up?" Bo couldn't help the dash of exasperation that crept into his voice. He'd started WCS with Vic almost a decade ago.

Vic bristled defensively. "It's just, well, it's not so easy to let go. What am I supposed to do with myself?"

"Rest," Bo suggested. "Take it easy."

"Don't put me in a goddamn nursing home just yet." Vic scowled.

Bo shook his head, his laughter very real this time. "You sound just like my dad."

The old guy's gruff face broke into a grin. "How's he doin?"

"Well. Still believes rest is something you do after you die."

Vic guffawed. "See? He gets it. Our jobs are our life."

"Not knockin' that." Bo held up a hand. "I'm not trying to put you in a nursing home, and I'm not trying to put you in your grave either, but come on, man. At this rate, you're going to be *thinking* about retiring longer than you'll get to enjoy your retirement."

"If I sound like your old man, you sound like my wife." Vic scratched his chin.

"She has a point. There's more to living than working, you know," Bo said, sensing the stubborn bastard might finally be wavering. "I thought you wanted to travel more."

Vic sighed. "Claudia wants to go on a cruise."

"That sounds nice."

"If by nice you mean boring."

"Oh, come on. Now you sound like my nephew. I bet there is all kinds of trouble you can get into. Show off how to cannonball from the high dive. Ride on a dolphin or parasail or something."

"Hmph." Vic was silent for a moment, watching as the crew taped down the last of the cords. "Ride a dolphin. Really?"

"Pretty sure." Bo hid a smile. "Tell you what. If you fill out the paperwork passing sole ownership of WCS over to me, at least to get things started, I'll see about arranging that dolphin ride. Consider it a retirement gift."

Vic made a face.

"I meant a bon voyage gift," Bo quickly amended.

"I've never ridden a dolphin before . . ." Vic narrowed his eyes, considering. He nodded to himself. "All right, cowboy. Let's see you get through this shoot. If all goes well tonight, I'll have my guy draw up the papers."

"You're serious?" Bo held his breath. After all this time, all his hard work—it was the suggestion to ride a dolphin that did the trick?

"Yep. Get this one in the can, and it's a done deal. I'll hand over the reins and ride off into the sunset." Vic held out his hand. "On a dolphin."

Bo grinned and exhaled. Elation swelling inside his chest as he shook his soon-to-be-former business partner's hand. Then he glanced around, taking in the bustle of activity, and the weight of responsibility settled over him. No one, and nothing, better fuck this up.

"Bo," Sadie said, heart pounding in time to the steady thrum of the escalator's motorized steps rolling up and up and, *oh God*, up. "I'm going to fuck this up."

"Abeja, I know you're scared." Bo's voice was calm, a steady presence at her side. "But I also know you can do this."

"Really?" Sadie squeaked, sarcasm mixing with fear. "Because I don't know that, and I'm the one that's supposed to be doing this."

Ryan joined them on the platform at the foot of the escalator. "Ready?"

"Almost," Bo said. "Right, Sadie?"

Sadie bit her lip. She knew they were on a tight schedule tonight, and she was holding things up. Her heart was pounding now, hard and fast, like it was getting ready to burst out of her chest and fly away. Sadie wished she could do that. Turn tail and bust through the ropes cording off the set. She glanced over her shoulder. Behind her, dozens of extras and crew members stood watching, waiting.

From up on her platform, Sylvia called Bo to come over.

"Have I ever told you what scares me?" Ryan asked casually while they stood waiting.

Sadie shook her head, throat too tight to speak. She knew what he was doing. She'd told him about her "escalator problem" when they'd rehearsed this scene earlier in the week. For some reason, she'd been fine then. No fear. Maybe it was because the escalator they'd practiced on hadn't been as big, or maybe it was because they hadn't been in a mall, and her childhood memories hadn't been triggered.

When she was little, she'd spend minutes standing at the edge of the escalator in Water Tower Place, talking herself into taking that first step. What if she missed? What if she tripped and fell? What if her leg got caught? As the questions piled up on top of each other, her lungs would freeze, and her stomach would twist and flop like she was already falling. And then, once she finally managed to get on, she'd watch in horror as the steps flattened, disappearing into a crack in the floor. Her heart would pound in fear, convinced she'd be sucked into that dark void too.

"Bananas," Ryan said.

"What?" she asked, exhaling the word in a puff of surprise. "Did you say you're scared of bananas?" Sadie turned to stare at her costar. His unexpected response had broken the choke hold on her throat.

He nodded. "Yep. Something about them weirds me out. The way people peel them before eating them, like Hannibal Lecter, peeling away the skin of his victims before devouring his next meal."

"I never thought about it that way." Sadie wrinkled her nose. "Gross."

"And then there's that stringy stuff," Ryan added, mouth turning down in revulsion. "What *is* that stuff?" Not waiting for her to answer, he continued, "But the scariest thing, the thing that haunts my dreams, are those damn dancing bananas."

"Dancing bananas," Sadie repeated. "Are you serious?"

"Those things are freaky as hell." Ryan shuddered.

Sadie pictured this tall, muscled action hero, waking up screaming from a nightmare about dancing bananas. She repressed a giggle. "Thanks for sharing that with me." She patted her costar on the shoulder.

Bracing her legs, Sadie clenched her hands into fists and stared up at her mechanical nemesis as she began to go through her breathing exercises. She'd already jumped out a window and somersaulted two stories to the ground, she could ride an escalator a few floors up.

By the time she counted to five, legs relaxed and hands loose at her side, Bo was back. Emily, Sadie's stunt double, was with him. So was Tanya, clipboard in hand.

"I talked it over with Sylvia, and it's going to be tricky to get right, but I think we can film the bulk of this sequence with Emily."

"We'll need extra time in the editing room," Tanya said, flipping through her notes, "and some of the blocking for the fight scene with Henchman One and Two had to be reworked, but Emily's already been prepped."

"That's not necessary." Sadie glanced up at Bo. "I can do it."

His brown eyes flashed, copper sparks warning her he was on edge. Bo leaned in close, voice so low she barely heard him over the hum of the escalator. "I told you at that first meeting, I'm not here to make anyone do anything they're not comfortable with."

"It's fine. I'll do it."

And there went the muscle in his jaw. Yep, he was pissed. It was odd how she could tell, even with the beard. But she did. She knew he was clenching up like a crabby little clam. Knew if she touched his cheek right now, it would be rock hard with tension.

Bo glanced at Ryan and Emily. "Excuse us for a moment, please." To Tanya, he said, "Tell Sylvia to have the crew take a short five."

Without waiting for an answer, Bo took Sadie's arm and led her off the set, past the gaping camera crew and through a side door that opened to a sparse, utilitarian hallway Sadie guessed was used by mall employees. He gripped her shoulders and turned her to face him. "I understand you're scared, abeja. It's okay to back off. Let Emily take over. There's too much riding on getting this right."

Part of Sadie wanted to take the escape he offered. But a bigger part wanted to prove to Bo—and the rest of the world—that she had what it takes. Like her character Jamie, she was going to face her fears. "Remember that first fight scene?"

"We don't have time for this." Bo ran a hand over his face, frustration written in every line of his body.

Sadie forged ahead. She had a lot riding on this too. "You asked me to trust you, remember?"

"What has that got to do with—"

"Now I'm asking you to trust me," Sadie interrupted, notching her chin higher. "I admit I panicked for a minute, but I'm over it. I'm ready to film the scene."

"If you get halfway through the sequence and start panicking again, we'll have to reset the scene and reshoot. There's not enough time."

"I won't panic."

Bo stared down at her, and Sadie knew he was weighing the pros and cons. She pressed her advantage. "Consider me a calculated risk."

His lips raised in a half smile, but she noted the tension didn't leave his body. He was worried she was going to fuck this up. Not that Sadie could blame him; she had told him she would.

"Okay," Bo said a moment later, surprising her. He nodded. "I trust you, abeja. If you say you can do it . . ." His lucky-penny eyes met hers, muted copper, warm but wary. "Then let's do it."

Relief flooded her. "Thank you," she whispered, wrapping her arms around Bo. "Thank you for trusting me."

"Don't make me regret it," he joked, squeezing her in a hug.

Beneath the teasing, Sadie could tell he also meant it. His body was strung tight, muscles tense with nervous energy. Getting this scene right was as important to him as it was to her. And he was putting his trust in her. A thrill zipped through Sadie, confidence roaring to life. It burned inside her, a fearless ball of excitement. Breaking all the rules they'd carefully been playing by, she pulled Bo's mouth down to hers, channeling everything she was feeling into the kiss.

He kissed her back with a fierce desperation, tongue thrusting deep. His fingers splayed across her back, drifting lower until he was cupping her ass, pulling her closer.

"Fuck, I can't wait for this to be over so I can be inside you," he groaned, kneading her bottom as he rubbed himself against her.

"Same," she panted. They had waited so long to be together, and were so close to the end of this, so close to finally being able to—

The door banged open, the sound echoing off the cinderblock walls of the barren hallway. "Ibarra!" someone barked.

Sadie didn't recognize the voice. She froze, staring up at Bo as footsteps shuffled on the concrete behind her.

"Did you get a handle on things or what?" The footsteps came to an abrupt stop. "Oh." There was an awful, awkward pause. "I see that you did."

Bo slid his hands off her butt, face full of embarrassed chagrin like a boy caught with his fingers in the cookie jar. He cleared his throat. "Vic, I'd like you to meet the lead of this production, Miss Sadie Gold."

Sadie turned around. "Hi." She forced her lips to move into what she hoped was a smile and waved feebly. "Nice to meet you."

"Vic is my partner," Bo explained. "Co-owner of Windy City Stunts." He paused, the ghost of a grin creeping across his face. "For a little longer, anyway."

"Ma'am." Vic tipped his head to Sadie, then turned his full attention to Bo. The older man's face was lined with concern. "I'm not too sure about that."

"Excuse me?" Bo went deathly still.

Sadie thought he'd been stiff with nerves before, now he was downright rigid.

"You've got a gag to run, an entire production crew is waiting on you, and I find you in here, manhandling the talent?"

As the talent in question, Sadie was about to interject that nobody had been manhandling her, but Vic continued.

"Where's your head, man? In your pants?"

"Mind your own business," Bo ground out, teeth clenched.

"This is my business!" Vic hollered.

Sadie almost laughed. Bo just got served the same response he'd given her when she'd tried the same argument.

But there was nothing comical about his face right now. Above the dark curve of his beard, his face was ashen. Her stomach churned. This was her fault. If she'd kept her shit together and just run the stunt in the first place, none of this would be happening.

The door banged open again. All three of them jumped, heads jerking toward the hall entrance.

"There you are." Tanya tucked her clipboard under her arm and marched toward them. "Sylvia says if you're not back on set in thirty seconds, she's going to tell the crew to start rolling with the double."

"She can't do that!" both men objected. They stared at each other for a moment.

Bo was the first to recover. "She can't run the stunt without the coordinator on set."

"It's against OSHA," Vic declared, aghast.

"Then I suggest the coordinator get back on set," Tanya snapped.

Whoa. Sadie drew back in surprise. She hadn't seen this side of Sylvia's assistant before.

"We'll continue this conversation later," Bo muttered to Vic under his breath.

"You bet your ass we will," the old guy shot back.

Sadie moved to follow the two men heading for the exit, but Tanya stopped her. "You might want to stop by Zara." She tapped her clipboard, eyeing Sadie's recently kissed mouth pointedly. "Have her give you a touch-up."

Heat fanned out across Sadie's cheeks, but she nodded mutely and hurried out the door.

She'd warned Bo she'd fuck up tonight.

At least she was a woman of her word.

Bo kept his gaze locked on Sadie as she ran up the escalator, dodging extras and stopping occasionally to turn, head tilted toward the camera, as she gazed back down the steps and checked on the progress of the bad guys who were in pursuit. He wondered how much of the panic on her face was real. True to her word, she'd committed to running the gag, and the fear her character was supposed to show as she fought her way to the top of the escalator appeared to be very, very real.

Beside him, Vic watched as well, grunting occasionally, usually after a particularly crafty bit of choreography. "Oooh." Vic winced as Sadie's character gave Henchman Number Two a knee to the balls. "Nice one."

"I wasn't manhandling her, you know," Bo said quietly.

"Really?" Vic kept his gaze trained on the action. "Then it was some other man's hands I saw on the leading lady's ass?"

"It's not like that. We're . . . she's my—" He stopped himself.

"She's what?" Vic turned to Bo, salt-and-pepper eyebrows raised. "Don't fucking tell me she's your girlfriend."

Bo ground his lips together.

"For Chrissakes, Ibarra. You know better." Vic paused, frowning. "At least, I thought you did."

Vic had every right to be pissed. He was right. If the roles had been reversed. If Bo had entered that hallway and found one of his crew making out with a cast member, he'd likely pull him from the production. "Are you having second thoughts?"

"You know I am." Vic shook his head. "You would too. At best, your behavior was unprofessional as hell. At worst, it could be construed as harassment. The actions of all WCS members reflects directly on the company, no more so than the head of the company. As the owner, we set the bar." Vic stabbed a finger in Bo's chest. "You lower that bar and our reputation, and the success of our company, drops too. Word gets around. Fast."

Bo had nothing to say to that. Again, Vic was right. He watched as the scene reset, cameras moving in for close-ups as the actors ran through the same sequence again. Depending on how long it took for Sylvia to get what she was aiming for, this part could take a while. Luckily, they had the time. Despite the delay at the start of the night, the shoot was running on schedule.

At least he'd done something right. All the hours he'd spent prepping the cast and his crew earlier this week were paying off. His jaw tightened painfully, a muscle spasming in his cheek. In a blink, everything he'd worked for was at risk. Jeopardized by one moment.

All these weeks of filming, he and Sadie had been careful to keep things professional on set. And then, when they were almost at the end, when it was almost over . . . *Pinche mierda.*

"You're right," he finally said. "I was so worried some-one would fuck tonight up, and here I went and did it myself."

"We all fuck up sometimes." Vic sighed heavily. "You're like a son to me, you know that, Ibarra?" He slapped Bo on the back. "And you are a hell of a stunt man. I know you can handle the company. I was just . . . surprised. I never expected that kind of thing from you."

Bo nodded. He didn't expect it from himself. But with Sadie, all bets were off. That wasn't an excuse, though. "It won't happen again."

"I sure as shit hope not," Vic said. "At least you were off set. Away from the rest of the cast and crew. You know what kind of shit a story like this would stir if word got out."

"I'll make sure it doesn't," Bo assured him. Vic was

still angry, but he'd laid off the f-bombs and had down-graded to shit. The old guy was cooling off. "Are we good?"

Vic sighed. "Don't take this the wrong way, but I think it's best we wait until we see how this plays out. If I draw up the papers now and then this shit hits the fan, the whole company'll be screwed."

"What are you saying?" Frustration simmered in Bo's gut.

"I'm saying I'm not doing anything until I'm convinced this isn't going to be a problem." Vic's mouth was set, his mind made up. "Let's get this thing wrapped. Wait it out a little bit. The holidays are coming up. If in the new year things seem to have blown over, then I'll get the papers drawn up. Sound good?"

Bo jerked his head in a nod. It's not like he had a choice in the matter. All his life, he'd just wanted to get to a place where he could be in control, call the shots. But right now, he felt as close to that goal as he'd been ten years ago.

Fucking hell.

CHAPTER 24

FUCKING HELL.

The words had been playing on a deranged loop in Bo's head for the last eight hours or so. He sat up in bed, staring at his phone. *Fucking hell. Fucking hell. Fucking hell.*

Clark lay curled at Bo's side, tail swishing over the screen. "Not now, buddy." Bo nudged the persistent pile of fur out of the way and swiped through the story again.

Unfortunately, no matter how many times he swiped, the details didn't change. The images didn't erase. There, for all the world to see, was video footage of Bo and Sadie, locked in a hot embrace. And even though the quality was grainy, the fluorescent lighting of the mall hallway captured every detail.

Bo groaned. He had to grab her ass, didn't he? That seemed to be the internet's favorite aspect of the clip. A glutton for punishment, Bo scrolled through the comments. They ranged from clever and inventive to lewd to downright invasive, some even threatening.

Fucking hell.

How did this happen? Based on the poor quality, and the angle of the shot, Bo guessed they'd been caught on a security cam. But how did closed-circuit footage from a mall security video end up on an entertainment news feed? And so fast? Was it someone who worked at the mall? A bored security guard looking to make a quick buck?

Possible, but Bo didn't think so. While the story had spread like dry grass in a meadow fire, it was initially posted on *411 in 312* . . . the same website that broke the story about *Fair is Fair* shooting on location at Sadie's family estate. The same website that posted the bullshit about Sadie getting breast implants.

Someone at that site had an in with the film, and Bo was determined to find out who the asshole was that was writing these stories, and more importantly, track down the even bigger asshole who was leaking them.

Bo scrolled through the three stories, checking the bylines. But the only thing listed was *staff reporter.* Not surprising. If he was shoveling this shit, he'd want to keep his name hidden too.

It was a big fucking mess, and he needed to figure out how to clean it up. He had to. Disgusted, Bo tossed the phone on his nightstand and fell back into bed. The moment his head hit the pillow, Clark was there, rubbing his furry belly all over Bo's face.

"I know, buddy, I know." Bo reached up and scratched the attention-starved feline under the chin. Clark purred, pawing at Bo's beard. "Watch the claws, you little demon."

Bo wondered if Sadie had seen the story yet. Should he call her? After the all-nighter filming the escalator scene—which had gone off perfectly if you ignored the unscripted escapade in the hall—the entire cast and crew had decided to descend on a local waffle house to celebrate with an impromptu party.

Too pissed to enjoy the moment, Bo had passed on the invite. He'd thought about inviting Sadie to come back to his place, to celebrate the way they'd been planning for weeks, but considering the current situation, he thought better of the idea. He'd come home and crashed, only to wake a few hours later to discover this fucking delightful development.

Bo decided to hold off on calling Sadie. It was Sunday. Since the shoot at the stable, she'd been heading up to the Murphy estate whenever she had a free weekend. Let her enjoy the day with her grandmother.

He'd be heading up to his parents for dinner soon anyway. He could tell her then.

Sharp little teeth dug into the tip of Bo's ear. "Clark, you asshole, what have I told you about doing that!" Bo growled, rolling out of bed and dumping his furry tormentor unceremoniously to the floor. "A saddlebag. You hear me?"

Whiskers twitching above that thin stripe of dark fur that had earned him his name, Clark stared at him, unimpressed with his threats. Like Sadie, the cat had the same ability to make it seem like he was looking down at Bo, despite his disadvantage in height.

"Come on, let's get you some breakfast," Bo said, heading for the kitchen. "I want to fatten you up before I take you to the tannery."

Clark squawked irritably. Bo swore the cat understood every word. "Oh, quit your bellyaching. You know I'd never actually go through with it." He grabbed a can and opened it. "Besides, you'd make one ugly ass saddlebag."

Another squawk. Bo chuckled ruefully and set the food bowl down. Clark munched away contentedly, not a care in the world. *Lucky bastard.* Bo scrubbed a hand over his face. "Between you and me, buddy, I'm the one who's likely to get his hide tanned today."

Bo parked his SUV in front of the Murphy mansion. Usually he waited until Thanksgiving to put his motorcycle into storage, but he'd been spending so much time with Sadie, it made more sense to drive his car. He checked his phone. *Shit*. He was going to be late for Sunday dinner. This day was just getting better and better.

Bracing himself, Bo called his mother. "Hey, Mom."

"Mijo?" Worry tinged his mother's voice. "What's wrong? Why are you calling?"

"Nothing's wrong. I'm just, ah . . . I'm just going to be a little late for dinner."

"What?" Worry turned to annoyance. "Are you bleeding? At the emergency room? Do I need to call the priest?"

"I'm not dying, Mom," Bo groaned. "I'm at the Murphys. I have to talk to Sadie."

"Well, invite her to dinner, then," his mother ordered. "And don't forget to invite her grandmother too."

"But, Mom."

"No buts, Bonifacio. You either walk through my door for dinner on time or arrive late with Miss Sadie and Mrs. Esther. You hear me?"

"I hear you." His mother would have made a commendable drill sergeant.

Pulling his shit together, he made his way up the brick sidewalk to the Murphys' front door and rang the bell. It still felt strange, coming to the front entrance. For years he'd sneaked into Sadie's room through a window or waited for her in the hayloft . . .

Bo's entire body infused with heat as an idea occurred to him. He tucked it away in the back of his mind, saving it for later tonight.

* * *

Considering how the first half of his day had gone, Bo had expected dinner to be an epic disaster. The shit icing on his shit cake. He kept waiting for the other shoe to drop. But the meal ended up being pleasant. Enjoyable even. Toby had taken a shine to Mrs. Murphy immediately, and the two of them chattered and chirped like a couple of barn swallows.

It pulled at something inside Bo, something raw and untapped, to see Sadie's grandmother dote on his nephew.

Even Luna was more mellow. Polite, almost *nice* to Sadie.

After dinner, Bo drove the Murphy women back over to the big house and walked Sadie and her grandmother up to the door.

"Would you like to come in for a nightcap?" Mrs. Murphy asked.

"I'd love to, thanks." Bo nodded and followed the women inside. This could be the opportunity he'd been looking for.

Settled in the parlor with hot tea and a splash of the late Mr. Murphy's very fine whiskey, Mrs. Murphy turned to Bo.

"Your nephew is a delightful young man," Sadie's grandmother said. "How old is he?"

"Seven." Bo stirred the amber liquid in his tea.

"Luna was eighteen, then?" she asked, not with judgment, but kindly interest.

He nodded. "Yes, ma'am." Bo didn't miss the glances exchanged between Sadie and her grandmother. Thankfully, if Mrs. Murphy was interested to know about anything else to do with Toby, she was polite enough to keep it to herself.

Remembering his own manners, Bo added, "I want to

thank you again for letting us film on the estate. Especially at such short notice." ·

"Any time. I told Sadie her poppa would have been tickled beyond measure to know a movie was being made on his land. And starring his granddaughter too!"

"It's a great location for filming. Far enough from the city to make it feel like we're really out in the country, but close enough to handle the logistics of getting a crew on site." Bo sat back. "I've always loved this property," he admitted. "There's nothing quite like walking across the meadow as the sun rises. I miss it, sometimes."

"Oh?" Mrs. Murphy set her teacup down and tapped her gnarled fingers together. "Then why didn't you accept my offer? You would have made a great estate manager."

"Wait," Sadie piped up. She'd been so quiet, Bo had thought she might have fallen asleep in her chair. "You offered the manager position to Bo?"

Nana nodded. "Yes, after the accident."

Sadie shook her head, turning her attention to him. "And you turned her down?"

Bo shifted in his chair. "It just . . . wasn't for me."

"Why didn't I know about any of this?" Sadie wondered.

"Well, dear . . ." her grandmother began, voice tart, "you never asked." To Bo, she said, "It would have made me very happy if you had accepted the job and taken over for your father, but I understand the need to make one's own way in this world."

"Thank you," Bo said, throat tight with gratitude. Even though he didn't regret his decision, he'd carried the guilt of his choice for years. "And thanks for the tea, but I should probably be going. Let you ladies get some sleep."

Stifling a yawn, Sadie stood. "Good idea. I'll walk you out." At the door, she yawned again.

Bo brushed a finger down her cheek. "Tired, abeja?"

"A little. I napped when I got here this afternoon, but I still haven't caught up on sleep after the overnight shoot."

Damn. Bo frowned. Maybe his plan wasn't such a good idea after all.

"What is it?" Sadie blinked up at him. "Is something wrong?"

He glanced toward the parlor. Mrs. Murphy was still there, waiting for Sadie to help walk her up to her bedroom.

"Talk to me Bo."

"Later," he said, voice low. "Tonight. After your grandmother is in bed." He paused, then decided to go for it. They'd come so close to sticking to their pact, had been within hours of succeeding. If they were going down in flames anyway, they might as well have some fun first. "The loft."

"Oh." Sadie sucked in a breath, a knowing smile drifting across her lips as she nodded. "Okay."

"See you soon." Bo pressed a soft kiss to her forehead and then let himself out.

Feeling as anxious as she'd been at sixteen, Sadie went to help her nana prepare for bed. Over the last month, they'd established a routine on the days she was able to stay over for a visit. Not only was Sadie happy for the opportunity to tune out the rest of the world and spend time with her grandmother, she was glad she could give Angie an occasional night off.

"Everything all right?" Nana asked.

Sadie shrugged and helped Nana get to her feet. "I think so."

"Planning to meet Bo in the hayloft tonight?"

"Nana!"

"Oh, you two have never been as sneaky as you'd like to think," Nana informed her, chuckling at Sadie's chagrined expression.

"I guess not," Sadie admitted, holding Nana's arm as they headed up the stairs. "We got caught on the set last night."

They reached the landing, and Nana paused to catch her breath. "Oh, my," she wheezed. "Dare I ask?"

"We were just kissing," Sadie assured her. "But it wasn't very professional. Of either of us."

"No, I suppose not." Nana elbowed her. "Fun, though, right?"

Sadie laughed. Her grandmother was the best. "Yeah," she agreed. "Very." She opened Nana's bedroom door, mentally crossing her fingers no one else had heard about their "fun." She could check her phone, but Sadie had made a habit of unplugging from social media when she came here on the weekends, and she was protective of this quiet time with her grandmother. Besides, if anything had happened, Bo would have told her."

In a few minutes, Sadie had helped her nana finish her bedtime routine.

As she settled into bed, Nana said, voice thick with emotion, "I'm glad to see you two spending time together again. It makes me so happy to see you happy, bubelah."

"I *am* happy." Sadie smiled, the sting of tears that was becoming all too familiar lately burning in the back of her throat. "I didn't think I was unhappy before, exactly, but . . ."

"A piece of you was missing." Nana nodded. "I know what that feels like, to be without the other part of yourself."

"Like how you miss Poppa, you mean?"

"Oh, your poppa might be gone, and of course I miss

him, but he'll always be with me here." Nana placed her hand over her heart. "But when we were younger, when things were at their worst, we were torn apart. There was a time I feared your poppa and I would never find each other again."

"I never knew," Sadie began. "I mean, I knew the two of you struggled. I've heard some of the stories, but I assumed you were always together. I didn't know you'd ever broken up."

"My family did the breaking up for us. Didn't think he was good enough for me. I had seven brothers who spent plenty of time pounding that opinion into your poppa. It was when they started inflicting those opinions on me that they convinced him. Your grandfather told me it was best if he didn't see me anymore." There was pain in Nana's voice now. "But if he was stubborn, I was even more so. I refused to give up so easily. And as you know"—she smiled—"I eventually got my way."

"That's why I've always held out hope for you two. Even after . . ." Nana stopped. Grew quiet for a moment. Then she glanced up at Sadie. "I know I'm being an old busybody, but at my age I'm allowed to get away with it— like stealing fruit from the farmers' market." She paused. "I only steal the grapes, just so you know."

"Your secret's safe with me." Sadie grinned.

Nana's gaze dropped, smoothing the coverlet down with her palms. "As are yours with me." Her gaze lifted, irises faded to a soft cornflower blue. "He still doesn't know, does he?"

Sadie swallowed. Ever since she'd watched Nana interacting with Toby at dinner—and caught the look on Bo's face as he'd watched—Sadie had a feeling they were drifting toward this conversation. Nana was the only one who knew what Sadie tried so hard to keep buried.

Not another soul knew anything. Nobody. Not her mother, not her closest friends, not even her best friend. No one. Only Nana had been there for her. She'd helped Sadie do what needed to be done. And then she'd helped her get through the rest of that painful, horrible summer. Her grandmother had been her shelter, her safe place, her home.

"No," Sadie whispered. "He doesn't know."

Down the hall, the clock chimed eleven. Bo would be here soon. Her stomach in knots, heart pounding with anxiety instead of passion, the thought of sneaking out to meet him in the hayloft was no longer as appealing as it had been a few minutes ago. Sadie sat at the edge of her grandmother's bed. "Aren't you going to tell me I should've told him? Try and convince me I should tell him now?"

"No." Nana shook her head, voice firm. "That's for you to decide."

"You're not a very good busybody," Sadie muttered with affection.

"I said, I like to stick my nose *in* people's business, not get it *up* their business." Nana smothered a yawn.

Sadie smiled faintly, squeezing her grandmother's hand with affection. "Night, Nana. Love you."

Nana's brittle fingers squeezed back. "Love you too, doll."

Sadie clicked off the light on the nightstand. As she moved to shut her grandmother's bedroom door, Nana's voice carried softly in the dark: "No matter what."

CHAPTER 25

STANDING IN THE Murphys' stable yard, breath forming puffs of ice in the cold November air, Bo watched
as the light in one of the upstairs bedrooms went out.
Sadie would be down soon. Grabbing the duffel bag he'd
hastily packed, Bo headed inside the horse barn, pausing to pilfer a stack of clean wool blankets from the tack
room.

Anticipation heating his blood, he shouldered his bag
and carried the blankets up to the hayloft, grateful the
barn had steps and not just a ladder. He pulled a camp-
ing lantern from his duffel bag and set it up, filling the
recessed space with a pale warm glow. By the time he'd
finished spreading the blankets over a pile of hay, Sadie
arrived.

"Hey," she said. She was wrapped in a sweater, cheeks
pink from the cold.

"Hey," he shot back, covering his sudden fit of nervousness with a bit of cocky swagger. He dropped the last
of the blankets on top of the others and turned to root
around in his duffel bag. Why was his heart suddenly

beating so hard? Why did he feel as flustered as a teenager?

Bo knew the answer. That was easy. Because, as a teenager, he'd made love to Sadie for the first time in this loft. And then countless times after that, more times than he could remember. No. That wasn't true. He remembered each time with her. Though, having sex as a randy teenager in a barn in the middle of summer was a completely different experience than attempting the same thing as a grown-ass man in late November.

"What are you thinking?" Sadie asked.

"Honestly?" Bo smiled ruefully. "I was wondering if this might be a mistake."

Her face fell, and Bo realized how his words must have sounded. "No, no. Not about you . . . about this. Well, not about this. I mean . . ." Jesus, he really was acting like a bumbling teenager. Bo pulled his shit together and tried again. "I'm worried it's going to be too cold."

"Oh," Sadie said, relaxing. "*Oooh,*" she repeated, gaze dropping to his crotch.

"What? No!" Bo shook his head. "That's fine, princess. Trust me."

"I don't know . . ." Sadie tapped her chin thoughtfully. "I think I'll need visual confirmation."

Without another word, Bo set to work removing his clothes. The barn was warmer than outside, the air in the loft even more so thanks to the insulating layer of hay and the rising heat from the animals below. But still. It was chilly. Naked, he stood before her, resisting the urge to hold a hand over his junk. Which, as promised, was not affected by the cold one bit.

In fact, as Sadie looked at him, violet eyes feasting on his body, his cock stiffened further, performing for the audience. Bo glanced down at himself. "Show-off."

Sadie giggled.

When her attention finally returned to his face, Bo raised an inquisitive eyebrow. "Tit for tat?"

"Tit for tat," she agreed.

He was pleased to see she didn't flinch at the suggestion. He was even more pleased when she was finally naked too, her lithe form bare to his gaze. She was so fucking beautiful. So perfect. In the pale lamplight, her body became a breathtaking landscape of gleaming slopes and shadowed hollows.

Over the last several weeks, he'd had the pleasure of relearning her body. They'd given each other pleasure in countless ways—but not that way. He still hadn't been inside her. Had yet to know once again what it felt like to press into her, feel her hot and wet and throbbing all around him . . .

His cock already aching past the point of pain, Bo stepped closer, hands sweeping up over her breasts. Her nipples were stiff peaks against his palms. Goose bumps prickled along her skin. "Are you cold, abeja?"

"A little." She shivered as his fingers trailed over her collarbone. "Maybe you can help warm me up?" she asked, her voice sweet and innocent, her smile anything but.

"Maybe," he agreed. "Let's get you under the blankets, and I'll see what I can do."

They slipped between the layers, and Bo rolled, trapping her beneath him. "You feel so good," he whispered. Everywhere their bare skin touched, a delicious tingle rippled through him. Bo dipped his head, brushing his lips against hers. "So fucking good."

"You do too." Sadie smiled, mouth curving beneath his.

He kissed her, then. Long and slow. Lazy and sweet.

Even though he was dying to be inside her, they had all night, and he intended to make the most of it. Bo explored Sadie's body, spending endless minutes savoring each part of her. The delicate curve of her ear, the soft skin at her wrist, the tender spot behind her knee—which he was delighted to discover was still extremely ticklish.

Only when he'd touched her everywhere, hands claiming every hill and valley, did he flip onto his back, giving her a turn. Tit for tat. Sadie explored his body with the same exquisite care, taking her time, finding all the places that made him growl with pleasure. By the time she'd had a chance to touch every part of him, they were both panting with need, skin hot beneath the blankets, done waiting.

Bo reached for the condom stashed in his bag. With Sadie beneath him once more, he positioned himself between her legs and held still. "Abeja," he said, unable to resist teasing her, "nothing happens until you're ready."

Sadie looked up at him, eyes flashing with desire, mouth curving with humor as she caught his reference. "Does that mean you're waiting for my signal?" She spread her legs wide, bringing his body flush against hers. "Something like this?" she asked, thrusting her hips up, pressing against the head of his swollen cock.

"That works," he ground out. As they'd done everything else tonight, Bo and Sadie came together slowly. Inch by steady inch, he pressed into her, tension curling at the base of his spine as her body clenched, hot and tight and sweet as hell. Until finally, for the first time in far, far too long, Bo was a part of Sadie, embedded deep within her, as far as he could go.

"God, that's so good," Sadie moaned, wrapping her legs around his waist, trapping him inside her. "You feel so good inside me, Bo. I never want you to leave."

He laughed, raising his chin to stare down at her. "If that's what you want, I'll stay right here forever." He held still, fighting the urge to thrust, reveling in the feel of her all around him. "I'll never move."

Her mouth quirked. "Well . . ." She relaxed her legs, loosening her hold on him. "Maybe you can move a little bit."

He grinned. "Christ, I love you, abeja." The words spilled from his lips, easy and true. And right. So very right.

She met his gaze, violet eyes shadowed with lust and something more. Something deeper. Sadie reached up, running her finger along the line of his beard. "I love you too."

Heart full to bursting, Bo dipped his head and kissed her. First her mouth, then her cheek, then her neck. "I'm going to move now, okay?" he asked, lips against her ear.

She nodded, gripping his shoulders as he began to slide slowly out of her. Back and forth, Bo advanced and retreated. Again, and again, and again.

"Don't stop." Her nails dug into his skin, her voice breathy as she begged him to keep going. "Please, Bo, don't stop."

He wasn't planning on it. He never wanted to stop. Need built inside him, winding tighter and tighter until he was unable to hold back any longer. Bo picked up the pace, driving into Sadie hard and fast until she began to shudder, convulsing all around him. He covered her mouth with his, swallowing her screams. He loved how she let herself go. Loved he could make her feel this way. Make her scream. Make her come. And then he was coming too, pumping into her, giving her everything he had.

A shiver slid along Bo's spine, and he stirred, disoriented at first as he tried to place where he was. And then he remembered. He smiled and the wool blanket, soft and a little scratchy, rubbed against his cheek. Sadie was curled against his back, humming softly, her fingers tracing patterns on his skin. Bo lay still, enjoying the quiet moment nestled with her beneath the blankets.

"Bo?" her voice drifted over him.

"Hmm?" he murmured.

"I was thinking about your tattoos." She continued to stroke his back, outlining the ink with her fingers. "I was wrong." Her hand drifted over to his right shoulder. "This one. The sun. I thought it was for you, but it's not. Is it?"

"No," he admitted.

"It's for Toby." She was quiet. Contemplative. But there was something else there too. An undercurrent he couldn't quite pin down.

"Yeah." He shifted beneath the blankets, rolling to face her. "I'm sorry I didn't tell you before."

Sadie's eyes met his. "Why didn't you?"

"At the time, I wasn't ready to let you know about Toby yet." He swallowed. "And it's not really my story to tell."

"Your sister made a comment a while back that got me thinking."

Bo frowned, listening carefully as Sadie told him about her conversation with Luna, trying to process what she was saying. "You think Luna got pregnant because she was lonely?"

"No. I mean yes, but not in the way you make it sound." Sadie fiddled with a piece of straw. "I don't think she set out on purpose to have a baby so she'd have someone for company. But I do think she tried to make a relationship something that it wasn't because she wanted it so bad."

"What did she want?"

"Love." Sadie dropped her gaze from his, studying the

piece of straw. "She told me all she ever wanted was to find someone who looked at her the way you look at me."

Bo's heart twisted in his chest. *Oh, Luna.* "I had no idea . . . I wasn't around much, then. When she got pregnant, I mean." He shook his head. "That's not an excuse. I should have been there for my family more. By the time Toby was born, I'd been living in the city for over three years."

"I get it," Sadie said. "I feel the same about my grandmother. I should have come to see her more often. I missed out on a lot of time with her."

"But you're making up for it now," Bo said, wanting to comfort Sadie. Reassure her. Take the sad, distant look from her eyes. "There's something else, isn't there?" he asked. "Something you aren't telling me?"

Sadie shut her eyes. And when she opened them, that deep soul-wrenching pain he'd seen in the depths of her gaze the night they'd fought in her apartment was back.

"Abeja." His breath hitched. "*Please*. Talk to me."

For a long time, she didn't answer. Finally, she said, "I just wish things could have been different . . . before." She took a deep, shuddering breath. "We missed out on a lot of time together too."

"We did," he agreed, voice rough. It had been his own damn fault. "But we're also making up for that." He pulled her to him, then, pressing a kiss to her forehead before nudging her to roll over so he could hold her. "That's all we can do," he whispered against her neck, telling himself as much as he was telling her. As he drifted back to sleep, arms wrapped around Sadie, Bo vowed, no matter what happened next, no matter what the universe threw at them, he would never let her go again.

* * *

The cold kiss of November moonlight washed over Bo. He stirred, eyes still heavy with sleep, and blinked. Vision slowly coming into focus, Bo gazed through the loft window, watching the glowing white orb drift lower in the early morning sky. Soon, it would slip below the treetops, and not long after that, it would be day.

Beneath the blankets, within their shared cocoon, he was warm, but in the icy air of the loft his nose felt like an icicle. Unable to resist, he nuzzled Sadie's neck, the heat of her skin passing into his.

"Hey," she grumbled, "that's cold, asshole."

He grinned, lips curving against her nape. "You sound like me when I talk to Clark in the morning."

Sadie shifted against him. "I do, huh?" She cracked an eye open and looked at Bo. "He's going to yowl the place down when you're not there to give him his breakfast."

"I'll be home in time." Bo rolled onto his back, pulling her with him. Sadie curled against him, breasts a soft weight against his ribs, one leg wrapping around his.

"What time is it, anyway?" she mumbled against his chest.

"Four . . . maybe five," he guessed. Time was slipping away from them. Before the clock ran out on this magic night, there was more thing he wanted to tell her. "Abeja," he began, his voice a quiet rumble in the semidarkness.

"Yes?" she asked, breath warm on his skin.

"I want you to know . . . no one has ever made me feel the way you do." He ran his fingers through her golden spikes. "There's never been anyone else for me . . . not like this. Not like us."

"I know," she said.

He laughed.

"I didn't mean it like that." Sadie poked him in the

side. "I wasn't trying to pull a Solo on you. I just meant, I get it. It's the same for me. All these years, I've tried to convince myself that I was remembering it wrong. That, because you were my first, I had romanticized everything and looked back on our time together with rose-colored glasses or something. I told myself what we had couldn't possibly be as amazing as I remembered it. And I was right."

Bo nodded at first but then halted as what she'd said registered. "Wait, you were?"

"Mm-hmm." He heard the grin in her voice even before she sat up and faced him. "It wasn't as amazing as I remembered . . ." She bent her head, brushing her cold nose against his. "It was even better." Sadie brought his hand to her mouth, pressing a kiss to his knuckles. "I'd been so young, then, so very young and naïve. I couldn't possibly understand what we had. Nor fully appreciate the way you made me feel."

"And now?"

"Now I do." She turned his palm up, pressing more kisses over the rough calluses at the base of his fingers, sending shockwaves of sensation up Bo's arms and down his spine. "I understand how special what we have between us is. How it feels when you move inside me. How it feels to be with you. Nothing compares to you."

His breath caught. Her words were a sweet sting, piercing his chest. "My little abeja." Bo pulled her to him, unable to put into words all the things he wanted to say. All the things she made him feel.

So he showed her instead.

As the gray light in the loft warmed to a pale gold, Bo stirred again. It had to be past six by now. He'd put it off long enough. Time to tell her. Sadie was going to find out about the leaked video one way or another, and he'd rather she hear it from him.

"Abeja." He nudged her gently. "There's something I need to tell you."

Sadie didn't speak, just tilted her chin and gazed up at him. Waiting. Listening.

"The kiss, the one on set. It's out."

"Out?" She struggled to sit up, tucking the blanket around her bare shoulders. "Like out on the internet out?"

He nodded. "There's video footage."

"How bad?" Sadie closed her eyes, as if not being able to see him would make what he said better.

"Bad enough."

Grimacing, she cursed under her breath. "There's got to be somebody on the inside doing this. Someone on the crew."

"That's what I think too." Bo sat up, impressed that she was keeping her cool right now. She was pissed, but it was a controlled anger, her temper in check. "We need to figure out where the leak is coming from."

Sadie got to her feet, holding the blanket close and scooting toward her clothes. "Come on." She tossed his jeans at him.

Bo dragged them on under the blanket, motivated by temperature more than modesty. "Where are we going?"

"To send out the bat signal."

CHAPTER 26

BY TEN A.M., after speedy showers, a speedy drive into the city, and a speedy pit stop to feed one miffed mustached feline, Sadie was seated next to Bo in Meg's office. The PR maven had sequestered them in what she referred to as her war room and immediately began pulling up footage of the hallway embrace for review.

"My goodness, Bo. You really got a good handful there," Meg observed.

Sadie's cheeks tingled with heat. Both sets of them.

When the clip ended, Meg clicked the file closed and opened a series of other documents. "Okay. Here's the damage we're looking at," she began, pointing to some graphs. "Sadie, your popularity appears to have increased. People either feel bad that your coach—"

"Stunt coordinator," Bo corrected.

Meg held a hand up to him, starting again, "People either feel bad that your stunt coordinator is taking advantage of you—"

"I wasn't taking adv—"

Meg's hand popped up again. "People either feel bad

that your stunt coordinator is taking advantage of you."
She paused, turning to glare at Bo through the panes of
her glasses, daring him to interrupt again.

For once, he opted to skip a dare.

"Or they cheer you on for going after what you want,
female empowerment and owning your pleasure and all
that. Or, frankly, people just think it's hot and like watching you two go at it."

Meg pulled up another graphic. "And these trending
hashtags are directly linked to you. Well done."

Sadie scanned the words, *#GoingforGold*, *#Grabbin-
gtheGold*, and *#HotAssGold*. "Who comes up with this
stuff?"

"Hot Ass Gold," Bo murmured, reading it out loud.

"Don't you dare laugh," she warned him.

"He shouldn't be laughing," Meg agreed, pulling up a
fresh set of data. "Because while this little mall make-out
session has been good for you—"

"It's been terrible for me," Bo groaned.

This time Meg let the interruption slip. "Indeed." She
adjusted her bow tie and tapped a graphic on her screen.
"People take issue with seeing a big, strong, bearded dude
manhandling a sweet young thing."

"*Manhandling.* Why does everyone keep using that
word?" Bo wondered. "And she's thirty for Chrissakes."

"Hey!" Sadie objected.

"Sorry." He glanced at her. "I didn't say that to mean
you're old, just that you're not young."

"Should I get you a shovel?" Meg quipped.

A-plus on the sarcasm, lady. Sadie knew she liked this
woman. She raised her eyebrows at Bo, wondering if he
was going to dig himself out of the hole or bury himself
deeper.

"All I was saying is that we're basically the same age,"

Bo tried again. "I'm not robbing the cradle here." He turned to Meg. "We've been dating since we were kids!"

Meg cocked her head, and Sadie swore it was like a bird spying a tasty meal. "What's this now?"

"We met when we were little," Sadie explained. "His family, um, worked for mine, and we spent a lot of time together during the summer months."

"Tell me more," Meg ordered, dark eyes bright as she pushed her thick-rimmed glasses up her nose.

Sadie glanced at Bo. He shrugged.

Together, they began to tell Meg their story.

That night, Sadie called for an emergency session of Monday Margaritas. Off with her duke in England, Bonnie was out, obviously, and Delaney wasn't up for dealing with driving into the city, but Cassie and Ana agreed to meet. Which was good, as Sadie missed Ana and she really needed to talk to Cassie. With just the three of them, their usual booth felt huge.

By the time they'd finished the first round, Sadie had brought them up to speed.

"Meg Fay is effing brilliant, you know that, right?" Cassie asked. "She's one of the best public relations managers in the city, maybe even *the* best."

"She wants us to come on your show," Sadie said.

"Absolutely," Cassie agreed. "I can shuffle around a few things and get you a spot. I just need to clear it with Therese." She wrinkled her nose. "We might have to get Tiffany involved too, seeing as this is all entertainment and social media news."

"Isn't she the one who tried to sabotage your career, Cass?" Ana asked.

"Yep." Sadie nodded. "She tried to make Cassie look like a fool on live TV."

"She had some help with that part," Cassie reminded them, lips pursing. "And it all worked out in the end. I took a negative story and made it a positive." Cassie flicked her straw at Sadie. "Which sounds exactly like what Meg is doing for you."

"Meg said she plans to use our history to spin the relationship out to be an epic love story rather than Bo just looking like a perv."

"Hashtag: Grab the Gold," Ana chortled.

"Hashtag: My friend is about to get her face smashed in the guac," Sadie retorted.

"I told you, Meg is brilliant," Cassie continued, ignoring Ana and Sadie's little skirmish. "The romance angle is going to be great for your movie. Everybody loves a good happily ever after."

"Here, here!" Ana raised her glass.

"That reminds me, before I forget, I met the *Fair is Fair* author."

"Valerie Rose?" Cassie perked up. "She's a literary sensation. Twenty-three years old, debut novel snags high six-figure deal, immediately optioned by a big studio."

"Well, she's also very sweet and loves your book closet segment."

"She does?" Cassie beamed, face shining with pride and excitement.

Sadie smiled too. Cassie had worked so hard to get to where she was now. Risked a lot. Sadie admired that. She hoped to emulate her friend. Like Cassie, Sadie had walked away from a job that was comfortable and safe so she could chase a dream.

Cassie had caught her dream. Sadie hoped she could do the same. *Fair is Fair* was done filming, aside from the occasional retake or vocal track to record, Sadie's job would now be marketing. Interviews and appearances to help build the buzz. The spin Meg put on the story about Sadie and Bo helped keep the needle moving toward the positive side, but Sadie would have preferred her relationship with Bo was kept out of the public eye. Thanks to that video, though, privacy for her and Bo was going to be impossible. And now that the file on their history was open, Sadie feared what else people would find if they kept digging. None of this would be a concern if it hadn't been for that leak, and Sadie was determined to find out who had been trying to sabotage her.

"So, how do we figure out who let the video leak in the first place?" Sadie asked, poking at the lime in her second margarita. "Or who provided any of the other details for the stories that *411* ran on me?"

"Let me do some digging," Cassie offered. "I've got plenty of contacts in that sector from my reign at *ChiChat* as social media queen. I bet I can find out who wrote the articles."

"That's who wrote them, which sure, that person sucks, but whatever," Ana noted. "What about the source?"

"That might be a little trickier, but still possible. If I can nail down who the reporter is, we might get them to spill, but unlikely. Unless it's court ordered, they usually don't like to reveal their sources."

"Sleazeball code of ethics?" Ana snarked.

"Something like that." Cassie leaned forward, voice dropping to a conspiratorial whisper. "But I might be able to get in through the back door."

"Sounds dirty." Ana sipped her drink, eyebrows wiggling.

"Everything sounds dirty to you." Sadie elbowed her friend, then asked Cassie, "What do you mean?"

"Track the payment," Cassie explained. "Figure out who *411* bought the video from."

"Wait." Surprised anger flashed through Sadie. "Someone made money off that?"

"Are you kidding?" Cassie blinked at Sadie as if she was from another planet. "Sites pay big dollars for this kind of thing. That clip that went viral last week, of the actor losing his shit in a parking garage? I'm betting $5k, easy."

Sadie sucked down the rest of her drink. She sat back, tequila thrumming in her veins, fueling the rage burning inside her. Someone had fucked with her life, and Bo's too. Put both their careers and reputations on the line, for money.

And she wanted to make them pay.

It had been three days since the footage leaked before Bo decided he was ready to face Vic. The hallway video from the shoot had been released on Sunday morning, and by the time he and Sadie had made it to Meg's "war room," it had been viewed and shared and reblogged or whatever it was people did with this shit more times than he wanted to think about. Meg's counter story, the one of their "epic love" had hit sites on Monday night, and now, on Thursday morning, three days later, the story had gone international. Meg was thrilled.

But when Bo told Vic about the steps that had been taken to handle the bad PR, his partner seemed nonplussed.

"They shifted the spin on this." Bo pulled up some of the sites that had been running the story. "See? Instead of a villain, I'm a hero."

Vic glanced at the stories but remained categorically unimpressed. "I'm glad your reputation has been cleared. But the fact remains that you acted unprofessionally on a job site." The older man's face darkened. "And you betrayed my trust."

"Betrayed? What are you talking about?"

"You weren't straight with me." Vic's chin jutted out. "You've been involved with that Gold girl since day one of the shoot and said not a word about it."

"What was I supposed to say, Vic?" Bo held out his hands.

Rather than answer him, Vic stubbornly continued, "And when you came in here to my office, and told me, right to my face, that you would be shooting on location at her place? That might have been a good time to mention what was going on."

"I never lied to you." Bo stared at his partner. "What was between me and Sadie was private."

"Ain't so private now." Vic snorted. "Here's a suggestion. You want privacy, don't date a movie star."

"I'm sorry if you feel I let you down, Vic."

"You did let me down. You know better."

Bo knew he'd made a mistake. And he was sorry. Sorry he'd disappointed Vic. Sorry he and Sadie got caught and put their dreams at risk. But the thing was, he didn't regret it. He didn't regret kissing Sadie. If they were back in that moment, and he was faced with the same choice . . . he knew he'd do it again.

"Is that it, then?" Bo asked, stomach twisting as he felt years of hard work, a decade of hopes and dreams teetering on the verge of collapse. "Is the deal off the table?"

"IT BETTER NOT BE!" Claudia yelled from the front desk.

Vic heaved a sigh. "No, the deal is not off the table. I'm a man of my word."

Bo didn't say anything. On one hand, Vic could claim Bo's actions put the entire company at risk and nullified their agreement. On the other, Vic had been stalling on moving forward with the deal so long that if Bo had been smart and included an actual deadline in the agreement, the old guy would be in serious breach of contract. In a sense, their actions could be viewed as a draw.

"I'll honor what I said at the shoot," Vic acquiesced. "After the first of the year, I'll see where things stand. And then I'll draw up the paperwork."

"YOU BETTER."

The two men stared at each other for a moment.

Bo headed out of the office, more disheartened than he cared to admit. Claudia stopped him. "He's just mad right now." Vic's wife pointed to the wall where a cruise ship calendar hung. "For years, I've dreamt of going on one of those." She nodded her head. "Give it time. He'll come 'round. I'm going on that damn cruise."

For the sake of both their dreams, Bo hoped she was right.

His boots had barely hit the sidewalk outside the office when his phone buzzed. Sadie. There was news.

Twenty minutes later, Bo found himself once again sitting next to Sadie in Meg's "war room" and decided he found the name fitting. He was ready to go to battle. Bo flexed his fingers, working out the tension in his knuckles. It had been a stressful week, and he'd spent more time than usual working over the bag in his apartment. It helped to try and picture the fucker who had sold that footage and put everything he'd worked for at risk.

Bo stared down at his knuckles. The problem was, he couldn't actually picture anyone. Who could it have been? Who was the leak? Annoyed Dave? Maybe, but Bo couldn't see the motivation. He glanced over at Sadie. Sitting next to him, she seemed a million miles away, lost in her own thoughts. He'd barely seen her since that night in the hayloft. The past few days had been a maelstrom of damage control. With his job on the line, Bo needed to be laser focused on his other work assignments. He'd had to get the stunt sequences set for the *Chicago Rescue* special, run through the gags, check with his crew, and lock in the schedule. But all the while, his attention had been split, trying to track down the leak.

But that was going to change right now. They were going to find out who'd started this mess. And then they would make sure it was over.

"Thank you both for coming on such short notice." Meg peered up at them from her pile of papers and adjusted her glasses. She turned to Sadie. "I must say, your friend Miss Crow was most useful in this endeavor." Meg glanced down, reviewing her file. "She has quite a web of connections. A tug here, a pull there, and eventually, someone knew someone who knew someone."

Bo shifted in his seat. Restless, nerves raw. What was with this cloak-and-dagger shit? Just give him the names of the people who did this so he can go kick their asses already.

"Before we begin, I must warn you that the inquiry led to some . . . sensitive information."

Sadie jerked in her chair. "What kind of sensitive information?"

Bo caught the note of fear in Sadie's voice and looked over at her, trying to catch her attention, but she ignored him, her gaze locked on Meg.

Meg folded her hands over the papers spread on the conference table. "I know it will be upsetting, but we've pinpointed the source of the leak, and I'm afraid to say, it is a member of the production team."

"Oh." Sadie sagged in her chair.

No shit, Sherlock. Beneath the table, Bo cracked his

knuckles, wondering what Annoyed Dave would look like with a broken nose.

Meg shuffled some papers, handing a sheet to each of them.

The reporter who'd written the stories for *411* was some guy Bo had never heard of before, but he made a mental note to look him up later.

The source of the leak—the person who had been cashing checks for selling information and video footage—was Tanya Fisk.

Assistant Tanya. Always hovering.

Little fucking clipboard-carrying Tanya.

Bo amused himself for a moment imagining unpleasant uses for that clipboard.

"Why would she do that?" Sadie asked, her lips pinching in a sad knot.

"Oh, the money, I'm sure." Meg fussed with her bow tie. "The problem, though, and the thing that our Miss Fisk failed to consider, is that she signed a—"

"An NDA!" Sadie straightened. "Everyone does, it's standard."

"What is it with you two? Stop interrupting me. This isn't some quiz show where you get a prize for buzzing in the fastest." Meg moved back to the pile of papers. "Yes, she signed a nondisclosure agreement. I've already conferred with Sylvia, who has assured me that steps will be taken to ensure Miss Fisk, as they say in our business, 'never works in this town again.'"

Sadie brushed a hand over her short blond spikes. "But why me?"

"Pardon?" Meg quirked a brow at her over her glasses.

"Why did Tanya focus all her leaks on me? I mean, the last one I get, she walked into that—literally." Sadie choked out a disgusted laugh. "God, that should have been a clue, huh?"

Bo agreed. He wanted to kick himself. He'd never even considered the uptight pencil-pushing coffee runner to be capable of this devious crap. He'd judged her. Made assumptions about her. The same way he'd hated people doing to him.

"As the lead character in the film, you were the obvious choice. And the sad fact is, women are generally easier to exploit in the media. To be blunt, you were not just the obvious choice, but the more lucrative one."

"The production company is going to sue her, right?" Sadie asked. "For breaking the NDA? If nothing else, just so she doesn't profit from messing up my life."

"Funny you should mention that." Meg picked up a manila folder. "When we confronted Miss Fisk, we discovered she'd been gathering material on you for further financial gain. Now, the reason for all this secrecy is that, as with everything, we'd like to contain the potential for . . ." Meg paused, ". . . nastiness."

Beside him, Sadie tensed right back up. Bo could feel the trepidation rolling off her. He glanced her way again, almost expecting the spikes of her hair to rise like the hackles on a hound.

What the hell was going on?

Meg slid the folder to Sadie. "Miss Fisk has stated she is ready to provide some very personal information to the right buyer."

"That sounds like blackmail."

"It rather does, doesn't it?" Meg agreed. "Save for the fact that Miss Fisk is not asking for money for her information. She simply wants to avoid having to spend money."

"She wants the lawsuit dropped," Bo guessed.

Meg nodded. "Otherwise, yes, she will sell this information to the highest bidder. And since it pertains to a situation that occurred long before this film was being produced, the NDA does not apply."

"Which means she can't be sued for leaking the information." Bo shook his head. *That clever little weasel.*

"Of course, if this *information* she claims to have is proven false, like her story about your enhanced endowments, then I move we take her on."

Sadie didn't answer, just continued to stare at Meg.

"But, if there is any chance this story is true . . . Well, like I said"—Meg pushed her glasses up the bridge of her nose—"we'd like to contain any potential unpleasantness."

Bo glanced at the folder again. Sadie was looking at it like it was a snake lying in wait to bite her. He was dying to know what the hell Tanya had dug up that made her think she could pull a fast one on an entire film studio. Whatever it was, it had to be intense. Or maybe that was just it. She was trying to pull a fast one and had nothing more than another invisible boob job story.

He considered the situation for a moment, realizing there was a factor at play that shouldn't be—him. "While I appreciate being kept in the loop regarding Tanya's actions and the footage she leaked involving me . . ." Bo paused, ". . . out of respect for Sadie's privacy, I'm not sure if I should be a part of the current conversation. If this is a story involving Sadie—"

"It involves both of you."

"Oh." Bo frowned. He and Sadie had done a lot of dumb shit together as kids, but never anything that could be worthy of blackmail. No petty crimes, nothing illegal. What the fuck could it be?

Bo's phone buzzed in his pocket. He ignored it, his

brain whirring frantically. That first time in the loft, he'd been seventeen, which made her sixteen . . . *shit*. Was it illegal if they were both underage? And who would even know about that besides the two of them?

His confusion would clear up fast if Sadie just opened the damn folder. But she still hadn't moved.

"Sadie?" Bo leaned toward her. "Look, I can't believe they'd send me to jail, abeja, but if you want to fight Tanya on this, I'm willing to risk it."

"Jail?" Meg cocked her head. "Things are pretty messed up right now, but that's still not a crime."

"What are you talking about?" Bo frowned at Meg.

She bristled. "What are *you* talking about?"

"Bo doesn't know." Sadie's voice was heavy and low.

"Oh." Meg blinked. "Um, well, ah, yes, then . . ."

It was the first time Bo had seen the PR woman get flustered, and that freaked him the hell out. "What don't I know?"

"Perhaps, you were right," Meg began, rising from her chair. "Maybe it would be best if you wait outside for this part of the consultation." She moved to open the door.

"But you said it involved me." He turned, trying to get a read on Sadie's face, but she was immobile, smooth porcelain, blank. "Sadie?" His voice cracked, desperation leaking through. "What don't I know? What aren't you telling me?"

She still hadn't touched the folder, still hadn't moved. She stared down at it, still as a corpse, save for the rapid rise and fall of her chest as she struggled for air.

"Sadie?" Bo grabbed her wrist. Her skin was clammy, cold to the touch. *Shit.* "I think she's having a panic attack." He stood, helping Sadie to her feet, gently, careful not to move her too fast.

"Should I call an ambulance?"

"No." Bo shook his head. "I don't think so. But some water would be good. And she needs air."

Meg hurried to open the door to the conference room. Bo held Sadie's hand and walked her down the hall. Still breathing in rapid, wheezing little gasps, she followed behind him, arm limp in his grip, like a rag doll on a string, about to collapse at any moment.

Bo stopped near a bank of windows where the crisp November sun scattered squares of light over the corporate gray carpet. Sadie's skin was almost the same color.

"Sadie?" Her eyes were wide open and unfocused, pupils swallowing the violet hue in a gaping darkness. Bo patted her cheeks, rubbed her arms. "Abeja, listen to me. Breathe." He kept his voice low and calm, reining in his own terror at seeing her like this.

"It's fine. You're going to be fine." Her heart was hammering like a fox caught in a snare. Bo pressed his palms over her chest, leaning into her, offering the weight of his body as comfort. "Everything is fine, sweetheart. Just breathe."

They stood like that for seconds, minutes, hours. Bo didn't know. But eventually her heart slowed, her breathing evened out, and her skin took on its normal shade. He slumped against the windows, cold glass a welcome chill against his back as he cradled Sadie in his arms.

At the soft thud of footsteps on the carpet, Bo glanced down the hall. Meg approached with a glass of water.

"How is she?"

"I think she's past it."

Bo's phone buzzed again. His mother now. *Fuck*. He straightened, throwing a glance toward Meg. "Stay with her. I'll be right back."

"Mom. What?" Bo snapped, immediately regretting it. His mother didn't deserve his shit.

"Finally," she breathed. "Your sister's been trying to reach you."

There was a thread of panic in her voice. Nerves already frayed, Bo's throat went tight and dry. "What's wrong?" He forced the words out. "Is it Toby?" Adrenaline already out of control, fear pumped through his veins. "Did something happen to Toby?"

"No, no, mijo." His mother's voice was soothing, but the worry was still there. "It's Mrs. Murphy, Sadie's grandmother."

Bo listened to his mother explain, anxiety lacing his gut tighter and tighter. He glanced toward the windows. "I understand, Mom. We'll be there soon." Bo ended the call and forced air into his lungs as he headed back to Sadie and Meg.

"We'll deal with the Tanya business later."

"We will?" Meg considered him, eyes assessing. Then she nodded. "Right."

Bo reached for Sadie's hand. "We need to go, abeja."

She glanced up, confused.

"It's your grandmother." Bo forced himself to meet Sadie's gaze. Her eyes were already so full of pain, he hated what he had to say next. "She's in the hospital."

CHAPTER 27

THE TOWERING STREETLAMPS lining the expressway flew by in a steady rhythm as Bo raced north. Sadie focused on counting each pole as it passed. It gave her brain something to latch onto, a place to direct her attention so she wouldn't sink into the panic spiral swirling at the edge of her thoughts.

Her compartmentalization system wasn't working. Whatever had happened to her in Meg's war room, it had ripped open every box, leaving the contents strewn all over every surface. Heart breaking, mind racing, soul aching. *She should have told him.* That night in the hayloft, when they'd shared so much, and he'd sensed the pain in her, begged her to let him in. She should have opened that box, then.

But she didn't. It was easier to leave it buried. Keep it submerged in the dark while she floated at the top where it was light and easy. No struggle. And now the choice had been taken from her. Instead of an act of courage, instead of a gift of trust, her confession would simply be that. A confession. An admission of guilt.

Not guilt over what she'd done. Sadie had long ago come to terms with that choice. She didn't regret it. No, the guilt came from keeping it hidden for so long. For treating her choice like it was something to be ashamed of. She'd locked the box up tight and never let any of those feelings out—and by doing so, she could never really let anyone in.

The only person she'd ever truly let all the way in was Nana, and now Sadie may have lost her forever.

Arriving at the hospital suddenly made it all too real. Sadie's mind started to spin like a carousel going too fast. Moving through the long white hallways next to Bo, she felt like she was still in the car, lampposts whizzing by faster and faster until their lines became blurred. She felt blurred.

"Breathe," Bo whispered. A quiet reminder to relax.

Sadie breathed. One panic attack was enough, thank you very much. Inhaling and exhaling slowly, she followed Bo into a waiting room, latching on to details. Luna and Mrs. Ibarra were there, little paper cups of vending-machine coffee in hand. Toby was sprawled out on the floor, coloring. Bo's mother caught sight of them and waved them over.

"Is she okay? What happened?" The questions spilled out of Sadie, scattering onto the waiting room floor. She'd been holding them in for what seemed like hours. Words sitting on her tongue as she rode in the car, waiting to get here, waiting to be able to ask, to find out, to know.

"Is she okay? What happened?" Sadie couldn't help repeating herself. She'd been holding on to those words too long.

Mrs. Ibarra took Sadie's hands within her own. Bo's mother's hands were smooth, but strong and confident, like her son's. She walked Sadie across the room and settled her onto one of the couches.

Sadie glanced around, noting the other people sitting and waiting for news of their loved ones, other families. "I should . . . I should call my mother." The words felt strange and wooden on her tongue. But Nana was in the hospital, her daughter needed to know.

"Angie is trying to reach her now," Mrs. Ibarra assured her.

"Why didn't she try calling me?" Sadie wondered, hurt that no one had tried to contact her, to let her know.

"That's my doing." Bo's mother patted Sadie's shoulder. "I told Angie to worry about tracking down your parents, I know they can be tricky to pin down sometimes."

That's an understatement. Sadie surprised herself. Even amidst the fear and worry, she could still be snarky about her parents without even thinking. Years of practice.

"And I didn't call you," Mrs. Ibarra continued, "because I thought it would be best if you had someone drive you." She smiled at Sadie, golden-brown eyes the same shade as Bo's full of compassion. "I know she means a lot to you, mija. I was worried when you heard what happened, you'd be too upset to get here safe."

"You were right." Sadie nodded. "Thank you."

"What did Bo tell you?"

"Honestly, I don't really remember much, the car ride here, it was kind of a blur . . ."

"She fell."

"Fell? How? Where?" The panic drifted closer, swirling, ready to suck her in.

"On the front porch, so not too far. But hard."

"Was she there long?" Oh God, her poor nana, alone and in the cold.

"I don't think so." Mrs. Ibarra shook her head. "Luna had dropped off some canning vegetables, and we think your grandmother slipped trying to bring them in by herself." Her gaze moved over her daughter and grandson. "Luna feels terrible about it."

"It's not her fault." Sadie followed Mrs. Ibarra's gaze, watching Bo's sister absently stroke Toby's soft blond locks. "I know my grandmother appreciates Luna's kindness. She raves about her flowers and vegetables."

"Maybe you can tell her that," Mrs. Ibarra suggested gently. "I think it would help, especially coming from you."

"I don't know," Sadie began.

"I do know," Bo's mother said.

Sadie pulled back, surprised by the vehemence of the response. Maybe Mrs. Ibarra felt her daughter was lonely and needed a friend.

"I'll tell her," Sadie promised. "Do you know what is happening right now? With my grandmother, I mean."

Mrs. Ibarra frowned. "I suspect a broken hip, which likely means surgery. The sooner the better. It's never a good idea to postpone these things."

"Why?"

"The risk for complication goes up the longer you wait."

God, wasn't that the truth? Sadie should get a tattoo of that phrase. She scanned the room, looking for Bo, spotting his broad shoulders in front of the coffee machine.

Again, Sadie chastised herself for not telling him before. She could forgive the scared, disconsolate eighteen-year-old who'd decided to keep the secret to herself, but she could not excuse the woman. The thirty-year-old woman.

"A doctor should be out soon to give us an update,"

Mrs. Ibarra said, and Sadie jumped from one emotional landmine to the next.

"Will I able to see her, then?" she asked hopefully.

"Depends." The older woman eased back in her chair, considering. "If they decide to prep her for emergency surgery, which is what I think they're planning to do, we should be able to get you back there for a quick hug."

Sadie was grateful Mrs. Ibarra hadn't used the phrase, *say goodbye.* "Thank you. For everything."

"Anytime. You know that." Bo's mother paused, a small chuckle escaping. "Though I don't want this to become a routine."

"Agreed." Sadie managed a smile.

Bo returned then, handing Sadie a paper cup of something that might be coffee.

"Thanks." She wrapped her hands around the cup, letting the heat soak into her palms.

"Don't thank me yet," he warned. "It's liquid, it's warm, and it's brown, but I'm not sure it's coffee."

Sadie sputtered into her cup.

"Glad I can still make you laugh," Bo said.

"That makes two of us."

"How are you holding up?"

"Okay, so far." She stared at the ground, tracing the patterns in the carpet with her toe. "I'm scared, though. I've never lost anyone close to me. I mean, anyone that I can remember." She loved her poppa, but her memories of him were vague, more fantasy than reality, and she'd been too little when he died to really miss him. "The only thing that comes even close was losing Flynn."

Bo's eyes kindled, lit with memories. "I remember Flynn."

A smile tugged at the corner of Sadie's mouth. "I hope so; you saved his life once."

"No." Bo nodded his head toward his mother. "*She* saved his life."

It had been Bo who'd first noticed something was wrong with Flynn. Yes, as a vet, Bo's mother had been the one to provide the care that cured the dog, but modest he may be, Sadie knew it was Bo's quick thinking that recognized Flynn was having an allergic reaction that saved him.

Sadie risked a sip of her drink. It wasn't great, it wasn't even good, but it was passable. And it had caffeine, which was really all that mattered right now. Sadie had a feeling she was in for a long night. She glanced over at Luna and Toby. "It means a lot that you're here, but you don't have to stay. If you need to get going, I understand."

Luna offered her a soft smile, and for the second time Sadie could ever remember, Bo's sister looked at her without chips of green ice for eyes.

Sadie thought about what Luna's mother had said.

"My grandma talks about you all the time, you know."

Luna pulled back, eyes wide. "She does?"

"Oh yeah, raves. I think she might be your number-one fan."

A pretty pink blush bloomed in Luna's cheeks.

"Hey, Mamá. I'm your number-one fan." Toby scrambled to his feet, hopping into his mother's lap and scattering his box of crayons in the process.

"Tobias," Luna groaned.

"It's okay. I've got it." Sadie set her coffee cup on a nearby table and sat on the floor, scooping crayons back into the box. "Hey, Toby, do you mind if I color?" She glanced up. Toby was curled against Luna, blond head tucked under her chin, already half asleep.

"Sure." He yawned, head bobbing, and gave her a drowsy smile. An arrow shot straight through Sadie. She forced herself to smile back, then shifted her gaze to the coloring book, focusing on letting the smooth repetitive strokes soothe her.

The sharp, sudden pain that happened like this sometimes always confounded her. Sadie could never predict what would set it off: a toothy baby grin, or a mom on a train, quietly whispering in her child's ear as they looked out the window, shared excitement in their eyes, watching the world go by. It didn't happen often. But when it did, it stopped her cold. A barb that pierced through the deepest part of her. The initial sting passed quickly, but the pain would linger, like a poison. Sadie had experienced this feeling before, at other moments in her life too, long before the summer that shall not be named. She called it the what-if feeling. Or sometimes, the if-only feeling.

At least, with Toby, she understood the trigger. He was Bo's flesh and blood. Sadie looked up from the page she'd been coloring. Toby was already out cold, head thrown back, mouth wide open like a little fish. She smiled at the tender picture.

Then turned to find Bo watching her.

Sadie dropped her gaze. She'd still been disoriented when he'd brought her the message about her grandmother. But she'd heard what he said to Meg. About dealing with the Tanya business later.

It had been a reprieve.

Time and space for her to deal with what was happening with her grandmother.

But after that . . . Sadie knew it would be time to deal with him.

Nana always said things looked better in the morning, and maybe she was right. Sadie's appearance, however, was not one of them. After a long night spent catnapping on two chairs shoved together to form an impromptu bed, Sadie was ready to hunt down a cup of coffee that actually tasted like coffee and scrounge up a toothbrush. By the time she'd found one and had used the other, a nurse came by with good news. Nana had been settled into a room and could receive visitors.

Things really did look better in the morning.

Sadie gathered up her things and cleaned out the little nest she'd made to sleep in. Last night, after she'd learned her grandmother would indeed be having emergency hip surgery as Mrs. Ibarra predicted, Sadie had only been given a moment to see Nana before they wheeled her off to prep. Afterward, Sadie had thanked Bo and his family for coming and encouraged them to head home, but they wouldn't hear of it.

Mrs. Ibarra insisted they wait until Sadie's grandmother was out of surgery before leaving. It was nearing midnight when news finally came that the procedure had gone well, and Nana was moving to recovery. Giddy with relief, Sadie had watched Bo gather up his nephew from Luna's arms and carry him out to the car. The sight of Toby's chubby cheek pressed against Bo's broad shoulder, golden curls bobbing down the hall, wrecked her.

Sadie stepped quietly into her nana's hospital room. It was a good size with a wall of windows looking out over a garden. She smiled. Nana would be happy about the view. Shuffling quietly to the bed, Sadie checked on her grandmother. Wrapped in one of those bedsheets turned into robe things hospitals made everyone suffer in, Nana looked small, childlike, save for the shock of white hair.

Smoothing a hand over Nana's cheek, Sadie was relieved to note it was warm to the touch, but not hot. Bo's mother had said post-op infection was one of the things to watch out for.

Drained, her tank completely on empty, Sadie collapsed into the lounge chair set up next to the bed, not sure which truck of emotional trauma had run over her the hardest: relief that her nana was okay after all the hours of worry, anger and angst about the Tanya situation, or fear and resignation for the Bo situation. And then, of course, was the emotional grab bag otherwise known as a panic attack. Fun times.

There was a lot she needed to deal with, but right now, she needed to be here. Popping the lever on the chair and easing back, Sadie relished the opportunity to lie down and catch a few more minutes of sleep. Lulled by the sweet sound of her nana's gentle snoring, Sadie drifted off, dreaming of her old dog Flynn.

Sometime later, Sadie awoke, knowing even before her eyes were open that her mother had finally arrived at the hospital. There was a distinct weight and pressure to the intensity of Maureen Goldovitz's stare. Once you felt it, you never forgot it.

Sadie sat up and turned to face her mother. As always, she had to fight the urge to straighten her spine and suck her stomach in. The instinct was bone deep—deeper—it was embedded in her cells. Her very DNA. Her mother had been telling Sadie to stand up straight and look pretty all her life. Like she was something to be displayed on a shelf.

Shoulders back, tummy in, smile on.

"Mercedes," her mother said.

That was it. No, "Good Morning." No, "How are you?" And definitely no, "It's nice to see you."

"Mother."

"I see your hair has yet to recover."

It took all of Sadie's willpower not to run a self-conscious hand over her short spikes. Now that filming was done, she'd been looking forward to growing it out again, but her mother's comment made her want to find the scissors and start chopping.

Instead, she bit the inside of her cheek and smiled, a trick she'd learned years ago. "Well then, it's a good thing you're here to see to your mother's health and not your daughter's hair." *Or your daughter.*

Nana stirred on the bed.

"Nana?" Sadie stood, brushing a hand over her grandmother's cheek. "Are you awake?"

Nana shifted under the pile of blankets, hospital white on hospital white, and raised the bed to an incline position. "I am now."

"It's nice to see you up." Sadie shifted the pillows around gingerly, helping her grandmother get situated. Thanks to their routine of the last two months, she knew how Nana liked things. It felt good to be able to help take care of her. "Can I get you anything?"

"Some tea would be nice, doll."

"You got it." Sadie headed for the door, but stopped, asking over her shoulder, "Anything for you, Mother?"

"From the hospital?" Her mother shuddered.

Wondering why she even bothered, Sadie left the room. Her mother's voice carried easily behind her.

"I'm worried about her."

Sadie paused, heart flickering with a spark of hope that never quite went out.

"Do you think her arms look bulky? They seem bulky to me. Goodness, combine it with that haircut of hers and . . ."

Before she could hear any more, Sadie hurried down the hall to the little self-service beverage station. As she reached for a cup to pour the hot water in, she inspected the toned line from elbow to shoulder.

Don't let her get in your head, Sadie reminded herself. She popped a teabag into the cup and grabbed a lid. So what if her arms were bulky? She'd worked her ass off for that bulk. She *liked* that bulk. Training for this film had taught Sadie to appreciate what her body could do. For the first time, her appearance didn't seem quite so important. Sadie headed back to her nana's room. Holding the steaming cup out in front of her, she admired the dip and swell of muscle sweeping up the curve of her arm.

As she approached the door, she heard the icy clipped tones of her mother's voice rising in volume. Sadie hesitated. Whatever was going on, it couldn't be good. Her mother did a lot of unpleasant things, but yelling, especially in public, was not one of them. Nana must really be pissing her off.

Not feeling even a smidge of guilt for snooping, Sadie moved to the wall, stopping just outside the door.

"You can't be serious, Mother."

"Do I look like I'm joking?" Nana said with her usual tart spunk. "My mind is made up."

"Surely you want to wait until you are home to worry about any of this; we can talk again after you recover and are feeling better."

"No. I want this done now. The sooner the better. Your husband can make the arrangements to have our lawyers come here."

Lawyers? Sadie bit her lip. What was Nana up to?

"And if I get the slightest impression he's dragging his feet, I'll hire someone else. I may have a busted hip, but these wrinkly old fingers can dial a phone number just fine."

Go, Nana. Sadie didn't know what her nana was planning, but if it irritated her mother this much, she was sure it was something she was going to like. She breezed through the door, all clueless smiles. "Here we go, some hot tea for you." She set the tea on the rolling tray by her grandmother's bed.

Her mother took a step back, as if she feared being contaminated by the steam rising from the cup. "Well, if you insist on pursuing this mad course of action . . ."

"I do."

Mom notched her chin up, and Sadie wondered if her mother had another tuck done recently. "Then I have nothing more to say on the matter."

Nana snorted. "I doubt that. But hope springs eternal."

"I suppose you're pleased with yourself, Mercedes."

"Yep. Whatever Nana wants." Still unsure of what her grandmother had done or how she herself might be involved, Sadie decided if it was enough to get this much of a rise out of her mother, then she was pleased as punch. She bit her cheek and smiled.

Her mother spun on her Italian heel and with a puff of designer fragrance, was gone.

Once the clicking of Maureen Goldovitz's shoes had faded down the hall, Sadie drilled her grandmother. "Nana, what are you up to?"

"You were listening at the door, you tell me."

Sadie grinned. "All I know is you want Daddy to bring the family lawyers to the hospital."

"Oh, you missed the good stuff, then." Nana's grin was delightfully mischievous.

"I'm listening."

"I'm tired, doll face."

A prickle of concern pinched her brow. Nana was just so *Nana,* Sadie almost forgot her grandmother had major surgery mere hours ago. "We can talk later if you need to rest."

"No, no. I'm tired of the way things are. This fall jarred more than my bones." Nana took a sip of tea. "I've decided to move."

"Move? Where?"

"One of those retirement places. You know, little old-people condos."

"I was thinking about that recently," Sadie admitted. "It would be nice if you had some more company."

"I also want to turn the estate over to you."

"Wait." Sadie jerked. "What?"

"Your poppa wanted you to have that land. And we both know if it passes to your mother first, it will never make it to you. She'd have sold it and spent the earnings before the grass started growing on my grave."

So, that's what had pissed her mother off. Sadie couldn't argue with Nana's reasoning in that regard, but she did have other reservations. "But I wouldn't have the first clue how to run the estate!"

"Pish, we have so many foreman and managers, the place basically runs itself. There's a good team in place. Good people who will help you make good decisions. And you can always hire others, if you want."

Sadie paused, feeling guilty and selfish but knowing she had to be honest with her grandmother. "Running Murphy Farms isn't what I want to do. Hopefully my career as an actress takes off, and when it does, I'll likely be living all over the place, shooting on location."

"Then you have a place to come home to."

"Would that work?"

"Why not?"

Sadie didn't have an answer for that. It was worth a try, at least. And she did love the estate. Had so many wonderful memories there. More than anywhere else, it was her home. "Okay." She smiled at her nana. "I'm in."

"That was easy." Nana grinned, the smile curving slyly as she added, "I do have a few caveats."

"Oh? Waiting to share details until after I agree to the deal? Pretty slick, Nana."

"You'll be happy with these terms," her grandmother promised. "I want to give the carriage house to the Ibarra family. Permanently. I plan to put the deed in Luna's name, so she and Toby never have to worry about moving."

"That's a wonderful idea," Sadie agreed, her heart getting all warm and fuzzy. "That will make Bo very happy too. I know he's worried about his sister's future once their parents are gone."

Thinking about Bo and the future, Sadie's mood suddenly took a nosedive as she recalled everything else that had happened yesterday. The war room. Tanya's threats. The file. Sadie hadn't opened the file, but she knew exactly what story Tanya was holding over their heads. She'd like to think it wouldn't have been possible for that weasel to ferret out such incredibly private information, but Sadie knew how horrifyingly easy it was to get access to a person's entire life with just a few clicks.

"Have you finally decided to tell him, then?" Nana asked.

Sadie nodded, everything twisting into knots inside her. "He's going to hate me."

"Shh, doll. He won't hate you."

"He will hate what I did, then. The choice I made . . . without him. Without telling him."

"It was your choice to make," Nana said firmly. She held out the hand not hooked up to monitors and IVs.

Sadie took her nana's hand, squeezing tight. Her

grandmother had been through so much yesterday, and yet, here she was, helping Sadie. "You're pretty amazing, Nana."

"I know." Nana winked, but then her expression turned serious. "You're worried he won't be able to accept what you did. But the important thing to ask yourself is do *you* accept it?"

"Yes." Without hesitation, Sadie nodded. "I've thought about this a lot, Nana. A long time ago, I accepted the choice I made was the right one for me at the time."

"Then that's all there is to it," Nana said, patting her hand.

Sadie gave her a weak smile. If only it were that easy.

After making sure Nana had everything she'd needed, Sadie let her get some rest and headed for the parking lot. Last night, after carrying Toby to the car, Bo had come back to the waiting room and handed Sadie the keys to his SUV. He would drive his family home in his mother's car, and when she was ready to leave the hospital, Sadie could drive his car over to the carriage house.

Which meant, unless she decided to be the ultimate chicken and ditch Bo's car and find another way home, Sadie would be seeing him today. She wasn't going to be a coward. It was time to have the talk they should have had more than ten years ago. It was time to haul that box out of the pit where it had been festering and clean up the mess.

On the drive from the hospital to Murphy Farms, Sadie decided she'd clean up another mess too. Tanya. That decision had been surprisingly easy. It helped that the idea of giving the traitor any kind of a break infuriated Sadie.

If she wanted to be able to go to Bo and tell him what

she'd done and not be ashamed, then Sadie had to be ready to prove the same thing to the world.

Was it anybody's damn business? No. But acting like her choice was something to hide wasn't right either. Besides, if Tanya had managed to dig up Sadie's secret, it was only a matter of time before somebody else did.

At least this way Sadie could get ahead of it, control how the story came out. And she already had a few ideas of how she wanted that to happen. But first, it was time to talk to Bo.

Before going to the carriage house, Sadie decided she'd stop at her grandmother's to shower and change. She'd been in the same clothes for more than twenty-four hours. Then, over a quick snack, she updated Angie on Nana's condition.

Finally, out of excuses, Sadie drove to Bo's.

Walking slowly down the stable aisle next to Sadie, Bo fought to keep his mouth shut and his patience intact. Ever since that bizarre conversation with Meg in the war room, he'd been unable to stop wondering, stop worrying. What the hell did Tanya dig up on Sadie? On them?

Meg had said it had to do with him, so how could be not know about it?

Sadie's panic attack had scared the shit out of him, and the stuff with her grandmother had been stressful too. Once he'd come home, and everyone else had headed to bed, Bo had sat up, unable to sleep. Wracking his brain as he worked his way through a bottle of Jack. Eventually, he'd crashed on the couch. Too wiped and too wasted to make it up the stairs.

In the morning, Bo's body reminded him, very unpleasantly, that he didn't drink to excess often. He liked to stay in control. Until last night, the shots of vodka he'd done with Sadie had been the most he'd drunk at once in years.

Hours later, the residual pounding in his skull was a reminder of all the time he'd spent torturing himself last night. He wished Sadie would just tell him. He didn't want to have to ask, but at this point he was getting ready to beg.

Reaching the end of the aisle, they stopped at Stella's stall. Bo dug in his pocket and pulled out some sugar cubes. He handed one to Sadie. "You can give her this, but you have to keep it a secret. My mom doesn't like the old girl to have any sugar."

"Okay." Sadie's smile was shy. She held the cube out to the mare, smile growing as Stella ate the sugar.

Bo smiled too. It was impossible not to feel happy while a horse licked your palm.

"Speaking of secrets," Sadie began, her gaze fixed on Stella as she stroked the mare's muzzle, "I need to talk to you about Tanya's file."

Finally. Bo held himself in check, not saying anything, waiting for her to continue.

In the silence, Bo's thoughts raced, mixing with the pounding of his skull as he tried to figure out what piece of their past—what scandalous piece—she knew and he didn't.

"That first summer, the one after . . . after we broke up," she began, her attention still on Stella, voice small and quiet. "I found out something had happened."

"What?"

"Before you broke up with me . . . before you walked away." She stopped, took a breath. "We, uh, spent some time in your car together."

The floor fell out from under Bo's feet. His stomach going with it. *No.* Not possible.

He hadn't used a condom, but Sadie was on the pill. Had been on the pill for more than a year. "But . . . you were on the pill . . ."

She shook her head, pink rising in her cheeks. "I'd stopped a few weeks before the dance."

He stared at her, dumbfounded. "Why the hell would you do that?"

She bit her lip and stared at the ground, cheeks flushing hotter.

"Did you *want* to get pregnant?" There. He'd said the word. It was out there now. Floating between them.

"No." Sadie shook her head fiercely. "But my reason was equally foolish. I'd heard taking the pill could make you gain weight, and I'd wanted to make sure the dress I bought fit for the dance so—"

"My God, Sadie." Bo groaned. He ran a hand through his hair, trying to wrap his mind around it. "When did you know?"

"My body is like clockwork, so pretty quick. I suspected early June. And knew by the beginning of July."

"Why didn't you tell me?"

"I tried." Her words were laced with accusation, a knife stabbing him in the gut and twisting.

"What do you mean you tried?" Despite his best efforts, Bo could feel his temper rising. "This is the first I've ever heard of it, so you couldn't have tried very hard."

"I came to see you."

"Where? When?" Disbelief punctuated each question.

"Here! I came here, to your house."

"When was this?"

"As soon as I knew for sure, right after the Fourth of July holiday," Sadie said.

"After the fourth . . ." Bo echoed, rewinding the days, going back to that summer.

Fuck. *The accident.*

"Luna answered the door, said you were gone, and refused to tell me anything else. Only that you wouldn't be back for a long time."

"So, you just gave up?"

"I gave Luna a message, told her it was important, that I needed to see you." Sadie paused. "I begged her, Bo."

She was telling the truth. Sadie had tried to tell him. She had wanted him to know.

"That was the summer of the accident. My Dad and I, we were likely still in the hospital . . ."

"And Luna never gave you my message." Sadie's words dropped like stones. Hard and flat.

Bo shook his head. "There was a lot going on. My dad—for a while we were worried he wouldn't pull through—maybe she forgot." He wanted to believe that, wanted to believe that in the chaos of that summer, Sadie's visit had slipped his sister's mind. But Bo doubted it. And by the look on Sadie's face, she did too.

A bitter laugh escaped Sadie. "Somehow, I'm not mad at her. She didn't know why I needed to see you." Sadie shrugged. "When you didn't call, I decided that you stood by what you said, and you never wanted to see me again. I could have tried reaching out again, but I was angry. And scared. I didn't want to force something on you that you didn't want. Didn't want to force it on myself. I had been accepted into the acting conservatory; it was a big deal. If you don't get in that first semester, you don't get in. If I'd given up my spot, I'd be giving up my entire plan for college, my plan for my career."

"Please. Your parents could have bought you another spot."

Sadie jerked as if he'd slapped her.

"I didn't mean that," he began.

"Yes, you did," she called him out, tone razor sharp. "You absolutely did."

"Fine!" Bo exploded, temper snapping like a twig beneath his boot. "I meant it. You have fucking *everything*. Who cares if you go to a different college or do some other acting shit. You don't even need to have a fucking job if you don't want one!" His angry words bounced off the stable walls. Rustling the horses.

"You're right." In contrast to his heat, Sadie was ice cold. "I've got a trust fund and a rich daddy, and now thanks to my grandma, I'm going to own this place. I didn't need to go to college. And I don't need a job. I did those things because I *wanted* to. And the thing is, I can, Bo. Because it's My. Fucking. Choice."

He froze. She wasn't talking about college anymore. "Abeja—"

"No." Her voice cut through his. "I came here thinking I needed to try and explain, to make you understand . . . but you know what? I don't. I don't have to explain myself to you." Sadie walked toward him, chin up, staring him down. "What happened is in the past. We can't go back. We can't change it. If this is our second chance, our chance to make it right, we have to be ready to let go of our mistakes and move forward."

"Mistake?" That word seemed too small, too insubstantial for what she'd done. Bo pictured Toby. Gutted by the thought of his nephew not existing, not being a part of his life. He shook his head. "This isn't some little accident. You had an abortion, Sadie."

Her face paled. But then her violet eyes flashed. "I know. I was there." She moved toward him. "I was young. I was scared. And I had to make a choice."

"So did Luna."

She reeled back. "Is that what this is about?"

He ran a hand over his face. "All I'm saying is that—"

"—Is that she faced the same choice as me, right?" Sadie crossed her arms. "The difference is, you think your sister made the right decision."

Bo was silent, jaw clenched. He didn't know what to say to her. He didn't know how he felt. There was so much jumbled up inside him right now. Anger, regret, frustration, fear. Resentment burned in his chest. Why didn't she tell him? Why hide it from him for so many years?

"This was supposed to be our second chance, Bo." Sadie held her hand out to him, palm up, the same as he'd done in her apartment. "Our chance to make it right, remember?" She sounded like she was on the verge of crying, voice thick with tears.

The sound ripped Bo apart, but he stood still. He didn't take her hand. He couldn't.

He didn't know if they could make this right.

After a long, silent moment, Sadie's hand fell away. "I guess this is it, then." She sucked in a shuddering breath. "I guess it's my turn to say this." Her voice was sharp, acid burning away everything but anger.

"It's over, Bo. For real this time." Sadie turned, shoulders back, spine straight, and walked away from him, footsteps echoing on the stable floor.

Dusk had just started to fall when Sadie stomped out of the stable and out of his life. Hours later, it was only six in the evening, but full dark, the November night cold and cloudless. Bo sat at the edge of the hayloft window, legs dangling, watching his breath as it puffed into the air around him

"Stay out here much longer and you're going to get icicles in your beard." His sister sat beside him, sliding her feet over the edge. "Shit, it's cold."

"Get used to it. Winter isn't even here yet."

"Thanks for the reminder." Luna sighed, legs gently swinging back and forth.

"I drove Sadie back to the big house. Figured it was too cold to walk." Luna hesitated, and Bo could feel his sister's eyes on him.

"Did she say anything?" He couldn't stop from asking.

"She said a lot of things."

"Let me guess, I'm an asshole."

"I think the word dick came up more frequently. Dickhead, dickhole, dickwad. You know, variations on a theme."

"So it was an artistic choice."

Luna snorted. Then her tone shifted. "She told me what happened, said it's going to be made public soon anyway, and better if I found out from her."

Bo sighed. "I can't believe she didn't tell me back then."

"Well, first of all, you dumped her, and second of all, to be fair, she did try to tell you. Your bitch of a sister didn't give you the message."

"I was hoping you'd just forgot," Bo admitted.

"Nope." Luna's feet kicked faster. "I did it on purpose." The kicking stopped. "I had no idea Sadie was pregnant. I just knew you'd broken up with her and figured she was acting spoiled, wanting her way. I'm sorry, Bo."

"It's okay." His heart twisted in on itself as he tried to imagine what might have been. "It's done."

"It is done. And I think, maybe it was for the best."

"What?" Bo stared at his sister. "You can't mean that."

"Why not?" Luna blinked at him.

"Because . . ." he sputtered.

"Because of Toby?" She shook her head. "What does he have to do with this?"

"Because you had to face the same thing! She was eighteen too. You had nothing, no resources, no help, and she had everything."

"Maybe if I had more resources, I would have done things differently."

"I can't believe you would say that." Bo shoved back from the edge of the window and stood. "I can't believe you would think that about your own son."

"That's not what I mean, Bo." Luna scrambled to her feet. "I was saying, if my life had been different, I may have made different choices. And who knows where I might have ended up. I did what I thought was best at the time. The same goes for Sadie. If you hadn't broken up with her, or if I had given you that message . . . do you think either of you would be where you are today?"

Bo grit his teeth. "I don't know."

"No one does! We're human. We have to do our best with the choices in front of us at the time." Luna took a step toward Bo. "You had a choice in front of you today, brother. Let's hope you didn't blow it."

CHAPTER 28

IT WAS FEBRUARY, exactly three months until the release of *Fair is Fair*. Sadie had spent the first month of the new year in LA, networking and getting a sense for what she wanted to do for her next project. The rest of the time, she'd been flying all over the country for interviews on talk shows and podcasts. She'd flown back to Chicago to participate in Cassie's new segment for *ChiChat*, a "Coming out of the Book Closet" special feature called "Book2Movie." Sadie and Valerie Rose were scheduled to be the inaugural guests.

The segment had gone smoothly, earning a thumbs-up from PR Meg. It had been fun to see Cassie, and Sadie enjoyed the chance to spend some time with Valerie as well. The author of *Fair is Fair* had become a good friend over the last few months.

Last November, when Sadie had gone to Meg and told her she wanted to be the one to tell her story and expose her past on her own terms, there'd been quite a bit of backlash. But there'd been an outpouring of support too. An abundance of positive energy outshining the darkness and hate, overpowering the horrible things being said about her.

From the start, Valerie had been a staunch and vocal supporter, declaring she couldn't be prouder to have such a strong, passionate woman bring the character of Jamie to life. Thanks to the author's legions of devoted fans, Sadie, or, more specifically Sadie as Jamie, became an overnight sensation, elevating the movie's launch into the stratosphere.

After wrapping the *ChiChat* taping in the city, Sadie had driven out to visit Nana, who was settled nicely in her new digs and already had a trio of gal pals. Her grandmother was officially a golden girl. Finally, Sadie faced the inevitable and headed to the estate, dreading staying in that big empty house by herself.

Worse, it was Valentine's Day weekend, and Sadie wasn't looking forward to spending it alone. On a whim, she invited Ana over for a slumber party. She hadn't seen her best friend often these past few months. They'd barely had time to hang out while Sadie had been filming, and when the abortion story broke, Sadie worried she might never see Ana again.

She'd been afraid Ana was mad at what she'd done. That she, like some of the nastier people on the internet, believed Sadie was unforgivable. A lot worse had been said too, but Sadie had learned to block all that out. Ana admitted she'd been angry, but not because of what Sadie did. It was her body, her choice. No, what devastated Ana was the fact Sadie hadn't trusted her enough to share her secret. Sadie's lack of trust had cut her best friend deeply.

Never one to wallow, Ana had forgiven Sadie and moved on. Now, on Saturday night, Ana was mixing decadent cocktails while Sadie sifted through a stack of romantic comedies.

"Ready for ovaries before brovaries?" Ana asked.

"I'm not sure you should be celebrating Galentine's day," Sadie teased. "Aren't you dating Ryan?"

Ana shook her head, the horn on her onesie wiggling. Since it was a slumber party, she'd insisted on the footie pajamas, providing Sadie with a black-and-white panda set, complete with stumpy tail. "First, Galentine's is for every gal. And second, I gave your costar the 'I just want to be friends' speech before he left to film that dinosaur movie in Australia or New Zealand or wherever the heck he swanned off to this winter. Told him it had been fun, but it was time to move on, thank you and Godspeed."

"So, he's not the one, huh?"

"My prince charming?" The horn wobbled again. "No, definitely not." Ana sniffed. "Ryan was grocery store cake. You don't fall in love with grocery store cake."

"What?" Sadie laughed, watching as Ana set about mixing a cocktail.

"Men are like cake," Ana explained. "And I love cake. But I'm not *in love*. Not yet." Ana drizzled chocolate syrup on the inside of a martini glass. "I have yet to find the perfect recipe. The right blend of richness, sweetness, and texture. The right balance of cake to frosting."

"That's really deep." Sadie lifted her glass in salute. "Respect." She sipped her drink, considering Ana's words. What kind of cake would Bo be? Not too much frosting. Sweet, but not too sweet. Indulgent texture. Decadent flavor. Sadie stirred her martini, smiling to herself as the answer came to her. *A donut.* Bo would be a donut.

"You're thinking of *him*, aren't you?" Ana demanded, settling on the couch next to Sadie.

"Guilty," Sadie admitted, downing the rest of her cocktail. Her moment of levity faded, and she stared into her empty glass. "I don't think he will ever forgive me."

"That's bullshit," Ana ground out.

"Ana—"

"No, don't 'Ana' me." She scowled, crossing her arms.

"You look like an angry unicorn ready to stab somebody with your horn."

"I'm not a unicorn, I'm a narwhal."

"A what?"

"A narwhal. They're like whales, but cooler."

"But you have a horn," Sadie insisted.

Still huffy, Ana stood, fisting her hands on her hips. "It's not a horn, it's a tooth."

"Now I'm really confused."

"Never mind." With a grunt of disgust, Ana grabbed Sadie's empty glass and headed for the drink cart. "Back to what I was saying, if he's not willing to forgive you, he's not worthy of you," she insisted, mixing more martinis. "I forgave you."

"And I'm not worthy of you," Sadie admitted.

Ana glanced up, emerald eyes sparking. "None of that. No pity parties allowed." She rattled the cocktail shaker. "It was a shitty thing to do, not telling me. But I told you, I'm over it." Ana topped off two glasses with chocolate shavings and returned to the couch.

Taking one of the martinis, Sadie smiled, a squeezing bittersweet ache deep in her heart. Love and gratitude for her friend. "It meant a lot to me, you know."

"Yeah, I know." Ana shrugged. "I wish you would have been honest with me in the first place. That hurt."

"I was barely honest with myself," Sadie admitted, rubbing at the familiar burn in her chest. "I just wanted to bury the past, forget it had happened, and move on."

"We've talked about this." Ana reached across the couch, grabbing Sadie's hand. "You can't move on from something if you don't face it. Hiding from it—or locking it in a mental box—doesn't make it go away."

Releasing Sadie's hand, Ana sat back. "Maybe that's the problem." She sipped her martini, green eyes thoughtful over the rim of her glass. "You haven't seen him since this whole mess exploded, right?" Ana set her glass down. "So, how can you know Bo won't forgive you if you *haven't talked to him*?"

"Isn't it obvious? He doesn't *want* to talk to me."

"Have you tried talking to him?" Ana challenged.

"I told him I never wanted to see him again, remember?" Sadie moaned, rolling into a ball.

"Oh, my said little panda." Ana sighed and scooted closer. "Haven't you learned by now?" She rubbed a soothing hand up and down Sadie's back. "Never say never."

CHAPTER 29

OPENING NIGHT FOR *Fair is Fair* had arrived and the crowd gathered outside in the warm May air grew even more excited with each new limo that pulled up. Local celebrities and politicians made their way down the red carpet to the movie theater hosting the premiere event, waving to the fans lined up on either side.

As promised, Bo had scored Luna a pass to the event, and his sister stood next to him on the fringes of the crowd, bouncing with excitement.

"Why do we have to wait all the way back here?" she wondered, standing on tiptoe as another limo pulled up, trying to get a glimpse of who was next to arrive.

"Because I like to make you suffer," Bo teased. It had been a long time since he'd seen his sister get this excited about anything. He was glad she was relaxing, having fun. The last few months had been good for her.

Now that the carriage house and surrounding property were officially hers, thanks to Sadie's grandmother, Luna had finally been able to indulge her passion, expanding her gardens, planting new crops, and adding a hoophouse, a greenhouse, and other landscape things Bo couldn't keep up with. Since taking ownership of that bit of land, Luna had blossomed, the happiest he'd ever seen her.

Bo could appreciate her excitement. Early in the new year, either because he was finally sick of the Chicago winters or Claudia had finally worn him down, Vic had finally signed the papers passing full ownership of Windy City Stunts over to Bo. WCS was officially his. And he was happy, in a manner of speaking. But it was hard to feel much of anything when there was a gaping hole in his heart.

No matter how hard he worked on set during the day or how long he spent working the bag in his loft at night, Bo would fall into bed, mentally and physically exhausted, and dream of Sadie. There was a sadness inside him, a bruise he didn't think would ever fully go away, but it was a pain he could live with. There was regret, yes. But not resentment. He'd come to understand what she'd meant about not wanting to go back and change the past. The choices they'd both made, for better or for worse, had brought their lives to this point.

Bo had made a mess of things that night in the stable. Luna was right. He'd had a choice to make. And he'd made the wrong one. He only hoped it wasn't too late to set it right. He should have gone after Sadie that very night. But it had taken him a while to pull his head out of his ass. And once he finally did, she was gone. Off somewhere in California or New York, doing movie-star stuff. That scared him too. That she was moving beyond his reach again, orbiting farther away all the time.

These last few months, while Sadie traveled the country, appearing on talk shows and chatting with late night TV hosts, it would have been so easy for Bo to listen to the small cruel voice in his head that told him he wasn't good enough for her, that he would never be good enough. Especially now. Now that her star had risen, that she was loved and adored by a legion of fans, the world at her feet.

But he refused to give in to those fears. He wasn't going to make the same mistake twice. He began to imagine what he would say to her, how he would reach out to her. Before long, it had become part of his dreams. And just like when he was a kid, once he'd dreamt of doing it, he believed he could.

Bo glanced over at his sister. "You remember your part in the plan, right?"

"Hand her the note." Luna waved an annoyed hand. "Why are we doing this tonight? You could have just walked over to the estate anytime in the last few months when she was there, or I don't know, *called* her."

"No."

"Or *you* could hand her the note."

"No. She has to come to me, and it has to be—"

"—In the meadow," Luna finished for him. "Got it." His sister slid him some side-eye. "I never would have guessed you to be such a romantic. Weird, but romantic."

"I'm not romantic."

Luna laughed. "Then we'll agree on the weird."

A sudden murmur ran through the rows of fans as another limousine pulled up. Bo braced himself.

"She's h-e-e-re!" Luna sang. "Good luck." His sister gave him a quick peck on the cheek and disappeared into the crowd.

Sadie emerged from the limousine. Bo had a clear view of her for a half-second before the throng of admirers swooped in. An instinct to rush forward, to shield and protect her, sliced through him, but he held his ground. He'd seen the security detail and knew she was in good hands. He remained where he was, watching from the sidelines as his abeja had her first big movie-star moment.

Dozens of girls, perhaps a hundred or more, lined the curb and sidewalk leading up to the theater. Many of them sporting "the Jamie," the name that had been given to the short spiky hairstyle of Sadie's character. All of them were shouting, eyes shining with devotion as they chanted, "Fair is fair!" and "My body, my choice!" over and over.

To the public, Sadie had become Jamie—in real life as much as on the screen. Like her character, Sadie owned her past and spoke her truth, earning respect and admiration from the media as well as from a growing legion of fans.

And from Bo as well. Putting aside his own tangled feelings, he could respect what she'd done, admired the way she'd handled herself through all that had happened. Watching her sign autographs, smiling and chatting with people as cameras flashed and the frenzy continued, people screaming her name, Bo's heart twisted.

She looked so beautiful, the folds of her long gown sweeping gracefully over her legs, fluttering out as she walked along the red carpet. Her hair had begun to grow out, no longer the cropped spiky locks of Jamie, short golden curls now framed the fine, almost elfin lines of her face, grazing her chin. His hands itched to tangle in her hair. He wanted to trace the curve of her exposed neck, skim one finger along the delicate line of her collarbone, kiss the top of her bare, elegant shoulders. More than anything, Bo wanted to pull Sadie to him and hold her against his heart.

Later. If it was meant to be. If they were meant to be together, he would hold her then.

He would hold her forever.

On cue, Luna skirted around the crowd, passing through security with a flash of the access pass around her neck. Then she was next to Sadie, and Bo almost did a double take to see the two women hug. Would wonders never cease.

Sadie took the note from his sister and turned, searching the crowd, her gaze colliding with his.

Bo sucked in a breath.

Maybe Luna had told her where he was standing, or maybe Sadie had sensed he was there, or maybe it was both. All Bo knew was that she felt it too—that same buzzing sensation under her skin. An awareness.

Their eyes held, and within the space of a heartbeat, everything slowed down, the shouts from the crowd, the flashes of the cameras, all of it fading to nothing as he and Sadie stared at each other. The moment stretched out like a rubber band, expanding. And then *snap*. The noise flooded his ears, and she disappeared beyond the door, Luna with her.

Bo eased back through the crowd. Luna had given Sadie the message. That was all that mattered for now. The rest would be up to her. If she came to the meadow, if she showed she was open to at least that much, it would be enough to give them a chance.

If not, he'd know it was well and truly over.

CHAPTER 30

WHEN SADIE ARRIVED at the Murphy estate, it was late enough at night to be called early in the morning. She parked in front of the house and reached into the little beaded handbag she'd brought with to the premiere, pulling out the note Bo had given her.

She opened it gingerly, careful not to spill the glitter tucked inside. He'd given her glitter. A tender smile tugged at her lips; she still couldn't believe it. But belief was what this was all about. Belief and hope. And trust. Sadie read his words again.

> *I'll be waiting where we first met.*
> *When we first met.*
> *Meet me there.*
> *I dare you.*

That was it. All through the premiere and the after-party, Bo had been there. Not for real, she hadn't seen a trace of him since that moment on the red carpet, but he was there, in the back of her mind, his dare taunting her.

There was no confusion regarding the place Bo was referring to. What Sadie wasn't clear on were his intentions. He wanted to meet her, back where everything started. Why? Was he ready to forgive her? Had he forgiven her already? And if so, did that mean he was ready to try again?

She wouldn't get the answers to any of these questions unless she took Bo up on his dare. All evening, Sadie had debated with herself, cruising on autopilot as she smiled for cameras, signed autographs, and made small talk. Meanwhile, the questions played on repeat inside her head—an endless loop of doubt. Should she meet him? What if he didn't show? What if she'd misunderstood? Should she go?

Her brain could have saved the mental energy. Her heart had known what to do since the moment she'd read the note.

It was Bo.

Of course, she was going.

Tucking her keys into the little handbag, Sadie got out of the car, the sound of the door clicking shut too loud in the predawn air. The sky was that strange inky blue-black that offered the promise of day, but held it back, the ocean of night fading into the brightening line of the horizon like the undulating curve of a shoreline.

Sadie folded the note into a tiny square, holding it tight in one fist. She glanced up at the dark and empty house. Silent windows stared down at her. Even though the house was now hers, it didn't feel like home anymore. Not without Nana living there. Her grandmother had said to give it time—whatever Sadie eventually decided to do with the estate, however she decided to proceed—she had her blessing.

The sky continued to lighten, now almost that same

indigo shade as the drapes on her Nana's canopy. Sadie turned to look east, where the faintest streaks of pink crept past the lingering shadows.

It was time.

Note still pressed tight in one fist, Sadie made her way toward the back of the house. As she headed across the meadow, she realized she should have ditched her premiere finery and changed into something more comfortable. But the thought hadn't even occurred to her. She'd had one goal—make it to the meadow by dawn.

Now, with the glittery hem of her evening gown snagging on thistles, stilettos slipping in the wet grass, Sadie wished she'd taken a few minutes to at least put on different shoes. She kicked off her heels, leaving the expensive Italian leather behind as she made her way toward the line of trees on the other side of the meadow.

Her bare feet padded across the carpet of wild clover as the sky continued to grow brighter. Clutching the paper in one hand, Sadie picked up her skirts and began to run, her heart pounding in her ears. She reached the edge of the meadow, and stopped, breath coming in gulps.

Filled with a sense of urgency, Sadie had to remind herself she was not literally trying to beat the dawn. There was no magical hidden path to discover. No fairy prince to trap and demand he tell her all his secrets.

To the east, streaks of gold and pink continued to fill the sky, but still she was alone, the meadow empty, save for herself. Doubts circled like ravens, casting shadows in her mind. Maybe she'd misread his letter. Misinterpreted it. Maybe he wasn't coming after all.

She scanned the line of trees, hope sinking in her chest as dawn crept toward the horizon. A faint rustle from behind her made Sadie's heart lurch, and she turned. Bo was here. Moving toward her through the trees from the west—always the west—heading into the sunrise.

Just like that first time all those years ago, when he suddenly appeared before her, riding a horse pale as moonlight, it was like magic. And now, like then, he seemed too good to be true. A figment of mist and shadows. A fae prince who would disappear with the coming light. But as the light grew, burning away the mist and dispelling the shadows, he didn't disappear. Rather, he became more distinct. More real.

Sadie stood at the edge of the meadow, watching Bo approach. Still in his dress pants and shirt, he hadn't changed clothes either. The suit jacket was gone, though, and the sleeves of his shirt were rolled up, powerful forearms flexing in the early morning light as he gripped the reins and guided his mount toward her. Back then, he'd been a boy with beautiful eyes and a dangerous smile. A fairy prince come to steal her breath and heart.

The figure who appeared before her now had the same beautiful eyes. But his smile was more dangerous than ever. No longer a boy. Not a fairy prince, but a man. One who still stole her breath.

But not her heart. That, he hadn't stolen. Because she'd given it to him. Freely.

And no matter what happened in this meadow, in this moment, deep down, Sadie knew he would hold a piece of it always.

Leaving the horse to nibble at the clover, Bo moved toward her. "You came."

"I did," she agreed. "Which means it's your turn. Truth or dare?"

He studied her, his light-brown eyes molten honey, a warm golden glow. "Does it matter which one I pick?"

She cocked her head at him. She'd thought about this on the drive and had prepared an answer. "Not really. If you say truth, I'll ask how you feel about me. If you say dare, I'll dare you to tell me."

"I see." He was quiet for a moment. "The truth, then."

Sadie's heart froze in her chest, ice spreading through her veins like frost despite the warmth spreading over the hill. She braced herself, set up protective shields inside. This time, if he said it was over, she would be prepared. This time, if he said they should never see each other again, she wouldn't shatter.

When he spoke, Bo's voice was low and etched with pain. "After you told me what you did, what you kept hidden from me, I thought you had been so selfish." His voice shook and he stopped, took a breath. "But everything I was feeling—it was all about me. I was the one being selfish. I never stopped to think about what you were going through. Didn't wonder what it must have been like for you to face that alone . . ." He made a desperate, choking sound, as if words were caught in his throat.

"I wasn't alone," she whispered. "Not completely. I had my nana. She helped me see my way through." Sadie wiped at the tears burning in the corners of her eyes. "She wouldn't let me hate myself for the choices I made. No matter what, she always, *always*, made sure I knew I was loved."

"She's a very special lady." He smiled softly. "I'm glad she was there with you, and I plan to thank her in person. But I should have been there too. I never should have abandoned you."

"Bo, we've been over this," Sadie said, suddenly very tired. "If you are looking to apologize, if you are here because you need me to absolve you of any lingering guilt you feel, fine. You're absolved."

"That's not why I'm here." A muscle worked along his jaw.

Sadie's temper snapped. "Why, then? What's done is done. I told you, we can't go back and change the past."

"This isn't about the past, abeja. It's about the future." He reached for her, then, pulling her fingers into his hands. "Our future."

"I can't plan a life with you, Bo." She pulled away, wrapping her arms around her middle. "Not if I'll always wonder if you resent me. If you resent the choice I made."

"Sadie, I love you."

"I know." Realizing what she'd just said, Sadie laughed, short and bitter. She shook her head, saying it again. "I know, Bo. But if you can't forgive me, *truly* forgive me, if that seed of resentment remains inside your heart, then I'm afraid love won't be enough. That seed will fester and spread. I can't worry that one day, if we do decide to have a family, this ghost from our past will rise up and come between us." She was trembling, her voice shaking now, but he had to know where she stood. "I refuse to let that one moment define the rest of my life."

"You wanted the truth. Right, abeja?"

She nodded. Heart too heavy and throat too tight to say more.

"I forgive you for not telling me. For hiding the truth for so long. I understand why you did it. And I forgive you." Bo paused and sucked in a breath before continuing, his voice softer than a prayer, "But I cannot forgive you for the choice you made."

Each word he spoke was like a shard of broken glass. Sadie swallowed, choking as they shredded everything inside her. She'd told herself she was prepared. That her heart would be protected this time. Safe. But no matter how much she'd braced for disaster, she still hadn't seen the hit when it came. She forced herself to look at Bo. To meet his gaze one last time.

But as he stared down at her, Sadie slowly began to realize something.

His face was not closed, his mouth not harsh.

And his eyes . . . his lucky-penny eyes were not glittering with anger or resentment or worse. They were bright and full of love. Glowing with warm compassion.

"I can't forgive you, Sadie. Because there's nothing to forgive."

"What?" she whispered.

"I mean it, abeja. I've had months to think about this. You did what you needed to do. What was best. For you. That's as it should be, and I accept it. I accept it as part of you." Bo brushed a hand over her cheek, touch tentative and featherlight. "And I love you. I love every part of you. Everything you've done and every choice you've made. They've brought you here."

Hope collected the tattered threads of Sadie's heart, weaving them back together, stronger than ever before. Like magic, as he spoke, his words became a part of her, healing the broken places inside her. "I love you too. Always. I've never stopped."

"That's good." Bo's smile was crooked. Hopeful. "Don't ever stop." He pulled her into his arms, kissing her once, his lips full of tender promise, before he turned her around, pressing her back to his chest, facing the horizon. The sun was fully up now, the sky bright with promise. "That first morning, when we were kids, you came from the east, bringing the sun with you."

Sadie shifted, pivoting so they faced the woods. "And you rode in from the west."

Bo nodded, chin brushing against her hair. "We came from the opposite ends of the earth, but we met here. Our worlds were so different, I always feared they would drift farther apart, pulling you away from me." He turned her to face him, his arms pulling her close. "It took me a long time, but I finally realized, all my life, I've been looking at it the wrong way."

"What do you mean?" she asked, searching his face.

"It's not about your world or my world. It's about our world. The one we make together."

Yes. Her heart soared. It made perfect sense. So simple, and yet, it had been so hard for either of them to see. "You're right." She went on tiptoe, cold wet clover tickling her toes, and kissed him.

"What now?" she wondered.

"I was thinking," he began, a note of uncertainty in his voice, "how would you feel about building a house? Right here."

"Here?"

He nodded. "In the meadow, but close to the line of trees."

Sadie could picture it. A tidy little house, the fairy cottage she used to dream about, with windows facing east to welcome the sun and a hammock in the back to watch the twilight fade in the west. A home made just for them.

"I won't always be around," Sadie warned. "I'm a star in high demand now, if you haven't heard," she teased, keeping her voice light, but still making sure he knew where she stood.

"Not a problem. Clark and I will here," he promised. "Ready to welcome you home."

"That sounds good to me." She beamed. "Actually, that sounds perfect."

"I do have *one* more question." He cocked a grin at her.

"Oh?" Sadie reached for him, placing a hand over his heart. "Lay it on me, bad boy."

Bo's fingers caressed her chin, his touch light as a bumblebee's wings as he tipped her face up to his. "Marry me, abeja. Let's start our new life together, you and me, right here." He brushed his nose against hers. "Our own place. Our own little world."

ACKNOWLEDGMENTS

This story is about fate, or at least, the possibility of fate. Considering all the various moving parts that had to connect, all the pieces that had to slide into place to lead me to write this story . . . yeah, I'd like to think there's a good chance fate exists. I know for a fact my editor, Jennie Conway, was a gift from the writing gods. If I made a wish list of all the things I hoped for in an editor, Jennie, the result would be you. Thank you for working so patiently and diligently and compassionately with me. You took the garbled ball of threads I delivered and helped me weave them into a story I am proud of. Thanks to my copy editor, Christa Soule Desir, for taking the time to balance craft with heart. The whole team at St. Martin's Press has been a joy to work with, and I appreciate all of you. To my agent, Pamela Harty; knowing you are there when I need you is priceless, thanks for being in my court.

Like the girls in my stories, I'm blessed to know some amazing women, including my Golden Heart© classes, the Mermaids and Rebelles (hello, pocket friends!).

Virtual hugs to my sprinting buddies Kari Cole and Alyson McLayne. No matter how we say we're going to do better next time, those deadlines always creep up on us. Lots of love to my Portland Midwest peeps, including my Sunday writing crew Melanie Bruce and Clara Kensie. Extra special thanks to Lynne Hartzer for making me feel so loved by checking in to see how things were going and surprising me with the most incredible writing weekend survival basket. Thanks to Ricki Wovsaniker, who spent the days trapped in her house during the polar vortex beta reading this story. Your critiques are always thoughtful and insightful Ricki, and I'm lucky to know you. A very heartfelt thanks to Katherine S. Lopez for providing a sensitivity read. I am grateful for your time and deft insights Kathy, and I'm thrilled I was your re-introduction to the world of romance!

Cheers to my Reading Lush Facebook group. You are the best virtual drinking buddies and it's a treat to hang out with my Lushes! Thanks to everyone who chimed in on my "research" questions ranging from the age of first kisses to nicknames for grandparents. Shout-out to my #8isgreat class at the gym, including my trainers James and Tim (who combined provided the inspiration for Sadie's trainer, Jim). I am grateful to the friendly faces I see every morning: Kat, Brenda, and especially Christine. Thanks for keeping me coming back and being so supportive of my writing, ladies! Also, a note of thanks must be given to Khai, a fabulous massage therapist. Many a writing-induced kink has been worked out under her talented hands.

Thanks to my mom for her unflagging enthusiasm. Much love to my daughters, who are each their own unique brand of awesome and amazing and who exhaust and exhilarate me on a daily (often hourly) basis. Love and thanks to my husband, who celebrated the moment I reached the end of this book by bringing home a bottle of white wine for me . . . and a bottle of red for himself. Hugues, your unwavering love and support is everything.

And finally, to my Readers. I'm lucky you're here, reading my work. Maybe fate led you to this book. Maybe you need this story. Whatever brought you to turn these pages, I'm glad you're here. Thank you.

Don't miss the Sometimes in Love series!